The Whole World in My Hands

To Sarah.

With much
love &
best wishes

Jeremy

XX

The Whole World in My Hands

Jeremy Vine

Hodder & Stoughton

LONDON SYDNEY AUCKLAND

First published in Great Britain in 1994 by Hodder and Stoughton
a Division of Hodder Headline PLC

10 9 8 7 6 5 4 3 2 1

A CIP record for this title can be found in the British Library

ISBN 0 340 61241 X

Typeset by Hewer Text Composition Services, Edinburgh
Printed and bound in Great Britain by
Cox & Wyman, Reading, Berks

Hodder and Stoughton Ltd,
A division of Hodder Headline PLC
338 Euston Road
London NW1 3BH

For Janelle, and for Barb

Staring down, Derek Weston simply could not believe it.

So he drew his fingers into a fist, looked up at the ceiling, then slowly lowered his gaze again until it settled, comfortably, on the clenched hand.

That's it, he thought. *Nice and comfortable. Nothing there of any importance. An ordinary Essex vicar's fist. How could there be anything of importance in it?*

He even gave his collar a little twiddle.

It can't be.

He hummed something. Thought about supper.

Nothing like a good supper.

Then, uncurling the fingers slowly, he held his breath.

Suddenly—

It is.

Suddenly he had let his breath go and inhaled and gasped, all together, all in a fraction of a second.

For there it was, still: winking at him.

He simply had no way on earth of believing it.

There was no way in heaven of believing it.

There was definitely no way in Evenham to believe it.

For at least five minutes, the Reverend Derek Weston just stared at the thing in the palm of his hand.

He winked.

The thing winked back.

He tried to blink it away, blinking furiously.

Blink-blink-blink-blink-blink-blink-blink-blink-blink.

It stayed. His eyes widened.

He pinched himself.

It pinched him.

Numb with shock and awe, he drew the longest, deepest

breath of his life, slumped into the armchair in the corner of the study and ran trembling, spare fingers through the generous waves of grey hair which a parishioner had once, unkindly, said made his head look like a milk chocolate truffle.

You are on your own now, he told himself.

Then he remembered the summer day the whole, fearful business began.

– 2 –

It was a brilliant afternoon. Gerald and Eunice Cooper, as well as John and Sonya Todd and Charles Mannox-Lloyd, all announced they had been praying for weather.

'We prayed for weather,' Mrs Cooper said confidentially, clamping her vicar's forearm tighter than any worktop vice and pulling him towards her. 'We succeeded,' she added. 'Something obviously got through.' A ray of bright sunlight cut across her face. 'My left eye has gone, Gerald!'

'It's just the sun moving, dear,' her husband put in, grinning. 'It's not your eye.'

The grip grew stronger, and Eunice Cooper's glasses slipped an inch down the bridge of her nose. 'It is a truly brilliant day for a fête, Derek.'

'Inspired. Brilliant. Really very well done indeed. Top marks,' her husband guffawed. He was a retired engineering lecturer who had written a controversial paper on the square roots of hymn numbers. He always seemed to be laughing. 'Last time we prayed for weather, it poured,' he chuckled.

'We were praying for rain,' his wife hissed, pulling Derek's face closer to hers.

'Aintree,' she added, mysteriously.

'—and just look at that marquee over there,' someone was saying. 'Derek, you really have done a marvellous job of all this.'

They moved away. There were crowds of them. Gradually regaining feeling in his forearm, the vicar of St Saviour's church, Nock Green, Evenham, shook other hands – nodding, beaming as he did. Yes, crowds! Dear Eunice Cooper was right, he thought, looking at the masses of backs and profiles and faces gliding around the expanse of lush field sloping down

3

and away from him: *it is a brilliant day, and I have done a brilliant job.* A thrill edged up his spine. *Christianity is about crowds.* He felt a tickle of guilt at not having prayed for the good weather himself, but how could it matter when a roasting sun was out – as were hundreds of people? And not all of them from the parish, either. That was what was so exciting. This fête . . . this might not even be a fête at all. This might almost be mission.

I have done a brilliant job, he told himself again.

For once.

Derek Weston was forty-six, with roughly a dozen years each in teaching and the church behind him: tall, statuesque even, lean-jawed and healthy-looking, handsome face always residually tanned, with enough grey hair on his head to stop any bookmaker ever giving odds on baldness or recession.

He often looked at the high-stacked, abundant hair in the bathroom mirror, pulling spectacles off as his wife undressed in their bedroom and watching himself come into focus in the glass. *I am not going to go bald,* he would secretly tell the reflection as it brushed its teeth – adding, on a bad day: *my ministry already has.* Not that it mattered. There were worse things than bald ministries. Hell, for a start. Theological disputes. Supermarket parking bays. Northolt. Junk mail from high street banks. Shouting. New Zealand.

My ministry needs a toupee, he would mutter.

A football sailed over, booted by a group of children using discarded shirts as goal markers. Suddenly elated, Derek Weston hopped a yard towards the ball and trapped it cleverly under a toe, flicked it up – there was a cheer from the players – and then, on the bounce, swung a foot back and sent it cannoning into the rear of a woman carrying a tray of juice.

'Sorry! Sorry, Ruth!' he called. She half-turned and gave him a forgiving smile, then bent to retrieve several glasses and a jug from the ground. He was about to rush over to help when he heard his own name skid to a halt with a question mark after it.

'Oh –' Derek Weston turned to see the speaker. 'Marshall – hello – I—'

4

'Sorry, Derek. I know you're busy. With all this – success. But can I have a word, just for a moment?'

Wiry and intense, Marshall Kampfner might well have spent his thirties training at a gym to punch his way out of middle age. Marshall – serious, diligent Marshall – was on the Parochial Church Council. That made him vital. He had certain useful gifts, too: as a librarian, he rarely displayed emotion and was skilled in not answering telephones.

Short, Marshall was, bony, slightly stooped, with rodent features. Today he wore a narrow T-shirt, pinching his trunk just as the milk-white skin of his face pinched in at the top of his nose. He was squinting at the vicar, dark brown eyes so close to each other that Derek wondered how he was able to see in three dimensions.

'Shall we get into some shade?'

'No, no, Derek. You have to get used to it. I do, I mean. One musn't waste a lovely day like this, that's for sure. You've done so well. I just hope the sun holds. There are so many here.'

A distant whoop seemed to confirm the fact. 'I'm sure you did most of it,' the vicar protested. In the blazing heat, he had the momentary sensation that his voice was the only part of him which existed. He raised a hand, putting the top half of his face in shadow. Perhaps in a minute he would get some squash from Mrs Atkins.

'Now – it's just – that – there was – um – something, Derek.'

'Something? Oh – now – it's – it's not another problem with the pebbledashing, is it?' Derek could not forget how the man standing in front of him had chided a team of builders weatherproofing the south side of the church for using what he authoritatively told them were malformed stones.

It was weeks ago now. As the vicar had squirmed in embarrassment beside his PCC member, a furious argument had broken out which touched briefly on issues of geometry and geography before the two of them were forced to withdraw after coming under a hail of pebbles. A small claims action the vicar should never have allowed himself to be drawn into was now being dragged out interminably,

5

and Marshall Kampfner had taken great delight in reporting back every detail.

'Nothing to do with our impending victory in the courts, no.'

'Then – what?'

Marshall sighed, blinked, screwed up his eyes and peered down at his watch, tipping his pencil-thin wrist to see it. 'I don't know if there's time to tell you before the bishop comes,' he said.

'Is he not here yet?' Derek Weston was always relaxed about visits by the Bishop of Basildon. *I am approved of,* he thought. *I might have blown the bishopric, but he can see I'm holding it steady here. Even-keeling it. Yes, he must see how happy I am at St Saviour's. He knows about the contented congregations.*

'Not yet,' said Marshall. 'I think one of the young mums said she'd spotted the hat moving on the other side of a fence, but it turned out to be someone carrying a dinghy. And he doesn't wear his hat at fêtes, obviously. No, this is – well, it's quite important. That's the point, Derek. I can't say it when he's around. And you must promise not to mention it to him when you see him. It affects you.'

An irresistible thought rocketed across the vicar's mind.

I might not have blown the bishopric.

He felt a shower of hot sparks drop down his back.

I might not have blown it up in a shower of hot sparks.

'Is it—'

'A rumour,' Marshall cut in. 'That's right. And a big one.'

More sparks, then a shiver.

'How – how big?' *How big a rumour would me becoming bishop be?*

'Only I know it.'

How small could it be?

They say that in the life of every vicar whose career fails to climb as it might, for whatever reason, there is a single moment when that vicar knows he has blown the bishopric. For Derek Weston, the moment had come after he gave the church choir permission to record a version of what they had described as a 'well-known pop song'. The vicar embraced the idea. Stupidly, he had not asked the title. At forty-plus, he knew nothing of well-known pop songs. Then the thing had come out. It attracted enormous media attention. Even at that point, warning bells were not ringing. The record began to climb the music charts. *Straight in at thirty-one . . . twenty-five . . . highest riser, up to number nine . . . seven . . .* Finally, Derek Weston investigated.

His choir, it turned out, had done a version of a song called 'Rocketbomb' by a band called Slaughter Mechanism. They were a young choir. They had seen no harm in it – no harm in the lyrics, 'I'm going to find a woman and bomb her/Find a village and rocketbomb the hell out of it'. They had apparently believed there could be an evangelistic interpretation. On the reverse side of the single was a Wesley hymn set to bongos, as if that made everything all right. Sensational publicity followed.

The record rose to third place in the music charts. Derek Weston had blown the bishopric.

Now Marshall Kampfner was hesitating, and the vicar was suddenly wondering if he might have cause, on this baking Evenham afternoon, to reassess everything.

'Well—'

'It's a rumour, that's all. Just a – well, a fairly big rumour. I don't—'

'Marshall – for crying out loud – what on earth are you trying to—'

They were interrupted.

'Derek – Derek, I'm so sorry to butt in—'

In an instant, the two men were surrounded by a group of three or four of the church's most distinguished members and their wives.

The vicar inhaled, deeply. 'Gentlemen, hello. Good to see you here, Mrs Foster. I do hope that sprain's getting better. Hello there, Eileen. Good afternoon, Lady Gearey.'

'And do you know Connie Leach here, Derek? Sorry, fellah – did we interrupt?' George Foster gestured at the back of Marshall Kampfner, moving away slowly, like a librarian called to collapsed shelving.

'Not in the slightest.'

7

Brigadier Sir Kenneth Gearey started: 'You weren't, ah—'

'—discussing anything important?' That was his wife, finishing the question. George had obviously dragged them all over.

'Rarely,' the vicar mumbled, ambiguously.

'A couple of things,' said George Foster briskly, thrusting a shoulder forward like the prop as a scrum collapses. He was a squat man with grey sideburns and a perpetual expression of wide-eyed astonishment. Long retired, he saw himself as a kind of lay caretaker to the church; it did not take much observation to confirm that his sense of tact and timing had also taken early retirement.

He opened his address at steel-bending volume.

'First, I gather the bishop's been sighted. We've lost the industrial strimmer, second. Third, the cricket looks like coming to an end soon, so it might be time to think about moving people to the marquee in groups. Fourth—'

'Hold on, hold on,' Derek Weston said. The rest of the group were laughing at the vigour of the outburst. 'You said the industrial strimmer—'

'Hired. To do the grass round the marquee. One of these things that'll take the top off your shoe as quick as look at it, let alone plug it in. We're just a bit worried the kids might be playing with it somewhere.' Always that look of stunned surprise on his face.

'We think the bishop's here,' cut in Sir Kenneth, hands on hips. He was Governor of the Tower of London, a military man, and Derek Weston always felt privileged that he had stayed with St Saviour's through the years. *We are both servicemen*, the vicar sometimes told himself proudly, *though in different senses*. The man's only irritating habit was that he kept referring to himself in the plural, like royalty; it had been a while before Derek noticed. 'We saw his car,' Sir Kenneth was saying now. 'My wife saw it too. One of the ladies is looking after the whole business.'

'Mrs Atkins, that's who,' Lady Gearey said firmly. 'Old Mrs Childs is deputising on the urns. She's already had to – well, send a few of the local hooligans packing. You know what they're like with these sorts of events. Usual thing. Delight

8

in sticking a spanner in. One chap with a beard was doing some sort of clever one-wheeled thing with a motorbike, I gather – put a tyre-mark on someone's leg. And they were asking Mrs Childs for milk with tea in, to confuse her. By the way, Derek – for heaven's sake, do try calling me Jennifer for once.'

They roared with laughter. All of them. Somewhere a loudspeaker was blaring details of a car number plate.

Itching to find Marshall to continue their conversation, the vicar asked himself urgently where he might be. He wondered: *will I ever be allowed to look?*

The laughter died down. He spoke across the warm, intimate breeze that blew between them all.

'I hope you might all be able to come into the marquee for the buffet and slides. Just a small show that all the churches in the Evenham region are doing, in turn, to give people an idea where collection money is targeted.'

'So you're targeting, are you?' That was Paul Trundell.

'That makes a lot of sense.' His wife, Eileen, a chartered accountant who had taken maternity leave to become a foster parent.

'Rather than just – since we're on technical words – chucking. Yes.' And that was the vicar. 'Targeting.'

They dispersed. All but George Foster, who turned out to be in the middle of a detailed account of just how precariously the marquee centre-pole was being held in place, and exactly what the vicar was supposed to be doing once he got inside.

'—so you'll be standing, okay—' He had an arm outstretched, back twisted, a hand jiggling as though he was about to try to limbo his way under a park bench, 'and the chap at the back will take his cue to start the slides rolling when the lights go down, straight after you take your place.'

'Fine.'

'He's in a booth, Derek, you understand, so he won't be able to see anything.'

'I hear you.' The vicar was not listening.

'A booth. He'll go by the lights.'

'Good.'

*   *   *

The bishop was looking slightly strained when they met. It was the merest strain: an emotional version of tennis elbow. Nothing that affected services, just a slight restriction on spin. So it was with the Bishop of Basildon's smile as they shook hands. It was a fifth of an inch narrower than usual. Derek lobbed him a grin.

They exchanged cursory greetings. The bishop, the Right Reverend Terence Stitt, was wearing a surgically-pressed black shirt and peculiarly-shaped sunglasses. Derek glimpsed an Italian word painted on the frame and wondered: *what does that continental word mean? What dark secret is dangling behind those black lenses? What was Marshall going to tell me?*

Whatever it was, Terence Stitt was not telling. He talked about puppets. He had a deep, booming, foghorn voice, a huge Adam's apple, big as a basketball; when he spoke, his eyes darted this way and that, as if he had just had a tip-off about a mugging.

'The Stitt household is full of all kinds of Punches and Judies,' he said.

'How wonderful.'

'A new pastime. Imported by my eldest daughter. We had a homeless man to stay for a period, and I think he made very much of them.' The bishop was known for emphasising social action. 'They just seemed to do more than anything else to resonate with his sense of humanity, throughout the time he was with us.'

'Really? How long did you have him?'

'Two or three hours,' the bishop said.

'Right.'

'I'm sorry to say he'd been knocked down by my car.'

'Oh, dear.'

The bishop added: 'You've done a sound job here today, Derek.'

The sun flashed off an Italian lens.

The two men were standing in the middle of the field, and for a moment it seemed to Derek Weston as though the whole universe was revolving around them – trees, parishioners, football sweaters, loudspeakers, stars, planets, everything. He wondered if he had become an existentialist.

'Thank you,' he said, half-agog, remembering the compliment as though it had been passed back to him through history.

'You enjoy it here, don't you?'

'I do. Very much.'

Someone walked by with a large stereo system perched on one shoulder, cranking out a deafening metallic beat.

The two paused. The bishop waved away an insect. The vicar raised his own hand to brush it away, uselessly, because it had already flown off.

Then, in the instant the booming music began to fade, the bishop said something that caused the trees and parishioners and sweaters and speakers and stars to crash to a standstill.

'I always think it's never that good an idea for a clergyman to treat any church as home, Derek, you know.'

The music was gone. Terence Stitt glanced away, as if to allow his vicar to grapple with the sentence privately.

Suddenly, silently, Derek was a sun, a solid shining in the midst of a log-jammed world, radiating certainty. *He is giving me a signal*, he thought. *He is giving me the signal that means I need to be ready to get the call that says—*

He is giving me the signal that comes just before that call.

I am going to be rung and told to become bishop.

Derek Weston, vicar of St Saviour's, Evenham, reined in his galloping breath.

I have not blown the bishopric.

His heart seemed to sing for joy. It sang everything, even 'Rocketbomb'. All it needed was Marshall Kampfner's confirmation. A wink, a nudge – either would do. But he had to have that confirmation. It could even be a wink and a nudge at the same time. Or a slap on the back – yes, you could slap vicars on the back without offending protocol. Not bishops, though. Bishops got telegrammed, not slapped. *Soon*, Derek Weston told himself, walking towards the marquee, exhilarated, feeling a fleck of rain on his forehead, *soon I will be telegrammed*.

When the moment for slides came, there were far more people in the marquee than anyone had planned for. Dark clouds had scrolled across the sky. A sudden shower drove the crowds towards the nearest shelter.

Four-fifths of this lot aren't even in the church, the vicar reflected, struck by a pang of guilt at what the size of this rain-driven crowd said about the size of his congregation. *My sermons are less powerful than water*, he concluded sorrily.

But soon Derek was standing in front of two hundred people with plates tilted under the makeshift marquee lighting, smiling broadly, catching the eye of the bishop and Mrs Stitt, of the Coopers, the Trundells, the Gearys, Mrs Atkins with a tottering stack of plastic cups made fluorescent in the light of a bare bulb somewhere . . .

'Ladies and gentlemen – and any of you who aren't usually with us on a Sunday morning or evening at St Saviour's—'

The conversation in the marquee began to fall away.

Is that a rumble of thunder?

Derek Weston tapped the windshield of the small microphone on the table.

'Hello?'

'Yes,' someone said.

'Ah – as I was – um – saying—'

There was a loud whirring sound outside the tent. He raised his voice, and leant down slightly, towards the microphone.

'We are planning to show you some slides of Africa, of the missionary work going on there. Many of us put our hard-earned money towards it, and—'

'Forty pence,' whispered an anonymous voice, which threw Derek slightly.

'—and, yes,' he went on, 'we believe we have much to gain from—'

The whirring sound outside grew louder, and nearer to the tent wall. Suddenly George Foster was there, making fast hand gestures where he stood to the right of the table. 'The strimmer – they've got the strimmer,' he was hissing, making sharp cutting motions with his hands. He started thumbing frantically with one of them, jerking a fist backwards and forwards. A few heads glanced in his direction.

Turn slowly away from him, the vicar thought. He turned slowly back towards his audience. 'Africa is important,' he said, raising his voice.

He saw the bishop and his wife nod unanimously. A drop

of rain that had found its way through the marquee canvas overhead fell, catching the end of the bishop's nose. 'Yes, Africa is a vast droplet – um – a vast – continent – and not too drip on us – ah – not too – um – distant from us,' the vicar went on. 'Hang a string on a map where London is, look down it, and there's Africa, if it's long enough. So we really must, all of us—'

In that instant, the whirring became a high-pitched scream. As one, the sea of faces in front of Derek Weston snapped away. Jaw slack, he looked for the bishop, catching snatches of movement all around the marquee, catching Terence Stitt flick his head too, all of them turning, turning to stare at the entrance . . .

The vicar saw the profiles of the long-haired hooligans for only a matter of a fraction of a second. Two of them seemed to be holding George Foster at bay, thrusting their arms out at him. It was not possible to tell if George was making any noise above the screaming of whatever it was the thugs were holding, leaning on, an object that looked like a huge metal plate on the end of long iron stalks, juddering—

The industrial strimmer.

—as they leaned into it, all of them laughing, all of them, in gales of—

Instantaneously, all the marquee lights went down. There were suppressed gasps from Derek Weston's audience. Lit now only by dim sunlight through thick canvas, the faces in front of him went ocean green. 'No fear,' said the vicar out loud, not thinking, hearing the nonsensical pair of words reverberate in the speakers and reflecting in that split-second that the microphone, at least, had not been cut off – and then suddenly finding his face caught in a box of light—

The slides.

—and now some people were laughing, and the vicar was wondering why, half-blinded in the beam of the projector that had been switched on as the lights were cut, squinting and peering through the square of coloured light, catching a glimpse of Marshall Kampfner in a corner of the luminous square and momentarily hearing a flash of their conversation rerun between his ears—

It's a rumour, that's all.

—and then Derek Weston was starting to move, realising what was happening a second too late, hearing the metallic whirring and screaming rise like an ambulance siren, then that judder again as though it had hit a rubber wall full-on—

Not a rubber wall, a rope.

—another judder, more high-pitched vibrating—

The vicar felt knowledge unfold second by second in his heart and head like pinmen jumping on the page-edges of a pocketbook, knowing as it happened that the hooligans would cut the guy-rope completely, knowing as it fell that the marquee had been about to collapse around his parishioners and their friends, around the bishop and his wife and scores of visitors to the parish, knowing it all and never really being surprised as it happened, not even being astonished as the thick folds of canvas blanketed him personally and he heard the muffled roars of fury and angry laughter rise at once around him.

And then the only tragedy he had not foreseen in the milliseconds before it happened.

The ominous creak of the centre-pole.

When the thing fell, he found out later, it toppled on to Marshall Kampfner.

– 3 –

'Well?'

The front door snapped shut behind the vicar, and he looked up the vicarage stairs to where his wife was standing, waiting for an answer.

'Well – well what, darling?'

Judy Weston stepped down one stair, put a hand on a thin hip.

'How is he, Derek?'

Derek Weston looked down at the fraying hall rug in response. There was no reply that would not sound just as ragged as that rug, maybe more so. He ran a hand through thick tufts of hair, and looked up again. 'How is anyone? Not too good.'

In fact Marshall Kampfner had barely recognised his vicar in the hospital, where he sat propped on fluffed pillows, a mountain of bandages piled high around his head, arms slack, nurses attending him fussily.

He had peered at Derek Weston as a rat peers at cheese, squinting through rodent eyes, nose twitching at the sides, chin raised with supreme effort as though trying to sniff out the stranger in the dog-collar seated on the edge of his bed.

'It's me, Marshall. For heaven's sake – Derek, Marshall,' the vicar had said. Gripping the edge of the mattress with a hand, he sent a fast prayer zinging skywards like a bolt from a crossbow: *Lord God, help this man recognise me. Give him back his orderly brain. Restore his memory, restore his—*

'Dalek Marshmallow?' the figure in the bed asked vacantly, as if on sudden inspiration. The vicar pictured the dud bolt tumbling uselessly out of the sky.

15

A nurse had cut across them before Marshall could go further.

'She explained that he shouldn't be reminded of anything,' Derek told his wife now, gazing up at her vaguely. 'Which is a bit strange, considering he seemed to be having a problem with his memory.'

'Memory loss?'

'I think so. Not so much lost as mislaid, they said. Animalesia.'

'Amnesia, Derek. Animalesia isn't anything.'

'No, that's what they said. I queried it too, but apparently he keeps hearing farmyard noises. There were so many bandages around his head it was stopping light coming into the ward. It's – it's very hard to see a Christian theme in this.'

'Oh, well,' Judy sighed. 'So – the Summer Celebration turned out to be a fête worse than death.'

Derek bridled. *Punch and Judy*, he remembered. It was typical of his wife to end the conversation with that kind of truncheon witticism. The two of them had long ago faced up to their differences. She was successful, for a start. She made money – in a bank, of all things. She had a convertible car. She was still thin, with a youthful hairstyle, a fetching way of tossing her head abruptly as she talked, fashionable taste in dresses and everything else.

She worshipped at the church; she believed in something they did not discuss; that was it, the sum of their similarities. After which the two of them went off at angles, like fenceposts hit by a truck. One pointing at the moon, one at the sun – only meeting below ground, where it was coldest.

On his way up the stairs, the vicar found himself thinking thoughts he could not help. *I am a kind man. I serve the Church, other people, tea, everything. Why, why did that big pole have to hit him? Why is that poor man sitting in a hospital bed, his mind jammed like a chocolate machine in an underground station? Before he could tell me whatever it was he knew?*

Then Derek Weston was begging for the most profound forgiveness for his selfishness and failure to check tent-poles, mounting the stairs slowly, plodding as though every step was a million-word prayer, wresting the dog-collar from his neck.

'I gather,' his wife was sighing from the bedroom, 'that up until it happened, everything was going swimmingly.'

'Sunnily. You saw the weather.'

'I would have seen it if I hadn't been working. And I really was, I promise you.'

'I don't doubt it. Yes, it had been going quite well. And the bishop was extremely understanding about the – um – incident. He managed to climb out of the marquee quite quickly, anyway, through a gusset. Besides, a few people did say complimentary things about the day.'

'A few?'

'One or two.'

'Two?'

'Well – one, actually. But a lot of the others were sympathetic.'

'I heard about the projector,' Judy Weston called as he reached the top of the staircase. 'I heard it threw a slide straight into your face, the first one – it was some African woman with nothing on. Not a shred of clothing. Nothing.'

'Oh – ah – yes,' Derek mumbled, asking himself: *was it really? Is that why they were laughing when the projector suddenly came on?*

'Is that what happened, Derek?'

The vicar suddenly felt very tired: felt forty-seven, not forty-six. 'I think the chap on the projector was waiting for a cue, and when they cut the wire to the lights he thought that was it. It was the easiest mistake in the world to make. His booth was plunged into darkness, so he switched the projector on. That first slide – I didn't know what it was of. I couldn't see it from the inside. I only saw a light. Everything went brown, with dots. It's not easy to see a picture projected on to your face. The script said it was something to do with the Zairian Shakespeare Company.'

'Have they caught them?'

'I don't think their performances are that offensive, on the whole. Apart from the way they interpret—'

'Not the people in the slides. The yobs with that lawn-mower, I mean.'

'The strimmer? The police aren't even bothering. For a

17

start, I didn't get a clear view of any of them. Everything was juddering. And the police said the only way they could do a criminal damaging something-or-other—'

'Press charges for criminal damage—'

'—yes, would be on the basis of a simple cut guy-rope, in which case the people could just offer to repair it and get off scot-free. Apparently you can't pull someone in front of a court for cutting a rope these days. The Director of Public Prosecutions has been dropping all the cases. They need to open fire on a crowded room as well. There's nothing very illegal in the act of – you know, strimming, *per se*.'

'That can't be right. Not in law. They've sold you a line.'

'I know, but who's to say that to them? We need police goodwill.'

'You're not a football club, Derek.'

'We have as many own goals as one.'

'True. Very true.'

Regretting his attempt at humour because she had used it against him and he should have guessed she would, the vicar moved to the bathroom and looked into the mirror, peeling off his glasses. *Sir Derek Weston*, he thought, blinking. *Nothing bald about Sir Derek. Lord Derek Weston, let's say. The head of some bank, maybe. POLLS MAKE WESTON FAVOUR-ITE TO SUCCEED PM AS HE SURVIVES STRIMMER ATTACK. That'd be the headline. Glass desks by the dozen. Pounds everywhere. Millions.*

Whoosh, he said to himself. *I can just imagine it.*

She appeared at the door, and the vicar switched off his imagination like a lectern light.

'Daydreamer, nightdreamer. You're always dreaming, Derek.'

He looked across from the mirror to his wife's face. Slim as ever, framed with immaculately spiked hair – black streaked with precise greys. Lips coloured scientifically; a tiny, tiny mouth, one of the smallest ever. Eyebrows dipping down in a steep line, efficiently, thin as cocktail sticks. Fine, bright, 42-year-old eyes, lids like perfectly manicured fingernails that became would-be claws if she fluttered them at you, he had long ago decided. *Stay clear of those eyelids*, he had to stop

18

himself thinking if he ever moved his face towards hers, ready to kiss . . .

Not that they did that too much.

'The TV serviceman came round today,' she said.

'Oh.'

'He found your first five sermons stuck inside it.'

'What?'

'Stuck inside the TV.'

'Really? Where? In the back?'

'Yes. But when he took them out the picture went funny. It started flickering and blurring. He said that sometimes happens. They'd been there so long they'd moulded with the electrics.'

'Moulded?' He was thinking: *we are both servicemen*.

'Melded, moulded, melted, malted. I can't remember which.'

'Paper doesn't melt,' he said, adding thoughtfully: 'Golly – that's amazing. I thought they were thrown away years ago.'

'I had no idea how they fell in there. Through the air vents, he said. I reckoned they could have been sucked in when the PCC meet. All the hot air they emit, you know – it might have created a slipstream, a sort of vortex effect, and . . .'

He did not hear the rest of the sentence, because she had walked out of earshot.

The vicar dried his face with a towel.

When he looked up from it, she was standing there.

'You still have your clothes on, darling.'

'I'm thinking, Derek.'

The vicar's heart sank. The formula was well known to him. His wife wanted to talk. She was upset about something.

He replaced his spectacles. A minute later, they were in the vicarage living room, sitting an ambiguous distance from each other on a peach sofa strewn with old newspapers.

Derek Weston caught the time on the ancient grandfather clock in the corner. Nearly midnight. Then he caught the date on a newspaper. It was two months old. He put out of his mind what had happened two months ago.

'I think I want to leave you,' she said.

He was struck dumb.

The clock counted out a minute like the referee in a ring, strangely loud, its ticking the only sound in the room.

Finally, he asked: 'For how long?'

The words had croaked out of his mouth. Absently, she fingered her wedding ring. 'You have no conviction any more, Derek.'

'I don't – feel that,' he said.

'I do.'

The vicar mumbled: 'I have a conviction for speeding.'

'You know what I mean.'

'But I'm never negative, Judy,' he said. 'I'm a positive person. Everybody tells me that. Everybody. I'm tremendously positive about us.'

'Presumably because you're a positive person,' Judy Weston put in. 'Otherwise, you couldn't be tremendously positive about us. I'm a banker, and I know when I'm looking at debit columns. Us two – we've created an awful lot of them, Derek.'

'We could wipe them. We could – bring in receivers, or—'

She waved his words away, her eyes suffused with tears. 'Oh, Derek. Oh, Derek. Oh, I wish you could understand the change I've seen you go through since we got married. All those millions of years ago – Derek, you were such a visionary before. When we came here, you really believed God could transform anything.'

'I still do.'

'And I was such a little thing, trusting in you – no, you don't. And you know you don't. You might just about think he can change the weather. But having said that, I bet you didn't even pray the sun would shine for your fête. I never see you praying now. The last time you were kneeling was to hunt for a socket. You're a good sort of man, but you know perfectly well you've settled in there—' she pointed at the living room wall, indicating the position of the church beyond it '—and Derek, dear Derek, after eleven years, we're basically staying, aren't we? For ever? And a day? For ever here, on Nock Green?'

'I—'

'Nock, Nock, who's there? Still us? Is that the joke? Still the Westons? Or are we just staying till the Day of Judgement? Will you try and get an extension then, too, Derek? Forget my commuting into London, forget new challenges, forget the congregation—'

'I shan't forget my congregation, Judy. That's why we're here.'

'Don't be so pompous. You know they need someone else. There aren't enough people sitting in the pews on Sundays to play Pass the Parcel. Not unless they used a courier service. Derek, I'm sick of seeing it week after week – all that space! A decade ago, the place was full.' Her voice was soft as she added: 'Full because of you, too.'

'They'll come back,' Derek Weston protested. 'When they've got tired of the tinsel wherever it is they are now. And it's not as empty as you say.'

'Compared to what it was, it is. You used to have – at the heart of yourself, Derek, right in the centre – you had a kind of – I don't know what the word is – it was like a jewel, a thing that glowed, something priceless, something that gave you the power to want more and more for God, something right at the heart of you, something that really—'

'It's very rare, that sort of thing.' The vicar urgently wanted to say out loud what he thought Marshall had been about to tell him in the moments before the pole had knocked it out of his head, explain to his wife that things could be changing soon, that everything could be—

'Well. Yes. Rare. For your information, Derek, I did some singing at the place down the road last – oh, I think it was Thursday. I don't know. But it's lively there, you know. The new person – I can't remember the name – but anyway, they—'

'At St Paul's? The new chap? I'm not sure. There was a mess until recently. But did you really—'

'—yes, they – no, it's not a chap there, Derek, it's a woman – and she has what you used to have, Derek, and it's getting lively over there, and they were having—'

'—turn up and—'

'—a little gathering of their choir—'

'—sing there?'

They paused. She coughed. Sheepishly, he thought.

'Did you, Judy?'

'Yes. So what? I sang there. They rang the house asking for you, trying to see if we had an alto. I said we hardly had a choir and most of the people who sing in our church think perfect pitch is what they use for road resurfacing.'

'You didn't.'

'Well – I said the first part.' Half of her face was in shadow. 'I suppose it's lucky I didn't think of the second at the time.'

Derek Weston felt blood reach his cheeks. Suddenly, he was standing over his wife, fists clenching and unclenching.

'It's not fair! That's not fair! I've got to be able to trust you, at least, Judy!'

'It was only a bit of singing.'

'That's not the point. It's a—'

She was on her feet in an instant. 'It's what?' She had almost spat the words out. 'What is it? Competition, Derek? Someone to show you up? Someone with ideas down the road there, and that's why you don't like it? You mind me singing for them, do you, because of that?'

'I—'

'Is it because it's a woman down there, Derek? A woman vicar?'

'I didn't know it was a woman.'

'Shame on you,' she concluded.

They both breathed deeply.

Then they went to bed.

Lying between the covers, big green covers, the vicar looked up at the moon where it hung in the triangle of space between the bedroom curtains . . . a vulgar, glinting medallion in the open collar of a Bermuda shirt. He reached over to where his wife lay, facing away from him, and put a hand on the petite freckled shoulder, threading his fingers through a delicate silver chain that hung slack from the back of her neck.

Her voice sounded small, muffled by pillow. 'We never do anything together.'

'You do a lot of – of banking,' he said hesitantly. 'Darling, why can't we just – if we tried, couldn't we – couldn't we face down our differences?'

'We're supposed to face up to them,' she sighed.

'We already—'

'Now that Caroline is settled—'

Caroline, their daughter, had married a year ago.

'Judy, she needs us to be together,' Derek Weston mumbled, his eyes drooping. He rolled his head and looked up at the ceiling. A female vicar, just down the road. It was almost incredible. How had he not found out earlier?

'Caroline would understand if the two of us decided to—'

'Don't say it again, Judy. We've been – we've managed to make it work for twenty-three years so far, and—'

'I don't see what that—'

'Judy – please.'

The vicar's wife was silent where she lay for a minute. Then, eyes closed, Derek muttered: 'The Geareys invited us to come and see the Tower again, as their guests.'

'It would only take one tiny thing, you know, to make me leave.'

'What shall I tell the Geareys?' he asked.

There was no reply.

Derek felt sleep overtaking his senses, one by one.

A minute later, his wife spoke again.

'If you want me to be really honest, what I am finding so hard is that business between you and Charlotte Davidson two months ago.'

But there was no answer. She turned in the bed. The vicar's features were slack, his mouth lolling. A sound like whistling from a smashed organ-stop was piping in his nose.

23

– 4 –

Three or four weeks later, Mirabel Weekling and Phyllis Childs were gingerly mounting the steps of St Saviour's, bright sun at their backs.

'Crumbling,' observed the first pensioner tartly.

'You wouldn't be the first, Mirry.'

'No, the steps. Creaking.'

'They told me it might after I had that plate put in.'

'Not your steps, Phyllis. These ones. We need another appeal.'

Most of the church was wooden. The inside walls and roof, the entrances, the doors. New forms of rot and fire risk were constantly being discovered, and the vicar had once launched an ambitious fund-raising drive to bring in forty thousand pounds for a flameproof cladding treatment known as Durable Stone Coating, or DSC.

But the drive started badly after a feature in the *Evenham Gazette*, headlined JUST ADD CANDLES AND WE CAN HAVE A PARTY, alleged that several buildings treated with DSC finished up looking like large cakes – 'iced by a chef who has been at the birthday rum', the paper said, under a photograph of a local sports centre. A ski shop had been nibbled aggressively by vermin because the coating had a nutty flavour, and a police station started being nicknamed 'Château Gâteau' by petty criminals. So the St Saviour's appeal drew only thirty-five pounds in the first month; the target was drastically scaled down, and in the end the donations went on a set of midget fire extinguishers and on paying someone to spray the pew Bible jackets with flame retardant.

As the organ cranked out a half-recognisable melody,

Phyllis and Mirabel found their usual seats with a kind of ancient grandeur, and waved.

The vicar tipped his head in the direction of the two nodding grey heads.

He tipped it at the Geareys, too. In pew three. Then looked over at his curate, and smiled. Otis Cheeseman was a shy, sandy-haired American who had proved invaluable, in a quiet way, since his appearance in the church eighteen months ago after taking advantage of something called a Transat Church Swap Program. He was closing in on thirty, serious-minded, a perfectionist with a mild streak of hypochondria who seemed a little gaffe-prone and unsteady in the pulpit and suffered a very slight tic in his right eye at times of tension – so Derek kept him mainly to pastoral work and notices. Irritatingly, Judy always referred to him as Notice Cheeseman.

Otis was a dedicated, almost compulsive theologian. He had brought so many thick books over from America that four-fifths of them had to be stored inside the church itself. Often Derek saw him creeping to and fro, late at night, with some vast volume in his hands. *He is fascinated by the jots and tittles of belief*, the vicar had decided soon after their first meeting. He wondered sometimes if Otis could ever fall in love – was he engaged to his books?

His library must have been shipped over at huge expense. In the weeks before the crates arrived, Otis seemed lost without them. 'Some people get off on grand feelings,' he had explained quietly, 'but I find myself keener and keener to look into the background detail, like what sort of hat Samuel wore at breakfast – or indeed, whether he might have eaten breakfast bareheaded. That way you know where you are.' He claimed to have 'learned every verse in the Bible', then scaled the claim down to the second half of it after Derek asked him a prepared question on how many acres Hoglah got when Joshua divided Hebron, and Otis was three out. 'Even so,' the curate said, unabashed, smilingly, 'I wouldn't even cross the street without looking it up.'

The vicar had offered a cautious smirk in response to that one, thinking a serious personnel problem might be looming – yet the curate had gone on to prove his value to the church time and again with conscientious good works. *Without Otis*, Derek had often begun thinking, *without Otis . . .* then, invariably, he would leave the thought there, as if afraid of where it would take him.

'Nice view from here,' whispered Mirabel.

Phyllis Childs, whose hearing was not what it used to be, agreed. 'They ought to clean them.'

There were sixty-five in the church that morning. Sixty-five, that is, until twenty-eight minutes past ten.

The vicar had been lost in his own thoughts as the moment to start the service approached. A wedding the day before had been the subject of a misunderstanding between the relief organist and the bride, who had wanted the ballad 'Everything I Do, I Do It For You' played as she appeared at the end of the aisle. But in rehearsal she described it simply as the theme from the film *Robin Hood*, not making it clear that the version her song appeared in was the latest of several remakes.

So when she appeared at the end of the aisle in shining white, braced for the romantic melody, the relief organist had begun a deafening rendition of the music from the original film: 'Robin Hood, Robin Hood, riding through the glen/Robin Hood, Robin Hood, with his band of men . . .' and for a short, feverish time, looking on in panic, the vicar feared court action. Luckily, it all seemed washed away in later celebrations.

Shaking off the memory, the Reverend Derek Weston looked at his watch.

Nearly half past.

A thought zig-zagged between his temples: *my life is three-fifths past.*

Never mind. How was it possible to mind?

Sunday. Time to clock on.

At twenty-nine minutes past ten, Derek reached for the hymn-book lodged on the narrow shelf above his knees. Then he saw the three figures silhouetted in the entrance of the church, white sunlight at their backs, and stopped his hand.

The shapes seemed frozen in the doorway for a fraction of a second.

He blinked: saw the image in reverse on the insides

of his eyelids. Three in fierce mauve against a Tippex backdrop.

Visitors!

He had not seen them before. Motionless in that moment, they looked like something out of a Western – and for an illogical sliver of time he dreaded fearsome, shotgun vengeance for the collapse of the marquee nearly a month ago, hot lead blasted at him for falling congregations that he had never really minded, spent cartridges tumbling to the timber floor . . . smoking for his marriage, his armchair life, insolent optimism and abundant hair, the tennis and the squash, the accidental playing of incorrect music at weddings . . .

But suddenly they were sitting, he was standing, and the service was under way.

'I don't believe it,' said Mirabel Weekling.

'What?' asked Phyllis Childs.

'I said I don't believe it.'

'What?'

'I can't see a thing.'

'Sorry, dear. I'm not picking you up.'

'I said – I can't see anything.'

As the opening bars to the first hymn hooted in the organ-pipes, the three newcomers to St Saviour's church had sat directly in front of them. Now the two elderly women were attempting to recover the view they were used to.

The congregation negotiated a path through the first hymn, like lost ramblers.

Derek Weston saw the two hillocks of grey hair bounce up repeatedly behind the newcomers.

At one point a piece of metal appeared to jump out of the back of the organ and ping on the side of the altar table.

Something is falling apart, the vicar reflected in a space between verse and chorus. He looked up from his hymn-book and glanced at the three new figures, eleven rows back.

The organist launched into another attack on a verse. It sounded like a surprise attack with ground troops, the vicar decided. The man had picked up the first line four words late, but late was better than never. The singing was worse than usual. There was no oomph in the alleluias. The choir had been depleted by something described by a doctor as hysterical flu. Having visitors gave the vicar a rare twinge of embarrassment.

As the sixty-eight parishioners took their seats, the man in the pew in front turned to Phyllis Childs and Mirabel Weekling. 'My wife and son,' he beamed, teeth jutting out, indicating the two next to him with a leaning thumb. His teeth seemed to point at a selection of airports. The wife shifted around in her seat and smiled warmly. 'We're new here,' she said, in a hushed voice. Her eyebrows were trembling. 'I hope we're not in your way.'

'Hello,' said Mirabel, sweetly. 'Not at all.'

Now, at the front, the curate was speaking. The husband and wife faced forwards again, the woman whispering something into the ear of the boy.

Phyllis Childs muttered at her friend: 'Couldn't you have said something a bit more pugnacious?'

'Keep your voice down, for heaven's sake. You'll send Otis into a tizzy.'

'I can't see him.'

Continuing his reading of parish notices, Otis Cheeseman was only momentarily distracted by the sight of a crest of crinkled grey hair rising over the three newcomers, a flat hand underneath it shading a pair of eyes.

He moved on.

'And thank you, all of you – most all of you – for praying in connection with the accident at the Summer Celebration. This week we received news that the two guests in the parish who were bruised after falling on to molehills are substantially better. I'm sure you'll also be relieved to hear that at long last, Marshall Kampfner is due out of hospital—'

He drew breath for what sounded like the beginnings of a ripple of applause.

'Well, we understand the medical details are that he suffered a concussion, followed by a memory misplacement and an operation of some sort. As all of you – as most all of you – will know, the doctors basically decided he must rest. I gather all of these things come normal in time. And

I'm pleased to say he expects to be back at work in Evenham library a mere eight days from now.'

There was an intake of breath at the good news. 'So – all that Marshall asks,' the American went on, blinking several times in rapid succession, 'is for your prayers that he should be able to recall a few remaining things easily, and I have – I think I have – a list of them here. Yes, got it.' He unfolded a small piece of paper. 'The route he normally takes to work, it says, the names of anyone he owes money to and the amounts, the names of his two smallest children, any outstanding PCC business, the arrangement of shelving in the library – he asks you to pray particularly for the large print section – and the place where he last parked his car, at least to the nearest county.'

Derek Weston coughed in his seat.

And whatever the rumour was that he has since been unable to remember.

He watched the curate replace the note in his inside breast pocket.

If you could pray for that to resurface, I'd be most grateful.

In a small voice, Otis was adding: 'We might remind ourselves at this point that Jehoiada lived to be a hundred and thirty.'

Always nervous when his curate improvised, Derek glanced about. He was suddenly caught in the gaze of the three worshippers he had never seen before. There was a glimmer of—

The faintest flare went up over his heart, then died.

'I think now we'll—' The vicar got up, cleared his throat and looked around. 'People, everyone, let's sing again.'

With each verse of each hymn, and all through the vicar's sermon, the sharp sunlight outside seemed to choose a different pane of stained glass as an entrance to the church. Every-coloured rays touched the heads of the parishioners in turn. Standing secure on the elevated pentagon of pulpit floor, preaching on 'Goodness Is Something To Be Aimed At', Derek Weston suddenly found himself rejoicing in the natural light, the beauty of the timber interior and the genial human warmth radiating from those within it.

29

There may not be hundreds, he reflected. *But it's been a good life leading them*. And as so often in past weeks, he began to wonder when next the bishop would be in touch, what the form of words would be . . .

We have chosen you as bishop for a large area of the country called—

'I can't hear him,' Phyllis Childs hissed at Mirabel Weekling. 'You're not getting anything at all?'

'Hang on.' She reached down to her waist and fiddled with the small cream button on the top edge of the matchbox-sized hearing-aid unit attached to her belt.

Derek Weston was concluding his sermon when he heard the piercing whistle in the twelfth row back.

'We can never know what happened after this parable was told,' he said. The whistling became an undulating plastic shriek. He thought of strimmers. 'But it – it may be – it may be that—' It was a howling now, like old kettles coming to the boil, and he was competing against it – the vicar turned his head in the direction of the noise.

As instantly as it started, the ear-splitting shriek stopped.

'I think that's it,' muttered Phyllis. 'I'm getting him again.'

'That's funny,' Mirabel whispered, 'because he's not speaking now.'

'Oh – perhaps it's Radio Five Live, then,' said her friend, reaching down to the unit. Mirabel Weekling looked up, a puzzled expression on her face.

The vicar had fallen strangely silent where he stood in the pulpit. At once, the whole congregation was attentive.

Derek Weston was lost for words.

Boxed inside the pulpit, he stared over towards where the two elderly women were sitting in the twelfth row back. But the vicar was not looking at them. He was gazing at the three newcomers to his church – at one of them in particular.

And it was a full thirty seconds before he returned to the final paragraph of computer-typed sermon laid out on the lectern.

'I know, Rex. It's unbelievable.'

The vicar was at the home of his friend, Rex Gobart.

'But you're paid to believe strange things. In any case, can't you just—'

'Get them out? Ask them to leave? Of course not, Rex. This is the Church of England. It's got a shocking case of claustrophilia at the moment – love of confined spaces, that is. This is supposed to be the Decade of Evangelism, believe it or not. Everything's done on a headcount now. The old notion of quality control has gone totally out of the window. If two people arrive who the vicar doesn't like, you put it to a vote and the vicar has to go. I think I'm only allowed to ask them to leave if they vandalise the pew Bibles, bring in unlicensed shotguns, or call for Michael Portillo to become Prime Minister.'

'Goodness.'

'Yes – or show unusual levels of goodness. That's another one.'

Brow creased like crêpe paper, the vicar put down his tea and looked over at his friend. 'It's bad, actually,' he said quietly. Rex Gobart – nicknamed 'Breakfast' because of several large early morning meals at university – could usually be relied on to offer crumbs of comfort. He was outside it all, that was why. But on this occasion he seemed lost for them.

'You're saying they've just – as it were – landed on you? And they'll stay?'

'Crash-landed, more like. They certainly didn't have their wheels down,' the vicar replied. 'And they weren't cleared by air traffic control, which is me.' He only had to cast his mind back a couple of hours to replay the conversation with the three newcomers as they filed out of the church. 'They said – well, first they said, sort of, "Hello. You don't know who we are, do you?" Laughing. And of course I said—'

'You said you thought you did.'

'No – how could I? I blurted out something about thinking I recognised her from a police reconstruction. I'm sorry, Rex – I couldn't admit it. We shook hands. Their son was pretty gormless. Zombified. That's when the mum and dad came out with—'

'That they were the Davidsons.'

'That's exactly how he said it, Rex! Like an announcement over the tannoy at a department store! "We are the Davidsons!" It was – well, as I say, I realised while I was preaching the sermon that it was them. I knew. I was somewhere near the end, talking about a parable, and dear old Mrs Childs – one of our oldest regulars, Phyllis Childs, aged eighty-four – her hearing aid made a nasty whistle. A shriek. It quite often does. It once went off during a parade by the Brownies, and they all started trooping out of the church with their flags twenty minutes early and had to be brought back. It caused chaos, actually. But I looked over towards Phyllis this time, because it sounded a bit worse than usual – that was when I caught the eye of the woman.'

'Mrs Davidson.'

'Marion Davidson. Yes. Marion Davidson. Her face – suddenly, Rex – it – triggered something. Don't ask what. It must have been the line of her jaw and the hair, I think. I just – I just knew who they were. Instantly. I'd never seen them before, but I knew exactly who. I stared and stared and stared. I couldn't speak for about two minutes.'

'Really? What did your congregation do?'

'Well – they suddenly became very interested, actually. One chap got nudged by his wife and woke up. Someone else pulled out a pad and made a note. And a lady at the back did a huge rasping sound into her handkerchief, which sounded like – what's that firework? An air-bomb? As if that was going to jolt me out of it.'

Rex snorted with laughter, an economist's carefully-calculated laughter, leaning into the threaded wicker of his creaking chair, pushing two pudgy hands into his cheeks. He was a big, square-headed man whose stomach seemed to threaten to pop the buttons on his Sunday waistcoat as he jerked his shoulders back where he sat at the kitchen table. The two men had met at university, lost touch, then renewed the acquaintance when the vicar came to Evenham. Rex, a City management consultant – twice married, twice divorced – had once described his religion as Mistianity: he'd completely missed whatever it was he was supposed to believe. He never went near a church. Derek Weston forgave him that. It meant he could tell him anything.

'She looked like Charlotte. Simple as that.'

Now the vicar was telling the management consultant everything.

'Mrs Davidson?'

'Marion Davidson.'

'Sheeeee—'

'She looked like her daughter,' the vicar broke in. 'That's why – I hope you don't mind me coming over, Breakfast. But it is – well, after that incident with Charlotte two months ago, after what I was saying about—'

'About Judy,' Rex Gobart broke back magnificently, booming voice making the kitchen shrink for a moment. Beyond a net curtain, sun was streaming into a lush garden; the vicar's eye dwelt on a majestic rocky pool, its surface flickering in the pure, golden rays.

He heard the management consultant say: 'As someone who's played two and lost two, I need to keep you on the straight path here. Just remember, Derek, this isn't about Charlotte. This is about Judy. This is about your wife. And from what you were saying last time we met, she was dwelling on it.'

'That's true. Of course that's true. She was dwelling. That's the whole point.' The vicar turned back to him. 'We had an argument. She said she wanted to leave me. Anyway, in the end I managed to change the subject. I don't think she really meant it. Then we went to bed. But when we were lying there together, she just said something like: "To be honest,

Derek, what I find most hard is what happened between you and Charlotte Davidson two months ago." She said it straight – just like that.'

'How on earth did you answer?'

'I didn't. I just opened my mouth and made a snoring sound, so she thinks I didn't hear.'

'You're a coward, Derek.'

'Rubbish. I've never been afraid to run.'

They had talked about Charlotte Davidson many times in the two months since she had left St Saviour's after a year of being there every week, so there was no sensation in that part of the vicar's account. The facts were simple. The vicar had not been in love with her or anything remotely like it, but something had snapped into place as soon as they had met: she, twenty-one and just out of an exclusive music school, the Royal College of Something-or-other . . .

'You have the whole world in your hands,' the vicar had said.

'In that case, I'd better put it down,' Charlotte Davidson had replied, smiling. 'I need to look after my fingers. If I'm going to play properly, like I want to. For God.'

In the vicar's head, the statement echoed as an outrageous question: *play for God?* He had heard of working, but *playing*—? The two had been standing exactly where Derek Weston found himself with her parents and brother, fourteen months later: in the queue of hand-shakers at the church doors after a Sunday morning service.

'I love these beams,' she had put in.

'Sunbeams?'

'All this wood. The beams across the roof.'

There had been a cough from someone further down the queue.

Shut up, cougher, the vicar thought.

'We're about to start pebbledashing the back, to stop the—'

'And these shelves! What are all these piles of books for? Stacked in long lines up there?'

'They belong to my curate. He brought more than five hundred over from—'

34

'Better move on,' Charlotte Davidson had cut in.

'What's your—?'

'Charlotte. Charlotte Davidson. Cheerio.'

It seemed older than a memory now – seemed more like a snatch of Ancient Britain. Picturing that first exchange as he sat with Rex Gobart, the vicar half-expected to see Roman soldiers riding through the church cemetery behind the girl's head, wobbling their shields, asking directions in Latin. He had described her to Breakfast several times. She was short and slim, with blonde hair always bunched in a band over her crown and the upper part of her back very slightly stooped – possibly from playing the highest notes on the piano or too much scribbling of complicated quavers and octaves, he had speculated. Charlotte wore hexagonal glasses, casual red gloss on thin lips; had narrow, fine, shining, glinting eyes, eyes which glinted and flickered like rockpool surfaces; was blessed with shaded, easy-tan skin like the vicar's . . . and that small dot in a cheek, of course, like a marker laid down for a first ever kiss. In some ways young Charlotte was a little like Judy Weston. Swap his wife's jet-black hair for blonde, subtract two and a half decades, put some colour into Judy's cheeks and soften those flinted features a touch . . .

Charlotte wore loose-fitting shirts and trousers with surprising slogans splashed across them, buttons undone or missing everywhere. Judy's outfits were tailored to avoid even a centimetre of sag, held together with every zip and catch done medically tight, embossed with prim designer trademarks in obvious places.

On second thoughts, Charlotte is not a bit like my Judy, the vicar had concluded, victimising himself and his endless stupidity.

Now Rex was saying: 'I don't see why this would make things difficult.'

'Judy wasn't there today, thank goodness. She was—'

'What makes you think they're going to keep coming, anyway?'

'They said so! They live nearby – down the road. They said Charlotte told them how much help I'd been, how welcome they would be – though I think she probably said the church was in a terrible state, the vicar was an emergency case, and they ought to get down here fast in a kind of spiritual ambulance.'

Rex paused, rubbing his forehead. 'I never knew this about you, Derek.'

'Knew what?'

'The spiritual ambulance bit.'

'I'm not saying I need one. I suppose I could do with a bit of oxygen, in that sense. Perhaps a drip, too, and a spot of electrical shock treatment – oh, I don't know. Things have just – well, slackened off a bit in that department. I don't mind telling you. And to be honest, I've been pretty happy recently.' He lightened up, thinking of the Bishop of Basildon, of brilliant, heavy news coming slowly towards him like American freight trains puffing steam . . . 'Very happy, actually. But you know what it was about Charlotte, Rex, why the whole thing got—'

'Unfortunate, I think would be the best word.' His friend's face was stern. 'It got extremely unfortunate. And I speak as someone who's off the rails with women. I'll tell all kinds of people I love them, just for a day. But – look, speaking as someone who's fought two, surrendered two, Derek – she was only nineteen, for Pete's sake!'

'Twenty-one. And she really believed, Breakfast. And – now, come off it, it wasn't like that. You don't understand. It was simply – for once, in my church, I had someone who was just – just glowing with it. Someone who was really in touch.'

'With what? The charts?'

'With God. Christ, if you like. She understood it. She knew what it was all about, and – it's been so long since I've felt I had that centre in me.'

'And she had it, did she?'

'Her beliefs were – well, it wasn't belief at all. It was like a relationship.' The vicar shrugged. 'That's why I tried to get close to her. It was – professional. I'm not saying – I can't – it's – it's hard now, for me to conjure it all up again, what it was like having her there.' Derek was beginning to squirm in his seat. 'I'm not saying it was right,' he added.

'But it was good, was it?' His friend's voice was toneless.

'She made me believe it was possible to have that power again, the power I had when I first believed in it all – when I felt so in touch with God, all the time. The pearl of greatest price, they call it in the Bible somewhere. Haven't you heard that description before? The pearl? But now I'm back to – well, it's like trying foreign telephone numbers for a hotel somewhere I haven't heard of, and the receptionist isn't even picking up the phone. That's how distant I can feel.'

'Have you tried using a fax?'

'I'm serious, Rex.'

'Of course it's – it's – hard for me to understand. As a management consultant.'

'A while back I thought becoming a missionary would help. Their eyes always seem to twinkle in photographs. I met some called the Cravens, and their eyes were twinkling all over the place. But I rang up this lot who co-ordinate work in Africa, anyway – and they – believe it or not, they said they didn't have any vacancies!'

'No vacancies?'

'Yes – "no vacancies in Africa". It makes you wonder, doesn't it? It's not as if they could have the whole place covered. You'd think there'd be a couple of coconut trees free, or, or – I don't know, Rex. Sometimes I pick hymn numbers by shaking the box and pulling them out with my eyes shut. Once I put 1249633 up there, or some seven-figure number, because I'd been vague and pulled everything out, and of course they were all goldfishing with nothing to sing when they saw it. And Charlotte – she talked to me about all that, even agreed to pray with me about it – which I've never done with Judy, not for years – and – she – well, something just seemed to make her glow with power.'

'Glowing with power? You're making her sound like a microwave.'

'Oh – Rex, never mind.'

'She's gone now, anyway. Gone, Derek. Forget her. Boom-boom. Bang. Gone.'

An eye in the vicar's mind was suddenly opened. A vista of the past unfurled. *She's gone now, anyway.* He remembered the day Charlotte Davidson said she was going, the moment two months ago when he had felt relief and sadness drench him in equal measure.

'Going where? Another church?'

'I've got that job.'

'What—'

'The orchestra in the north-east I told you about. They decided they want me.'

'I thought you were applying to places where they spoke English.'

'Silly. It's a good job.'

'But you didn't want to play in a band, Charlotte.'

'I'll be doing a lot of solo work.'

She had chewed her lip casually and looked away from him. He bit his tragically, stared up at the stars. They were among a group doing something: leafleting, perhaps . . . one of her ideas, anyway, that had bucked up his unbucked church.

Days later, she had given him a lift back to the vicarage.

'I was just getting to know you,' he had said, pocketing a scrap of orange paper she had passed him with a long-distance telephone number on it. He sat on his hands in the passenger seat of her battered Mini and stared at the primitive dashboard.

'Well – thank you, Derek, for—'

'Oh, thank you.' He realised it meant far less to her than to him.

'I'll be sad to go. You must make sure you keep on with your praying, Derek.'

'I want to be like you.'

She had giggled, seemed suddenly embarrassed, and dropped her head so that her chin came to rest in the folds of her pink sweatshirt. But when the vicar climbed out of the car, anxious to leave it there, Charlotte climbed out from her side too.

'I must shake your hand, Derek.'

She had moved around the turquoise Mini bonnet.

Furtively, Derek glanced up into the darkness towards the upstairs windows of the vicarage. Was Judy in? It was not that

38

late. The lights were out. He guessed she must be out too. He looked back down, at Charlotte.

'Cheerio, Derek. It's been really nice. I did enjoy getting to – oh—'

He had grabbed her to him, thrown his left arm around her shoulders and suddenly had his face within an inch of hers, his right hand in the stray hairs at her temple. Then he stopped. She was looking up at him, stars drowning in her sparkling eyes.

Her chest was against his. The girl in pink and the vicar in trouble.

Her perfume—

Her perfume.

She moved a foot to regain her balance, and he felt a thigh move against his.

Then, slowly, her face turned away from his. As if from invisible aerosols, tension and anguish were scrawling themselves over it like tube-train graffiti.

Already regretting himself, regretting everything, regretting that someone had even given birth to him, Derek Weston pulled Charlotte Davidson closer where they stood in the vicarage drive. But the pull was half-hearted, formal . . . and by the time his cheek had stooped to brush dutifully against hers, the two of them were already drawing apart – and a moment later had done, and then in the instant after that there was an exchange of stuttered goodbyes and good wishes and a final disassociation, all together, all at once.

Those were bald farewells. She did not look as shaken as he felt, the vicar noted. Guilt rinsed him. Walking up the vicarage steps, he had run a hand through his hair and thought: *I shall never be as bald as those farewells*. Then, turning the key in the front door as her car pootled off down the drive, Derek Weston had yelled at himself from within: *what on earth were you doing?*

What happened to everything they taught you at theology school?

You crazy idiot! Keys bunched in his hand, the vicar grimaced. *You idiot! Your daughter is a year older than her! You're a senior citizen! You remember where you were when Jim Reeves died!*

Derek turned on the hall light and made his way up the gloomy staircase, reprimanding himself on every stair.

By the top he decided that maybe, just possibly, it was not that bad. What had he done wrong that was not contained in that minor fraction of a second?

And who in this world has not done a sin lasting a fraction of a second?

And would not Charlotte have been – would she not have been somehow flattered, the vicar had wondered, perhaps even slightly pleased, somehow, to be—

Then, on the way to the bathroom, Derek Weston drew level with the bedroom door, glanced in, and halted in his tracks.

A familiar outline was visible against the diffracted moonlight outside, a black shape before a shut window.

The vicar breathed in and peered into the room.

Blinking, he said: 'Darling – darling, what are you doing here?'

There had been no answer from Judy Weston, barring a tiny noise that came from somewhere in her throat that might have been a cry or a gasp.

'Why are you standing here in the dark, Judy?'

There was still no response. Eyes adjusting to the light, the vicar thought he saw his wife put her hands in the pockets of her skirt and look down.

'I saw you, Derek,' she said, finally. And Judy Weston had begun to weep.

In the vicar's mind, the vivid image rolled up like a blind. Some sort of eyelid came down on it, a final curtain.

Rex Gobart was looking at him now, searchingly.

'What's on your mind?'

'You don't need to ask, do you?'

'Well, surely it's good to have these Davidsons, anyway. To boost things.'

'The chap put a – a hand up in the middle of the service. During a hymn. I thought he was asking a question. I'm not sure we need that sort of boosting.'

'You don't want people with feeling?'

'His wife put both hands up during – no, I don't, Rex.' If I don't have any feeling, how can I take them? The place for feeling is politics or opera. And boosting is something you do with polio vaccinations. Frankly, our church is the place for – for groping.'

'Well, from what you were saying about that incident with Charlotte Davidson, I'd probably be on the verge of agreeing with—'

'No, no, no – come on, Rex, I'm not talking about—' The vicar breathed in, intertwined his fingers and placed his hands, carefully, on the kitchen table. He looked down at them. 'You know what I mean. Or maybe you don't. I've got all the surroundings, but I'm missing the centre.'

'The pearl?'

'The – you've got it! And -- and in that situation, it's disastrous to have people coming in with their own – their own centres. It'll start getting like local government,' he added, lamely. 'But—' Derek pulled his hands apart, slapped the palms on the tabletop and drummed with the fingers of one hand. 'There's a far more important factor to worry about now.'

'Which is?'

The drumming stopped. 'Well, listen, I can't go into details, but I think after all these years that I'm just about to be promoted. Seriously promoted. Not just to a rectorship – something higher.'

'A woman priest?'

'It's not been confirmed,' the vicar went on, ignoring the question. 'For a whole host of reasons, I'm finding it impossible to get it confirmed. So I can't tell Judy – I wish I could. I really want to do something to make her happy. But I just can't risk her getting hopes up that something might change, then have them come crashing down.'

He wiped a cheek with a hand.

'She's told me, Rex, that one tiny thing would be enough to make her leave. Just one thing. This is it, Rex. The Davidsons in the church. That's all she needs. And if she walks out, Rex, if Judy goes now, even for a fortnight, that's it – *finito*. The end of us, the end of everything. No promotion, no nothing. That's how the Church works. Extraordinary problems are all right, like not being able to believe the Bible or having a history of biting people. But if you have too many normal problems, like marriage or credit card debt, they pull the hatch lever on you. And – she'll go, Rex, if she meets the Davidsons. She'll go. I absolutely, utterly, know it. So how do I stop her—'

'Finding out who they are? Not at all easy,' Rex put in breezily.

'Am I sounding selfish?' the vicar asked, the words faint.

'Shellfish or selfish?'

'The second.'

'I was going to say – if it was the first, you're just a political prawn in all this.'

There was a long pause, and then his friend said, in a sober voice, 'No, Derek. You don't sound selfish. You love your wife.'

'I do,' the vicar said.

'Love needs to be expressed when it blooms,' the management consultant muttered, almost to himself.

Both men stared out into the garden for a while.

Finally, Rex Gobart announced: 'There's only one thing I can think of that might get you out of this. Only one thing.'

Derek twisted and untwisted his fingers for a while.

Then Rex told him what it was.

6

With a loud bang, the cork flew out of the bottle, shot across the room and out of an open window.

Everyone cheered. 'That must mean good luck,' someone called.

'The Lord is my shepherd,' said Marshall Kampfner, gazing after the cork, then looking down at his glass as the bottle arrived to fill it. 'Lovely. Sparkling wine. There. That's it. Thank you.'

'Welcome back, Marshall,' the chief librarian intoned. He was a tall man with an intricate moustache, inch-deep spectacles, a warm smile and an analytical mind. 'We've been devoting recurrent thoughts to you during your thirty-three day absence.' A dozen of them were standing inside a hoop of tightly-packed books at the library. 'You do look to be at premium fitness, and we also welcome that warmly.'

'What temperature?' a voice asked in a whisper, and there was a giggle.

'I'm much better,' said Marshall Kampfner, addressing all of them. 'From what I've been told about it, the way the pole hit me won't have any long-term effects.'

Someone asked: 'How did it hit you?'

'I can't remember,' said the librarian.

Everyone was hushed for a moment.

'But,' said Marshall, looking up from his glass with a hesitant smile, 'they said I probably wouldn't get that back. Everything else is on its way, or here already. And look – I must say, it's so kind of you all to lay this on for me.'

Buoyed, the librarians talked for a while. One said something about bookshops not being as good as libraries because they were louder, and someone else was commenting on how well the weather seemed to be holding up in Evenham this year, but that didn't mean there couldn't be a cyclone tomorrow. Another staff member slid off to deal with a member of the public who wanted to complain about being hit in the cheek by a large cork while walking past. Easing herself along a row of odd-sized gardening books, one of the trainees approached Marshall to ask what sort of physiotherapy he had been told to do.

'Head exercises, mainly. Funny jerks. Just to get my neck moving. All painless.' He did one as an example, striking his forehead a glancing blow on the spine of a thick volume about turf cultures. 'Except that one,' he squinted.

'Mind yourself! So you had quite a long list of exercises, did you?'

'Ouch. Nothing exotic. By the way, Cindi – what's happened over there?' He pointed.

'Oh, they finally took some action on historical fiction,' the trainee said. 'We had to move one lot of books up after they closed a section. It's all poetry now, that bit.'

Marshall stared at the shelving, overjoyed to have remembered so easily the way it had been stacked before the day of the accident . . . but then, as he looked, something else moved in his mind – some kind of absent memory, moving so subtly and with so slight a shift in his consciousness that he could not even tell what it was. Something connected with historical fiction, perhaps?

He looked over at the shelving.

No. It was not connected with historical fiction.

We had to move one lot of books up, she had said . . .

Cindi was still talking to him, but Marshall was not listening. And when the lunch hour ended and the library staff ambled back to their posts, Marshall Kampfner was still deep in thought.

Not long afterwards, the librarian picked up the telephone beside his computer and dialled a number he took great pleasure in being able to recall instantly.

Derek Weston was three feet from his phone when it sounded, faintly, in the vicarage study. Springing up from an armchair, he yanked two bulky directories off the receiver to get to it before the ringing stopped, sending an empty coffee cup tumbling off the back of his desk. 'Oh – come on – here – golly – ah—' Uncovered, the phone sounded startlingly loud. The vicar pulled the handset up and away from the debris, held it at arm's length while he fished for the cup, then pressed it to the side of his head. 'Derek Weston here.'

'Derek, it's Marshall.'

'Marshall! How are you? Back at work today, I hope! Sorry – I'm upside-down. Just reaching for a coffee cup.'

'Yes. I've done my first morning. Someone put all the books on slimming back under horror, so they needed a bit of a sort-out. And we've had a kind of celebration lunch hour.'

'Goodness. Wonderful.' Derek suddenly fell down the back of his desk. 'Ah – just – oh – just hold on a moment, Marshall, I—'

'Derek, I haven't got long,' said Marshall, interrupting him. 'First day and all that. I just wanted to – something a bit strange has just happened.'

The vicar grappled for position on the desktop.

'What?'

'I was just – it's to do with that question you kept asking me in hospital. About a rumour, wasn't it? The thing you kept telephoning about, every other day, insisting I try and think what it was?'

In one sudden, smooth movement, the vicar moved up and back in an arc and dropped, bolt upright, into a slat-backed wooden chair.

He blinked out at the gravel driveway beyond the window. *He's remembered.*

The vicar's grip on the receiver tightened.

'You know the thing I mean, Derek. Like on the day you took me to that spot on the Green next to where the marquee had been—'

Keep your breath steady, the vicar told himself. *Just keep it steady. Here we go.*

'—and we stood on it because you said it would refresh my—'

'Yes—'

'—memory of the conversation, of this rumour you said I'd

45

mentioned, and I stood there with you, and all I could bring to mind was that chap with a cat and a twitch from one of the James Bond films – and you said that wasn't right, and then you started getting a bit—'

'Marshall—'

'—aggressive, and—'

'—what is it you've remembered?'

The librarian sniffled down the line, and then began: 'Well, just now I was talking to someone about the shelving of one of our categories of book—'

To the vicar, the thin voice coming down the telephone wire sounded suddenly distant, absurdly clinical, as if the words had been individually donated by Reformed Presbyterian preachers on Horlicks.

'—and they used a phrase that jogged something, Derek. She – Cindi, her name is, the trainee – she said, "We had to move one lot of books up." She was talking about historical fiction after they closed a section of shelving or some such thing. It just – as I say, it just—'

'Jogged something?' The vicar leant forward at his desk, elbows pressing hard into the leather. 'Marshall, what? What did it jog? Moving books up? For heaven's sake, Marshall – the rumour!'

'I—' the voice at the other end faltered, then came back sounding clearer and closer. 'Gosh – I just can't remember.'

'Try!'

'I—'

'Try, Marshall!'

'What was the question again?'

'Your memory! The rumour! Whatever it was that got jogged!'

'It wasn't so much a jog as a hobble,' he said. 'But it's something to do with those words . . .'

Alone, the words were enough to exhilarate the vicar when he put the handset back in its cradle and whispered them in the silence of the study: 'We had to move one lot of books up, we had to move one lot of books up, we had to move one lot—'

It must be, Derek Weston thought. It simply had to

be. *I am about to be moved up. Not like books, not like shelving—*

I am going to be moved up to the bishopric.

So it was confirmed. It was as close to confirmation as church youth groups. You could not get closer to confirmation than what Marshall had just said. That was what had triggered him, wasn't it? Moving books up? All right, it would have been nice if he had settled it absolutely, but . . .

Paper was piled in front of the vicar: forms from a charity for autism he was donating to after seeing *Rain Man*, two red electricity bills and three letters from prisoners serving life sentences he corresponded with, all needing replies, some press cuttings about Derby he was using for a sermon on hell – now Derek Weston could not focus on them. He leant back in the chair, looked up at the ceiling and linked hands behind his head, awash in a surge of the most profound relief.

Judy will love me again, he thought.

The bishop-to-be might have been sitting, contemplating, for all of fifteen minutes.

She will realise I'm rocket-fired, dual-cylindered – maybe quadruple.

Sextuple-cylindered.

You don't get closer to confirmation than this.

Turbo-vicar.

The vicar sat up, jerked bolt upright by the sound he had just heard.

It was unmistakable.

A car, hitting something?

How long had he been sitting there thinking?

It sounded like a car.

A crash. Something crunching.

And not far away, either.

That was glass breaking, wasn't it?

Disorientated, he pulled his spectacles off and threw them on to the desk, jumped up from the chair, raced to the front door and out of the vicarage, catching his jacket on the knocker as he dashed past it.

At the top of the gravel drive the vicar pulled himself up for a second. He listened. The bush-lined driveway curled out of sight before it came to the road, and Derek thought he could hear the yawning creak of a car door being eased open.

He started running towards the end of the drive.

Twenty-five yards later the car came into sight, its front crunched against the elderly yew at the entrance to the vicarage driveway, bonnet corrugated by the impact, someone visible leaning away on the far side, the driver's side . . .

'Hey! Are you all right in there?'

The vicar ran up to the open passenger window.

To his left, the windscreen had smashed into thousands of pieces. Only half of it was still in place. The driver had his back to the vicar, sitting at a right angle to the seat, leaning forwards out of the door on the other side of the car. It was a red Renault. Derek noticed a wheel at a strange angle. Gingerly, he placed his hands on the upper edge of the lowered passenger window and poked his head inside.

'Are you all right?'

There was a sigh. And then the response, directed at the quiet road.

'Fine, thank you.'

The vicar turned his head and saw the creased red bonnet jutting up beyond the shattered diamonds of window, and past the hillock of crumpled metal the church yew marked with a streak of livid yellow where there should have been bark.

The driver sighed again. 'Praise God for seat belts.'

'I always do,' Derek agreed, intrigued by the form of words. 'This looks terrible. You've had an almighty crunch. I'm speaking as a vicar.'

At that, the driver straightened his back and made an effort at turning his head. He was Indian, the vicar realised – pausing for instant reflection on how few Asians he saw in Evenham, and simultaneously regretting the shocking snootiness of the place. The sort of town where you get refused entry to the park if your dog isn't wearing cuff links, was how he had once described it to his wife. The vicar stood up and walked around the rear of the crashed car.

'If there's anything I can do—'

The car driver pulled his head up shakily, blinking in

48

the sunlight, and the vicar realised he had seen the face before.

'I think I'll live,' the man said, brushing down his suit. 'I'm so sorry – you probably recognise me. From the Bishop of Basildon's office. Wazim Bhatia. Head of the steering committee.'

Derek was not sure. 'Wazim – yes – oh – now – wasn't it—'

'I think we might have met at the Lent conference. You made a joke about lending you ten pounds.' The driver was shaking his right leg now.

The head of the steering committee crashes into my tree, the vicar thought. *That's really rich, that is. That's a better joke than my one about the ten pounds.*

Comfortingly, the vicar narrated the story of how the team of British Telecom engineers, on a winter visit to a telephone box thirty yards down the road to investigate a clicking noise on outgoing calls, had managed to put their van into a sudden, screeching skid whose impact left the booth upside-down in someone's front garden on the far side of the intersection . . . all the time barely able to contain his curiosity. Why was Wazim here?

Could it possibly be—

Could it?

Wondering if the moment of great news might even be upon him, even now, barely an hour after Marshall's call, the vicar ran into the house and quickly combed his hair in front of the hall mirror. *That's it*, he thought. *Flatten it. Make it look intellectual, like C. S. Lewis.* He rushed to the fridge and brought out a glass of lemonade, pulled a dustpan and brush from a cupboard, and then, as the head of the steering committee leant in the shadow of the yew tree, absently sipping the drink, Derek Weston swept the debris off the car seats and floor.

Things are moving quickly. Just act naturally, he told himself, trying to winkle a piece of glass out from under the handbrake mounting. *Don't let him know you know.* Bending towards the mounting, he thought: *that's it. Service.*

He pulled a metal pen from his pocket to prise away the piece of glass.

It came free suddenly, flicked into a plastic tray in grey moulding below the car radio and bounced for a second. A ray of sunlight caught the fragment as it rattled to a halt in the tray, flashing brilliant white straight into the vicar's eyes.

There it was.

In that instant, as his gaze fixed on the small, countless-sided thing, glittering there, the chip of broken glass was a many-faceted diamond . . .

And, longing for pure, flawless power at the centre of his ministry, remembering the conversations with Rex Gobart and Judy, the vicar brushed the tiny blinding fragment into the dustpan as though sweeping away an image of perfection against which he would always lose. Taking care not to bang his head on the car door-frame, he got to his feet.

'I think that's cleaned it up a bit.'

'Oh – oh, thank you,' Wazim Bhatia said, moving away from the tree. 'I am rather shaken, actually. I felt one of my knees shake. I was in a daydream. Thank you for this.' He proffered the empty glass and pointed with a free finger. 'You've torn your jacket, Derek.'

'Oh.' The vicar looked down at a hanging strip of cloth. 'Knockers.'

The head of the steering committee held his gaze steady on the jacket.

'The door knocker must have caught the material when I ran out.'

'Oh. Zowee. I am very sorry. I've caused a lot of trouble. I feel extremely bad about this, Derek.'

'No problem at all. Why don't we go into the vicarage?' the vicar suggested, easily. 'I'll make us a cup of strong tea, or herbal, and we can talk there. I've got Gunpowder, too.'

'Gunpowder Two? What's that – a video of some sort?'

'Tea. Gunpowder tea. Low caffeine.'

The atmosphere in the kitchen was strange, Derek thought, pouring. When would Bhatia get to the point?

The vicar tried offering prompts. 'It's been glorious working here at St Saviour's, you know. But there is, I suppose, a

50

moment when every vicar looks towards the distance, the horizon – and sees something he never before, perhaps, realised he would see there.'

'Eyesight trouble, is it? Do you get a fuzziness? I had a bit of that.'

'I – oh, no matter.'

'Floaters?'

'No, no. Just burbling away here.'

He tried word association. 'I was playing chess the other day with one of the very good people in our parish, George Foster. And you know – he's very clever indeed in the way he moves bishops. He really is. He'll take a bishop and just move it suddenly across the board, just like that. Once he took several pieces with a bishop before I could do anything.'

'Oh.'

'His speciality is changing a pawn into a bishop.'

'Mmm, I don't mind chess,' Wazim Bhatia said vaguely, taking a gulp of his tea. 'Nigel Short,' he mumbled, glancing up. 'Very good with castles, did you say?'

The vicar let it rest. They swigged from their mugs, the conversation coming and going in stops and starts.

'This Dynamite's jolly good, Derek.'

'Gunpowder.'

'Of course. Blow it.'

They both saw the joke, and chuckled for a minute.

Finally, Derek Weston lost patience.

'Well, it's funny you should ask,' the head of the steering committee began hesitantly in response to the question, contemplating the inside of his mug. 'It's slightly embarrassing, in a way. I was actually on my way to St Paul's, just down the road. But I don't come round here that often, you see, and as I passed the entrance to your church I suddenly thought – "That's the St Paul's entrance!" The trouble was—'

'That turn of ours—'

'Exactly – and up came the yew into my bonnet.'

The vicar was offended, in some faint way. *Why am I always like the racehorse that falls in the paddock? Where is the perfection promised in the Bible?* He wondered if he was always too hard on himself, then decided he was always too easy and felt worse. He wished Wazim Bhatia had been coming to see him, and pledged, inconsequentially: *when I am bishop, I will read the gospels again.*

'You were on your way up the road?'

Wazim swallowed, and nodded.

'Do you still want to go? Shall I take you?'

The head of the steering committee looked uncomfortable again. 'It's too much trouble, I'm sure. You were doubtless preparing a sermon, or—'

'No trouble, no trouble,' the vicar said. 'Let me take you.'

Wazim pulled some documents from the back seat of the Renault before they set off, and placed them protectively on his lap as he sat beside the vicar. Derek realised he had left his spectacles on the study desk. He tutted to himself.

They were driving in silence, when suddenly the vicar thought: *hold on. I don't even know her name! What is Wazim going to think when he finds out we haven't even been in contact? Two vicars right down the road from each other?*

'I've been busy.' Derek Weston tossed the sentence at the windscreen.

The other man was not listening.

After a minute, he murmured: 'Nice car.'

'Yes,' Derek said. 'Not often you have a vicar in a soft-top. My wife's.'

'Battery-operated roof?' Wazim Bhatia asked, vaguely.

'Yes. Are you getting too much wind?'

'My hair is swirling.'

'Shall I put it down?'

There was no reply.

Roadwork barriers snaked up and down the pavement directly outside the vicarage of St Paul's, so Derek pulled the car into the kerb fifty yards from it, feeling his heart race as he unfastened the seat belt. He turned to his passenger. 'Everything all right, Wazim?'

'A bit bleary, actually,' said Wazim Bhatia, shutting his eyes and opening them again. 'I'm not taking in much detail.'

Take in as little as you want, the vicar thought kindly.

As they climbed out of the car, Derek pointed to the dashboard. 'Don't forget your documents.'

'Oh – goodness—' the head of the steering committee scrambled for them, knocking a shoulder on the trim around the door-frame as he barged himself back in.

'If you get that shoe any further inside the cassette machine, it's going to start rewinding your laces.'

'Sorry, Derek.'

He withdrew.

'Important, are they?' Derek Weston gestured at the sheets of paper.

'Routine,' the other replied, shuffling them.

What is her name? the vicar was asking himself. *Think!*

The other vicarage was an ordinary house in a street around the corner from the church building. At the door Wazim Bhatia took pole position, shuffling around a bit before knocking.

Just behind his right shoulder, Derek Weston was wondering how to play it. As bishop, he must not have stories circulating anywhere in the country about him not contacting neighbouring vicars. He would have to be—

'Quite important, this,' said Wazim at that moment, as if on reflex, speaking to himself almost. 'One of the first – um – women priests. And right here in Evenham, too.' His voice was measured, professional.

'Priestesses,' the vicar murmured, staring down at Wazim Bhatia's right trouser leg and noticing a rip in the back of it. *Right here in Evenham, he says. As if someone just spotted Wild Bill Hickok at the butcher's. It's not as amazing as all that.*

Derek Weston curled a lip in disapproval.

But then a thought struck him – that the door in front of them was about to open on a kind of history.

And, appreciating the massive significance of it for a fraction of a second, hearing Synod votes echo in his outer consciousness, the vicar uncurled his lip.

Wazim Bhatia knocked.

7

No more than half a second later, there was a rustling of curtain in the bay window to the left of the door. The flowered material was snatched back and a face appeared against the glass, instantly smearing it with circles of breath.

Derek Weston was aghast.

The woman was ancient, a mass of wrinkles. Toothless, she was screwing her eyes up behind spectacles that appeared inches thick, her face framed with grey hair, jaw cupped in Victorian lace, wrinkles everywhere. She looked ninety. She might have been a hundred. She grinned, winked, and did an absurd thumbs-up sign.

This is amazing! the vicar thought. *Was she Oxbridge, or something? What are they doing, appointing someone like—*

His head turned, shot round to the front again. The latch on the front door had clicked. Now another woman was standing there, grinning.

'Wazim!'

'Hello, Helen!'

Helen? Is this her?

'And—' the woman in that instant Derek positively identified as the new vicar of St Paul's was leaning slightly, cocking her head in his direction '—and – yes, of course – Derek Weston! I've seen your photo in the *Gazette*!'

'Helen!' the vicar said. 'Um – hello, Helen!'

'You've met before, haven't you?' the head of the steering committee said, uncertainly, turning to Derek.

'We—' the vicar began . . .

'I have been trying and trying and trying to reach you on the phone,' Helen said.

'And so have I!' the vicar agreed triumphantly, not thinking.

'Really?' she inquired, over Wazim's shoulder.

Change the subject, the vicar urged himself. 'My telephone has not been ringing properly because something has been – there has been a fault,' he explained, picturing the bulky directories hauled off it. 'It was ringing faintly.'

'I had a car crash,' put in Wazim Bhatia, saving him. 'I am all right.'

The story over, the two men moved across the threshold a minute later.

'Thank goodness you're in one piece.'

'He is,' Derek confirmed. Now the two vicars were shaking hands. 'Derek Weston,' he said, hoping it would act as a prompt.

It did. 'Helen Silverstone.'

'Thank you,' the vicar said. He felt her slender hand release his.

'It's great to see you at long last,' she enthused.

'The turn was incredibly sharp,' Wazim explained as they walked into the kitchen, making a crooked snaking movement with his arm.

'I can't take you into the lounge, I'm afraid,' said Helen. Derek felt there were three entirely separate conversations going on at once. 'A few of my old ladies are in there at the moment, playing with packs of cards.'

Derek Weston observed: 'Your trousers are slightly torn at the back, Wazim.'

'Are they?' The head of the steering committee raised his right foot and looked round at the loose material, tottering slightly, putting a hand on a kitchen cupboard for balance. 'Oh, golly. Slightly? I can see it flapping.'

'And your jacket seems to be coming apart, too,' Helen Silverstone told Derek in a puzzled voice. 'It looks ripped there. Were you in the car when—'

'No, no,' said the vicar of St Saviour's. 'I was in my study.'

There was silence between the three of them for a second or two, and Derek Weston looked carefully at the woman priest and logged his observations. Thirty-five, he reckoned. Married: she wore a ring. Neatly-cut black hair, shoulder-length, a ragged fringe. Quite a pretty face, with a small nose. Extra weight around the chin, but not much. Professional and intense-looking. Maybe given to anxiety – or maybe not. Black tights, thin ankles, shop dummy calves, no make-up. Serious, pale-faced, the sort who might veto something if she was in a committee. Lines from her nose going deep, past her mouth, as if trying to trap it, stop it spreading too far in a smile – nice, for all that. A decent, generous lady, the type who bought clothes from charity shops knowing they would never fit, pressed lift buttons for people and always had exact money on buses. He forgave the business with Judy, the singing she had done. Derek inhaled magnanimously. After all, it had kept Judy from church the morning the Davidsons rolled up, the second time she'd sung for them. He breathed out benevolently. No, the Reverend Helen Silverstone would be treated preferentially when he became bishop.

She might even find herself being head-hunted.

Then his eye caught the documents under the arm of Wazim Bhatia, and for the first time since he had seen them, he wondered what they were.

'We have the prayer group leaders in a get-to-know-you session in the living room too, so I'm afraid we can't go in there either,' Helen was explaining. 'It's jolly nice to see you both, I must say.'

'Right-ho,' Wazim Bhatia put in airily, looking increasingly shifty where he stood, leaning against the cooker. He suddenly blinked rapidly, and blurted: 'Do you mind if I use your—?'

'Toilet? Of course not, Wazim. Um – let me see – I think it'd be best if you went to the one upstairs. Past the bedrooms, and then it's on the right.'

'Thank you,' said the head of the Basildon diocese steering committee, and left the kitchen.

There was a brief pause between the two vicars, and Derek thought he heard a distant siren wailing.

'You're very busy,' he observed at last, beaming.

'Well—' she spread her hands modestly, and her black jacket fell open at the front '—well, no – not really. Not that much – business.' She pulled the sides of the jacket together and buttoned them. 'Pleasure! I mean – I don't feel – you know, it's just a part of settling in, isn't it? You have to assemble everyone, get everyone moving.'

'Yes,' the vicar said. 'Assembly's vital.' He laughed a bit. 'Lego.'

'I'm afraid I still have no knowledge of the area.'

That made him feel superior. 'It only takes a few years, don't worry.'

'We have a good bunch here.'

'How many?'

'A hundred? Hundred and ten, maybe?'

The wind went out of his sails. *Forty more than me. I hope she doesn't ask.*

'You?' she asked.

'Seven – sev-en – seven—' the vicar struggled '—sev-en-teen – hundred.'

'What? Seventeen hundred?'

'Yes,' he gasped, not thinking.

'Really?'

He coughed into a fist. 'Between seventy and a hundred.'

'Right.'

'Seventy, at least.'

'Yes.'

'Roughly,' Derek put in. 'Usually. Sometimes seventy-three.' He regretted the clarification as soon as he had made it.

'So we're about equal,' she said. 'The power of the gospel to change men's lives.'

'And women's,' Derek added, laughing nervously.

At that moment, a door out of sight across the hallway opened with a yowling squeak. A man appeared at the entrance to the kitchen, caught Derek's eye and looked horribly embarrassed.

'Hi, Glen,' the vicar of St Saviour's began. 'What are you doing here?'

Pointing at the kettle, the man mumbled something about tea for ten.

'Do you know each other?' Helen asked.

57

'From my church,' said Derek, suddenly grasping the horrible truth.

'Ye – y-yes,' Glen said. He gathered himself, breathed in and stepped forward. 'Nice to see you, Derek.'

'I didn't realise you—'

'Just for a ch-change,' Glen stammered.

'I thought you had simply left the church,' the vicar said. 'I'm pleased you're still coming to one. My fault. I should have followed you up.' A suffocating tension seemed to have built up in the enclosed room, and the vicar of St Saviour's wondered if he should switch on the extractor fan. *If I can be this cool under pressure I ought to try for a career as an American astronaut*, he caught himself thinking haltingly as he turned to Helen Silverstone. 'Well done, Helen,' Derek started breezily, 'I'd better make that seventy-two, I think—'

Before there was a chance for anyone to laugh, two more faces had appeared behind Glen.

'Derek!'

The vicar looked over the shoulder of his former parishioner. The faces were blurred without his glasses, but he recognised them instantly.

'Moira! Goolie! Hello! I thought you—'

The truth seemed to land suddenly in all their minds, like the back wheel on a stunt bike barrelling through newly-laid turf in a front garden, and the vicar caught his sentence midway, just before repeating the very words he had said to Glen . . .

He felt himself break out in a cold sweat. *Forget space travel, if it's like this*. Now all three at the kitchen door were blushing, fidgeting, and then there was a fourth making his way through them . . .

'I see what you mean about these trousers,' Wazim Bhatia was saying. 'Excuse me. Sorry. Just making my way through. Helen, I've left those documents on your – um – windowside table – sorry – didn't mean to barge past you—'

'I'll boil the kettle, Glen,' said Helen Silverstone. 'How many for?'

'Ten,' piped Thomas Gould, a balding, moustached man in

his mid-forties everyone knew as Goolie during his years at St Saviour's.

Five, he was with us! The vicar saw scarlet numbers scrolling across an inside edge of his forehead. *She's nabbed half my church!*

'We'll go into my study,' Helen said.

There was confusion as the three at the doorway moved into the kitchen, all looking somewhat ashamed of themselves.

That was like watching the Day of Judgement rewinding. The thought whistled round Derek's head, a stray firework. *Never again do I want to go through that.*

Feeling flat, dazed almost, he said: 'I imagine whatever it was you came to talk about – the routine meeting, or whatever it was you came to talk over, Wazim – well, look – I – um – ought to go now, anyway.'

'You've been very kind,' said Wazim Bhatia. 'Don't worry, Derek – I'll find my way back to your place later, and organise my poor car.' He ran a hand through the tousled black hair hanging over his forehead. 'Please send me any bills for the tree, including roots.'

'Stay,' insisted Helen, leaning forward. 'Go on, Derek. Do.'

'I must – no, really, I must go. Perhaps – I have a lot of dirt on my hands from the car thing. Could I just use your washroom, before I—'

'Upstairs. Past the bedrooms, and then it's on the right.'

'Thanks, Helen. Look, we must meet—'

'Through Judy!' she cried, springing up. 'Listen, Derek, I'll talk to Judy when she next comes to sing. That's a wonderful idea. We'll have a Chinese meal together. I'd love you to meet my husband Mickey, too.'

'I'll let myself out,' he said, smiling. 'Thanks.'

Mickey, the vicar reflected as he plodded up the stairs. *Don't tell me – your children are Donald and Minnie.*

All the same, he could not resist liking her.

He kept going back to Marshall's call, thinking: *at least I have that.*

On the upstairs landing, Derek paused. He coughed into

a fist. Out of interest, he looked left and right. The first bedroom he saw had to belong to a teenager of some sort: the door was ajar and he could see bed covers everywhere, posters of rock and film stars on the walls. There appeared to be another bedroom at the end of the corridor. Two children were there then, in the Silverstone household? Or was Silverstone just her maiden name? So what was it then – the Mouse household? Mickey Mouse? Is that what this was – the Mouse House?

For a second, Derek felt jealous at the woman vicar's gleeful, sincere enthusiasm. Then he jettisoned the feeling, like sandbags from a balloon. Two children? He ought to know. He should be ashamed of himself, not jealous of her.

The vicar glanced right, at the second bedroom. The walls were half pink, half blue – half something else, he noted, wincing at the effect. So this must be theirs. The vicar and the vicar's husband. Helen and Mickey. He craned his neck, his head going just over the threshold, and peered in – he could not resist it. Matching bedside tables. Mahogany, they looked like. Or stained. One with a pile of papers. Windows looking out to the street, one open, white curtains – but wouldn't they make the room very bright early on summer mornings? How could you sleep through that, with the sun beaming in?

Perhaps she doesn't sleep. Perhaps she gets up at five thirty every morning, he concluded, walking into the bathroom and running a tap. *Perhaps she gets up with the sun*. He looked into the mirror. 'I am not,' he whispered at the reflection, soaping his hands, 'going to go bald.'

Drying himself, rubbing a turquoise towel between his fingers, Derek Weston hummed on old hymn. Why always analyse one's feelings, like some lab technician surrounded by test tubes? He felt a gap in him where something had been, but the space was not aggrieving. *Faith is tonsils and appendix*, he thought, mistily. *You can live without them*.

Walking out of the bathroom, Derek was struck by a sudden, tantalising picture of the documents Wazim Bhatia had clutched tightly under his arm, and wondered: *why on earth did he bring them up here?*

60

Almost at that instant, the answer came to him. The vicar stopped in his tracks on the landing. The floorboards creaked.

He brought those papers up here to keep them out of my sight.

Derek made a small move with his feet, glanced around the bedroom door again.

It must be.

There on a bedside table . . .

The vicar stared at the documents, perched dramatically on the mahogany tabletop underneath the window sill . . .

No one coming.

The vicar imagined he must have looked quite official as he walked into the bedroom. He did not creep. He walked straight in, if slowly. *They'll assume I've gone by now*, he thought. *Let myself out. They can't see the front door from the study. And the car's out of sight*.

He felt bad about it – but not that bad.

I'm just reading, he told himself.

Glossing.

Shin brushing Silverstone quilt, he pulled himself up sharply and looked round, seeing a shape move on the other side of the bedroom . . .

A hazy shape. He tutted. *My glasses*, he thought. *I've forgotten them. That's hopeless*. He was seeing his own blurred reflection, caught in a small mirror hanging on a chain above the headboard.

A second later, Derek Weston was lifting the stack of documents from the bedside table. He opened the loose-leaf folder they were pinned in and looked at the shapes on the top sheet.

It was a map of some sort. The lines and spaces were very much like Evenham, he decided. He peered at large letters at the head of the page. Yes. Evenham. The vicar flicked through the rest of the pile. An elderly laugh rose through the carpet. Helen Silverstone's old ladies were directly below. Another map. Then a sheet crammed with what looked like figures . . .

Ducking away from the open window, feeling worse about

it all, Derek pulled out a piece of paper halfway into the bundle. It was packed with dense type. He squinted at the sheet. Portions of sentences came together, then drifted apart in waves.

Downstairs, Wazim Bhatia and Helen Silverstone had arrived at a break in their conversation.

'I think,' the head of the Basildon diocese steering committee was beginning, 'I may actually need to bring down one or two of my papers to help us with this.'

'Let me go,' Helen said, rising. 'I know where you put them.'

'The bedside table. I am sorry, again.'

Helen Silverstone shut the study door behind her and began walking up the creaking vicarage stairs. She looked at her watch, coughed to clear a tickle in her throat, and reflected on how very pleasant it was to be able to meet Wazim again. Good to meet Derek Weston, too. He had such a very kind face, and spoke so positively – with so much warmth and humility. There was little enough of that around, after all. Too much of church was politics. Too many churchmen were compulsive handwashers, albeit with perfumed soaps. But Derek seemed untouched by that, she thought. He looked like a golfer, with his wavy grey hair and sun-blessed skin.

She reached the top of the stairs.

Without pausing for breath, she walked into her bedroom.

Helen Silverstone, vicar of St Paul's, Evenham, moved directly to the bedside table and pulled the documents off it.

Then she heard her name called from downstairs.

'Yes – yes? What is it?'

'Just—' it was Wazim's voice, shouted upwards '—just a problem with your elderly – um – your elderly ladies, I think.'

'Coming down now,' said Helen, trotting down the staircase holding the papers.

When she reached the foot of the staircase, she saw the back end of Wazim Bhatia, leaning into the front room. 'Don't worry, nobody worry, that's okay—' He pulled his head out from the doorway. 'Zowee,' he added. 'I think one of them had a bit of a – a turn of some sort.'

She winked at Wazim and walked past him into the lounge. Several of the women had gathered around a frail lady in a chair by the window.

'You didn't, Beryl, you didn't,' one was calling into her ear.

The final word seemed to register with the woman, and she shot an angry glance at her friend and shouted back: 'I tell you I did!'

Someone peeled off and approached Helen and Wazim.

'Is everything all right, Mrs Reed?'

'Yes, dear,' the older woman told Helen. 'It's all fine. We just had a spot of excitement here with – um—'

'Beryl,' Wazim murmured in a concerned voice, looking past Mrs Reed.

'Exactly,' she said. 'During cards. Beryl wasn't playing, and she suddenly burst out, calling silly things, saying she'd seen – oh, I can't even remember – a man's legs dangling at the window or something, and we had to interrupt just as Pat was dealing the second hand because she lost count of the Jacks.'

Helen Silverstone tittered. Another lady threw a curtain open.

'See? See?'

'They were there, I tell you!'

'What were, Beryl? For heaven's sake!'

'The legs! Dangling legs! Behind the curtain!'

'Well, I think we should keep all curtains open from now on,' the woman vicar said gently, striding up to the frail figure in the chair and putting a hand on her shoulder. 'Beryl, don't you worry about them. We'll get you some more tea.'

The elderly woman looked over the rims of her glasses, saw the joke and chuckled to herself. Wazim Bhatia and Helen Silverstone laughed. Then nearly everyone else in the room laughed too. The head of the steering committee and the woman vicar went back to the study with the documents and continued their discussion.

8

Swinging the hanger from his index finger, lifting the polythene-wrapped material clear of the post, Otis Cheeseman walked through the open gate and cut past a holly bush, hopping across a long evening shadow on to the gravel and turning on a heel to walk up the drive.

He whistled an American tune to himself, and closed his eyes for a moment.

Otis was thanking God for everything, even for working at St Saviour's with Derek Weston, which was not the easiest job he had done (and that was including time with the Los Angeles Aggressive Pianists' Clinic), but was somehow made worth it by the vicar's enduring optimism, English geniality and eccentric, charming carelessness in all matters of administration. Which reminded him – that 'Rocketbomb' record by the choir, and the pebbledashing, they had been absolute classics . . .

Judy Weston opened the vicarage door when he knocked, and the curate modified his smile.

'Hi, Otis.'

'Hello there!' He felt ecstatic, somehow.

'Are they for—?' She was pointing at the jacket and trousers, visible through the polythene.

'Yes, for Derek.' Otis held them up by the hook on the hanger, blinked rapidly at them. 'The laundry people seem to know we work together.'

The vicar appeared behind his wife. 'Oh. Oh, oh, oh. Thank you so much,' he said, beaming and taking the clothes swiftly. 'You really shouldn't have bothered.'

'It was a bit pricey, actually. Because of the ripping.' Otis named a figure.

'Thirty-what?' Judy asked. 'How much?'

The curate repeated it.

'For what?' Judy Weston turned to look Derek in the face.

'I told you, darling.' He was pulling notes quickly from his wallet. 'Of course I did. That business with Wazim Bhaji's car on Monday. The suit got torn when I rushed out of the house. They were mending it for me.'

'And the trousers, too,' Otis added, helpfully.

'Yes,' the vicar confirmed, with a shade of reservation in his voice.

'Torn on a metal gutter, they said you'd told them at the laundry. They thought it was hilarious,' Otis put in.

'A gutter, Derek?'

'Judy, it was all part of the same incident,' Derek was saying, breathing in nervously, flicking the notes to check they were singles. 'You remember what a dreadful day Monday was—' He handed Otis the money.

'We're going out,' Judy told him. 'Anniversary.'

Otis thought she looked strained. 'Tonight?'

'Tonight,' Derek confirmed. 'Yes. I'm treating. Oh – now listen, Otis – I've – I've been trying to ring you for a few days. I completely forgot you were off for a bit. Can we just – Judy, do you mind if we just have a very quick – boring—'

'Go ahead.' Judy waved a hand at the curate and walked back into the house.

'– chat—'

'Shall I—'

'No – no, I'll come out to you, Otis,' Derek cut in, shooting a glance over his shoulder as his wife disappeared up the stairs, gingerly placing the repaired suit on a chair in the hallway. Straightening up, he moved out on to the doorstep, adjusted his tie purposelessly, and pulled the front door to.

'Did you enjoy your time away?'

Otis looked into the vicar's face. Derek was staring into the middle distance, as if the answer mattered even less than his question. 'Fine,' the curate said. He put his hands in his pockets and looked down at the redbrick doorstep. 'Yes, it was nice. I did some touring around Scotland with a – well, a friend.'

'Friend?' the vicar repeated, absently.

'Kind of. By the way, Derek – down the end of the driveway, there was a huge scorch mark.'

The vicar sighed. 'This is something the police are looking into. There was – well, it's a long story, but essentially someone from the Basildon office left his car down there and it caught fire.'

'You're kidding,' the American said.

'There were a lot of sirens. No one saw it. We were down the road, at St Paul's, when it happened. The police aren't sure if it was because the fuel tank had split, or what,' Derek said. 'It had crashed,' he added, still staring into the middle distance. 'They are treating the flames as suspicious.'

The curate's eyes goggled for a moment.

'Otis—' Derek's head moved. Looking up, the curate felt himself caught in an anxious, tremulous gaze. 'Otis—'

'I am here.'

'Something – um – difficult has happened.'

The curate asked the question that tunnelled to his tongue. 'How difficult?'

The vicar seemed absent again, murmuring: 'I have taken – measurements.'

'Measurements?'

'Measures, I meant.' The vicar breathed in sharply, as if dismissing everything. 'Small ones. The problem is minor, actually.' He made a brushing motion with a hand. 'A new family has arrived in the church with an – well, um – an unfortunate name.'

'Really?'

'They came again last Sunday, but since you were in Scotland—'

'What name is this, exactly?'

'The Davidsons. Do you know them? The family of Charlotte, the musician. Anyway, her parents and her brother, they rolled up, and – I just thought you might appreciate the sensitivity with some of our older members, given the nature of—'

'With the older members? What – the name "Davidson"?'

'I should explain. It was before you were here, Otis, actually. There was a very much loved member of the congregation called – um – Bart. Old Bart Davidson. And he died in – in circumstances that really were rather unfortunate.'

'Really? How?'

Not expecting the question, the vicar grabbed at the first answer that came to mind. 'He fell down a well.'

'Did he?' Otis's eyes widened.

'Yes. He was quite young.' *Forgive me, God.*

'Really? Old Bart?'

'For his age,' the vicar lurched on, thinking: *forgive me seventy times.* 'It's just something that people like Sonya and Mrs Atkins and a few of the others – the Coopers, Mrs Weekling, Jot ffitch – are sensitive on. They don't like being reminded. So I rang the Davidsons yesterday and asked them, you know, if anyone came up to them and held out a hand and introduced themselves, or whatever, that they should not say their name, really.'

'But Davidson is quite a common name. It has a mixture of antecedents which can be traced back to a fair number of family groups.'

'Otis – look, I did tell you a while back – I did say, you know, not to be quite so literal about everything—'

'Yes, yes. Of course.'

The vicar breathed in. 'Essentially, they've agreed to be known by the name "Peterson" for the moment.'

'Peterson?'

'It's not that different—' The vicar looked searchingly into the face of his curate and detected nothing, not even a puzzled smile. Otis had a crooked nose. The vicar's eyes moved up it slowly. Then he leant forward secretively. 'I haven't even told Judy.'

'Really? Did she – did she know – er – Bart? Bart Davidson?'

The vicar ground his teeth as the lie passed over them. 'She heard the splash.'

Hands empty of Derek Weston's mended suit, Otis was walking back down the drive a minute later, grimacing. Every day there was some new incident! He thought of the healing meeting the vicar had tried to organise, thrown into chaos just as it was supposed to start, after a parishioner broke two fingers when a stack of plastic chairs he was lifting toppled sideways and hit a woman who had recently started attending the church, leaving her, in the words of an ambulance crew who arrived at the scene, with a frozen neck and a rotated fibrous wrench in her left shoulder. She had fallen across a table which had collapsed on someone's knee. Otis had not been there. Later, when he asked the vicar what the result of the evening had been, Derek had replied simply: 'The result was three–nil.' Even in a million years the whole of America, the curate reflected, could never be as exciting as Evenham.

As he reached the end of the drive, a man in the back seat of a small green car parked half on the kerb at the mouth of the driveway looked up sharply and tapped the driver's shoulder. A third man, in the passenger seat, glanced over at Otis and said something to the other two behind the shut window.

In a moment the car was revving its engine. It rolled into the road with a bump and a screech of tyre on tarmac, and shot off. Scratching his head, Otis watched the vehicle disappear, the heads inside silhouetted against a distant, pink horizon.

Twenty minutes later, the Westons were ready.

Derek walked down to the car. He looked back at the vicarage as Judy stepped out of the front door and pulled it shut.

'Darling!' he called up. 'You look so beautiful tonight!'

She could not stop the blush the remark drew.

'Now my cheeks are the same colour as the sky,' she said softly.

Derek had promised a restaurant, surprising her. Turning out of the drive, they pulled the visors down across the windscreen simultaneously, shielding their eyes from the setting sun. Judy glanced over at her husband as they accelerated away from the church. His hair was patted down on his head, tidily, as though supreme effort had been put into the patting. And he was wearing a checked jacket, the one she liked. She momentarily felt sorry for him, deeply sorry, for the life he had been allotted by the Church. But then she hardened her heart, abolishing her pity, remembering he loved it and was always saying so.

Judy clenched her teeth at the thought, raising ridges in her forehead.

All the old irritations resurfaced.

Did she love him?

Sometimes she wondered if she had ever known the answer to that.

She supposed she must have done, once.

Maybe twice.

'. . . and that twitch in Otis's right eye has got a lot better,' Derek was saying, but she was miles away and offered nothing in response. He hooted the car horn at a cyclist, then turned excitedly to Judy. 'Do you remember, darling, years ago, when we were driving down here, and someone you knew was cycling past, Libby I think, and she gave us this merry wave and we waved back, and then we looked round and she'd hit the lamp-post and come off in the verge?'

He chortled. His wife simply mumbled, 'Not really,' though she did, and had to look away and bite her lip to avoid grinning. She gazed out at a parade of shops gliding seamlessly past the window.

They were slowing down.

'This is where I'm taking you, my dear,' Derek said, pulling the car into the kerb. 'French, in Norton Mortimer. Your favourite place, your favourite food.' The keys clinked in his hand as he pulled them from the ignition.

They took their seats at a table at the window, and she could not help relaxing instantly. He seemed so alive, so alert – so attentive to her. Different, somehow.

'Darling, let's order.'

'Thank you for bringing me here, Derek – so much,' said Judy. She sighed, as if duty bound to place the generous remark in a context of ancient hurt and bitterness.

He ignored the sigh. 'I couldn't wait to see you today. I know you've had such a busy week, with everything you've been doing in the City, with all your digits—'

'Oh, dear – did I give you that impression, Derek? Of not

69

being around? I suppose I did.' She felt guilty, suddenly. 'I'm sorry if I did.'

'I always think, you know, with such hard commuting, I understand it,' Derek said. 'It's all my fault. They were thinking of sending up a satellite to photograph the face of Evenham, it's so far out. It always has been.' He thought of the hazy maps that were all he had been able to make out in Helen Silverstone's bedroom before scrambling out through the window after hearing her cough on the stairs. 'Evenham may be picturesque, but it is—'

'Well,' said Judy briskly, flicking open laminated halves of menu, 'don't let's worry about that now.' She did not want him to stray in the direction of the subject they had so often argued over. 'By the way, the Geareys—'

'Have invited us to the Tower again? Don't tell me – yes?'

'Yes. They rang. And I've set a date, at last.'

'Well done,' said Derek. 'Now – what are you having?'

The meal was wonderful. There was a cheerful hum of candlelit chatter around them. Then, two glasses into the wine, Judy brought up the late-night discussion of a month before . . .

'Look, I'm sorry, Derek. Truly. I was just – really frustrated.'

'I know.'

'I didn't mean to say you weren't – well, you know what I said. All of that.'

Derek Weston's eyes suddenly gleamed at her across the table. He wondered: if someone had taken a photograph at that moment, would he have looked like a missionary?

'Judy, listen. You're right,' the vicar said suddenly. He looked down at the table, released his hand from hers and adjusted the position of a spoon minutely. 'I've been so complacent. My last sermon was gibberish. An ad lib, you know. My beliefs have slacked off. Even my squash has. All my serves are out. As you say, I don't have—'

'I really didn't mean to bring all this—'

He looked up into her face, his eyes flashing. 'But you're

70

right! Judy! Do you realise how much I love you? How much I want to keep you?'

'Derek, I never meant I was going to leave when I said it.'

He straightened his back. 'I suppose I knew you didn't. Anyway, you wouldn't have got very far with a passport photo like yours.'

She was earnest. 'I really didn't mean it.'

'But you deserved to be able to say it.'

To her surprise, she felt a rash of annoyance break out, fleetingly, on the surface of her soul. 'Yes,' she agreed. She scraped her front teeth across her bottom lip. 'I suppose I did deserve it. I've been very upset, Derek.'

'I know.'

'The last straw was Charlotte Davi – Davids—' She brushed her lips with a napkin. 'I don't even want to say her name.'

'No. Well—'

'I don't even want to hear that name again.'

The restaurant seemed to go quiet for a moment, and Derek skewered a broad bean on a prong of his fork and pushed it into his mouth. 'I don't either,' he murmured, chewing painstakingly, as if he had the name in his mouth and was biting it to pieces. He swallowed. 'I know. But it wasn't—'

'It doesn't matter what it was,' Judy cut in. 'She was a symbol, wasn't she? I can't bear even being reminded. That whole business – never discussed, never explained. I didn't get any kind of explanation. Just heartache. Just tears.'

'I was preparing a sermon on discretion.'

'Derek,' Judy Weston chuckled emptily, 'you're doing it again! It's just cut-out, isn't it? Like a chap with a pneumatic drill wearing ear protectors. You keep blasting away, and everybody gets a migraine but you.'

'I—'

'Your first sermons, Derek – Derek, they were so beautiful, you know, all those years back – they were wonderful! Where are we going now, the two of us?'

There was silence between them. Then, in the corner of

71

the room, a man in a waistcoat with a scarf tied on his head began picking at a guitar. Judy leant forward again, pointing her cutlery at the plate. A single, ice-pure tear ran in a line down her cheek. Derek watched it. Strains from the guitar filled the restaurant.

Then he whispered across at her: 'Judy, you don't have to worry any more.'

The guitarist moved closer, stopping at another table by the wall.

Judy looked up at her husband.

'What?'

A sudden sharp guitar-chord flew across the room.

She wiped her cheek with the heel of a hand.

'You don't have to worry, Judy.'

'What? Why not?'

Just then the musician came close, strumming into Derek's ear. Angling his head away, the vicar thought of pneumatic drills. The man was singing. Derek gave an answer, but Judy heard no words, just saw his lips move across the table . . .

She leant forwards. 'What did you say, Derek?'

The strumming became intricate picking, the guitarist issued an off-key whoop, stamped a heel and spun round to face another table.

'I am going to be promoted to bishop.'

Judy only needed to hear the sentence once. Her reaction was extraordinary and instantaneous. The taut skin around her forehead which always seemed to hold her eyes in a permanently firm gaze loosened, and her expression appeared to fold inwards on itself for a moment. Then her eyes suffused with tears and, lips trembling and thickening, Judy Weston lowered her face, cupping her forehead in a hand.

'Oh, Derek, I don't know what to—'

'Just praise God,' said the vicar, reaching across the table and placing a hand on his wife's forearm. 'Just praise God for recognising it really was about time.'

She was laughing through her tears. 'About time, too.'

'Is that the title of a film?'

'What?' Judy brushed at an eye with her napkin, but the tears kept coming.

'The sequel to *About Time*. I was just thinking of a silly conversation I had with the chap from the steering committee,' Derek chuckled, his chuckles chiming with the picking of the guitar. 'Sorry. He was going on, and I said "Gunpowder, too" talking about our tea, and he thought I meant a video.'

Judy Weston was laughing into the napkin, laughing and crying at the same time. She lifted her handbag from the floor and pulled a silk handkerchief from it, wiping her nose and mouth. Then she inhaled deeply, ending in a gasp that shook her chest with relief, and looked up at the ceiling, blinking rapidly and rubbing the sides of her face with her palms.

'Brilliant,' she said at last, grinning. 'I don't think I've ever heard anything as brilliant.'

'It might not be Basildon or London,' Derek put in. 'We'd have to move.'

'I'd love the change, though. Think of it! As long as it was near a big city – how did you hear? Terence?'

Derek fumbled with the spoon again. 'Intelligence,' he said, adding quickly: 'Information, I mean. I can't really go into it. It was Marshall, basically. But he couldn't confirm it because of his knock.'

Judy seemed suddenly bored by the detail. She clasped both her husband's hands between hers, sandwiching them flat against each other. 'Prayer! That's what it is, Derek! Prayers! Going up and finally getting somewhere!'

'The pearl!'

'The pearl, Derek! And all I said about you losing your centre—'

'I've been recognised, I suppose,' Derek sighed, sweeping gravy to the side of his plate with a knife. He felt a lone tear wobble on an eyelid rim. 'That's all. I hadn't blown the bishopric, after all.' He was overwhelmed with pride and daring. *We had to move one lot of books up*.

She was staring at him.

'I love you, Derek.'

'And I love you, so much,' he said.

'I really do love you.'

'I am so glad to be with you. You make me feel such a success.'

'You are one, Derek. You are one now.'

'I wanted it for you, Judy. For us.'

We had to move one lot of books up.

'I'm sorry we've argued, my darling Derek. It's all been my fault.'

'And mine.'

At that instant, simultaneously, the vicar and his wife raised their glasses, unprompted, and brought them together with as much vigour as they dared.

'Happy anniversary, my dear husband!'

'Happy anniversary, my sweet wife!'

Judy added: 'There's some wine on your shirt.'

'My cup runneth over,' the vicar muttered. He looked down. 'Oh. I think my glass just broke.'

9

15 Summers Row Terrace
Jesmond Hill
Newcastle
Tyne and Wear

Dearest Otis,

You're so kind to me! And to think you covered it all up with all those books at first! I'm still glowing from the weekend – so tell me: are all Americans like you, or just the preachers? I love you Otis, I think! Don't quote me!

Perhaps I'm utterly off my rocker . . .

Gulp.

Talking of rockers, know what? After you left on the Wednesday or whatever it was, I got a shock in a super-market. You are now going out with Jesmond Supersaver's fifty thousandth customer. They were just putting my stuff through the till when an alarm went off, balloons started dropping from the ceiling and some burly northern councillors appeared, laughing etc, balloons bouncing on their bald heads and them heading the biggest ones around. Photographers too! Like the moment the final ends at Wimbledon and all those famous Royals line up in toupees and the ball boys scuttle about. I won ninety pounds in groceries. (A voucher, so no I CAN'T and WON'T spend it on a book.) And this chap in punk gear behind me in the queue started going on – this is why I mention rockers – saying I had barged past him and he ought to have been the fifty thousandth, etc, it would have made a better story because of his hairstyle . . . on and on. I said it wasn't very punky to want to shake hands with Conservative councillors. But the voucher's burning a hole in my skirt pocket slightly

75

and I'm thinking of sending it off to a charity, maybe one that helps rehabilitate punk rockers through some sort of therapy involving old Abba albums and pictures of safety pins being used unglamorously, e.g. on nappies.

How is the church, then? How is dear Derek? You know he needs a LOT of care and attention. A LOT. He needs reminding all the time of why he's there, a bit like a mouse in a maze has to keep getting a scent of the cheese. This is what you MUST say to him every time he slumps, if you know what I mean – say, 'Derek, the reason we are here is because Christ came to save sinners.' Say it in capital letters. JESUS CHRIST CAME TO SAVE SINNERS. I said it a couple of times and it was like a voltage going through him. Afterwards he said he felt like a four-pin plug. Trouble is, the wires coming out of the bottom are fraying.

Remember Ronald Reagan? He used to start every speech by saying, 'What this country needs is a spiritual revival.'

Plus – did you know there are thirty-six thousand people in America who are over a hundred?

The orchestra is going well, but I wish you were here. Shall I tell you what I love about you? It's that you look so lost, so incredibly lost and studious, with all your books and your frowning . . . you just seem to be a kind of walking bag of words, twisted up in yourself like tangled string. And then when we started talking and going out, all secret, it suddenly seemed you had this great mass of love, a big bag of love to break over my head! And all the string went everywhere! Not that it hasn't been done before – the love, I mean, not the string – I suppose people did use to tell me they loved me quite a lot, on playgrounds, mostly – ha – but it never happened with such style and surprise and such a loud, deafening bag-breaking sound! Good grief! So tender, your touch! You really care! You make me sound like a poet! How far down does it go? In you, I mean? Scotland was fantastic, Otis. The Isle of Skye. Tell me everything you have ever thought about anything. I'm not good enough for you, that's the problem.

I can't believe my parents have turned up in the church.

I think maybe I said something to them, I can't remember. They are having problems (big ones) with Adam. Perils of adoption. For goodness sake tell them NOTHING about us – you won't, will you? Derek doesn't know, they don't know—

Please don't go, don't ever leave England. Come up here and let's drive north and buy a farmhouse in Pitlochry and own an untrained goat. Forget this Transatlantic Church Swap business. Let's do really exciting things instead, like getting rescued from wells in remote districts. Forget less glamorous places like the Blue Ridge Mountains and Beverly Hills. Give Beverley or Hull a chance.

Otty, don't for goodness sake make a big thing with my parents, or any kind of thing, because if they find out about us they'll think, 'Disaster, she's off to the States tomorrow' and start treating you like an unexploded bomb and trying to defuse you. They'll probably spray you with foam or something, like a fire. They DON'T have to know. Pretend to remember me only vaguely if it gets dodgy – try saying 'Wasn't she a visiting speaker?' or 'That sounds like a character in one of my theology books,' etc, then start mumbling about the book and they'll soon get bored and you'll see their toes curl up and be able to slip away.

I know I've sounded silly to you. Don't think me silly.

I'm just excited, that's all.

Mammoth, musical love from the north

Charlotte

10

'Five–two.'

Derek threw the ball up, brought his forearm round in a narrow arc and drove the racket-head through it.

The blob of green flashed at the opposite corner of the court, ricocheted on to the far wall and bounced high in front of Rex Gobart, who stepped aside and took a wild, heavy swing as it buzzed for a fraction of a second in the air in front of his stomach. The stroke sent the ball leaping off his racket at an absurd angle, curving over his friend's shoulder and into the door behind them.

'Sorry,' Rex wheezed.

Derek was momentarily concerned. Squash was hardly Rex's game, and his unlikely invitation to book a bank holiday court had come out of the blue. Perhaps, the vicar reflected, Breakfast had some troubling matter he wanted to raise, and forgot playing would leave him too breathless to do it.

Certainly, Derek thought, sending an underarm serve looping into the corner of the receiving box, *if life was as simple as squash, God would leave us all to it and concentrate on other planets*.

'Thanks a lot.' They shook hands at nine–three in the fifth. The vicar yanked the court door open. 'I bet we would have been three times faster twenty years ago.'

'Twenty years ago I wouldn't have been here. I would have been listening to 10CC, or something.'

'You had a motorbike, did you?'

'Eh? An Austin.' Rex tucked in his shirt, hands trembling. 'You're very fit, you know.' His face was a dark shade of beetroot red. 'Five–nil. Whoops. You win.'

'But you played well. I'm in the league here,' the vicar

said. 'My great achievement. I've beaten five people with sweatbands, one who said his racket was made out of tensile aluminium, a chap from a cult who made a death threat against me if I won, and a bloke who used to do funny footwork on his service return.'

'Wonderful.'

'He tripped on a match point.'

'Marvellous.' They were in the locker room now.

'Well, he broke his wrist.'

'Oh.'

In the bar, drinking coffee, Rex seemed to be checking his watch as often as he brought the cup to his lips, so Derek asked: 'In a hurry, Breakfast?'

'Supper,' said Rex Gobart quickly. He leant back in the chair, sending his stomach exploding out of his unbuttoned jacket. 'Hmmm – um – just trying to work out how long it'll take to get ready. I've got a couple of people coming round. Trout.'

He blew his nose, then added: 'That's what I'm cooking.'

The explanation, delivered in Rex's sonorous drawl, sounded strange, as if suddenly invented. Derek inquired: 'Do you want to go now?'

'Give it fifteen minutes. No problem. Oh – by the way, Derek, did you ever happen to see—' now Rex was fishing in his jacket pocket, then carefully pulling his hand out with a scrap of paper between forefinger and thumb '—this article?'

Derek took it and stared at the printed words. 'From the *Gazette*?'

'Yes. Last week's.'

It was a single piece, with the headline FAT MAN THANKED BY ANGELS stretched over the top and a large picture of a violent-looking bearded individual in a black crash-helmet embossed with a skull and crossbones. Derek read the first paragraph out loud. '"A leading member of the Evenham Gross Angels motorbike group yesterday telephoned this newspaper in a dramatic bid to thank an anonymous man who saved a dozen bikes from daring thieves." What—' The vicar looked up. 'This isn't you, Rex, is it?'

'I'm pretty certain it is.'

'Really?' The vicar looked down at the article again.

'I was out walking in the country with Abigail,' Rex explained, taking a swig of coffee and glancing up at the ceiling. 'I just saw these blokes loading about a dozen black Harley Davidsons into a truck outside a pub. We were about to go in. It was actually so obvious, I didn't get at all suspicious. But inside the pub I saw all these – well, whatever they call themselves—'

'The Evenham Gross Angels,' the vicar mumbled, still looking at the article. He glanced up. 'As far as I know, they used to be called the Evenham Angels. But then they decided the name didn't sound unpleasant enough, and they changed it.'

'Nice. Well, they were all in there. In the pub. Fairly boisterous and so on, leather jackets, shouting – and I suddenly twigged the bikes must be theirs and told myself, "Hold on, that's a big operation to lift them going on outside." So I mentioned it to the lads at the bar.'

The vicar read out loud: '"The truck had already gone, but the Angels rang the police, who stopped it further down the road." This is brilliant, Rex! "And last night," it says here, "the group's leader rang the offices of the *Evenham Gazette* to ask us to thank the portly man they say alerted them to the theft as it happened." Wonderful! And there we all were, thinking you were just an ordinary management consultant! But then I suppose it was ages before we suspected Clark Kent, too!'

'Obviously, I'm a bit miffed about that,' Rex said, putting a fingertip on the first word in the headline.

'Oh, it's probably inaccurate.'

Rex chuckled. 'Now – just as guidance, Derek – it probably isn't a good idea to mention anything about this to Judy, is it?'

'What – this article? Why on earth not?'

'Just the bit about the bikes, I was thinking,' he said, taking the piece of paper back and folding it. 'The make. Harley. I thought the name might be—'

'Eh?'

'Davidson. I thought it could be—'

'Oh – now, Rex, don't get—'

'—offensive, perhaps, or—'

'No, now don't be ludicrous,' the vicar laughed. He scanned his friend's face for a sign he was joking. 'Anyway, that Davidson business, that's all sorted out,' he added in a murmur as he lifted his coffee cup. 'Thanks for your advice. I won't go into it.'

In Rex's car, a purring white BMW, the management consultant told the vicar: 'You know, this week, for the first time ever, I thought about Christianity seriously.'

'Really?' Derek shot a glance at the beaky profile of his friend's big face.

'Looking at the world about us. The crime, the collapse of morals, ethics and everything – and my dishwasher, by the way. Plates keep coming out with pieces of spinach on. I never eat spinach. The whole world now is like that joke about the chap who calls the RAC and says he's had a breakdown, you know, and the mechanic pulls up on the motorway and asks him what exactly is the cause of it, and he says, "I just can't seem to hold down a relationship." Really, it all seems to get worse and worse. Lying by politicians, barefaced lies. Shares falling, even ones you get pretty decent tips on. And – well, look at us, Derek, we're getting on now – and there's just no end to it, is there? No end. It gets harder to climb stairs. It gets harder to understand the words of pop records – and I'm just talking about the titles. Last week an old woman was mugged in Slough for a tin of dog food. Did you read that? All right, I know we say, "Oh, Slough" – that joke about the bomb going off there and causing ten million pounds' worth of improvements – but the arson attacks in this area, even! Don't get me wrong, Derek—' Rex blurted out '—I am a Conservative. A bullish one, too. I believe in tax relief on mobile phones, and so on. And I agree with all the manifesto commitments. Privatising slip roads, deporting illegal invalids. But the—'

'Immigrants.'

'What did I say?'

'Invalids.'

81

'But I'm actually beginning to wonder if politics is ever going to solve anything.'

Quick, God, Derek prayed. *Remind me what your manifesto was.*

'What does it mean, Derek – becoming a Christian?'

The vicar became a Viking, and plundered his memory. 'It's a mixture of faith and action,' he said. 'You have a feeling in the pit of your stomach, and you go around doing things to try and stop it going away.'

'That sounds like the opposite of an Indian meal.'

'Don't get me wrong. I didn't mean to make it sound – well, metaphysical. It's more like a commitment – a promise.'

'To God?'

'To do better.'

'Right.'

Derek wondered: *have I made it sound too interesting?*

'It's not all excitement,' he added, cautiously. 'There are dull patches too.'

'Sure.'

'You should talk to my curate about it. Otis Cheeseman. He's excellent on the detail. He's read a lot of books.'

When they arrived at the vicarage, Rex invited himself in for tea. Walking up the gravel drive, Derek asked: 'You haven't seen Judy for a while, have you?'

'Er – not for a while.' Rex seemed suddenly nervous, looked at his watch again, and coughed.

Derek turned the key in the front door, opened it, and showed his friend into the vicarage hallway.

'The great thing about squash is that it allows you to take out all the aggression you want to take out in church, without being arrested,' he said breezily, wiping his feet as he closed the door behind them. 'The number of parishioners' heads that are saved from being bashed to a pulp by the simple invention of the squash ball is quite amazing.'

Rex cleared his throat. 'Right.'

Derek called: 'Judy!'

There was no answer.

'Let's go through to the living room. I've no idea where she is,' the vicar said. He walked across the hall, towards the living room door. 'Perhaps she's decided to hop on a train somewhere.' He put his hand on the living room door handle. 'I suppose she might have had a call from a friend.' He began to open the living room door. 'Though I must say, most of the calls we get on a day like this tend to be—'

The sentence jerked to a halt.

Derek's jaw dropped.

The cheer from the forty or fifty people standing in front of him hit the ceiling of the room just as the friendly slap from Rex Gobart hit the vicar's back.

'Surprise! Surprise! Hooray!' A dozen of them were still shouting and cheering half a minute later as the vicar began to collect his senses, one at a time, from the faraway corners of his mind where they had been catapulted . . . asking himself urgently: *what was I saying about squash balls and parishioners' heads? How loud was I saying it?* and then, giddily: *a surprise party! But what for? What for? What have I done to deserve—*

Judy was at his ear suddenly, whispering the answer. 'What you told me in Norton Mortimer. It's a celebration.'

The vicar stared around the room, blankly.

'We were standing here in complete silence waiting for you, darling. They hid their cars.'

Dozens of faces . . . some turning to each other to talk, others clapping and calling still . . . John and Sonya Todd, Charles Mannox-Lloyd, red-haired Karen Pemble and Connie Leach standing next to each other, winking over at him as if they all had some private joke in common . . . the Turners, the Pasarells . . . Gerald Cooper, laughing his head off . . . Otis . . . Guy Portch, Reg Zrobny, Caroline Pridgeon, friends of Judy from work . . . some faces he could not even place, neighbours perhaps . . .

'Do they know?'

'No, darling.' Judy's answer to his whispered question was instant. 'I thought you'd like to be the one to tell them. That's the big joke, you see – a surprise party!' She released his arm, took a step back, raised her voice. 'Surprise for you, surprise for them! I'm the only one who knows everything!' A few people on the other side of the room laughed. 'You're hyperactive, Judy!' someone shouted, and she called back: 'No I'm not! I haven't got time to be!'

Derek was about to say something through the broad grin he had only just managed to paste to his face when Rex leant on his shoulder. 'Sorry, mate! I knew you'd enjoy it! The squash was Judy's idea, to get you out of the house while she got ready. I said you'd never believe I was serious about playing, but you did!'

'I'll know next time, I suppose,' Derek said, trying to alter the position of the grin and failing. 'It was the game you got four points in that threw me off the scent.' He gave out a raw, unnatural laugh. His face was numb.

Soon the guests were evenly spread around the room, the discussion was loud and merry, and two of Judy's colleagues from work were bringing round a tray piled high with cracker biscuits and cheese as George Foster leapt to and fro with bottles of lemonade and wine. 'Wonderful, Derek!' he called to the vicar at one point, pop-eyed. 'Just what a bank holiday Monday needs! No marquees this time, either!'

Derek Weston felt himself going into shock. Surreptitiously, he pulled his sleeve up and gave his forearm a merciless pinch. *This is real life*, he told himself amid the babble of conversation, hardly able to believe it. *This is incredible*.

Then he saw a familiar figure in the corner of the room, talking to a woman from the choir whose name had momentarily been scrambled in his head like egg with squares of salmon. The conversation seemed to end just as he looked over. The woman peeled away and began another with someone else. Grin riveted in place, Derek edged towards the figure.

Everyone spoke to him as he did. 'Did you expect this, Derek?'

'Not at all, no.' *Smile widely.*

'Not at all?'

Wider. Now laugh. 'No.'

'I can't wait to hear what the surprise is, Derek.'

'We're all excited, Derek.'

'What is it, then?'

'Oh – it's a surprise.' *Chuckle and wink.*

84

He was handed a glass of wine.

'Can't you tell us, Derek?'

'No, Marshall, I can't. Not yet, anyway. I was just coming over to have a chat.'

Marshall Kampfner reached out his hand and shook the vicar's. 'You saw me being abandoned just then, did you?'

'I just wanted to ask how you were.'

'Oh.' The librarian looked puzzled, almost. 'I'm fine.' He reached over to the end of the mantelpiece and picked a palmful of peanuts from a bowl. 'How I am? You must be talking about—'

'The marquee pole,' the vicar said.

'I'd forgotten.'

'You couldn't have forgotten about—'

'I'm joking, Derek. It was weeks ago, that's all I mean. One doesn't want to keep harking back to it. There are more important things to worry about, like shelves.'

'And you're all right now, are you?'

'Oh yes. Fine. In the clear – literally. A lot of people were praying for me, as you know. I got a stack of Get Well cards – one addressed to "Marshall Capsule", actually, a misprint, but it seemed a bit appropriate considering the number of things I was taking for a while. But I'm easing my way back into church things now. There's so much to thank God for, there really is. Which reminds me, Derek, if you happen to recall the pebbledashing case, there are several fairly important things to do at this juncture. Someone needs to recover any pebbles that were thrown at us, if they can, to prove a principle the lawyers call—'

'Marshall,' the vicar cut in, 'you've left something out, haven't you?'

The librarian paused for a second.

'The mix of the cement?'

'Something else.'

Marshall said: 'If you're worried about the protest over the songbook order, I thought I'd already passed on the fact that the publishers have agreed to black out all the choruses which mention world domination.'

'Not that, not that,' the vicar said, laughing edgily.

'Um – let me think. Next door's Dobermans, do you mean? The restraining order comes into force next month, so if they ever start that awful howling again during something by the choir we can just nip round the back of the vestry and—'

'Not that, Marshall. No.' Putting an elbow on the mantel-piece for balance, Derek leant towards the librarian and whispered in his ear: 'We had to move one lot of books up.'

Marshall pulled his head back. 'Really? Where?'

Nervously, the vicar reached for a peanut. 'Don't worry if you can't remember.'

'We had to – we had to – move – oh, yes,' he said confidently, 'I do know what you're talking about. Yup. The thing I heard in the library that prompted—'

'Well, I just wanted to say how grateful I am.'

'—me to – oh. Right.'

'For your – remembering.'

'Fine. No problem. I wasn't at all sure that—'

'I just wanted to say—' Derek paused, then went on, 'thanks – for the memory.' He heard the opening swirls of one of Judy's jazz discs, and added in a voice hardly recognisable as his: 'Good, Marshall. Grand. I'm glad you're better. Thank you.'

'Not at all,' the librarian said, looking a little confused, flicking a peanut up in the air with a thumbnail and catching it in the palm of his hand. 'Not at all, at all.'

'I thought you were going to catch that nut in your mouth for a minute.'

'That's the only thing I can't do because of the accident, actually,' Marshall said. 'I was mentioning it to Otis just now. If I jerk back my head, I black out.'

'Oh.'

'We had terrible trouble at Chelmsford Planetarium.'

'Oh, my.'

'The stars suddenly went out. But they say that'll get better, too.'

Someone was banging a fork on a glass.

The vicar looked over his shoulder and saw only the backs of heads.

He raised himself on to the tips of his toes.

Fork in hand, his wife was beginning to speak from the other end of the room.

'I don't know how to thank you all,' she called.

A hush descended on the place.

Nor do I, the vicar thought.

Judy Weston was wearing a pleated cream skirt and red top, a string of pearls around her neck, skirt narrow as a pencilcase. 'I want to thank you all so much.'

I want to thank you all a bit less, the vicar thought. He slugged half his glass of wine back in a single, unusual movement.

'Both Derek and I have enjoyed many of the friendships here for a great deal of time. A large part of our lives,' Judy went on.

Some faces turned back to the vicar. He was smiled at, warmly, and returned the smiles indulgently. Just then, as everyone was looking, a peanut hit the upper part of his left cheek. He flinched. 'Sorry,' Marshall whispered beside him.

Judy raised her voice. 'This has been a surprise party with a bit of a difference, as some of you may have noticed.' There was a titter somewhere. 'It was a surprise for Derek, thanks to the fact that we all managed to stand here in silence for fifteen minutes and hide our cars—' another bout of chuckles '—and, as I think I may have hinted to some of you, it may bring a bit of a surprise to some of us.'

More widespread laughter, more faces turning back to the vicar.

Silence.

Then, from Judy, two further syllables.

'De-rek.'

Unable to help himself, the vicar spluttered on to the back of his hand.

What do I say?

Like zombies suddenly activated by a code word, everyone in the room wheeled round to face the vicar. He drew himself up where he stood in the corner. Took his elbow off the mantelpiece.

You are used to this, he told himself. *Employ all the old rules of speaking.*

In an effort to look casual, he put hands in pockets and bent one leg.

The vicar breathed in, inflating his chest.

'Hello, everyone.'

A few people said hello back.

'I'm so pleased you could all come.'

No one said anything to that.

Derek Weston's thoughts slipped their leashes and tore off, greyhounds from traps, before he could catch them.

'Judy – thank you, too,' he went on. Like a bandleader introducing musicians, he gestured over at her with a hand. 'My wife.'

'Yes,' someone out of view agreed.

Bracing himself where he stood, the vicar said: 'This is a very exciting occasion for me. To have you all here in my – our – living room. I imagine many of you will have been here before. Perhaps I could extend a special welcome to those for whom this is a first visit.'

There was a moment's pause, and Derek put in: 'In fact, perhaps you might like to introduce yourself to the person you're standing next to, whomsoever it happens to be, so that those who are here for the first time feel at home.'

Instantly, a hubbub started. The vicar took a swig from his glass, emptying it, wishing he could drain his mind of panic as easily. A minute later the noise of conversation had died away. He looked down at his shoes.

'There are surprises and surprises,' he said loudly. He tilted his head up at the scores of eyes glued on him. 'When I came into the room just now and found you all here, that was – well, a big surprise. My wife is absolutely right when she speaks of another surprise, a second one – but I have to say I think by any definition that particular surprise would be described as a small one in comparison!'

'Oh,' someone said, in disappointment.

'—which is,' the vicar went on, 'not to disappoint you all, by any means. I am so grateful that you are here, and I know you must all have gone to great lengths to keep it secret.'

He winked at Judy. Two or three people laughed.

'Doubtless,' he added, 'you had secret passwords, and so on.'

Four or five more joined in the laughter.

'Perhaps "Bishop" was one of them,' he said.

The laughter was suddenly choked off in some parts of the room, as if smothered by creeping legislation.

Heart in mouth, the vicar swallowed and went on: 'I am, as you can see, not wearing my vicar's garb this afternoon. There is a chance I may not be wearing it for much longer.'

Before anyone could react, the living room clock struck five with a sequence of ear-splitting hoots. A wooden bird on a spring jumped out of a hole at Derek's right shoulder and flopped forward across the front of the clock in a tragic manner, as though it had given up an escape bid at the last moment.

There was a snorting splutter from someone in another corner of the room, which stopped with an abrupt sucking sound.

In the lull, Derek Weston's courage failed.

He felt his face suffuse with blood. Somewhere, someone coughed, as if giving him a prearranged cue.

'Um – that's – that's about it,' the vicar said. 'It was a false alarm.' He caught puzzled faces in every line of vision, and tried to clarify. 'I just wanted you all to be on your guard for – well, those of us in the parish, at least – for changes. Good changes.'

Connie Leach was the first to clap. Derek caught her eye as she brought her hands together, slowly at first, at waist level; then others joined her, starting staccato and slow as if from upper circle seats at a bad ballet . . . speeding up now, smiles spreading, getting louder, Connie and Karen bringing their hands up to their chests simultaneously, grinning broadly, others clapping in waves and smiling, one – Charles Mannox-Lloyd, Derek thought it was – even letting out a small cheer . . . several others following him with cheers too, George Foster doing a kind of a jig with a bottle of Raspberry Tizer in one hand, whooping and laughing . . . the vicar nodding now, beaming but feeling the ends of his mouth tremble with the tension of keeping the beam there as they all stared at it, applauded it, celebrating the joy of the grin and the news the vicar had just conveyed . . .

But what have I just told them?

He could not imagine what it was they thought they had just heard.

Later, Otis Cheeseman shouldered his way towards the vicar. 'It's a wonderful party,' he said, adding in a low Arizona drawl, 'though I didn't quite get that bit of yours about undressing.'

'Undressing?'

'The change of clothes. The garb deal.'

'Garb deal? Oh. Did you – did you think anyone else got it?'

'Someone said they thought you might have been making a prophecy about Oxfam. I wasn't sure what Oxfam—'

'A charity. Finds foster parents for oxen,' the vicar added, mischievously. 'That's probably a little bit too exotic for me.'

'Phyllis Childs didn't hear much of it at all, and she asked Charles what had happened, and he just said it was the moment for congratulations, and she should congratulate you.'

Before Derek had a chance to reply Rex had joined them, looking as if he had drunk several glasses of wine, spreading his feet wide on the living room rug for balance.

'Lovely stuff, Derek. You have a terrific wife.'

He gave the vicar a melodramatic wink, and swayed.

'Thanks, Rex. Yes, the weather is—'

'Judy is utterly terrific. You know,' Rex went on, 'the more I think about it, the more amazed I am at that conversation we had about – um—'

Derek snapped round to Otis as Rex grappled for the unmentionable name.

'Otis, what was it you were doing in Scotland? Anything exciting?'

The curate turned from Rex Gobart, who was obviously in a gargantuan private struggle for a word, to the vicar. 'I was with a friend.'

'School friend?'

'Charlotte!' Rex said suddenly . . . and then, catching sight of the vicar's face, blushed, coughed, and began apologising profusely. 'Something – sorry – something caught in my throat. From earlier. Some apple charlotte.'

'Yes,' said Derek.

'Perhaps if you lie down—' the curate was suggesting '—perhaps if you went into a horizontal position for a few moments—'

'I need to press on,' Rex muttered, uncertainly. 'Another act of heroism awaits! Angels to help!' He turned to the vicar with a lop-sided grin, but Derek's face was blank. 'Strange,' Otis said as the management consultant weaved his way unsteadily towards the living room door, 'to have that kind of delayed action with a pie.'

'I am going to become bishop,' Derek murmured, watching Rex reluctantly get drawn into a conversation with Karen Pemble. He looked over at Otis.

The tic in the curate's right eye went, once. He said slowly: 'I thought that was what you were saying.'

'It needs to be confirmed.'

'I guessed that was what you were trying to say.'

'It seems to be,' Derek told him.

'Wow,' Otis said.

'I had a tip-off.'

As guests began to leave, Judy caught her husband by the elbow. 'Why didn't you say it properly? I was about to jump in and spill the beans.'

'I lost my nerve,' the vicar replied. 'But some people got it, darling. Connie Leach came up to me and asked me if she had heard right, and I said yes. And I've just told Otis straight out.'

'How did Notice take it?'

'Vaguely. You know how sensitive he is. Sometimes I just can't resist teasing him. He's such a lovely fellow. He probably didn't want to react in an inappropriate way. I think he's in love with someone in Scotland.'

'I'm so excited for you. That's why I—' Judy gestured around the room at people still deep in conversation, large porcelain plates emptied of sandwiches and cakes. 'That's why all this—'

'It was so kind of you, Judy.'

'And we got loads of people. The Geareys said they'd try, by the way, but in the end they obviously—'

'Bye Judy! Bye Derek!'

'Thanks again! Thanks, both of you!'

'Bye!'

'Goodbye!' the two of them called back. Derek turned to his wife, and whispered, 'And I'm so grateful, Judy.'

'Things are so much better between us since—'

'I know,' Derek put in. He inhaled, long and slow, and looked up at the ceiling. 'What a difference a bishop makes.'

She giggled.

'I just feel – sort of activated,' she said.

'Before I go to bed tonight,' the vicar went on, 'I think I am going to pray.'

11

Standing at the window of his bedroom, the vicar looked out
at the black Evenham sky. Behind him a snore rose through
a heap of blankets whose outline, struck by moonlight,
was faintly reflected on the pane. Judy had gone out like
a short match.

I must pray something, the vicar thought. *If someone was
running a meter on my prayers, I would only owe 2p.*

He peered out at blocks on the horizon.

'Come in, God.'

A stuttering snore rose and fell behind him. The moon-
struck outline shifted minutely in the pane.

'God – come in,' the vicar murmured again, more quietly.

I'm talking like someone who hires out boats, he thought.

Still, he tried again: 'Hello, God. If you're receiving me,
please come in.'

*Come in number ninety-one . . . come in number ninety-one
. . . hold on, we don't have a ninety-one . . . number sixteen,
are you in trouble?*

Tiny cubes of yellow light twinkled at him in the distance.

Weston to God. Come in, please.

The vicar teased himself. *The trouble with this sort of prayer
is you keep getting taxi drivers cutting in. Hello, God – oh, sorry
– yes, I'm hearing you – car for three into Windsor centre –
Temple six-six – pick-up in ten minutes – sure – you're breaking
up a bit—*

The vicar longed for secure lines. Longed to be able
to jettison the feeling that every prayer was a tannoyed
announcement . . . longed for it all to be personal, all
this stuff, not just public; for a conversation with God
to be a conversation with God, not a scripted address

read from scruffy paper over the heads of a congregation.

He envied his curate, too. He envied Cheeseman. Otis was so clean-cut, so very twenty-nine . . . he was a Precision King, the American, while Derek's life was all jammed bumper-cars and bleeding noses. Christianity was about perfection, not imperfection. With attention to detail, the vicar guessed, the claims of Christ must simply become obvious. Faith was simply another word for perfectionism. Lucky, thorough Otis, a slave to precision and books, would have had no problem accepting the facts when they were presented, instantly equipping himself with every scrap of evidence to back them up – whereas the vicar had lost count of the number of times he had mislaid his Bible even, let alone forgotten vital verses. He had once called the Garden of Eden the Forest of Dean three times during a sermon.

Christianity for him had been kick-started on emotion: a sudden realisation, years ago, when he had been teaching, that his life was stained yellow with wrongdoing like a smoker's finger. He had walked off the street into a church, and found a Peruvian man in a green anorak shouting from the pulpit—

'Do you really believe zat you can go srough life wizout confronting zat sacred cross on Calfry Heel?'

Derek had fumbled for his A to Z of Essex, started looking up Calfry in the index at the back.

'Do you really believe zat what ze Son of God did on zat cross can be just ignored by you? Zat you can ignore his dying and what it meant?'

Derek had looked up, and something had rolled back across the top of his mind, like Judy's sunroof opening on to a sky he had never seen before.

Calvary Hill.

His had been an emotional conversion, as conversions went. There had been tears, prayers, some wheezing and a sprint round the block propelled by joy. He had crashed into a pillar box and apologised to it gleefully. Amazing to think Peru, with its shattered economy and amateur terrorists, could send a missionary who so comprehensively overturned the certainties of a British geographer. But it had been done. Derek had gone down on the floor like a wrestler hit illegally, was instantly surrounded by well-wishers – the Peruvian's cronies, no doubt – and confessed everything openly, including something about hiding a calculator in his sock during a Maths examination and even, embarrassingly, that he had slid on a piece of discarded soft fruit when the preacher made his appeal just then, rather than being felled by anything spiritual.

Not that it mattered: long hours later, he had opened a Bible at the sole verse he still knew by heart, and it had taken his breath away as he sat waiting for Judy to come home. 'This is the will of him who sent me, that I shall lose none of all that he has given me, but raise them up at the last day. For my Father's will is that everyone who looks to the Son and believes in him shall have eternal life, and I will raise him up at the last day.'

Oh, his stomach had flipped, and all that sort of thing. He bet Otis's stomach would never have flipped at any of that, at least not flipped at so acute an angle: America was a vastly overpopulated country, he imagined, massively over-run with bespectacled lawyers and film extras and people who said they had been propositioned by the President, and there was precious little room for wild stomach movement.

Lucky, lucky Otis, the vicar thought. *You brought maps. You read as you travelled. If the trail ever goes dead for you, as it has for me, you will be able to look back and know exactly what brought you here*. It was something he had never been able to do, even though Judy had taken fire in a similar kind of way a year after the Peruvian had got to him. For they had long since ceased all talk about their very separate faiths, and when the vicar opened his Bible these days he discovered a new, even more chilling sensation: verses stared out at him blankly, like Bosnian road signs. Did the villages they seemed to point to even exist now?

What I need, he reflected, pressing fingertips against the window, *is the pearl of great price*.

He had it in the early days. Those days, his sermons were like TNT.

The police would have had the bomb squad round to defuse them if they'd been tipped off.

Derek pressed his nose against the glass.

They would have sealed off Evenham.

The glass went misty with his breath.

The pearl.

He squashed the tip of his nose against the pane.

That would make it personal.

Yet the vicar could not bring himself to be the slightest bit unhappy about anything. Not even about the terror of the surprise party that day. Yes, he might be conscious of empty space within himself, but no one could be unhappy about empty spaces – no one with experience of trying to park in central London, at any rate. And Derek Weston was, after all, about to be made bishop. But it would be so nice . . .

It would be more than nice, he reflected. *It would be so desperately spiritual – never again to have to search for God on a squeaking dial, never to have to yell for him like an airman from a cloud-covered cockpit, never to have to wait for Sundays to get through . . . it would be so wonderful just to start talking and find him there.*

He thought fondly of young Charlotte, who had known all that and told him so, then looked down at the dark driveway, flinching as a diffracted streetlight beam caught the side of his face and – oh, no . . . had rays from the same lamp, coming from the same angle, caught Judy's cheek as she stared down on that pitiful, dreadful night? Shivering at the recollection, he put his rude fondness aside.

Long ago, the vicar had a secure line. A private line to his creator. What had happened to it?

Was I disconnected for not paying the bill, or something?

Or for not using it enough?

His brow creased. He rested his palms on the sill, bent his elbows.

Did God's number change?

It must have done. God, the vicar concluded, must have gone 081. He had certainly become unobtainable. And it was hugely ironic – massively, sensationally ironic – that a being who seemed to boast in the Bible that he was running a lifelong surveillance operation against everybody on earth was so desperately difficult to contact in person.

If this was a James Bond film, Derek thought, *I would find the microphone hidden in the lampshade and shout into it.*

He felt sleepy, and wondered if Caroline, his daughter, was up now too. Chatting, perhaps, with her husband of one year? He hoped they were both acutely happy with each other, and was almost certain they must be. Jeff Massey ran a thriving wargame company out of Sudbury Hill, ferrying his customers into the countryside on Sundays and issuing them with camouflage jackets, visored helmets and pump-action airguns so they could shoot high-speed paintballs at each other to their heart's content. He was a mechanically-minded man who had once boasted he could fix the solenoid on any make of car. Serious, Jeff Massey was; responsible. He knew about clutches. He would make sure he kept Caroline in his.

Something to the right of Derek's eye made him turn his head.

Three, perhaps four miles away, across Nock Green – what was that? A bright light in a home?

The light seemed to grow brighter as he watched.

A fire.

Mesmerised by the glimmer as it grew into a glow, illuminating nearby roofs, the vicar must have watched for all of ten minutes. Then there were distant, barely audible sirens, blue and white flashes, small movements in and around the blaze.

It must have been rapidly extinguished, for the spot that had caught his eye went dark again and the vicar turned his head back to the night sky.

'God,' he murmured, 'wherever you are, please come in.'

Another snore from behind him.

'Nothing big. I just wanted to – to thank you for this – promotion.'

His voice was the only sound in the room.

'To thank you for the transformation it has caused between me and—' he thumbed over his shoulder '—and Judy. My wife,' he added in a low whisper, afraid of waking her. 'To thank you that I had not, after all, blown the bishopric. And – one more thing—'

The Reverend Derek Weston ran front teeth along his bottom lip as far as they would go, one way and the other.

The room felt cold. *If God is in here, he has suffered a drop in temperature*. The vicar wondered: *have I – might I have – just been talking to myself?*

'Please, if you can, give me back the centre. Give me the jewel at the centre.'

Nothing came in reply. One last time, he tried.

'God, come in.'

Derek Weston stood there in the silence, but the silence stayed silence and he could not detect any kind of answer, anywhere, not even in a momentary rustling of branches as wind licked trees by the vicarage. 'You may need me when I'm bishop,' the vicar murmured, turning away from the windowpane and reaching for the top button on his shirt. 'You know, you may just need the odd job done.'

Then he undressed, put on his pyjamas and climbed into bed.

12

There had been three weeks to do it. Now there was only a day. And they were panicking.

'We always seem to panic,' said Ruth Richards.

'I know,' Ken O'Driscoll put in. 'We always leave it too late, that's why.'

'We're like the Gadarene swine.'

'What?'

'Darting.'

Ruth, Ken and Claire Stupples were putting final touches to the layout of the parish newsletter, bunched on the floor of the vicarage study in a sea of cut paper.

'Where is Derek, anyway?' asked Claire, a rotund girl who had briefly been a missionary in Russia, but flew home after suffering a panic attack during a hardline coup in Tomsk. Pigeon-shaped, with a streak of immaturity that made her difficult company and an ear-piercing voice, she asked: 'Shall I shout for him again?'

'No – no,' the other two said instantly. Ruth's lean face was topped with a shock of tightly-curled ginger, arms covered in freckles, delicate white legs folded underneath her like struts on a deckchair. A nurse, she always spoke with a hint of reservation, as if conscious of the impact of incorrect diagnoses. 'I thought I – er – I told you yesterday, Claire. Derek passed a message on to us that he'd be away visiting someone who says she's had a prophetic dream about the result of the next general election.'

'Oh – of course. I suppose I thought he'd be back by now.'

'Well, perhaps it's a hung parliament.'

'He did apologise,' Ken put in, crusty-voiced, looking up

from a pair of scissors and adjusting his spectacles with a free hand. 'He told me he had to go, because the last time this person phoned up she was going on about Kuwait being invaded imminently, and Derek wrote her off as a crank, and then of course – well, you know what happened. I think Derek's always blamed himself for it, actually.'

Ken O'Driscoll had the furrowed, marbled look of a man who had taken early retirement from a printing firm where he mostly worked nights. 'You have to be so careful,' he added seriously, as if giving advice gleaned from years of so-carefulness. 'You really do.'

The telephone rang. Claire Stupples jumped up, threw a baggy-trousered leg over the cut-out shapes on the floor and stretched awkwardly for it.

She giggled into the receiver.

Marshall Kampfner said: 'Hullo?'

Claire put a hand over the mouthpiece and whispered: 'It sounds like a nutter.'

'Hullo? Is that the right number?'

'Sorry,' Claire chuckled into the handset, turning towards the window. 'This is St Saviour's vicarage. I'm afraid Derek Weston and his wife are out at present.'

'Claire, it's Marshall. Marshall Kampfner. I'd forgotten you and Ruth would be there, doing the—'

'And Ken—'

'—doing the – and Ken, yes – putting the newsletter together. Hullo. Look Claire, can you do me a favour? I'm calling from work. It's actually quite urgent.'

'Sure.' She covered the mouthpiece again, hissing 'Marshall' at the other two and rolling her eyes melodramatically. Ken went back to a stencil he was fiddling with.

'I have a very urgent message: can you please ask him to ring me?'

'If it's about the result of the next election, he already knows.'

'It's – I don't—'

'Sorry,' said Claire, 'sorry. Humour me. No problem at all. What's the message?'

'That's it. To ring as soon as he can.'

The receiver went dead.

'How rude,' she mumbled, negotiating a clumsy landing on the carpet. 'I must get a pen.' She reached under the armchair, grabbed a pencil. 'That'll do. Now—'

'Ken,' Ruth said suddenly, looking up from a sheet of card, 'this thing about arson – does it have to go in?'

'Derek says yes,' Claire sighed. 'Apparently the police have been asking if he can get people to keep their eyes open.' She had just found a used envelope to write the message on, when the telephone rang again. 'Oh – heavens.'

'Language,' said Ken.

'Flip, then.'

Ruth laughed as Claire heaved herself upright and reached for the receiver.

'Madhouse Number One!' she shouted into it.

An assured voice came back from the other end. 'Hello. This is Beverly Gardner-Laing, secretary to the Bishop of Basildon.'

Claire gulped. 'Right-ho.'

'Is that Mrs—'

'Claire Stupples here.' She blurted: 'Newsletter team, Evenham parish. Unmarried.'

'Claire, could you give Reverend Weston an important message from the bishop, please?'

By now both Ruth Richards and Ken O'Driscoll were staring at Claire intently.

'Er – yes. Yes, of course.'

They watched in silence as she made a careful note on the back of the envelope.

'Two o'clock, Friday. This Friday, is that?'

A pause.

'Right,' Claire said finally. 'Right-ho. Cheerio then.'

She replaced the receiver very carefully, as if trying not to leave traces.

'Who on earth was that?' Ken asked.

'An assistant from the Bishop of Basildon's palace. Asking to see Derek for a very important meeting.'

'Really?' That was Ruth.

'Yes.' Claire.

101

'Heavens.' Ken.

They worked on for a while, talking about items in the newsletter as they pasted them to card. One paragraph, in italics, expressed a belated welcome to the new vicar of St Paul's. 'We hope Helen Silverstone and her husband Minty will enjoy their time in Evenham enormously,' Derek had written. 'And that Helen's work will add greatly to the sum total of worshippers in the two parishes.'

'Strange way of putting it,' Ruth said, shifting her bottom on the carpet. 'And listen – I'm sure it's meant to be Mickey. Um – you'd better – change that bit.'

Ken got to his knees and pulled the computer keyboard towards him. 'These wretched things.'

'What things?'

'Computers. They've ruined the art of anonymous letters, that's for sure. All letters are anonymous now.' He coughed into a fist. 'By the way, weren't they celebrating something here on Monday?'

'Who?'

'Judy and Derek,' Claire said. 'Yes. Actually, they mentioned it to me—' she positively swelled at the social significance of this '—but I couldn't make it.'

'I couldn't either,' Ruth murmured, and Claire went down like a punctured pack of ground coffee. 'But now you mention it – I heard there was a surprise at the party, something to do with – um – with Derek wearing a different uniform.'

'He doesn't wear a uniform,' Ken advised, typing at speed. 'He wears a garb.' A grey-cornered cube expanded on the computer screen. He struck a key.

Ruth said, 'I don't know, someone told me he was going on about changes in the parish. Apparently – er – it was to do with wearing different clothes.'

The printer was rattling. A sheet of paper jiggled out. Pinching the top edge between thumb and forefinger as it came, Ken suggested: 'Promotion?'

'Come on now.' Claire turned to him, waving a set square dangerously. 'You don't get higher than vicar. When I was in St Petersburg people used to talk about English vicars as if they were kings.'

'They shot all their kings, that shower,' Ken said over his shoulder.

Ruth was scratching her neck. 'At least vicars don't get shot here. Not – um – openly, anyway.'

'They get stabbed, sometimes,' Claire mused, glancing up as if on inspiration and finding the other two frowning at her. 'In the back, I mean.' She persisted. 'Well, if you just think about all the little comments we've made about Derek from time to time – totally unnecessary things – like when someone was saying there'd been no conversions here, saying Derek couldn't even convert foreign currency—' she was picking up steam now '—and when we were harping on about how he shouldn't have let those karate people use the coffee hall for practice sessions—'

'Oh, not that again,' Ken protested. 'It wasn't karate, anyway. It was Ju Kwon Wok, someone said, which is apparently much more defence than attack.'

'It still involved flying kicks. And everyone agrees Derek shouldn't have said yes to it – it's just not Christian, that's why.'

'Judas needed a pretty good kicking,' muttered Ken.

'Well, he didn't need a flying one. I think so too,' Ruth piped sheepishly, concentrating on drawing a line with a fine felt tip. 'I mean, I agree with Claire. The karate was the last straw for Moira and Goolie. I know that for a fact. And frankly, as I was about to say earlier, the – um – the way most things—'

She was interrupted by a knock at the window.

'Otis!' Claire squealed.

'Hi, matey,' Ken said. Ruth beamed up at the American.

'Hi. How are you all?' Otis Cheeseman's voice had a through-glass timbre. The tic under his right eye triggered. He tossed his head, throwing the sandy fringe back.

'Well!' the three of them called in unison, then laughed.

'I'm just looking in,' the curate said, smiling broadly.

'Literally!' Ken called.

'Have to do a couple of things in the church.' He picked at a hard speck stuck on the other side of the pane, wrinkled his nose as it came away mushily in his fingers and threw it to the ground in distaste.

'Do all the looking you want,' said Ken warmly. 'Derek's not here, by the way. He's seeing one or two people.'

'We've had a very important message for him!' Claire shouted, and explained.

Tramping down the gravel drive towards the path that cut across to the church entrance, Otis reflected on the news.

The vicar going to see the bishop on Friday? What on earth for? Was this the moment he had been talking disjointedly about on Monday, the moment of great truth?

Hearing his feet crunch in the tiny stones he felt suddenly melancholic. What if he had to take over at short notice? Preach? Read banns?

Crunch, crunch, crunch-crunch-crunch.

Otis Cheeseman knew what the real problem was, the cloud cutting sunlight from his mind. He was a perfectionist. After hearing humid weather could cause hair loss, he had worn a shower cap indoors. He tested the bristles on his toothbrush with a tweezer. He could not bear listening to a badly-tuned radio, piano, car or choir; had secretly rejoiced when the dogs next door to the church seemed to be agonised by ultrasonic noises and started the cacophony that forced the choir to abandon its annual demolition of Handel's *Messiah* and issue refunds.

Otis drank bottled water. His theology books were meticulously catalogued. Told his parents planned to visit England on an autumn bus tour, he had rung the vehicle registration office in Swansea to check the service history of the coaches. He was known at the supermarket in Evenham for returning bread.

In that sense, Derek and he were opposites: the scatty mismanager and King Stickler. But perfectionism had been no asset to Otis in church. Faith, it seemed, was the very reverse of it. You believed you were being transformed into the image of God, you kept being told you were, but when you glanced in the mirror the bridge of your nose still looked like a ski-jump hit by a downed helicopter. Scattiness had the day as far as faith was concerned, for sure. Don't ask questions. Don't look. Don't tidy your desk. Just jump.

Crunch.

Perhaps he was jealous of Derek, soon-to-be-bishop, Weston. Would the vicar's elevation somehow move him closer to heaven?

If Derek thought so . . . that was like trying to reach God with a step-ladder! Goodness knew, if that was even slightly possible the queues around hardware shops would feature on national traffic reports. Slowly, over twenty-four hours, the curate had become astonished by what the vicar had said to him at the party, was perhaps feeling as great a sense of shock build up within himself as he had when, during less worldly-wise days in Arizona, he had read of the disrobing of a former tutor, the leading Tutt County televangelist Dr Michael Wraggage, after a court case in which the preacher was accused of circulating copies of Matthew's gospel with an appeal for uncrossed cheques to be sent to his home address inserted in the Sermon on the Mount.

Had he any cause to be shocked now? To be melancholic? Strictly speaking, he had very little cause to be upset by anything.

Otis was utterly in love, so far as he was able to define it.

He had never played host to these emotions before. Charlotte Davidson was the most beautiful, musical, perfect being ever to set foot in or out of Evenham; loving, caring too. The curate was determined not to reveal the depth of any of this until he had accurate confirmation that the foundations of his feelings were secured on something more than just – well, just feeling. Feeling was no proxy for an empirical determinant.

As for Derek's impending promotion, the curate tried to tell himself that Christianity was about imperfection, not perfection. Which meant the big truths were on Derek's side. Belief was not, could never be, any kind of precision tool – not least because so many of the people who resorted to it would find ways of electrocuting themselves if it was.

Which made Otis wonder. If he viewed the years since he had first felt the wiper of Christ on the windscreen of his soul, he knew he would see years of checking this, checking

105

that; of worrying if a certain wrongdoing here or there might have slipped through the net, of fear about a lurid thought crash-landing in his mind for the second time in an afternoon, of dread that he might utter something unforgivable in his sleep, of sheer terror that perhaps Americans would simply be excluded from paradise, for all the obvious reasons; or that somewhere, hidden in the Bible, was a verse he had missed which would keep him from ever entering what he imagined heaven would be: a blinding, searing light; mercury plummeting in the mouth of a million-foot thermometer; a warm voice drifting through pure oxygen, calling out every name he had ever been known by; no barging; complimentary library cards, free ice cream, raspberry ripples..

Perhaps he was further from that than Derek Weston. Perhaps he was the one who had missed the point.

Reaching the open door of the church, Otis stepped in without hesitation. He needed just five minutes to check a book.

Then he glimpsed a woman sitting halfway down, head bowed.

Praying? Otis Cheeseman failed to recognise her from behind, and would have ignored her altogether had something familiar not popped up in his mind like blackened toast. He stepped up behind the figure, and stopped in his tracks.

Now she was turning, smiling, drawing fingers across her forehead as if wiping something away . . . the toast was smoking . . . and he was holding out his hand to her, taking in her face, thinking she was around fifty, probably . . . an attractive face, it was, too: tanned, hair slightly bleached, big-eyed, young-looking . . .

He could not quite believe the pop-up trigger his memory was giving him. He almost felt he was in a dream. Maybe he was. Perhaps he was about to be offered a shimmering raspberry ripple.

'We've met before, I'm sure.'

'I don't think so,' she said. 'Actually, I was at the service on Sunday, but—'

'Were you?' The curate was genuinely surprised. He did

106

not remember seeing her there. He felt a twitch under his right eye, making everything suddenly real.

'I'm Otis Cheeseman.'

She blushed. 'Marion.'

'Marion—?'

'—er – Peterson,' she added, staring down at the floor.

Reality rushed him, a snorting warthog. He was staggered to have run into Charlotte's mother like this. She was looking upset. Tearful, almost. 'I'm the curate here,' he explained succinctly. He realised why his memory had been fumbling for recognition. They had exactly the same jawline, same hair.

'I know,' she said. 'I think our daughter mentioned a curate to us when—'

Later, details of the conversation had been swept out of his mind by waves of shock and bitter anguish.

Otis had felt his face reddening at the mention of Charlotte, and as he blinked several times at Marion Davidson he found her blushing too. Twisting in the pew, she had glanced absently about the empty church and gone on: 'I say "our daughter". That's rather given the game away, a bit. But you probably know – Derek did ask us if we wouldn't mind being, well—'

'Petersons?'

'—yes, just for a while – you obviously do know. Because of—' she laid special stress on the phrase that followed '—the situation here.' Then, crossing her hands on her lap: 'It's not a bad name. But it does mean we aren't really able to mention Charlotte, because people instantly start wondering why our surname has gone away. But never mind. Your accent – American, aren't you?'

'From Arizona. Is – is everything all right? Other than that?' He could not help noticing the smudged mascara at the corner of one eye.

There was silence in the place for a minute, during which her lower lip trembled. At last, she said: 'We're having some trouble with our son. Adam.'

Marion Davidson suddenly threw her head sideways, as if recoiling from an object thrown at her. She said nothing for several seconds.

Then, looking back at the curate with a tear wobbling on the lower lid of each eye, she said: 'Nothing in life is simple, Otis. You know, ever since Clive and I got married, we've trusted in the simple promises in the Bible. Love God, love your fellow man. You'd call that simple, wouldn't you?'

'Yes, I would,' said the American confidently.

'Well, we thought so – think so. We still do. But our son, Adam, has a condition called something like craxio – craxiodormano – er – exfusti – um – something. I've forgotten the short word for it. Has that ever crossed your path, at all?'

'I don't think so. But I don't do that much walking.'

'It doesn't cross many paths, I don't think,' she said. 'It's a behavioural thing.'

Otis chewed his lip.

'It's not – don't get me wrong, it's not anything – ah – catching. The problem is just that—' she seemed to gasp in the middle of the sentence '—Adam is not able to make ethical choices. He can't tell right from wrong.' She brushed a hand across her brow. 'He is very difficult to control.'

The curate breathed in. 'Oh, dear.'

Marion Davidson shuddered. 'He's so unlike Charlotte – our daughter. She's always been such a happy thing, always so hippetty-hoppetty, she's always had a lot of boyfriends – she's got millions up there in Newcastle now, I gather. But Adam is very, very difficult to control.'

Most of what followed was lost utterly to the curate of St Saviour's church, Evenham, in the diocese of Basildon. He simply kept reminding himself of who he was as seashell sounds roared in his ears; found himself staring deep into the nest of hair on Marion Davidson's head, the droning from her mouth a swarm of killer wasps.

'. . . someone like him used just to be called a problem child, apparently. But now they can give it the proper name . . .'

He was blinking.

'. . . and he's already been expelled from one school for cutting down a hedge, plus there was a written warning because he attacked a lad who supported Arsenal and was caught trying to mould his head into the shape of a cannon. But by far the worst thing about it all is—'

Marion Davidson paused, moving her head an inch so that Otis's stare was thrown miles off it, bouncing and skidding to a halt somewhere near the far end of a pew. She opened her handbag, pulled out a crumpled tissue and blew her nose into it. The blast echoed around the wooden interior of the church. He pulled his gaze back on to her lips as they moved again.

'He can't ever really become a Christian.'

Otis Cheeseman inhaled.

His mind went blank.

He spluttered: 'Oh – sorry – who can't?'

She looked at him. Deciding she had misheard, she continued: 'Well, I did read an article giving examples of one or two people being cured when San Marino got that goal against England in the World Cup, because very high levels of shock can do it. But – no, that's for the birds,' she said, voice wavering. 'In any case . . .'

The sentence wound on. On and on. But Otis had lost track of the words completely at that moment, sent his gaze zooming about the inside of the church.

It came to a sickening halt on a violent red glass apostrophe set among ochre rectangles in a stained glass window. He decided it was tear-shaped. The tear was a mosaic of a million bruises, each a boyfriend of Charlotte.

The tear was shed for his dying love and his crumbling American heart.

– 13 –

LIST OF THINGS

1. Check paper clip fastening collar
2. Wear <u>pressed</u> shirt
3. Practise answers [e.g. Ministry – what future direction?
      Preaching? Subjects?
      Why do you want to be bishop, what could you give, etc?
      What is point of it all?]
4. Practise vestry joke
5. Remember newspaper, books, address list
6. Learn names [Hawkley Castari, Terence and Audrey Stitt, Cliff Camping, Peter Selwyn, Beverly Gardner-Laing, Bill Venerick]
7. Shoes
8. Memorise list of achievements

The vicar spread the piece of paper on his study desk and looked out on to the gravel drive. *What are my achievements?*

He scrutinised individual pieces of gravel.

How many million achievements can I shower them with if they ask?

The Reverend Derek Weston permitted himself a wry grin. It had not been his intention to learn lists of successes to emit suddenly in the direction of Terence Stitt. The idea had come from someone else. He lifted his head. 'Judy!'

She appeared, suddenly, at the door. 'Are you ready?'

Standing with his back to her, Derek asked dreamily:

'What were my achievements again? What was I going to tell them?'

Judy walked up to him slowly, saying nothing. Drawing level with her husband, she put an arm around his waist.

'That I love you.'

'Not that,' he said. He looked down at the arm snaked around his body. *Why did the two boa constrictors get married? Because they had a crush on each other.* 'The other achievements, I mean.'

'I was just being romantic, Derek,' she said stiffly, pulling away. He turned to look at her. After debate, Judy had taken the day off work to accompany him. But she was wearing an outfit as businesslike as any he had seen her in: a surgically pleated royal blue skirt, hiptight around the waist, calf-length; that brief cream jacket with arms which always seemed overlong to him, front sporting great big round flashing buttons, rough swirls encrusted in terrifying gold; a thick black patent leather belt; spiked hair immaculately, frighteningly coiffed. *The fear of women is the beginning of wisdom*, he thought, then retracted the near-blasphemy with a wince. Around Judy's perfect neck, resting on the collar of a deep red silk blouse, was a single string of pearls.

Derek's eyes lingered on them for an instant.

He lowered his gaze.

Oh – and Judy had her best high heels on. He knew them by their buckles.

'My, my, my,' the vicar said, laughing, reaching out to her.

'Don't – sorry – Derek, my hair!' she giggled, drawing back and tossing her head. 'I hope I look all right to you.'

'All right? All right to me? If Saul had seen you, he would have called off the massacre at Nob.' The vicar's reference, to an Old Testament bloodbath whose details he had long forgotten, was one he frequently used in connection with almost anything.

'You and your massacre,' she said, brushing a hand down the jacket.

'I was just asking, darling – my achievements. Tell me them again.'

111

She replied without hesitation. 'Stamina, commitment, imagination. The summer party – don't mention the marquee. Enthusiasm. Staying with Tara Staveley that day, for seven or eight hours, in her home, helping her when she was about to die of viral bronchitis. The sermon you preached which made three people come up to the front afterwards and ask questions about predestination. Generosity. The vision you showed by placing confidence in Otis. The way you—'

'The Tara thing is a bit inaccurate. I got locked in the house accidentally.'

'Yes, but you never complained,' she said quickly. 'Also the way you've counselled a succession of people from outside the church against getting married, where the choice was obviously wrong. Do you remember the couple from Melbourne who said the only thing they had in common was surfing? Your honesty, too. Tell them that. The sermon series you preached on Genesis—'

'Well, there were a few complaints when I said—'

'You don't have to remind them about that Darwin comment. Talk about the smooth way you do communion, the way you know everyone's names. Unflappability, Derek. And the Reach-Out Week three years ago – why don't you mention the clever thing you did to get so many people to sign up, you know, hinting on the poster it was something to do with aerobics and making the payment non-refundable? Plus your relationship with George Foster. The way you've brought that man into the church, given his life a real meaning—'

'God's done that,' he interrupted, adding quickly '—or someone other than me, at least.'

'But you helped, Derek. Really, truly, there's an awful lot for you to tell them.'

'If they ask.'

'Exactly.'

The vicar glanced at the calendar on his desk. Friday, September 7th. There was a Bible verse in capitals below the coloured squares. 'A MAN CAN RECEIVE ONLY WHAT IS GIVEN HIM FROM HEAVEN.' Under that, in italics: *John, chapter three, verse twenty-seven*. Derek wrinkled his nose. A

112

shard of sunlight cut across the windowpane as he turned back to it.

He was nervous, but utterly exhilarated. From the moment he had picked up the message Claire Stupples had left for him, in fact, he had been utterly and completely enslaved by exhilaration. Exhilaration had been his King and Queen, his Jack and Joker. It was as though everything was logical at last. The air he was breathing went down like pure oxygen. The vicar felt a clear-as-glass sense of himself, of his marriage, of anything he could mention. *When I am told the news this afternoon*, he pondered, *I shall begin to be more methodical about Bible study and Christian thoughts*. Yes, method would come easier then. He would simply stick out a foot, feel with a toe for the bottom rung of the ladder, and start to climb.

'Have you checked your collar?' Judy was asking.

'I put a paper clip round – just round here—' he was arching his neck and pointing into it.

'It won't spring up?'

'Shouldn't.'

'Sure?'

'No.'

'Let me have a look.'

In the last hour before they left the vicarage . . . *my last hour as a vicar*, Derek told himself dramatically . . . they prayed together. For the first time in months, perhaps years, they prayed together.

The vicar and his wife thanked God for second chances, for not giving up on them even though they had let him down so very often and so badly, for this awesome new vista that had electrified everything in their lives, for friends in Evenham they would surely miss, and for spiced chicken. Derek was not sure why he brought in the chicken, except that there was a Thai restaurant in Evenham he had never been to and which he supposed, kneeling there on the living room floor with his eyes closed, he might now never visit.

Blinking in the light, they were looking at each other.

'Chocks away,' Judy said.

14

Flowers leapt out of a fat vase on the desk, wrenching Judy's eye from the receptionist. Big bold chrysanthemums, morning glory, a spray of pink aster. Judy felt Derek's hand tighten around hers, then let go. Her arm fell like lead to her side.

Absently, she looked up. Halogen lights!

She felt removed from the moment, as if the vicar was nervous for both of them. Irrelevant thoughts queued in her mind like Moscow shoppers in fox fur hats: that Caroline had not even been told about today; that they were guests of the Geareys tomorrow and Derek had probably forgotten; that the Basildon diocese headquarters looked like an American investment bank; that the best film she had ever seen was *Magic* with Anthony Hopkins, and that the vicarage was out of kitchen paper.

'Reverend Weston. Hello.' The Bishop of Basildon's receptionist was definitely new. She wore a roomy green dress and large spectacles with bright blue frames. 'And Judy Weston, of course. Hello. I'm Cassie Hayhurst.'

'Are we early?' Derek sounded nervous.

'Bang on time.' Cassie Hayhurst took the top off a fountain pen with a rattle that sounded something to do with expensive metal. 'I think they're nearly ready for you, actually.' She was gesturing at a fawn sofa by the wall.

When they were both seated, Derek called: 'What happened to Edith, Cassie?'

The receptionist was tapping a number into the telephone keypad, and answered without breaking the rhythm or looking up. 'Her shorthand – lengthened.'

'Oh dear,' the vicar mumbled. He turned to Judy and whispered, 'They've got very money-conscious. Because of the mistakes with property in the eighties. They're still trying to sell some offices they bought in the Isle of Dogs. There's a new sort of efficiency in the air.' As if to prove it, the receptionist appeared to have begun dictating a lengthy pager number down the telephone, digit by digit. 'Poor old Edith,' the vicar added under his breath. 'She knew everyone, didn't she?'

'She even knew me,' Judy whispered back with a grin and a wink.

Cassie Hayhurst was saying into the receiver: 'Please fax amended audit figures within two hours. End of message.'

They had been waiting for ten minutes when suddenly a door opened across the hall. A slim, tall woman bustled towards them, her shoulders heavily padded. A second person was closing in behind her. Cassie was doing something official with an arm. *Indicating us*, the vicar realised, and shot to his feet, virtually pulling Judy to hers.

'Beverly Gardner-Laing. Good afternoon, Derek. Welcome.'

The vicar goggled. *Have those shoulders been padded with bicycle saddles?*

'Good afternoon, Beverly. This is—'

The vicar's wife got there before him. 'Judy.'

'Julie – of course.'

'Judy – Judy,' they said together.

Now take me to your leader, Derek thought.

They were led briskly down a long corridor. They arrived at a lift. Derek's heart was thumping, thumping as though he was reaching the end of a marathon sprint, coming within yards or metres of unbroken tape . . .

All you have to do is stay upright, and you've won it!

They ascended. They ascended to the fourth floor. Beverly explained how the second and third were rented to a charity of some kind – the vicar was not listening. Judy kept glancing at a large mirror set into the rear wall of the lift, radiating certainty, tension and pleasure all at once. She looked intensely beautiful.

Now they were moving down another grey-carpeted corridor at speed. The building looked newly refurbished, newly everything. 'It's just at the end here,' Beverly Gardner-Laing was saying. 'The reception room.' Walking at full tilt behind her, Derek glanced down and saw tiny blue bows sewn into her stockings over the tendons at the back of her ankles. He imagined them rare butterflies, just landed.

The room was large. It was furnished with old chairs and a sagging couch, with stately lampshades dangling from the ceiling on chains. In the rest of the building everything had been new, voguish; here there were reproductions of classical paintings on panelled walls, an old oak desk standing stolidly in the thick pile of a dark rug. The curtains were an ancient Arabian yellow. The ceiling arched high above an elaborate moulded cornice. The windows were high. And set in the tall panes, Derek Weston could see the backs of the heads of the people now standing to greet him.

'Hello, Terence,' Judy was saying.

The bishop stepped forward warmly, pressing one of Derek's hands between two of his.

Someone else was coming forward too.

'Wazim Bhaji!'

'Yes, Derek. Bhatia. Hello, hello. Do sit down. Judy, do sit there too. You probably know Cliff—' the head of the Basildon diocese steering committee indicated one of the others '—Cliff Camping, our flying deacon, do you?'

'Of course. Hi, Cliff.' Derek leant forwards on the sofa as it sagged further, intertwining his fingers presidentially. He felt indescribably warm and noble.

'Hi, Derek.' Cliff Camping always looked very serious, as if he had recently flown into something. He nodded to them both as he resumed his seat. 'Hullo, Judy.'

'Hello, Cliff.'

Bill Venerick was introduced, head of Strategy and Planning; 'Peter Selwyn you know,' Terence Stitt went on, 'our diocesan officer for mission'. Another man at the back, small and muscular and with a pointed grey beard, whom Derek had never seen or heard of before, was named as Roger Banks, the acting administrator of finance.

Beverly Gardner-Laing smiled at them both and said: 'I know I've already introduced myself, but I didn't want anyone to leave out Michael here. Michael Beltway, who is overseeing our review of the various types of hymnals we use across the diocese. He was in the lift with us.'

'We have songbooks,' Derek chipped in. 'Uplifting.'

'Right on, chum,' said Michael Beltway.

Everyone nodded soberly.

Then the bishop's assistant rose from her chair, moved over to Terence Stitt and bent down to whisper something. In response, he raised a hand and quickly removed an object from the side of his head. He chuckled. 'Beverly tells me I am improperly dressed, in that I have had a pencil behind my ear all day.' The depth of the bishop's voice was always a surprise: he was a beanpole of a man, with a stiff back, sunken chest and non-existent shoulders, and a round tub of belly no jacket ever effectively hid. His eyes darted around the room as he added in bass tones, 'It doesn't ever do to be improperly dressed.' The remark drew staggered laughter, and Derek said:

'Did you hear about the vicar who asked a quartet of musicians round because he was freezing? He told them to play at the back of the church and, when they started, he said, 'Thanks, I've already got woollen leggings: what I really needed was a string vestry.'

The laughter staggered away into nothing, and the vicar felt himself blushing. He had timed it wrong. He felt Judy's knee press sideways into his, a reprimand. Terence Stitt was twisting the pencil between his fingers.

'Well,' said the bishop.

Here we go. This is it, the vicar thought.

'I imagine you will probably have been wondering why—'

Soon, he told himself, *I will be telegrammed*.

'—we asked you to come here this afternoon.'

The vicar felt nineteen nervous thrills surge within him, his throat constricting with suppressed excitement.

'Yes,' he breathed, barely able to speak. *No*, he thought.

'You will be aware,' the bishop said, 'of the pressure that exists right across the church on every single position – from bottom to top.'

'Yes,' Derek Weston confirmed. He heard an echo in his

head: *to top*. Beside him, Judy was agreeing quietly. 'Oh, yes. Yes. In all institutions.'

Terence Stitt turned to the small man with the pointed beard. 'Would you like to underline that, Robin?'

Thumbing through a thick sheaf of papers, the man corrected him. 'Roger.'

'I'm sorry.' There was momentary embarrassment. The bishop whispered at Derek: 'There were just too many puns on Robin Banks, from the finance point of view – you know, the diary people in the *Church of England Newspaper* would have gone bananas over—' He shrugged. 'Well anyway, he was happy to alter it. For safety.'

Ignoring the aside, Roger Banks had got to his feet. The vicar noticed he was barely six inches taller than the stiff-backed chair he had just occupied. *This is it*, he thought. *They're going to tell me all the figures, then say why they've chosen me*. He remembered the bishop's words from – oh, long ago, aeons and moons ago: *it's never that good an idea for a clergyman to treat a church as home, Derek, you know . . .*

The bearded figure at the end of the room was now reading out a long list of mammoth numbers which were passing miles over Derek Weston's head. The vicar kept thinking he could hear classical music somewhere.

The administrator ended by saying, very slowly: 'Four-hundred-thou-sand.' Then he coughed in several racking splutters from deep within his chest and sat down, slapping a sheaf of documents hard on his knees.

They were suddenly all looking very grave indeed, Derek noticed.

All of them.

Even Beverly Gardner-Laing was looking grave. This would be the moment for the bicycle saddles to fall out, break up the atmosphere a bit. Roger Banks curled the fingers of a hand and dragged them through his beard.

Derek felt the minutest frown lingering on his brow. He wiped it away, a stray insect. Now he was desperately trying to remember what those figures had been, what they might have meant.

Before he could, Terence Stitt's voice boomed across his

thoughts. 'And it is for precisely that reason, Derek, that we felt we had to come to our decision.'

The vicar's heart was leaping!

'So either,' the bishop continued softly, 'we close your church, Derek, or we close St Paul's. It simply is not possible, we think, for both to remain open in such proximity to each other. One of them really is going to have – to go.'

The vicar felt all blood drain from his face.

What the—

'I'm very sorry, Derek. Judy, I am sorry. That's not to say you won't be the ones to stay. We'll make the decision in a month, and we'll be along sometime before then to assess your – well, your church profile.'

There was silence before anyone spoke again.

'When?' Derek's voice was a croak.

'Say – three weeks?' That was Wazim Bhatia, coolly consulting his diary.

Terence Stitt said: 'It'll be good for the parish, Derek. I know your congregation is full of the most – um – flexible, warm and – ah – and sincere people. And clearly, whichever vicar is – um – moved on, there'll be a post found for them. Be it he or she. Possibly in a curacy again for a time, for a brief time, and then a substantive posting elsewhere.'

'Right.' That was Derek's voice. Judy did not speak. He turned towards her on the sofa, caught the ridges in her temple going up and down furiously as she sat there mute, and turned back. 'Okay. Right, fine,' he said again. Everything was racing. He pressed his right foot hard into the floorboards, trying to find a brake. 'I – I do – completely understand. Of course I do.'

'It's been a great innings, yours has,' the bishop said, leaning forward in his seat, eyes twinkling. 'Botham,' someone said quietly. Michael Beltway.

And then an extraordinary thing happened. In the silence, Wazim Bhatia began to clap. The noise was like gunshots. The vicar's mind leapt back to the applause at the end of the surprise party. The huge yellow curtains even seemed to move slightly with the sound.

Watching, the vicar saw Roger Banks carefully place his

119

documents on to the varnished floor and join in, bringing his hands together slowly and forcefully. Then the bishop started to clap too, loudly, with significance. His assistant followed next, pitter-pattering her palms delicately against each other, glancing up and flashing a grin across the room. Soon everyone else was applauding: Peter, Bill, then Michael Beltway, performing some kind of complex syncopation with his hands . . .

The vicar and his wife could do nothing but sit and listen, grim-faced. The clapping seemed to go on for ever, gathering and deepening in the large reception room until it was hanging in the air above them like a huge pregnant cloud, and Derek and Judy were two tiny raindrops in it about to fall.

15

'I don't believe it! I don't bloody believe it!'

'Please darling, don't swear.'

They were back at the vicarage. Facing each other in the hallway.

'I have never been so humiliated in all my life. Those jerks! Those stupid, stupid jerks! I tell you, they wouldn't even get jobs as doormen in our bank, Derek! They wouldn't get a temporary try-out in the canteen! Sitting there, smiling pompously like that – leering at us! Like grinning shop dummies!'

The vicar felt his mouth trembling. He felt his whole face trembling. 'I know, darling, I know. It was a bit of a surprise to be told—'

'And that woman with the shoulder-pads! A surprise? What – a surprise? A touch startling, was it? The odd raised eyebrow, was there? Derek—'

'All right, it was a bombshell.'

'No, Derek. Hiroshima was a bombshell. Bishopsgate was a bombshell. This was bigger than that. There were worse injuries, anyway. I'm talking about you and me, Derek – that's who! They've cut us through our hearts! They've blown us up! To think we drove all the way over there in complete ignorance, chatting away to each other about all those questions you had the answers to, questions they were never in a million years going to ask—'

'But that was your idea, Judy.'

'The joke wasn't – doing that stupid joke about the vestry! When did you think they were going to find the time to get the punchline to that one? They'd have to take a year off! Mind you, they'll probably be able to after they shut our

place down for once and all, shut us both down, shut down
for good and—'

She was so angry, so incandescent with rage, she was
getting her words jumbled. Judy's face was red. Derek
stared into her eyes. His knees were shaking. Her pupils
were flashing. The telephone rang.

'Hullo, Derek. It's Marshall. Look, you never returned that
call. The message I left.'

'What message?' Derek's palm was spreading the receiver
with sweat.

'Oh, golly, didn't Claire pass it on? It was to do with – have
you got a moment?'

The vicar was silent for an instant, getting his breath back,
catching Judy on the edge of his field of vision, still standing in
the hallway, hands on hips, swaying, looking off into a corner.
'Go on,' he said gravely into the handset.

'That thing I heard in the library. Well, before that. The
rumour. The one I was about to tell you before I got hit by
the marquee. I've remembered it, Derek.'

'Oh,' the vicar said.

Marshall went on: 'Someone was saying to me – on my first
day back in the library – they said something about books.
"We had to move one lot up after they closed a section."
That was what they said. And I kept concentrating on the
bit about moving books up, you see. That's why I couldn't
make sense of it.'

'I see.'

'But it jogged me, Derek. And now I've remembered.
Closing the section – that's what must have triggered me,
but I didn't realise. The rumour was that they were going to
shut a church in Evenham and move one of the vicars up to
take charge of both congregations.'

'Thanks, Marshall, very much.' The vicar's voice contained
no trace of sarcasm or bitterness. Nor gratitude. It contained no trace of anything. 'I'll speak to you soon,' he
said, and hung up. As the handset clicked in the cradle,
something clicked in his mind. He remembered the bishop's loaded words at the summer fête – and his stupid,
muffed interpretation of them: *it's never that good an idea*

for a clergyman to treat any church as home, Derek, you know . . .

Judy was no longer in the hallway. Derek walked through it. She was slumped in an armchair in the living room, crying softly, one hand covering her face.

He stood over her, looking out towards the vicarage garden.

'I took a day off work for this,' she moaned.

'Will you have to go in tomorrow?'

'I can't, can I? We're going to the Tower. Early.'

The vicar felt a chasm opening between them, with him trying to bridge it by nailing a foot to each side and now finding his legs stretched a hundred miles each way, like elastic.

Tears sprang into his eyes. 'Darling, Judy, don't give up hope.'

Judy Weston breathed out in a gasp, as though involuntarily. Through sobs, she said: 'It's so awful. It's so horrible.' The words were almost wails. 'To think of you going off to be the dogsbody in some Birmingham outhouse. To think of the number of people we're going to have to tell.'

'They haven't closed us down yet.'

'We'll have to tell Otis,' she murmured.

'But they haven't shut us yet.'

'The other church is going to win, Derek.'

At that moment, the vicar felt his heart capsize. It went down like a scuttled dinghy, without drama, just bubbles. His insides were wrenched by the most agonising sense of loss and tragedy he had ever experienced, and he groaned in pain.

Judy took the hand away from her brow and looked up at him. One side of her face was streaked with run mascara. She rose shakily from the armchair, reached out and touched his arm. He was still staring into the garden.

'We can't win,' he heard her say grimly at his side, tugging twice at the sleeve of his shirt. 'We won't win, Derek. Stop dreaming. The whole problem has been your dreaming.'

The vicar felt the skin on his face sensitised. He opened his mouth. His lips were dry. He brought a hand up and wiped salt water from his eyes.

'I won't sing again at St Paul's,' Judy was saying. 'That's the best I can do. The rest is up to you, Derek.'

He turned his head towards her, and spoke in a hushed tone. 'You're not going to leave me, are you?'

'I'm not going – look, I'm not going to Birmingham.'

'They said it would be temporary.'

'What?'

'A curacy. Wherever.'

'They're full of garbage. I wouldn't trust them an inch.'

'They're men of God,' Derek mumbled.

'Yes, and Herod was good with children.'

'Look, Judy,' the vicar croaked, 'I think I just need to take a minute to digest all this. It's a bit like – like being made redundant.'

'That's exactly what I was thinking,' she said, pensively. She wiped a cheek roughly with the heel of her hand. 'Those – skunks.'

'If only we—'

Derek Weston had been about to say something about the Bible, about prayer, about the past and the way they had both begun by believing so much and somehow let it all decay within them . . . let it all go cracked and blue, like old Cheddar . . . but now he left the sentence dangling three words in.

'If only – what?' Judy prompted, her voice frosted with indifference.

He paused.

'Nothing,' Derek mumbled, finally. 'Hard cheese.'

Judy Weston turned towards the garden, and her husband watched her face set icily. He looked down at the carpet, dropped his shoulders, put his hands in his pockets, walked out of the room.

In the study he pulled the chair out from under the desk, lowered himself into it and rested his elbows either side of the blotter. The vicar dropped his head into his palms, so that every inch of his face was covered.

He pressed his face deep into the palms of his hands, and pressed the palms deep into the flesh of his face. Then he wept. Even if he had been able to speak through the tears, there were no words worth uttering. He felt his lips thicken.

In the silence of the study, the vicar's shoulders jumped with grief. Derek Weston saw history sliding back from this moment, as though everything that had ever happened in the universe had been building up to it. A huge, smelly foot had crashed through the clouds and stamped on his world. He wept and wept.

After fifteen minutes the pain had not lessened, but Derek looked up and blinked out at the gravel beyond the window. Then the vicar did something he might never previously have imagined contemplating, let alone carrying through. He reached over and pushed with his fingertips at the study door, checking it had clicked properly shut, then drew a scrap of orange paper from somewhere near the bottom of a drawer.

He read a number off it, and dialled the telephone.

The ringing on the other end did not last long.

'Hello?'

Derek recognised the voice instantly, and felt flesh bump on his forearms.

'Charlotte?'

'Yes.'

'It's Derek Weston here, of Evenham.'

There was some crackling on the line, so the vicar did not hear whatever it was she said first. He told her so.

'I asked how you were,' she said.

'Good, thanks.' He glanced over at the shut study door.

Neither said anything for thirty seconds.

Then: 'My orchestra's doing a thing in London at the end of the month.'

'Oh.'

'Might see you.'

'Yes – yes, lovely.'

'You're talking very quietly.'

'The line isn't much cop,' he said.

There was a momentary silence, and then Charlotte volunteered: 'I heard from my parents that they've been enjoying the church.' She added, 'I'm sorry, Derek – I didn't know they were going to land on you.'

'It's nice having them.'

In a concerned voice, she put in: 'They told me a funny story about Petersons, or something.'

'It's too long to explain now,' Derek said quickly, then hesitated. Slowly, he went on: 'Charlotte – I just wanted to – to ask – or to – tell you something.'

'What?'

'I'm in trouble, Charlotte.'

At the other end, she was saying, 'Oh. Right. And—'

'And I need your help.'

'Yes.'

'The pearl, Charlotte. We always talked about it. The jewel. The pearl—'

'Of greatest price,' she cut in. 'Don't tell me you've forgotten all the conversations we had!' She was laughing.

'It's not—' Derek suddenly heard movement outside the door, and paused.

'Hello?' Charlotte said at the other end.

'Derek?'

That was Judy. On the other side of the study door. Grimly, she was announcing: 'I've made some tea.' She knocked. Three times.

The vicar's heart raced. He froze. 'I'll be out in a minute,' he called hoarsely, pausing for a moment with a hand covering the mouthpiece, chest pounding, and then, as the footsteps moved away across the hallway carpet, turning back to the window and leaning forward into the telephone. 'Look, Charlotte,' he said, lowering his voice. 'Please help me. They're going to close my church. The whole lot of—'

'Derek, where are you?'

'At home, of course.'

'Why are you talking so quietly?'

He rubbed his eyes. 'I'm not, Charlotte. I'm just leaning into the telephone.'

'What do you mean, close the church?'

'If I don't get something together in the next three weeks.'

'Get something together? What do you mean, Derek?'

'I'm talking about organising a revival,' he whispered. 'And pronto.'

Charlotte Davidson's voice, when she next spoke, was edged with nervousness. 'Derek – are you whispering because you don't want Judy to hear?'

Urgently, Derek hissed: 'The pearl, Charlotte! The pearl! Help me!'

Suddenly he heard a creak on the floorboards outside the study, Judy's voice again saying something in the hallway, and then – as his head shot round to look at it, his eyes widening in their sockets – the squeak of the door handle turning.

He put the handset back in the telephone cradle. His wife looked in. 'It's getting cold,' she said vaguely.

'It's September.'

'The tea, Derek.'

She walked back into the kitchen.

For a few seconds, the vicar could not remember how to stand up.

'. . . and once they got into this position, they did not usually stand up again.'

The vicar glanced sharply over at Brigadier Sir Kenneth Gearey. Hands on hips, Sir Kenneth wheeled half-round and looked at him quizzically. 'For heaven's sake, Derek – not upsetting you at all, are we?'

Derek felt a light breeze blowing through his hair. He was certain he did look upset, but it had nothing to do with anything his most distinguished parishioner was saying. Judy's face was blanched and impassive, which was no help.

'Not at all.' The vicar hauled the corners of his mouth upwards, concentrating on unfurrowing his brow. 'I think Judy and I are both just a bit tired.' He saw his wife smile glassily.

'Thank goodness for that. Now, as I was saying, this is where Anne Boleyn asked to be beheaded, not by the axe, but by the sword, which was her way of . . .'

A cool September Saturday. Crowds of bedraggled tourists shuffling past them. In the distance the great iron blues and whites of the bridge, gold towertops flashing moments of sun. Here, outside the Chapel of St Peter ad Vincula, within the curtain walls of the Tower of London, below flagpoles, cupolas and arrow-slits, Sir Kenneth Gearey pointing at the small black execution block on Tower Green. Jennifer Gearey delayed in their official home, Queen's House the name of it, up in Princess Elizabeth's Walk, but coming out very soon – just attending to a few things, he had said. The three of them trooping past floors of weapons behind the fifteen-foot-thick walls of the White Tower, through the Council Chamber where Guy Fawkes was sentenced to be sliced into small pieces under a yawning timbered ceiling that made Derek think suddenly of his church, except that there was rather more yawning in St Saviour's; into the bedroom of Sir Walter Ralegh via the portcullises of the Bloody Tower – Ralegh, Sir Kenneth was now telling them, spent fifteen years imprisoned in comfort, brewing homemade beer and writing *A History of the World*.

'. . . but then he was executed, right here, in October 1618.'

'Really?' That was Derek, looking down at the block in the grass. It was so small. 'Pretty bad luck, I suppose, considering how much history there's been since.'

'Quite. Quoted Peter at the final moment, he did. "The end of all things is at hand," Ralegh told them. Do you know that verse? He was unfairly dispensed with, to say the least.'

Judy cocked her head at the comment. Gazing stonily at her husband, she asked: 'Why did Anne Boleyn want to be executed with a sword?'

Sir Kenneth Gearey looked momentarily unnerved. 'Not sure.' He was tall, barrel-chested, obviously every inch ex-army, slightly lame, with a jet black moustache draped over an upper lip that shivered every time he spoke, as though filtering out militarily sensitive words. He had generous, twinkling eyes, two stamp-sized patches of scarred skin over a cheekbone, and large hands.

'Perhaps it was sharper,' Derek suggested. He saw the sun edge behind a bruised cloud, as if disassociating itself from the comment. A distant bus horn blared. Several Americans on the other side of the Green were doing something with a video camera.

'Before she died,' the governor was saying, 'Anne Boleyn told her executioners to pray for the King. "Pray for the author of my doom, for he is a man of God, and I shall end my existence willingly," she told them.'

Judy shot a glance at Derek that had something to do with ended existences.

Not seeing the glance, or at least not registering the feeling in it, Sir Kenneth went on: 'Catherine Howard, of course, asked for the block to be brought to her cell so she could practise laying her head on it.'

Derek's gaze darted at Judy, then down at the block.

There was a brief silence between them.

The end of all things is at hand, the vicar thought.

'Right, then,' Judy said breezily.

'Is that where the expression "Knock your block off" comes from?' he asked a minute later.

'No,' the governor answered.

One of the Americans shouted: 'Come on, Melton!'

'I've timed this especially for you,' Sir Kenneth Gearey was telling the Westons as they doubled back towards another tower, 'because this is the fortnight when the two lowest floors of the Waterloo Block are closed.'

'Closed?'

'Closed to the public, Derek – ah – now – one second. Down there is what they call Mint Street. Where William Foxley made coins. In 1546 he is recorded as having fallen asleep for fourteen days and fifteen nights.'

'Didn't know your sermons were being circulated that early, Derek,' Judy said.

The vicar blinked down at the path as the governor roared with laughter. 'And this,' he continued, 'is the Beauchamp Tower. That's why I stopped us.' Sir Kenneth threw his hand out at the medieval brickwork. 'Reserved for prisoners of rank. Up there is where we live. With Jennifer. Um – Elizabeth, you see, came here in 1554. And she said, "Here landeth as true a subject being condemned a prisoner, as ever landed at these steps." Just over there, that was. At Traitor's Gate.'

Judy was staring at Derek, and suddenly commented: 'There's a lot of injustice in the world.'

'Injustice?' Sir Kenneth spun round to face her, arms folded tightly. 'But she gave her name to a golden age of English history, Judy. She was never executed. After she was released she came back to stay here as Queen for two days. Show who's boss.'

'She escaped the block,' Derek muttered.

Sir Kenneth breathed in, filling his chest with air. 'She did indeed.'

'But most times they didn't.' Judy glanced away, face pale and drawn.

There was an instant of discomfiture, of subtle dislocation. A crowd walked past them, through them, and they were momentarily separated from each other.

What an awful day this is, Derek was thinking. He wanted it over quickly. He felt utterly exposed. Naked. As though someone had seared his shirt off with a bunsen burner. The sky had gone grey, his heart and soul barbecue black. Insides groaning like slatted wooden bridges with long vehicles passing over them. What would the Geareys say when they found out? And Judy – Judy was so patently distracted! He shot a glance at her. *Try, Judy, try!* The vicar dreaded his wife suddenly collapsing in tears and spilling the broadest beans in history, but – no, no, never, she was too strong.

The tourists cleared, and suddenly there was Lady Jennifer Gearey.

'Hello! Hello! Hello to you both! Well, what a day!'

Lunch was superb, but Derek did not taste it. He ate quickly, as if trying to submerge his failures in food. Judy did the reverse. She left a slice of chicken at the side of her plate, and peas. The four were served by a pair of waiters in white jackets and black trousers. 'Just one of the little perks of being in charge here,' Sir Kenneth guffawed. The vicar looked down at the tablecloth. Pure white, a gold braid rim.

'After lunch,' Jennifer was saying between munches, 'we'll go to the Waterloo Block. Did you see the coverage of the move? Of the jewels? Yes? They're on the ground floor now. But they're being cleaned, you see, so it's not open at the moment.'

Sir Kenneth chipped in: 'It used to be. I say that – I mean the Wakefield Tower, where the Crown Jewels were kept until 1967, was virtually open house even during cleaning. Then they went into the Waterloo Block basement, which was a bit tighter. But this is the tightest security of all. Absolutely airtight. We fitted a moving walkway, too, a sort of metal belt, though of course it's not switched on today.'

A waiter arrived at Derek's side, offering a second helping of potatoes. 'Oh – yes please. Spuds. Thank you.' His father used to have a rule about no seconds, but he had always got round it by going straight to thirds.

'Tell me something, Derek,' Jennifer Gearey began. 'What was that surprise party of yours in aid of on Monday? I'm terribly sorry we couldn't make it.'

'It was – um—' the vicar chewed on a potato with deliberate slowness, buying all the time available '—excuse me.' He looked down at his plate, jaw grinding, mind galloping. 'Spuds. The party was—' finally he swallowed, glancing across at Judy and knowing instantly there was no prospect of rescue from her. *You are on your own in this*, her eyes were telling him. 'Well, it was a kind of marker, really.'

'A marker?' Sir Kenneth asked. 'We had heard—'

'A punctuation mark in the parish, if you like.' The vicar looked around the table, setting his cutlery on the side of his plate and laying his palms on the cloth. 'A semi-colon, of sorts.' How desperate, how urgent was his need for inspiration!

'It was a party, really,' Judy put in generously. 'Just fun.'

'Fun? I remember that,' Sir Kenneth joked, and they all laughed out of relief.

There was a long queue stretching out of one entrance to the Waterloo Block under a large notice announcing TOILETS, TORTURE INSTRUMENTS, EDUCATION CENTRE. 'That's not us,' Jennifer Gearey told them; 'the sign wasn't us, either.' Sir Kenneth launched into a brief history of the building. 'This place was made for a thousand men, you know.' As he said all this, they were going through a corridor marked PRIVATE. 'It's become a – ah, hello there.'

The four of them came to a halt at a junction of passageways, by an arched doorway where two yeomen were standing importantly.

Their faces broke into smiles when they saw the governor and his wife. The yeomen bowed. There was an exchange of pleasantries. Then the four passed through.

'The front is shut, you see, Derek.' They were going down a narrow staircase.

Completely to his surprise, the vicar had a sudden sense of

excitement. He could not remember the last time he had seen the Crown Jewels. Perhaps two decades ago. Maybe more. Sir Kenneth was explaining that the glass screens in front of some of them had been unscrewed so teams of cleaning and preservation specialists could get access. 'Right now, you see, the place is closed. We have to go into what's called an Alarm Sealed Area. ASA, for short. See, when you close all this off, security isn't even an issue at all.'

They reached a grey steel door with a wheel in the centre of it, set into a corner of solid Victorian wall. The governor picked up a telephone without a dial and asked someone to come down. 'Most of the jewels are seventeenth-century,' he was saying as they waited. 'Made to replace the ones the Parliamentarians destroyed. This door is nine inches thick.' A man with serious sideburns arrived, dangling a set of keys from a chain. 'It's unusual to be going in this way,' Sir Kenneth explained, 'though I – thanks, Andrew – I have taken a couple of others in here—'

He was interrupted by a clank as the wheel in the door was turned.

Sir Kenneth gave the other three a small bow.

'The Holy of Holies,' he breathed.

'Kenny!' his wife reprimanded him, thumbing at Derek.

'Sorry, Derek,' the governor said with a roll of his eyes. 'Forgot ourselves.'

The door opened.

'Not at all,' the vicar replied as they walked in.

The place smelt musty.

'One thing,' the governor said, stopping them just as they caught sight of the jewels. 'Oh – if you would, yes, Andrew – thanks very much. Andrew will have to stand here while we go round, just for form. I hope that's all right. Don't let it put you off looking. I was just going to say – another bit of small print, this – none of us is permitted to reach our hands out anywhere near the cases. It's just an in-house regulation we have to adhere to, for all kinds of dull reasons. So please, if you can, do keep your arms at your sides.' He coughed. 'Behind one's back is best.'

They began to move. The room was illuminated by fluorescent squares in the ceiling. Some jewels were spotlit. Their names were lost on Derek. Sir Kenneth was commentating, saying something here and there about everything, but the monologue seemed to reach the vicar's ear in pieces, as though broken up in gem-generated white heat – 'labels missing from this case, but if you get close . . . and here you'll both be able to see . . . well, these dishes alone worth more than all restoration work done on the Tower since . . . two coronets here, very interesting point I'd like to . . .'

Many more of the glass screens had been removed than the vicar expected. A sceptre was missing from one tall case. Odd velvet cushions were gone too. Bending forward, hands clamped at his back, Derek brought his head up against a dazzling pair of silver spurs, as if tanning his face in perfection. An air-conditioning vent hummed above him. The governor's commentary at the next exhibit whistled overhead: 'original string rotted . . . so restrung each time we clean . . . pearls love-gift in 1637 to Henrietta Maria, wife of Charles the First, who comforted him after death of favourite courtier George Villiers, Duke of Buckingham . . . curtain torn here, which means extra work for . . .'

A spotlight up on the wall flashed off one spur. The vicar blinked and caught a pulsing black circle on the inside of an eyelid. Perched on a ledge at the back of the case was a gleaming salt server, brilliant and pure and fat. Looking up, he drew level with a reflection of his face in the curved silver: egg-shaped, one eye popping, sweat on his brow.

'Don't get left behind, Derek!'

Jennifer Gearey's voice sounded strangely offensive amid such dazzling perfection. Utterly mortal, unfinished, cracked, flawed – the vicar swallowed the sound of it away, moved on. He felt his heart gulp like a goldfish. At the door, Andrew was looking at his watch and tapping a foot. Pearls now. A dozen clustered on coloured velvet. Pearls. The ones Sir Kenneth had been talking about. The buzzing of a housefly somewhere. *How did it get in here?* The vicar's fingers twined tighter around each other behind his back, then came undone.

'Hey! Sorry – sir!'

'What – oh, okay – but don't worry, Andrew,' Sir Kenneth was laughing by the furthest cabinet. 'Rest easy. But – um – Derek, probably not a good idea to—'

'Sorry,' the vicar said, moving towards them.

'—stretch our hands forward too much at all. No reaching! Rule made up by one of these silly governors. Not us, we hasten to add.' He whispered at Jennifer and Judy: 'Andrew's overkeen. Marriage problems.'

Derek caught up.

'I was just saying, Derek dear,' Jennifer was pointing out, 'this set of medals is the oldest here. What are they, Kenneth? I can't remember.'

'We think they're probably eight hundred years old. Silver-centred.'

'Really?' Judy said. 'What was that – Henry the Second?'

'One out. Richard the First. Derek, your wife is—'

Sir Kenneth left the sentence uncompleted.

They all turned to look at the vicar.

'Are you all right, Derek?' Jennifer Gearey took a step towards him.

'Yes.' The vicar beamed suddenly.

'Derek—?' That was Judy. She saw the pearls of sweat jumping out on his brow.

'I'm fine.' He was grinning.

'Do you know about Richard the First, Judy? He was so desperate for money he actually offered to sell London – Derek, your wife is truly impressive.'

Perkily, Judy said: 'He built a castle in France. I know that.'

'Château Gaillard. That's right. On a clifftop. He claimed he could fight off any attack, "even if the walls were made of butter," he said – but in the end the place fell when people climbed in through the drainage system. True.'

'You know everything,' Judy Weston told the Brigadier, and he swelled with pride.

'It's all selective,' he said. 'Just the odd gem.'

For some reason, they turned to Derek.

'You've gone terribly quiet,' Jennifer Gearey chuckled.

'Overwhelmed,' the vicar explained in a hushed voice.

'It's been a wonderful day,' his wife sighed. She looked quizzically at her husband, and sighed again. 'I sense that – well, Derek and I had a difficult day yesterday. I sense we could have been better company.'

'Not in the least,' Sir Kenneth protested airily. 'To be frank, we've been looking forward and looking forward to having you. Normally, of course, you have us – at St Saviour's. It's such a change from just brushing past each other on the way out of church.'

'Oh – come on – there's much more to see,' Jennifer was telling them. 'Over there, by Andrew, are the royal sceptres . . . diamond collet necklace, round stones in claw settings . . . India in 1851 . . . arc lights really quite bright just there . . . longest sceptres . . . right next door to fringe tiara, worn by . . . alcove . . . the current ones are . . . you'll be amazed . . .'

17

Staring down, Derek Weston simply could not believe it.

He had no way of believing it.

For at least five minutes, the Reverend Derek Weston just stared at the pearl in the palm of his hand.

He went through everything. Judy, Marshall, the rumour, the marquee, Charlotte, Wazim Bhatia's car, Helen Silverstone's bedside table . . . Rex . . .

The Jewel House in the Tower of London.

It had all spiralled in towards the centre, all of it, like grooves in a record. The jewel was the centre. Derek was the old needle, a rusted turntable stylus, swept towards it as everything spun around him. Now he had it in his hands.

The pearl of great price.

He had snatched it. Snatched the royal pearl, from whichever king it was, from whichever coloured cushion – he could not remember any of that. Could barely recall his hand shooting out a second before Andrew had looked over . . . it had shot out! His hand! He had grabbed it!

Almost unable to do it without screaming, Derek looked down at the pearl. It was big and perfect and full of panic, sitting pretty in his palm. He swallowed. Hanoverian, was it? Hapsburgian? *Good gracious and heavens above.* It was as flawless a gem as he had ever seen in his life. How much of his life was unlike this gem! It must have been one of the biggest on the cushion. Must have been. And how many were there? *More than a dozen*, he thought. *A good fifteen.*

The vicar breathed in slowly.

I only took one.

His heart raced. How much was it worth? Billions? Zillions, squillions? His brow began pouring with sweat. Beads of perspiration ran down the back of his neck. The study seat was suddenly an electric chair. A grim-faced prison warder was pulling a creaking lever to loose megavolts of crackling current.

He pinched himself.

It pinched him.

For heaven's sake – they'll find out! This afternoon! I'll get a call from the Geareys, the police . . .

But then he brushed his brow with a hand and wondered if he really would. The Jewel House had been in a kind of mess. Covers were off. Cleaners were about. The four of them had been strictly supervised. And he, after all, was a vicar. Who would ever decide to count the other pearls, and when, and why?

At that moment a thought struck the Reverend Derek Weston, of St Saviour's church, Evenham – struck him so hard he thought of the Peruvian in the green anorak all those years ago, and wondered if some kind of a voltage might actually just have passed through his tatty, flower-covered study armchair . . . wasn't this, precisely this, exactly what he wanted? What he had always needed? Just what he had been asking for when he prayed – *God, give me back the jewel at the centre?*

Slowly, clenching the thing in a fist, the vicar rose from the chair. He felt giddy. A moment after he had straightened up, white dots pinged in his eyes like solar objects. He still felt giddy. He placed his free hand on the desktop to steady himself. Looked out on to the church drive. Blinked.

He could post it back, of course. Easily. He could use a brand new, self-sealing envelope, write the address left-handed, moisten the stamp with tap water that would cause any DNA profiler to send his equipment in for a service, drive into the middle of London and pop it into a pillar box. What could be simpler? And the Tower people would cover it up, wouldn't they? If they got it one day in the post? Of course they would. They would probably lie if they had to. Why would they want to admit it had ever been taken? How could they, with all those Alarm Sealed Areas?

When the vicar looked down at his fist, though, some

strange wave lapped at the edge of his heart. He tried to open his hand, but – momentarily – could not. He brought the knuckles close to a cheek. He felt a huge thrill, suddenly.

I have the whole world in my hands, he told himself.

Derek inhaled, nostrils flaring, fist vibrating. The fact exhilarated him. And fact it was. No more the loser, no more the man ever looking inward at empty space inside himself, the velvet cushion in his heart with a dip in the material where a gem had been; no more the vague pursuer of precious things other vicars seemed to have by right, the man who spent his life navigating by rear mirrors . . . Derek Weston had the jewel at the centre of the world.

'Fact,' the vicar mumbled. 'Fact, fact, fact, fact.'

It was a fact. It was a beautiful fact. And now he felt a huge, humbling power stream through him, crashing against his soul like a Hawaiian tidal wave, coursing through every bend and pocket in him as if it had only been waiting for his acknowledgment to do its work. 'I have the pearl of greatest price,' he whispered. His heart was pounding. Twenty years slipped from his shoulders like a bathrobe. 'The pearl, the pearl, the pearl.' He remembered ages ago, when he first had it – yes, and the congregation in his church had been double, triple what it had fallen to now . . . he could hardly believe the words he was uttering, but something deep within him registered them as truth, ringing cash tills in the caverns of his soul . . . one-armed bandits screaming million-dollar jackpots . . . fluorescent fruits and bars flipping in plastic windows . . .

Where did the Bible speak of the pearl? It hardly mattered. He would look it up. He knew it was in there. Now he had a church to save, and nothing could convince him it was not possible. What had Helen Silverstone got that he could not just flash this flawlessness at and demolish? What obstacle towered so high that it could not be cleared by the vaulting radiance of this priceless treasure? What sun could he not outshine? *She may be Helen Silverstone, but I will be Derek Goldstone*, the vicar thought. *I have the whole world in my hands*. Telling himself that, telling himself that again and again, he became exhilarated beyond

139

words. Goose bumps shot up all over his arms and back and legs.

He opened a drawer and pushed the thing carefully into a half-empty box of staples, but the instant the drawer was shut an emptiness chewed at him, and he felt the point of having the pearl was gone if he was not going to keep it on his person.

So the vicar removed it from the drawer, just as carefully; brought it up to his face, close up, right up to an eye . . . his right eye.

The pearl blurred.

The pearl blurred as he looked at it.

He was crying. Derek Weston was crying with joy.

18

'Shhh.'

'Don't shush me.'

'I'm listening.'

'So am I.'

'Turn it down, then. It's feeding back again.' Mirabel pointed at the hearing-aid.

'I'm listening. That's why.' Phyllis Childs shifted rebelliously in her pew seat and gestured past the shoulders of the family in front. 'I've never seen him like this before.'

'Nor have I,' murmured Mirabel Weekling.

At the front, Derek was bringing his sermon to a climax. He was leaning into the big pulpit Bible like a meatpacker putting his shoulder to carcasses coming off trucks, shouting verses as if trying to attract attention all the way down the road into Evenham town centre. The vicar had waved a finger in the air – people looked upwards, thinking the unprecedented gesture meant something was happening in the roof. Then he used leaden silences to let strong points sink in, wiping the corners of his mouth with a handkerchief. He had been preaching power and purity, preaching them at top volume, and suddenly he was finished with a slap of Bible closing and a puff of dust flying off it.

'Let's pray.'

Seated to one side, Otis Cheeseman blinked. The tic went under one of his eyes as he closed them and leant forward. He could not quite believe what he had just heard. He adjusted himself in the wooden seat. The sheer loudness had been remarkable. The mix had been like octane after years of flat pop.

The curate opened his eyes and raised his head, slowly, as

the vicar sent a closing prayer over the bowed congregation. Otis peered through his sandy fringe at the vicar's wife, expecting to see her bowing too. But she was sitting up at the end of one pew, back straight, and as his gaze caught her face and he tried to read what was written on it she glanced over at him.

Judy Weston swallowed as the curate averted his eyes sharply, pushed back his fringe and bent forward again over his knees, his head down. She dipped hers an inch. A million thoughts were buzzing in her mind, none to do with anything Derek was praying for. She could not even hear what Derek was praying for. It was usually a combination of future projects and former Yugoslavians. She had been surprised by the tone of his sermon, maybe even moved by it . . . but against the backdrop of what had happened to them, it did not even register. How could it?

What was he trying to do? Turn his slipped disc of a church into the backbone of the diocese in three weeks?

After the service, Derek stood at the door with Judy.

The Geareys were the first to shake their hands.

'Judy,' Jennifer was saying, 'you look tired. I hope we didn't wear you out.'

'We really enjoyed yesterday,' the vicar told Sir Kenneth.

'That was a truly marvellous sermon. Real conviction,' he replied, and the vicar's heart soared as the governor's handshake slowed. *They don't know! They didn't find out! They haven't counted them!* He gasped at the cool air blowing in through the church doors, and said: 'I just want people to realise some of the truths in the gospels, which can energise our lives.'

'It was powerful,' Sir Kenneth said. 'Hell Is Near.'

'I hope that title won't have distressed anyone.'

'I liked the whole thing. Especially that stuff about jumping out of aeroplanes.'

'Taking risks,' the vicar said. 'Putting your faith in a greater power. Dropping.'

The Geareys were gone an instant later. The vicar shook a queue of hands, firmly, being sure to say names as he did so. And then something happened which made his stomach somersault. It came a moment after Claire Stupples and Ruth Richards drew level with him. 'Claire, Ruth – hello there,' he had said. 'Keep firm in the faith to which you were called.'

Neither of them smiled.

Ruth shook Derek's hand, grim-faced. Then she leant forward and hissed into his ear: 'We just wanted to say, Derek – we're both really, really sorry.'

She drew back.

'Yes,' Claire whispered.

The vicar felt queasy. 'Um – right,' he murmured.

Claire Stupples added: 'We both wanted to tell you that we love you.'

'Okay,' the vicar said, conscious that others were waiting to leave. 'Thank you.' He was wondering: *what on earth are they talking about? Have they got me confused with someone else?*

'We don't think they should close it at all,' Ruth hissed. 'Not at all.'

'Close what?'

'The church.'

Like a lead balloon, his heart fell out of the sky.

'—but the main thing is that we love you very much,' Claire was saying. 'And so do a lot of people.'

The vicar's insides turned inside-out. His outsides nearly went outside-in. He caught Ruth by the arm as the two of them began to walk off. 'How did you—?'

'Oh. Otis,' she said in a matter-of-fact tone. 'Otis told us. But we haven't said anything to—'

'Don't worry, don't worry,' the vicar interrupted. *Otis? How does Otis know?* He started shaking other hands, faster now, pulling at the hands, hearing one person at the back grumble that the queue was getting as slow as the M11 link road, feeling panic gorging itself in his chest. *Otis? Otis Cheeseman? How does he know?* The panic seemed to be flowing from the rock-hard bump in the breast pocket of his shirt, under his jacket, which was where he had put – where he had put – where – *where I put the pearl*, he reminded himself forcefully, determined to spell it out and not panic. *The pearl of great price.*

He shook another hand, beamed winningly. He would send

it back in three weeks. Two more hands came at him. He shook them, calming down.

That morning, waking early to prepare the sermon, he had rejoiced. The words poured out of him like light, just as he had expected.

'Hello, Mrs Peterson.' That was Judy, at his side. The vicar spun round.

'Marion, please! Please!' Marion Davidson was saying. 'Hello to you both!'

'Is Clive not here?' the vicar asked.

'He's spending some time with Adam,' she replied flatly. 'I wish he'd been able to come and hear you this morning, Derek. I really enjoyed it.'

'Thank you,' he said, desperate for her to move away.

Back at the vicarage, Judy lectured him. He was trying much too hard. Far too much. There was no point in him trying at all. 'Derek, they've done for us. That's it. It's over. You're not Lazarus. You're not even Frank Sinatra.' But when she looked into his eyes, which locked on hers as the vicar ran a hand through his hair, she saw nothing of the defeat she could have sworn would be there.

'It doesn't have to be like this,' he whispered. 'Always losing.'

She was silent for a moment, biting her lip.

'I haven't made any lunch,' she said.

'Lunch is for wimps,' he told her, seriously.

'Well, I haven't made any.'

'We can go out and get a pizza.'

She fell silent again.

Then she asked: 'You're not going to fight it, are you?'

'Not through the courts.' The vicar put his hands in his pockets and did a kind of shuffle on the hall carpet. 'There's a better way.'

'What? Declaring independence, or something?'

'Having a revival.'

'A – no, come on, Derek,' Judy said in an exasperated tone. 'What – floats and things? People selling popcorn?'

'That's a carnival. I'm talking about a—' he straightened

his hands and made a single cutting motion in the air in front of his stomach '—a controlled revival.'

'A controlled revival?'

'Uncontrolled, then. However you want to describe it, go ahead. I know what I'm saying, Judy. I intend to show leadership.'

She looked into his face and was astonished by it.

Judy Weston screwed up her eyes, folded her arms. She moved her legs so her thin calves crossed, bowed her head and began chewing the inside of a cheek.

She heard: 'I know what I'm saying, Judy. I'm not going to lose this place – and I'm not going to lose you.'

Quite to her surprise, the vicar's wife felt a kind of thrill drop down her spine. She looked up at her husband. 'What makes you think you'd lose me?'

'You virtually told me so. I know so, anyway.'

'All I meant, if I said anything, was that I couldn't bear to—'

He cut across her words with his. 'You won't have to! You won't have to! You won't have to bear to anything! I know exactly what I'm doing. I feel – Judy, I can feel a power – yes, power – just beginning to touch my life again. I really can. The power we've been missing for years. The power we've been talking about. I know what I'm doing. I know what it's about – perfection, Judy! Blamelessness. Flawlessness. Holiness. If we once catch on to what that means, we're saved.'

'We may be. The church isn't.'

'It will be.'

It was only after Judy walked away from the conversation that she realised she was staggered by it. Her husband was going to fight. During the afternoon a work colleague rang, apologising for the call on a Sunday and asking for credit details of a company the bank was dealing with. She had the conversation, but felt tarnished by it afterwards. It was office knowledge the man was attracted to her. He had bought her half a dozen lunches over the years, always asking for mineral rather than spring water because he had a lisp. He was tall and tanned, like Derek. He was successful, a money man, unlike Derek. Now she felt bad talking with him on a Sunday, this

Sunday, not just because of the lunches but because it was business – except that the real business, the really serious business, was somewhere else altogether now. She felt a whiff of raw reality had suddenly blown over her, fanned by her extraordinary husband, and called out for him.

'Derek!'

There was no reply.

He must be upstairs, she thought.

Judy walked into the living room. Then she walked into the hallway. She walked into the study. She looked over the desk and the shelving, ran a hand across the back of her neck.

Then she pulled a Bible with a tatty green cover, one of Derek's, from between two books about films. Outside, it was sleeting. She could not even remember when she had last picked up a Bible in her spare time. Judy opened two pages separated by a card bookmark, and read a passage ringed with thick red strokes.

Derek Weston did not hear his wife call because he was in the bathroom at that moment, washing his hands. He picked a comb from the edge of the basin, twirled it cleverly around an index finger and ran it through his hair. Soon the thick grey strands sat contoured neatly on his head. The vicar looked searchingly at the reflection. *I am not going to go bald*, he thought.

It was real. A new kind of reality was unfolding. Something vivid and awesome was happening. He was in touch with a power – he was in touch with something, anyway, that he had not been in touch with for years, and he could rule out nuclear power because there was not a single long-haired protester in sight, and it was nothing to do with New Age rubbish because it was not rubbish, simply because it resonated with something deep within him, deep within his simple Church of England vicar's heart; it was pounding against his chest wall, this brilliant, brilliant thing he had in his shirt pocket – a thriller, a fiction, a reality, a stunner, a weepy, a cataclysm and a balm in one, a burst of raw brilliant burning light that he could not explain or understand, that he could only follow his instincts and grab at, lurch at, just as all humankind lurched and grabbed suddenly at truth in the fraction of a second in

146

which it chose to flare up like science lab magnesium, just as he had grabbed at it instinctively in the Tower and wound up staggered, the pearl sitting there in his hands . . .

Derek Weston looked at his reflection. He suddenly thought of all the possibilities, all the chances he had been given. It was the pearl, doing that. Without it he would only now be bending his mind to failure and destruction. Since he had first touched the gem, felt its cool purity and virtual sanctity in his palm, the nearest to an instrument of God he felt he had ever been, something delegated by its creator to sum all truth up in spherical millimetres that he, Derek Weston, could understand as if he had been born to do nothing in life but grasp it . . . since he had first grasped it, pocketed it, sheer live energy had pulsed through his spirit. Where had it come from? It was as though seven engines in his soul had suddenly started ticking over, then come roaring to the rescue of the clapped-out eighth as it finally coughed itself into oblivion.

Derek Weston breathed in, smiled humbly.

Then he shocked himself by having one brilliant idea after another.

19

Otis cleared his throat. It was becoming a habit of his, along with a number of other things. One was rolling his shoulders after clearing his throat, which he now did. Another was worrying. Worrying was becoming a habit. Thinking too much was becoming a habit. So was watching *Empty Spaces*, a weekday television soap about Australian culture. He wondered if his life was draining of discipline. He felt burdened. He wanted to think of Charlotte for relief, but he was too upset to.

Derek and he met every Monday, at what the vicar described as a civilised hour. After working with Otis for a while, Derek had suggested they make the venue the Continental, a café in the centre of Evenham which was within walking distance of both homes. Often they just rolled up, ordered coffee and Danish pastries, and chatted.

Today was different. Otis knew it from the moment he walked in. The bell above the door buzzed, the OPEN sign clattered on the inside of the glass, and the man behind the counter – Italian, with a Jim Bakker quiff – looked up from a plate he was rubbing with a dishcloth and called: 'Derek is already here. He sits around the corner.' He flicked the quiff towards an alcove.

The curate thanked him. Never before had the vicar arrived first. That's why he knew today was different.

'Otis, hello there.' Derek jumped up and pulled the chair opposite him out from underneath the table, a movement which started as a flurry of hands and ended with the sugar bowl inverted. 'Oh, golly.' They spent a minute scooping the brown grains back with a spoon, and then Derek made an announcement.

'Otis – this could just be the biggest three weeks of our lives.'

The curate had no answer to that, so the vicar beckoned at the waiter.

'Scones, Otis?'

'I'm afraid I am allergic to scones,' Otis said. 'And, at the moment, to some types of tea.'

'Of course. Forgot.' They ordered two cream buns and two large coffees.

With a fingertip, the curate drew a question mark in the sugar left on the tabletop. He cleared his throat and rolled his shoulders. Then he crossed his arms, pursed his lips and placed a forefinger over them. None of this would happen in America, he thought. This could only ever happen in Evenham. He remembered finding the thought more amusing when he last had it.

'Perhaps you already know about the current state of play,' Derek said carefully. 'In fact, I should admit that I've been told you do. I spoke to Ruth and Claire in church yesterday, you see, and they did both say you had told—'

Reddening, Otis glanced up as though something had suddenly jolted him from a dream. He snatched the finger away from his lips. 'Well, yes, I suppose I did know,' he said. 'And then I – um, yes – I – I saw the two girls early Sunday morning, you see, Ruth and Claire, buying a paper in the centre of town – and it all came out.'

'But if you don't mind me asking, Otis, who told you? Marshall, was it?'

'No, it wasn't Marshall,' the American murmured. 'This is all a bit embarrassing, actually.' He ran his hand through his fringe, sweeping it back. 'This is all terribly embarrassing.' Now he was blushing deep red. He cleared his throat.

'Was it – it wasn't Judy, was it?'

The waiter came back with two cups of coffee. One black, one white. The curate stared into his for several seconds before he spoke again.

'It was actually – it was actually a friend of mine called Charlotte,' he said at length. Without looking up, Otis tipped sugar into the cup and stirred. He was getting a headache.

149

The vicar's eyes widened slowly in their sockets. *Scotland*, he suddenly thought. *Scotland, Scotland, Scotland*.

'Um – Charlotte Davidson, would that be?' he asked innocently.

'Yup,' the curate said.

Derek spoke next. He grabbed at honesty like a lifebelt. 'I was – in other days, Otis – I was close to Charlotte, spiritually. When I got this news, it was almost instinctive to ring her. I didn't realise you and she had been to Scotland.'

'No, sure. I understand. I'm glad you did ring.'

The vicar felt himself trembling slightly. He reached inside his jacket, felt for the bump in the breast pocket of his shirt. He needed a surge of inspiration.

He got it.

'That's wonderful,' he said.

'Are you all right?' Otis peered over the top of his cup.

'Yes.' Derek withdrew the hand. 'Yes. Absolutely. I was just—' he curled the fingers into a fist and rested it, decisively, on the table '—I think that's great. You and Charlotte. You'd make a tremendous couple, actually. It's lovely.'

Otis looked distant, suddenly. 'Oh. Well, we're not a couple any more. We didn't speak for a week. I was avoiding her. Then she rang on Sunday, while I was reading about Spurgeon.'

'I think I've heard of Spurgeon. What is it – a type of caviar?'

'A preacher from the Victorian era. I must admit I was cold with her,' Otis went on, dully, almost as if he was speaking only to himself. 'I thought we were in a holding pattern, but I don't think we're even in that now.'

'A holding pattern? Otis, Otis! She's not a jumbo jet! She's not some sort of a charter flight! She's a very nice girl!'

Then the curate did something that shocked the vicar. He showed emotion. His mouth pursed, and his cheeks inflated like oxygen tents.

'I'm sorry – I'm sorry – I know this isn't a very precise way to behave—'

The vicar rushed around the table, dropped into the chair

150

next to the curate's and put a hand on his shoulder. 'Otis, whatever it is, it can't be all that bad—'

In a minute, the curate had gathered himself. 'Love is – almost impossible,' he said. 'It really feels that way.'

He sounds like a Vulcan, the vicar thought, saying: 'I hear you. Well, she's a fearsomely attractive girl. I won't ask what might be the trouble.'

'Sometimes I think I get too involved in details,' the curate mumbled.

Derek moved back to his chair, leant sideways against the armrest. When he began speaking again, it was slowly and very deliberately. 'Otis, we are at a stage in the voyage of our church where we need to throw the details overboard. You heard my sermon on Sunday. I do think we have to give a very powerful message now. I know you and I are very different – you're very big, for example, on theological points. But I think now is the time we need to operate on thrust.'

'Thrust?' Otis dabbed at his eyes with a paper napkin.

'A very simple message, preached extremely loudly. I hate to make it sound simplistic, but we essentially have three weeks to save the church.'

'I thought it was going to be abolished,' Otis said, still dabbing.

'Abolished? Who's been using that word?'

'I thought that's what the news was.'

'Whatever you might have been told, Otis,' Derek began stiffly, 'there is no question of any bulldozers rolling down the hills on to our steeple. This is sheer economics. I think they called it a rationalisation. It's the sort of thing that happens all the time now. There isn't any question of a vendetta.'

'My parents are coming over here that week on a coach tour.'

'Really?' The vicar whipped a pad from his jacket pocket, and made a note in it. As he wrote, he was saying: 'Look, nothing is closing. They're not even going to close a door. At least – that's what the two of us have to decide for ourselves.' He put the block of paper back in his jacket. 'We won't close if we make ourselves—' he took a swig of coffee, his eyes brightening '—if we make ourselves shine. If truth shines out

151

of us. We do need to be clear about the message we're going to be giving people in the next three weeks.'

The American looked into the vicar's face. Something was very, very odd about all this. Never before had Derek Weston made any reference to messages, let alone being clear about them. There was a sparkle in his eyes the curate had never seen before, and it unnerved him.

'If I were to ask you, Otis, what your message is, what would you say?'

Haltingly, the curate answered: 'It would be something like – God looked down on the world and saw it was full of sin. People were damned. He sent his son, Jesus Christ, to die on the cross as a sacrifice for it all. Now, like the Israelites in the desert with the snake up the pole, if we look upwards to the cross we can find salvation. If we trust in Christ, our wrongdoings are forgiven.'

The vicar stroked his chin. 'Yes. Right. Well – all that is technically correct, of course. But it needs an awful lot of trimming, you see. There are too many specifics in there. We've got to whittle everything down.'

'Whittle?'

'Whittle and thrust,' the vicar repeated. 'We're working on inspiration from now on. We're focusing on raw truth. I honestly believe we could get the whole gospel message down to a single word.'

'Ri-right,' Otis said, not understanding very much at all. 'What would the word be?'

'I haven't worked it out yet. But you get my meaning.'

Feeling he must be missing something of massive significance, wondering if perhaps a whole field of belief had been closed to him because of his stupid fixation with detail, the curate watched as the vicar straightened his back and pushed half the cream bun into his mouth. 'Good,' he said through it. 'Good, good, good. That's settled. Now, I've got a strategy all laid out. I want to check it over with you, Otis.' There was a long pause as he swallowed. 'Is that okay? It's actually going to involve one rather difficult telephone call for you, I think, in the circumstances.'

Without taking his eyes off Derek Weston, the curate

picked up the bun on his plate and slowly pushed the narrower end into his mouth.

They both chewed in silence. Otis Cheeseman felt utterly exhausted. Between chews, he cleared his throat. His head-ache was getting worse. When he had finished the bun he sat back in the chair and rolled his shoulders as the vicar talked. Luckily, he told himself, curates were trained in swallowing things, or he would not have been able to believe a word of what came next.

20

All through the house, all afternoon, deafening bangs and crunches had been coming from the lavatory.

She had been unable to concentrate, and had gone out. But when she came back the noise was as deafening as ever. She went up to her bedroom, closed the door, switched on the television. He was definitely drunk, she thought. Never having had experience of calming a plumber, she had taken it all on the chin – complaints that the house was not adequately heated for tools, a string of bossy calls for tea and even an argument about broken custard creams . . .

She thought she had heard a human – some kind of human yelp.

The plumber was standing with his back to her when she arrived at the lavatory door. She gasped. The room seemed to be covered in blood.

'Nothing's happened,' he said groggily, making a go of hammering a bend in a pipe. She saw a thick line of blood trickle over the heel of his raised hand.

'Look, you're going to need stitches in that.' Charlotte was suddenly scared; wished Yan and Philip were in the house. Head spinning, she caught a wave of whisky full in the face. 'Can't I do anything for you?'

So a job supposed to have lasted a couple of hours ended with the man bleeding into Charlotte Davidson's sink and trying to staunch a deep gash with a tea-towel. Finally he had it woven around his entire hand and knotted, big as a boxing glove.

They stood there in the kitchen, facing each other under the harsh yellow light of a bare bulb. She really did feel quite frightened. The sun had gone down.

'Your boyfriends coming back soon, are they?'

'Boyfriends?' She had whispered the word.

'Fan and Tan, or whatever they're called.'

'Yan and Philip. They're flatmates, not boyfriends. My boyfriend's in Evenham.'

He leered at her. 'Loaded, are you? Rich?'

'Nope.'

He suddenly threw his head back and yelled: 'Wooooaaaa-aaaaaar!'

Then – a blur. The plumber blundered sideways a yard, mumbled something, swung the arm with the bandaged hand out like a huge match flicked from a book, sweeping a line of tumblers off the drying rack by the kitchen sink and sending them to the floor with a crash as Charlotte jumped away, tripping and falling over a table. The impact sent a casserole dish to the floor, where it broke into a dozen pieces.

She straightened up. Her vision blurred. Charlotte did not look at the man, who had moved back. She looked at the myriad glass shards and splinters on the floor. She was not quite sure what had happened. Only that she felt sick.

His voice sounded very small in the kitchen. 'My – oh, my goodness,' he was saying. 'I don't know what I'm doing.' His words were vibrating with fear now, not slurred at all. The Newcastle accent suddenly thickened in it. 'My – oh, heck. I've got myself into the most shocking trouble now.'

Charlotte heard herself tell him: 'Don't worry, don't worry.'

Eventually he asked if he could go back to work in the lavatory. Face crimson, angering, she said yes, yes please, it's the right place for you, finish it as quickly as you can and go. In her bedroom, shaking with delayed fright, she reached for her sketchbook but could not focus on it.

The banging started again, but not as loudly. Eyes glazing, Charlotte found herself halfway through a news programme. She heard it in snatches. Prime Minister attacks Tory critics . . . *bang, bang, crash* . . . violence in Italian local elections after candidate makes a joke about corruption . . . *bang, wallop, bang, crunch* . . . something about an internal inquiry at the Tower of London . . . *crash, crash, bang* . . . French

155

footballer with glass hip transferred to Oldham . . . *crunch, bang, bang* . . .

After half an hour she was still shaken but feeling a little better, when she heard his voice raised outside the bedroom door.

'I won't come in. Just to let you know it's all done.'

'Thank you,' she called back.

There was a pause.

'I won't charge you,' the plumber said, nervously. 'I cleared up the – er—'

'Right.'

'—um—'

'Thank you.'

'I am – Miss Davidson – I am very, very, sorry about – about all of – erm—'

'Don't worry, never mind,' she called, exasperated. 'Thanks for doing the work. I'll come down and see it later.'

'I was lashing out at society.'

'Yes, right.'

'I've got three children,' he added, without further clarification, and a minute later Charlotte Davidson heard the man let himself out of the front door and scoot off in his van. She breathed a lingering sigh of relief.

The telephone rang. She walked downstairs and picked it up.

'It's Otis,' a long-distance voice said.

She sighed, realising her hand was shaking as it gripped the receiver, and tremors were going up and down her arm and across her chest. 'Hi, Otis.' She did not want to upset him. She would not say what had happened. She had better rein it in.

'Are you – well?'

'Yes,' she said hesitantly. 'What have you been doing?'

'Today, just helping a guy with a limp collect a cactus from a garden centre.'

'I haven't heard from you, stranger,' she said, voice wavering.

He seemed cold and nervous. Perhaps it was just her imagination. She supposed she must seem the same. 'I decided it wasn't appropriate, in the circumstances,' she heard the curate say.

'What – sorry – what circumstances, Otis?'

'I'm sure you know. Anyway,' he hurried on, 'Derek's asked me to call, Charlotte. I hope you might be able to help. It is – slightly – a professional matter. Do you have a minute or two? Perhaps four?'

Confused, she wanted to say, 'For you, I've got hours and hours and hours', but ended up with a weary: 'Half a second. I need to drag an armchair over here.'

When she had done, Otis started. He said he was very worried about the vicar, who was showing conviction. She was the only person he could talk to about it. Was there any kind of action he could take?

'I think he's gone – kind of wild,' he went on gravely. 'He just goes on and on about Christianity being "about crowds". It's this deadline the bishop has set.'

'What's he been saying, then?' She brushed stray hairs away from her brow, wishing her concentration was sharper. Her head was turning over, Moulinex-blending her thoughts. She pressed the handset harder against her ear.

'All kinds of things,' she heard the faraway American voice say. 'On Monday he asked me if you could bring your orchestra to the church. For the last service in the month. He said he knew you'd all be in London that weekend.'

'Good grief. Would we all fit?'

'He says the church can take two hundred and twenty.'

'But we're a hundred and thirty.'

'He asked me to call you. It's got to be full, he says. He says the seats are my job – literally. He's thinking of having loudspeakers outside.'

'I'll see how many can make it. Some have got things on.'

'He wants you to play. The tunes of the hymns. He wants you to bring your instruments.'

The sentence took several seconds to register with Charlotte. When it did, she sat up straight in the chair. 'He wants what?'

'This is why I'm saying I'm getting worried.' The curate was speeding up, as though in panic. 'He says he's going to condense the gospel into a single word, he won't say what the word is, he said something about whittling I didn't understand, he claims if he starts calling in favours he can have all the motorbike riders in Evenham there, people called the Evenham Angels or something, plus he says he can get some martial arts people, plus others, plus he wants me to get my parents to divert their coach tour so everybody pulls up outside the—'

Charlotte stopped him. 'Your parents?'

The curate paused.

'Um – yes,' he said, eventually..

'When are they coming?'

'The weekend before,' he replied. 'Their thirtieth wedding anniversary is at the end of this year, and they wanted to celebrate by—'

'And you didn't tell me?'

'They were settling on a date,' Otis said, nervously. 'Pa wanted to leave it till the last minute to get a bargain.' He cleared his throat.

'But when they did settle on it – when was that?'

He breathed the words out. 'A few days ago.'

'Oh,' Charlotte said. Her head was still in a spin. She wanted to ask Otis questions, dozens of questions, especially about why his parents were coming and she was apparently not on the list to see them, why he had not telephoned or written, why his voice sounded far more distant than Evenham was from Newcastle – but she was feeling queasy and slightly ill, as if she had eaten bad tripe, or maybe even good tripe, and was getting worried she might burst into tears. 'Oh,' she said again. 'Oh, right. Look, Otis, I'll ask around on the orchestra. I'll get it announced. I have to go.'

'Right-ee-ho.'

Neither said a word for several seconds.

Then Charlotte Davidson summoned up enough of herself to say: 'God bless you, dear Otty.'

Putting the receiver down, the curate of St Saviour's church reckoned he had probably just heard the most final dismissal in history. It was even more final than the one Derek had given after the service that had been interrupted by a couple from a hippy convoy who wandered in selling maggots.

Gasping, he remembered the day his sister had died, long ago, after a sudden illness. Everyone had crowded around the door to her room. A child, he could only see the backs of legs. It was an image that shredded his stomach every time it resurfaced: rectangles of flannel trouser, someone crying somewhere. He wished he was not always so constrained and bookish. He would like to streak into the road, jump between car roofs, smash streetlights and yell at the moon.

Otis got to his knees on the spot, carefully hitching up his black trousers, and begged God not to think him at all melodramatic – but now that the only love of his life was confirmed lost, and since he also seemed about to be catapulted out of his chosen vocation into deepest, darkest space, could he order up a fatal lightning strike for himself?

'Please,' the curate added, getting to his feet.

Then he felt guilty about the selfishness of the prayer, which would be certain to disrupt the holiday his parents had planned, and asked instead that any strike should be non-fatal. 'Just to stun,' he mumbled. 'To get me through to the end of the month.'

How his Arizonan heart ached. He had loved her so much!

21

The patrol car came gently to a rest at the roadside, the edge of a front tyre squeaking against the kerb.

It rolled back a yard. The doors flew open like wings. Two policemen climbed out. The younger took great pains to smooth down the lowest edge of his jacket, adjusting his radio and then carefully putting his helmet on and tightening the strap under his chin. Walking forward, he saw the other turn to him and whistle.

'What?' the first policeman said. He was tall and wiry, with a moustache.

The second tapped his head. 'Church,' he hissed. 'We're not at a flipping riot.'

So they paused at the entrance to St Saviour's driveway while the tall, young policeman unstrapped his helmet and put it under his arm. He threw his shoulders back and smoothed his hair with his free hand. The other, a square-jawed man with a pasty face, rolled his eyes behind a pair of silver-rimmed rectangular glasses. They started walking up the gravel drive.

At that moment, thirty miles away in the centre of the City, a bulb blinked in a panel on a credit department desk at one of London's biggest merchant banks.

From behind a sheaf of computer-printed paper, a slim hand reached towards a cream telephone beside a styrofoam cup, knocked the handset out of its cradle, pressed a button, picked it up.

'Judy Weston speaking.'

'Hello – Judy?' said the caller.

'Yes, hello.'

'It's Kenneth. Ken Gearey. I hope you don't mind me ringing. We couldn't get through at the vicarage.'

A quarter of the way up the church driveway, the tall policeman stopped.

'I think I've forgotten my notebook.'

'It's lucky we don't get many riots, Leslie, or you'd probably roll up at the front line in swimming trunks. For crying out loud—'

'Got it,' the tall officer cut in, waving the thing in the air. He saw his colleague's forlorn expression and wiped the smile off his face. 'All set. Off we go, then.'

On the telephone, Sir Kenneth Gearey's voice was sounding gently breezy. 'Don't know if you saw the news at all last night, Judy.'

'The story about the problems in the Church of England?'

'Ah – no. That was a documentary. The main news, I mean. Presented by John Maitland. Well, you obviously didn't catch it. They had a little item on us.'

Judy scratched her nose with a finger and looked up at the digital clock above the Vice President's office door. She was busy. She tapped her biro on the desk. 'Did they? How lovely.' That was her banking voice.

'Wasn't quite as "how lovely" as all that,' Sir Kenneth said, and told her.

She frowned when the story was over. 'Really?'

'Yes, I'm afraid so. The cleaning specialists rostered that fortnight have been asked all kinds of questions, as you can imagine. Politely, of course. And there is one, teeny weeny thing to boot – ah – which is that they do just have to do a little bit of asking of the other people who went near the displays during that period.'

'Really?' Judy said again. 'Who were they?'

'Um – mainly my guests, actually,' Sir Kenneth said stolidly. 'They've been taking quite a lot of names off us. We're afraid we have been rather – embarrassed. So has Jennifer.'

Well out of earshot of whatever reaction Judy Weston gave the Governor of the Tower of London, the policeman in silver-rimmed glasses was pressing his thumb hard on the vicarage doorbell.

'I can't hear a thing,' the tall constable told him. 'Can you?'

'He's not exactly going to be out at work,' the other mumbled. 'One day a week, this lot do.'

The tall one said: 'My uncle was a vicar. He did two.'

'Hold on – what's that?'

They listened, the policeman in silver-rimmed glasses standing at a diagonal, leaning his entire bodyweight into the doorbell; the tall one crouched forward, an ear cupped in a hand.

'Ringing,' said the younger man, straightening up.

'It's the flaming telephone, isn't it?' He released the button. 'I can't tell.'

'It is the telephone. But I thought I heard two ringings.'

'What do you mean? Two consecutive rings?'

'Concurrent ringing, two separate notes. One suspended. Undulating.'

'But sometimes with these phones you've got all kinds of notes going on.'

The tall policeman touched his colleague on the arm. 'Just a second. Someone's turning into the drive.'

Half a minute later, a yellow Morris Minor appeared around the bend, gliding up the gravel towards them. The officers' eyes widened. The car had a wooden chair tied to its roof, a forward-pointing megaphone lashed to the seat of the chair and a set of striped red cables feeding into the passenger window. Loud electric guitar music was blaring out of the speaker.

They watched as the car slowed in front of them then ground to a halt at an angle. The engine died as if someone had shot it. The music cut out. A lean, rangy, healthy-looking man with a large mound of thick grey hair on his head jumped from the car. He was smiling. 'No prizes for guessing,' whispered the policeman in glasses.

'Afternoon,' the younger one said, stepping towards the vicar.

'Hello there, officers.' Derek Weston nodded as he locked the door.

'Nice bit of music coming out of that thing,' said the older constable, pointing at the loudspeaker with an amused expression. They were all shaking hands now.

'Really?' Puzzled, the vicar turned back to look at it. 'Music? Was there?'

'The Beatles, I think,' the policeman said. '"I Am The Walrus."'

'Oh.' Derek looked momentarily disconcerted. He put his hands on his hips. 'Oh, dear.' He put a hand over his mouth. 'I must have left the microphone sitting next to the car radio.'

The tall one wrinkled his nose, disguising a smile. The other stroked his chin. They watched the vicar walk back to the Morris Minor, lean in awkwardly through the driver's window and fiddle with something inside, calling out: 'I've just been—' he withdrew his head from the car '—spreading the message. Actually it's been a kind of a – um – a "snatch raid", I suppose you police would call it. On another parish.'

Derek wiped his hands on his trousers; then looked sheepish, as if unprepared for his own honesty. 'Borrowed car. But that's what it's all about, isn't it?' He strolled up to them again, grinning suddenly. 'Strimmer?'

The policemen exchanged glances. 'Strim – strimmer?' they both said at once.

'I thought that's what you were here for,' the vicar said. 'We had some trouble with a rogue one.'

'I don't think I knew about that,' the tall policeman said. 'Let me get my notebook out a second.' As he patted each of his pockets in turn, sneezing, the other constable told the vicar: 'Actually, it's just a routine check. Tower of London asked us to pop out. Shall we—?' he gestured at the front door.

'Oh. Y-yes. Of course,' Derek said quickly, taking some keys from his trouser pocket and sending them flying on to the gravel, trying but failing to catch them as they fell. 'Gosh. I'm all fingers and thumbs. I think I can hear the telephone.' He scooped up the keys, jogged to the front door and opened it. 'Please go in. Make yourselves at home.'

Mind in turmoil, the vicar leant towards the study telephone. He noticed the policemen standing in the hall. 'Go in, go in,' he said. 'Please.' He felt breathless. *Keep it steady*, he told himself, *keep it steady*.

'Derek. It's Judy.'

'Hi,' he said.

'You weren't in five minutes ago.'

'No.'

'You sound breathless.' Her voice was flat.

'Not at all.' He inhaled. 'See?'

The line crackled. 'I've got a message from Kenneth Gearey, a bit upset,' she went on briskly at the other end. 'He's just phoned me here. He says the police may want to speak to us about a jewel missing from the Tower. He was saying don't worry if they do.'

Carefully, Derek said: 'Yes. Here now,' and hung up.

'My wife,' he told the policemen, who were standing at the door to the living room. 'Trying to make me look guilty. Ha, ha.'

They gazed at him blankly. He showed them into the room, and they sat down together on the sofa. One tall, one shortish. The vicar dropped into a chair opposite them, leaning forward intently, his brow furrowed, hands clasped.

'I know this will seem a tiny bit silly to you,' the constable in silver-rimmed glasses began, 'but they seem to have managed to lose a diamond from the—'

'A pearl,' the other policeman put in, earning himself a vengeful glance.

'—have *managed*,' the first continued through gritted teeth, 'to lose a precious stone from the vaults of the Tower of London.' He sniffed. 'One can only assume that the job of guarding them was left to Group Three, the name I believe that particular private security firm has asked to be known by since its most recent escape.'

They all roared. But as his chest shook with his own laughter, Derek became conscious of the fear throbbing in it. He really did need to leave the room now.

'—and you and your wife, Reverend Weston, were on the list Mr Gearey has put together of people he invited around the place, you see—'

'He's in a bit of trouble, actually,' the younger policeman sniggered.

'Leslie—' The other man shot a blistering glance at his colleague. He turned back to the vicar. 'So, sir, we've just

164

been asked to pop round and ask you if you remember anything out of the ordinary, at all.'

The vicar nibbled at a fingernail, staring at the carpet. *Do I remember anything out of the ordinary? Where do you want me to start?* He glanced up. 'Could you excuse me – just for a minute?'

'Of course,' they both said.

'Do – um – make yourselves at home here.'

'Thank you,' the younger policeman sighed, leaning back into the sofa, folding his arms, stretching his legs out and gazing up at the ceiling.

In the upstairs bathroom, the vicar looked at himself in the mirror. He urged himself to remember the reasons for everything; not to panic, not to panic, not panic, not panic, not even for a moment. His face looked calmer than he felt. *Thank goodness.* He pulled at his cheeks, stretching the skin under his eyes. No mistiness. No perspiration. *Good. Good. Thank goodness. Now, don't panic. Don't panic. For heaven's sake, they musn't suspect . . .*

Gingerly, he pulled open the front of his jacket.

Keeping his breath as shallow as he could, standing there in the bathroom, motionless as a man before a dribbling tiger, Derek Weston reached carefully into the breast pocket of his shirt.

He swallowed as his index finger and forefinger and thumb settled on the perfect surface of the pearl, seeking sudden and total assurance that there could have been no other way, that this truly was as close as he would ever get to an agent of God – and, almost to his surprise, getting the confirmation in a lurch of his heart the instant the pads of his skin found purchase on the outside of the gem and he began to lift the beautiful thing clear of the fabric of his shirt pocket.

Impossible, he thought, *for me to sit in front of the two of them with this—*

It caught on the lapel of his jacket and was dislodged from between his fingers.

The pearl was dislodged from his fingertips. Without fuss, it fell to the bathroom floor, bouncing on the uneven lino like a big glass marble . . .

Crack, crack, crack . . .

Deafening cracks! The two of them sitting directly below! The vicar gasped, bending down madly, cracking his head

Crack

on the edge of the basin as the pearl went this way and that, rolling left towards a gap in the floor between the wall and the radiator piping . . .

His eyes were bulging in their sockets. He had been giddied by the blow against his head and was not breathing, was holding his breath and could feel the blood ganging up in his cheeks, closing in at his collar as he swung his arms, he was swinging his arms madly at the thing, rushing it with his hands as it curved around the uneven floor, fingers crazy tentacles, nails extended like cat-claws, palms scampering at it across the surface of the lino, chasing, chasing, chasing it at a million miles an hour – *come here, come here, come here* – he must only have been bending down for five seconds in all, maybe ten, but it seemed like an hour spent grabbing at the—

It seemed like an hour spent chasing the pearl before he had it secure in his fist. He had it there. He had it. He rose – *I have it* – feeling something relatively unimportant crunch in his back, feeling his arms and legs ache, rubbing his head with the unclenched hand.

Derek opened the bathroom cabinet and put the pearl into his shaver case, where no one ever looked. Then he washed his hands and walked slowly down the staircase, steadying his breath.

'Sorry about that,' the vicar said mildly as he appeared back in the living room.

'Not at all,' one of them laughed.

Determined not to lie, he gave details of what he had seen in the Waterloo Block as they asked for them. The younger policeman with the moustache seemed to be reading from a list of prepared questions. 'And do you remember, sir, how many pearls were in that case?'

'No,' he said, truthfully.

'And did you see anyone lurking in the – oh,' the constable said, snorting and turning to his colleague, waving a sheet of paper, 'this is absolutely ridiculous. "Did you see anyone lurking in the Jewel House?" it says here.'

'Ask it anyway,' the policeman in silver-rimmed glasses advised, turning his eyes to the light in the ceiling and pinching his nose like a snorkelling contestant about to dive.

'Did you see anyone lurking in the Jewel House?'

'No,' said the vicar, truthfully. He thought: *If I was a criminal, this is where I would mention the man with the stocking on his head. Easy.*

'And is there anything else you can think of that might help us?'

There was a moment's silence.

Outside, the trees on Nock Green rustled in a gust of wind, suggesting answers.

The vicar stared into the eyes of one policeman, then the other.

You are not a criminal and you are not a liar, he told himself.

He breathed in, spread his hands. Turned his open palms towards them both.

'Salvation is from God alone,' he said, finally.

Their faces were like bottles, filling up with blood. One licked his lips as his chin went purple. The other drew a finger across his brow as the red moved there. The officers exchanged uncomfortable glances. 'Um – well, right, okay,' the one in glasses began, groaning as he lifted himself from the sofa, gesturing that his colleague should do the same. 'Yes, fine – I don't think we want to take up any more of your day, Reverend Wrestle. Thank you.'

In a moment, they were all standing. 'Thank you very much, thank you.'

'Thank you,' Derek told them. 'Weston,' he added.

'I hope your ministry goes well,' the tall one said, waving vaguely in the direction of the megaphone.

Shaking his hand, both constables seemed suddenly to draw their faces closer to Derek's, staring at a point on his forehead.

'You seem to have a king-size bruise coming up there,' the tall one said.

167

The second added: 'A whopper.'

Derek Weston reached up, groped at the painful swelling in his skin. They were right. 'Professional hazard,' he blustered at them, desperately hoping neither would ask him to explain.

Neither did.

After the policemen had been seen to the front door without further incident, the vicar retrieved the pearl, carefully replaced it in the breast pocket of his shirt and put on inspirational music to support his spirits and stop his whole body shaking like a leaf – Denby Constant and the Heart of Gold band, on cassette, singing: 'Paradise Is Yours Whenever You Want It', 'Claim, Claim, Claim', and 'We Shall Destroy The Gates Of The Ungodly, Including The Hinges'.

22

What sort of day had that Saturday been? Years later, Judy Weston could only remember one thing clearly. It began with a doorbell.

She walked across the vicarage hallway, seeing the outline of an extra-large head through the dimpled glass in the front door, not quite able to place its owner.

Reaching for the bronze doorknob, she reminded herself to ask Derek to see if he could raise the volume of that bell. It was ringing faintly, with undulating tones. Not always healthy to encourage Derek in DIY: she had known that from the day, years ago, when Caroline's rabbit had been seriously injured in a hutch collapse.

But then the vicar's wife wondered if the bell mattered very much at all. It could undulate as much as it liked – they were probably going to be forced to do their own undulating very soon, to undulate right down that gravel drive for the last ever time. Faint ringing might even help them do their undue packing undisturbed.

Yes, it was sad. It was very sad. It was as sad as any tear-jerking movie about ill swimming-medallists or pilots with one leg, as tragic as the Bishop of Basildon's pathetic attempt at diocese strategy, as miserable as homes for the elderly, Cuba, illiteracy, Oregon, actors, pyramid selling, sonnets, single-cup water heaters, student unions, busking or the Turkish economy; yet something had happened to reroute her ferocious merchant banker's anger, maybe even close it off altogether.

Quite to her surprise, Judy Weston had been awed by the last person in the world any woman ever expected to be awed by. Her own husband.

She had stood deliberately aloof from the frantic activity that began after they were given notice of the impending decision in Basildon. She kept recalling with disgust how the bishop's big nose had twitched like a sensor as he spelled it out, how his eyes had flickered here and there around the room, his inflated Adam's apple twanging in his throat; and she was convinced that even a second's involvement in Derek's exertions now would set her fury and frustration rocketing.

Her husband never once complained. He just kept repeating, 'Conviction, Judy, conviction – that's all it needs, Judy, darling, you know . . .' until she had swung her gaze on herself, directly on to her own heart, like a coastal spotlight.

Judy Weston found herself reading her Bible again after discovering it under a misfolded mauve beach towel. Her fury at Derek evaporated. Before the crisis began, she would always be awake before her husband; now, morning after morning, she glimpsed him already dressed while she fumbled blearily for the alarm clock.

Often he would press the snooze button for her, leaning over the bed gingerly, holding his jacket to his chest and setting a cup of tea on the bedside table as she struggled to sit up. Once she woke to the sound of him whispering into her ear: 'The gem at the centre, darling. The jewel of greatest price.'

Whatever else in the world might be sad, this was not.

For so many years, Derek had been the meteorological equivalent of cloud with scattered showers. Now, suddenly, he was the apex of a cyclone. She was staggered. Big bonfires burnt in his eyes! He had been passing out leaflets about his church in Evenham shopping arcade! He was planning, he said, to use St Saviour's overhead projector to throw a 'special logo' he had designed into the sky! He reminded her of a man at the bank who won so many promotions so rapidly he virtually shot through the roof.

Moments of the old Derek – she came home one day to find him trying to fix a kitchen cabinet he said had blown off the wall when he opened a window – almost served to prove the transformation. It was like simultaneous miracles.

So Judy read her Bible again. She read it on the train

because she did not want her husband to know, and he was around now to see her reading it over breakfast; she worked her way through the gospels, one at a time, quick as she could without losing the detail. She felt her eyes suffuse with tears at one verse she came to while the rear end of Brentwood station was gliding past the window.

Gaze darting from text to platform sign and back to text, she read: 'The stone the builders BRENT rejected has become WOOD the cornerstone; God has done STAT this, and it is marvellous ION our eyes NO LITTER'. She thought of Derek, instantly, and was suddenly moved beyond words by the loneliness of his mission, undertaken without her support or assistance.

'Are you all right?' That had been the man sitting opposite. Wearing a bowler hat, of all things. Nose in the *Financial Times*. She compared him to Derek. The man shrank. A gnat in a hat. 'Yes, thank you,' she smiled. 'Fine.' She turned back to the crinkled pages.

One morning a man without a bowler hat was facing her, pointing jollily at the book. 'That yours, is it?'

She became uncomfortable, wriggled in her seat. 'Um – yes,' she said.

'Spotted it from the cover. I'm a social worker. Trained to spot. Ha.'

'Right,' she said.

'Mind if I show you my favourite verse?'

She minded quite a bit, but the man was so open to a rebuff, so stupidly gleeful, with a tuft of starched blond hair springing up in the middle of his forehead, that—

'There you are,' he was saying, passing the Bible back with a thumb pressed into the middle of a page. 'Sorry to bother you. My name's Dave from Bristol.'

Pursing her lips, she read the words around his thumbprint. 'This is the will of him who sent me, that I shall lose none of all that he has given me, but raise them up at the last day. For my Father's will is that everyone who looks to the Son and believes in him shall have eternal life, and I will raise him up at the last day.' She glanced over to thank Dave from Bristol, stiffly, but he was deep in a copy of the *Sun*.

171

She recognised the words as the only ones she was sure her husband knew by heart – but what did they mean? A passenger announcement squawked overhead. She looked over at a pile of faxed audit figures, her normal train reading, then back to the Bible, then out of the window. BARKING STATION, NO LITTER. Something growled inside her.

Derek confronted Judy one evening with a tremor in his voice.

She had just finished assuring the local police she could add nothing to what her husband had said about the Tower, and hanging up the telephone, told him: 'Quite exciting, you know. Really quite exciting. What do you think it was? A thief? It can't have been because he would have taken everything. The poor Geareys. The cleaners must have just sucked it into a hoover, or something, or eaten it.'

'Judy—'

'Yes?'

'Can I tell you something?'

'Yes. But don't strain yourself.' She was buoyant; she wasn't sure why.

There was a very long pause.

Judy Weston felt herself become nervous.

Derek's dog-collar sprang up suddenly, striking him on the chin. Breathing heavily, he fiddled it back into place.

She tried to catch his eye but was unable to.

'Something – on my mind,' he mumbled.

'Oh.'

She could hear children playing on the Green.

Then, cautiously, he began: 'Otis has a girlfriend.'

'Wonderful! Fanfares.'

'Well – um – yes. Fanfares. Literally. She is in an orchestra. In the north.'

'Great. Is she American as well?'

'No, she's pretty civilised.'

They laughed, then the vicar added quietly. 'It's – um – well, it's Charlotte Davidson, actually.'

Judy Weston did not know what reaction her husband was

172

expecting, but she was sure she could not come up with it. She just said: 'Oh.'

'She might visit the area. I was going to ask if you minded.'

She bit her lip. 'How can I mind? You're busy saving the universe.'

'Do you mind?'

'Like I say – oh, Derek, don't start asking stupid questions. Just do whatever it is you're doing. Just do it. I'm a banker. I work at a bank. I'm not Wonder Woman. I've no experience saving universes. If I spin round in a phone box I get dizzy.'

'I never said I was Superman. I can't even get my overhead projector downstairs at the moment. My back crunched. I've pulled it. Bending.'

There was a pause. Then he told her: 'She's coming to the service in ten days.'

Judy just said: 'Oh. Why?'

'Um – Otis asked her.'

'Fine.' She wrinkled her nose.

'She's bringing something.'

'What?'

'Oh, nothing. Her orchestra.' He added: 'Er – apparently.'

'I don't mind. I don't mind, Derek. Stop looking at me like that.'

'Like what?'

'Like I ought to mind.'

Judy wanted to say something then, something tender to draw them together. But she found herself lost for words, and blamed him. Just as all the howling wolves in their marriage were settling down, he had thrown a firecracker into their caves. She felt the gap between them widen, and wondered if anything could ever close it.

Yet her Bible reading continued, because even she could see the change in her husband and now longed for the return of her own purpose and conviction. One morning Judy prayed silently on the train. She had read the crucifixion story, subconsciously pushing the audit papers to one side as if

173

they offered no solutions, not even solutions to audits; urging God in her head, 'Please identify yourself. Forgive me for everything.'

She felt a movement in her soul like someone opening a crisp packet.

Judy Weston breathed in.

'Show me,' she went on daringly, 'the love of Christ.'

Then two inspectors asked her to show them a ticket, so that was the end of that. Later Judy wondered if she had been like a climber at that moment, drawing close to the edge of the precipice in heavy mist and never knowing. Would she suddenly fall into heaven?

That Saturday . . . that Saturday morning she had tutted as the doorbell went. Derek was out, being interviewed on BBC Radio Essex about rapid church growth. She had been reading – yes, reading it again, in the kitchen this time, ready to slam the Bible into the fridge if her husband returned suddenly. But this could not be him. He was speaking on the radio at that very moment.

Seeing the large head silhouetted in the opaque glass, she turned the bronze doorknob and pulled the front door open. Her quizzical expression cleared instantly.

'Rex—'

'Hullo, Judy!'

'—how are you?'

They exchanged deft hugs in the hallway. He asked: 'Is Derek not in?'

'No, sorry.'

The management consultant was well-dressed today – expensively dressed, she thought – with a fluffed-up yellow cravat at his neck and a large blazer hugging his heavy frame. He chuckled, blushing slightly, big cheeks pneumatically raising his thick-rimmed spectacles an inch. Judy detected a waft of exotic aftershave.

'I have a message for him, that's all.'

'Do come through. Would you like some tea?'

'Lovely.'

He stood in the kitchen as she fussed with the kettle. 'This

174

is Derek, isn't it?' Rex was pointing at the little portable radio by the sink.

'Yes,' said Judy. 'He's doing a half-hour interview.'

'Right,' he said. 'Yes. Hmm. I was listening in the car. Interesting.'

Oh, she should have been alerted by that. A minute ago he had asked if Derek was in.

Mashing tea bags against the sides of two mugs, she heard him saying: 'It was about this service of yours, that's all. Sunday week. This big one. He was asking me to do him a favour.' Rex rubbed his pudgy hands together, as if the house was too cold for him. 'If you could just tell him it worked out rather well. The people he wanted me to get in touch with thought it was a hoot. They'll be there.'

'Do I need to write this down?'

'Just say they're coming. He'll understand.'

'I'm keeping out of all this,' Judy said.

Rex pointed in the direction of the kitchen table. 'Are you doing some reading? What's that, then? I've just been reading Roderick Liddle's biography – you know, the Millwall manager. *Liddle by Liddle*, it's called. It was actually very—'

'It's a Bible.'

'Oh. I am so terribly sorry.'

She handed him a mug. 'No, no need to be. It's not private. I'm just, er, catching up.' She looked at Rex through her fringe, sipping at tea. 'I suppose I haven't read it as much as I ought to, as a vicar's wife.' Judy regretted the limp way the sentence ended as soon as the words came out.

'But who's asking?' Rex blurted. 'It's not as though someone's suddenly going to test you, is it? Don't worry, Judy, don't worry,' he breezed. His expression straightened. 'I don't – I don't like to see you getting worried.'

She felt momentarily uncomfortable. They wandered through to the living room. 'Ah, the surprise party,' Rex chirped, choosing an armchair. 'Indeed. Nice time. And this service Derek's been telling me about, it seems to be quite significant, make or break I think he was saying—'

'Oh, yes. People from the diocese headquarters are going

to be there. It's a turning point.' She did not want to say more.

Rex Gobart clearly did not want to know more, because he did not pursue it. He sat there for a few minutes, just sipping at the tea and glancing cheerily around the room. At one point he laughed to himself and shook his head. His cheeks were blazing red, Judy noticed. She sat with her knees together on the sofa, hands cradling the warm mug, strangely nervous.

He volunteered: 'I used to talk about "Mistianity", you know.'

'Really?'

'Made Derek laugh a bit. I missed it. All the Bible stuff. Wish I could have it.'

'You can,' she said. 'I'm sure.'

'Yeah? And win the free Fiat Uno?' He flicked a finger in one ear. 'Well, maybe so. I've definitely given up trusting the Tories, even though I think I recall they were offering some kind of eternal salvation at the last election.'

Judy laughed. 'It's a matter of trusting God, I think. That's all.'

'Voting Conservative?'

'Christianity.'

'Throwing caution to the winds?'

'Yes.'

He leant forward suddenly. 'In that case,' Rex began, placing the mug carefully on the carpet, 'I would like to tell you that I am deeply in love with you.'

All Judy could think of was that his mug might burn a hole in the floor.

'It was the party,' Rex said. 'It was organising the party that brought this on.'

'Oh,' she said. 'Look, Rex – I think your cup might—'

'Yes, Judy. The party.'

'I see. Um – that mug is—'

'It was doing all the work with you.'

She inhaled. 'The cheese pieces, and so on.'

'Absolutely. I just need some kind of – of enlightenment in my life,' he added, scooping the mug off the floor suddenly.

'Y-yes.'

176

'Don't get me wrong, Judy,' Rex said quickly, taking a gulp of tea. 'I'm not – this isn't a takeover bid, or anything. I'm Derek's friend. I just wanted to tell you. I heard him on the radio and jumped in the motor. Came straight over. I think you're one of the most beautiful people in this hemisphere.'

The vicar's wife was speechless.

'Possibly in any hemisphere. I haven't travelled widely enough to swear on that. Actually, to tell you the truth, I've never been to Wales, now I come to think of it. I suppose it's possible I'm doing the women there an injustice, but from odd bits and bobs I've seen on television I rather doubt it.'

Hesitantly, she asked: 'More tea?'

Rex ignored her. Just kept staring into her eyes with that baseball-sized face. His rosy cheeks flushed deeper red. He said: 'The other day, you know, I went into a church. In a lunch hour. I've been trying to figure out what it all means. I suppose you've inspired me, in a way.'

She smiled, weakly, reflecting that inspiration could spread in all directions at once, brushing hair from her fringe. 'We all have – um – trouble, I suppose, working things like that out. It comes down to – oh, I don't know if I should be talking to you like this at all, Rex,' she said, changing tone, scratching the backs of her hands with her long nails. 'You can't find me inspiring. I'm not inspiring. I've been trying to discover what – what lies at the heart of it all this past fortnight, too.'

'You?' He beamed. He winked. 'A vicar's wife?'

'Try merchant banker, and then you'll get the picture.'

He stiffened his back. 'I'm worried I've said too much. And I was only joking about Wales. You won't say anything to Derek, will you? I just – I'm not married, Judy, you see. I've been married twice, actually, and they didn't work. And when love flies overhead with me, you know, it flies ever so fast and so briefly. Like a swallow. Of course one wants to trap it somehow, with a net or something, just for a few minutes, a few days – one – one wants to – to tell someone.'

She was silent for a time. Then she said gravely, 'Perhaps you should have told someone else.' But she suspected the tiniest hint of a smile had flashed at the corner of her mouth.

'Well, I felt like telling you. Goodness,' he roared, 'how seriously we financial people take anything that looks like a meeting!'

She laughed too then, catching another blast of the pungent aftershave and realising the whole outfit had probably been thrown on, splashed on for her, feeling the intimidation all but drain from the room; she felt more sorry for him than anything. Somehow she desperately wanted to give Rex a flicker of the enlightenment he was searching for – but what, a stirring quote from the Bible? No, come on. She told herself not to be silly. The man was a management consultant.

'Thank you for coming round, anyway.'

He swigged the dregs of the mug, mumbling: 'The Man Who Said Too Much.'

'I don't really think you did.'

They might have parted then, but she had just remembered a comment Derek had made, and now had no qualms asking Rex if he could stay a moment and do something for them.

'An overhead projector?' he said. 'I haven't seen one for years.'

'It's upstairs. Derek needs it for some plan of his. But he's got a crick in his back – so would you mind—?'

'Not at all,' he laughed, plodding heavily up the staircase as she told him the story of the Spaniard they had in the church, a few years back, whose surname was Broyecta. 'But everyone called him Overhead,' she said. 'He seemed to love it.'

The stairs were rather steep for Rex, and when he reached the top he was out of breath. He stood there for a moment on the dim landing, wheezing, gripping the banister rail. 'Phew,' he said, swaying, pushing up his glasses with one set of knuckles and wiping his forehead inaccurately.

'Are you sure you're going to be all right?'

'No problem, no problem,' he wheezed. 'No problem at all. Goodness, the last time I had exercise like that was the squash against Derek.'

'Take it easy, Rex, for goodness sake.'

'Okay. Don't worry.' He coughed. Then he took his jacket off, used the label to swirl it stylishly around a fingertip, and said: 'Right. Where is it, then?'

'Through here. It is heavy, Rex.'

'No problem, no problem,' he said. He threw the jacket to the floor. 'Remember George Orwell. Heavy is light.'

She giggled. Her heart reached out to him. She decided she would perhaps raise Christian things, maybe even subtly mention the love of God, when they got to the doorstep and he was about to go. They walked into the spare room. 'Recognise it? In the corner,' she said. 'Under those books. You can see the focus thing.'

'Focus thing?' He bent down with a throaty sigh, scooped a dozen hardbacks this way and that, his rear and legs bulging massively inside a pair of trousers Judy was sure, standing behind him, were several sizes too small. Finally the square plastic top of the projector was exposed, the lens attachment sticking up on its metal stalk like a periscope.

'Okay,' he said, 'here we—'

'Rex, for heaven's—'

'—go—'

'—sake, be—'

Whichever word Judy was about to use was drowned out by a groan that came from deep within Rex as he heaved the object up to his chest, emitting an animal roar as he got it there, then quickly throwing his right arm around the outside of the contraption to stop it crashing back to the floor.

There was silence for a moment.

'All right?' said Judy, in a concerned voice.

Rex's face was going a shade of deepest crimson. 'I'm taking my inspiration from the Russian Olympic weightlifting team. Just don't force me to have a drugs test. Phew. The only way is down,' he breathed, straining at the thing, the metal stalk pressing a deep furrow all the way up his cheek, dislodging his spectacles.

'Are you sure you can make it?'

'Take it from me,' grunted Rex, beaming lopsidedly, 'the best way to do something like this is with a lot of speed and very little fuss. Can you just push my specs back down for me?'

Judy did. Then she tried to put her hands underneath the projector, but Rex turned from her, cheerfully groaning that the staircase was too small for two, lumbering out of the room on to the dark landing, sliding his feet across the carpet to feel for the space where the steps began.

Walking behind him, she said something, put a hand forward to touch his shoulder and urge him not to go so fast; then, a second later, begged him to put the projector down; afterwards she could not remember what she had said.

Rex Gobart descended the vicarage staircase faster than he ever imagined he could: in a deafening, whirling flurry of arms and glasses and legs, a shoe, a hand, a snatch of yellow cravat and undone shoelace – and, somewhere in the middle of it all, a blurred open mouth and bulging terrified eyes flashing momentarily, projector overhead.

23

She had been unable to sleep for two days since, had just about managed work on Monday. There had been no blood. Derek did not seem able to get through to her whenever they spoke at the weekend. He was not surprised. They talked in snatches. They were both deep in shock and grief. The wallpaper was badly ripped halfway down the staircase. On Sunday there were ninety-eight in the morning. He recognised a family he had leafleted by the cinema, which was showing a rerun of *Goldfinger*.

Derek looked out at the enlarged congregation and saw hope spelled out in capital letters, in every kind of fount. *Goldfinger*, he thought.

The man with the Midas touch.

But when he had held the pearl up in front of his eyes in the vicarage study hours before that Sunday service, begging it to hold him in its hands for just another week, to get him through the funeral, then to save his precious church, he had been run through by raw anguish as if by a curved Moroccan sabre. He put the pearl down on his desk and turned his head away.

The thing blazed on the desk. It was always blazing.

Derek had gazed out at the church drive. The pang stabbed him. *I lost Rex*, he thought. *Rex wanted the truth and I did not give it to him*. He was not good enough to set eyes on any kind of truth. Not even to shut one eye and set the other on it. He was not even good enough to set a dog on the truth. Heart in mouth, the vicar dialled Otis, closing the pearl in his fist as the telephone rang.

The voice that answered had been sleep-saturated: 'Oh. Hey. Oh. Hi, Derek.'

'You not up?' He dragged the gem off the desktop, not looking as he did so.

'It's seven,' Otis had said. 'My alarm goes off at six minutes past, so I start the day with the fourth item in the news.'

'Look – I'm sorry,' Derek said. 'I need to ask you something, Otis.' He used his thumb to push the jewel into the box of staples in the top drawer of the desk.

'Don't worry. Is everything okay with you both? Are you managing to get over the dreadful—'

'Things are a bit difficult, actually.'

'Oh.'

The vicar asked: 'Could you preach this morning?'

The poor curate had done his very best. He stumbled his way through a pile of old theology college notes, the increased size of the congregation making his nervousness worse. His hands were shaking. They kept bumping against a microphone Marshall Kampfner had wired to the lectern during the week. New speakers screwed to the wooden panelling at the back of the church were emitting a low whistle. Sitting off to one side, Derek had closed his eyes and squirmed in his seat. *This is not what they need to hear*, he told himself. The sermon was on something to do with a comparison between the prophets Nehemiah and Obadiah. *No one wants to hear about those old windbags*, the vicar thought.

'. . . and if you turn to your Bibles, to page four hundred and ninety-seven, you will see that the number of so-called "associates" working on the temple was eight hundred and twenty-two, which was more than double the figure . . .'

The vicar gritted his teeth. He looked over at the congregation. *Christianity is about crowds*. He felt for the pearl in his chest pocket, catching Judy's eye and removing the hand as innocently and as quickly as he could. Her gaze lingered on him for an instant longer than he would have liked.

A recent hoax advertisement in an Anglican newspaper had fooled everyone into believing that the Decade of Evangelism had been cut to five years because of a shortage of funds. *Well*, Derek thought when he saw it, *we're doing eleven here. We've got the funding*. He had imagined his church a breakaway movement, attracting millions with a message of raw joy. *The Decade of Elevengelism.*

There was far too much detail in the Church of England. There was far too much crawling over little bits and pieces that people had said. There were far too many people in silly hats. There was far too much sex; far too much worrying about it, anyway. There was far too much standing around drinking coffee. There were far too many people with problems. There were far too many funny-coloured socks and fat arms. There was far too much Nehemiah and Obadiah. *This is what must have confused Rex*, the vicar decided, sitting there at the front of his church as Otis preached. *People whingeing on and on about technicalities.* His spirits lightened. He saw hope spelled out in the numbers in front of him. *I have the pearl of great price.*

After the service, he had told Judy not to worry about attending the funeral. 'You don't have to come,' Derek said. 'He was my friend.'

'He was ours. The surprise party, Derek.'

'Oh, yes – I forgot,' the vicar said. 'The cheese pieces, and so on.'

'Well – yes.'

It was held in thick mist.

The mist was so thick that Derek, who took the service, accepted the offer of a cycle rear-light as he made his way out of St Saviour's church. George Foster pinned it to the back of his jacket collar. 'I think you'll have to wear it,' Judy said at his side. 'Otherwise they're not going to be able to follow.'

'Too right, Derek,' George agreed.

'Thank you,' the vicar murmured. Tugging at his collar, the lamp threw a flickering red triangle down his back. *Mistianity*, he remembered.

Rex Gobart had left instructions for a medley of Elton John songs to be played in the church. They included 'Someone Saved My Life Tonight' and 'Bennie And The Jets'. He had also wanted 'Set The Controls For The Heart Of The Sun', by Pink Floyd, but his brother said the cassette copy left in

183

his home had honking sounds in the middle because of a fault on the tape.

His ex-wives both shed tears in the chorus of 'I'm Still Standing'. One produced pink tissues out of a sleeve like a magician. A number of people in suits were there, work colleagues, Derek had imagined, glancing about the place sadly as the music began, brow furrowed, thoughts fractured. *God*, he prayed, *bring these empty people into our ranks. Swell them*.

Tuesday morning. He could only ever remember meeting one of Rex's sons. Wally, was it? He could only ever recall hearing about another. Now it turned out there were three, plus two daughters. Trudi, did one say? Wally, Trudi, X, Y, Z! How had he not known? Perhaps he had hardly known his friend at all. One daughter apologised for the manner of her father's death as though he had picked it in a rash moment, like a bad seating plan. *Maybe he did*, the vicar pondered. It was as quick as you got. And in Anglican terms, dying in the arms of an overhead projector would probably rank top among approved exits from the world.

Now, stumbling on a divot at the edge of the graveyard, he could only hope the mourners were following the lamp at his back. Without even thinking, Derek reached up for the jewel. *Gorgeous thing*. He touched it through the fabric of his shirt, felt power stream through his fingers. *Please, God*, he prayed, regaining his balance, *never let me lose the light you have given me*.

'This way,' Derek said, turning. 'Follow the glow.'

A minute later, someone went sprawling and had to be helped up.

'I think he got your lamp confused with the brake light on that car,' a female voice was murmuring behind Derek. He half-turned, saying, 'Mine can't be a brake lamp because it doesn't get brighter when I slow down,' tramping ahead slowly, feeling his way with an outstretched foot. 'I think we are very nearly there.' The ground was uneven, lumpy.

A loud male voice called: 'Oh, for God's sake.'

Derek stopped. He heard a score of feet shuffle to a halt behind him. Turning, he saw white faces bobbing in the mist like party balloons. 'Please,' he said, brow knitted with indignation, 'let's remember where we are. We're at a church.'

'We can't see one. It's all fog,' a voice bleated.

'Just because you can't see something doesn't mean it isn't there. Please, let's watch what we say in the grounds.'

Someone grunted an apology. Then they were shuffling forward again. A mobile telephone rang at the back of the crowd. The vicar heard righteous tutting.

What happened next struck Derek Weston as extraordinary. He carried on walking, feeling the tugs at the back of his jacket, climbing a short, steep bank to reach a narrow path worn in the grass. 'Are you okay?' he asked Judy.

There was no answer.

Finally he came to the spot, and found her already there. Already there! She was smiling at him in a way she had never smiled at him before. In her face was a kind of – of understanding, of deep sympathy . . . concern, even.

The group shuffled to a halt behind the vicar. 'This is it,' he said over his shoulder, never taking his eyes off his wife. 'I took a quicker way,' she said softly. Something struck him; he was not sure what. He smiled uncertainly, moved carefully round to the head of the grave, feet slipping in mud.

With all of them standing in silence, jaw numb with cold, Derek read from the *Book of Common Prayer*. You took nothing into this world, you can take nothing out. Someone clapped arms against sides in the fog, and for a moment Derek imagined he was hearing a mourner with gloves trying to start a round of applause. He thought of the Bishop of Basildon's office, the surprise party.

Mouth set lopsidedly, Derek read two verses from a Psalm out of the corner of his mouth, cheeks burning in the cold: '"For he knows how we are formed, he remembers that we are dust. As for man, his days are like grass."'

His spectacles were smeared with vapour. He saw another flash of pink tissue.

Looking down, he read: '"He wraps himself in light as with a garment."' He had lost his place. He peered at the print and read, stupidly, without thinking – a textual note. *Silly,*

silly idiot. As he raised his head from the prayer book, the fog appeared so thick that for a second the vicar thought he must be utterly alone where he stood.

He said: 'Rex was a truly loyal friend.'

Derek Weston glanced down, over the top of the book, and saw only gaping black below him. Was he about to be transfigured, lifted up? But no. Just as he had been before the service two days before, the vicar was stung by sudden doubt and loneliness. *My life is such garbage*, he thought, astonished by the blasphemy even as it crackled across the telephone lines of his mind. The mist thinned. He saw the mourners panned out around him. He would miss the portly management consultant, his frank, free advice, so very much. Yet what would become of him and his church if he doubted now?

24

He woke with a start. He was sitting in the living room armchair, legs splayed across the carpet. 'Wha-what – what did I—?'

Judy was leaning over him, stock still, looking down, a hand extended in his direction, her arm frozen in mid-air.

'You fell asleep after the funeral.'

'Oh.' The vicar rubbed his eyes. 'Phew. Did the front doorbell just go?'

'Yes. You're exhausted, Derek,' she said, straightening up and looking over her shoulder towards the hallway. 'It's exhausted us both. Listen, I'm going to have to zip into London in a minute.'

'How long have I been—'

The doorbell rang again.

'An hour? Hour and a half? Not too long. I'll get it.'

'Goodness.' Derek rubbed his eyes. He muttered to himself, 'I've got things to do. Can't sleep now.'

'It's for you, darling.' That was Judy, in the hallway. 'Sorry,' she was explaining to someone, 'it's not ringing properly. The bell sort of swerves in and out.'

'Undulates.' A crusty male voice Derek almost recognised.

He muttered, 'Gosh,' getting up and walking to the door, catching a glimpse of himself in the hallway mirror. His hair was standing in wild waves, like a rug a comedian had tripped over. A real mess. He brushed a palm over it, heavily, seeing Claire Stupples, Ken O'Driscoll, Connie Leach and Sonya Todd all suddenly come into view, on the doorstep, spread out, all beaming at him. *I am not going to go bald*.

Before Derek even saw it in his hands, Ken was pushing

a bouquet of flowers at him. 'We wanted you to have this, Derek—' Connie said, beaming.

Reds, greens and blues flared in front of him.

'—just to show we all love you. A lot of people here love you. We know things are a bit difficult at the moment.'

'Yes, very,' said Sonya and Claire, together.

'Flowers,' the vicar said.

'Luckily it doesn't look like your sleep pattern has been disturbed,' Ken observed drily, earning a fierce nudge from Claire.

'That is so kind of you – of all of you,' the vicar said. 'It is so kind of everyone.' He wanted to tell them something majestic, something about victory and pricelessness, something about purity and blamelessness and coming on Sunday because it would be the best sermon and service they would ever attend—

'We're coming on Sunday,' said Claire. 'We know it's important.'

'Thank you,' he smiled. 'We're expecting quite a few.'

'There were a lot more last Sunday, too, when Otis preached,' Sonya put in.

'Yes,' Derek agreed. 'I've been reaching out. We both have.'

'Well, there's a lot of love for you here, Derek,' she went on talking as if they were in some sort of Wild West location, and Derek was the sheriff, and they had come to say someone was gunning for him on horseback. 'We are all rooting for you, we really are,' she went on. 'You don't deserve to be just blown away.' Claire was obviously the spokesman. 'Not after so many years,' she concluded.

Holding the flowers, the vicar wanted to say: *years? What do they matter? Only a fortnight, surely, since I found the pearl of greatest price* – but Connie Leach had started crying for some reason, and was being comforted by Ken and Sonya.

'Don't worry, don't worry,' the vicar said. 'There's no use crying over spilt churches.' Connie spluttered some laughter through her tears. 'Not that this one is, of course,' he added. 'Spilt, I mean.' *It isn't, and it will never be*. He glanced over their heads to the horizon. The sun looked as if it was considering going down. *I see the light, they see it reflected in my face*, he told himself. *They need me.* He added: 'You are all so – I don't really know how to say it the way it has to be said – so genuine, all of you. So caring towards me. And to Judy, of course.'

'Yes,' said her muted voice behind him.

'We just wanted to say,' Connie sobbed, 'that market forces are *wrong*.'

'I think we've all learnt that in the last fifteen years,' the vicar said easily. 'It would have been better if the Greens had got in.'

'You say that, but they don't have anything remotely like a foreign policy.' That was Ken again, but everyone ignored him.

Sonya Todd said: 'We were very, very sorry to hear about your friend. John and I met with Gerald and Charles last night and had a time of prayer.'

Claire said: 'Me and Ruth did too.'

What's that? Me and Ruth did too? A film sequel of some kind?

'I wasn't invited,' Ken muttered.

'Your thoughtfulness,' the vicar began, 'makes me speechless, almost. I think Rex's death really has knocked us both for six.'

They were gone a minute later. Flowers hanging from his fist, Derek felt his head sprinkled with conviction, like sticky silver stars. He was thrilled.

Judy was in the living room, pulling a purple raincoat on. 'I'll drive. It'll be against the traffic.'

'Drive – where?'

'Work, Derek,' she said. 'I told you. Just for two or three hours at the end of the day. Has to be done, I'm afraid. Especially as I wasn't in yesterday.'

She stopped doing up the buttons on the coat, and looked at him.

'Are you okay, Judy?'

'I'm just thinking, Derek.'

In other days, before the pearl had transformed the value of his life, the vicar's heart would have sunk at that. Now it did not. He wondered if the jewel had even transformed their flagging marriage. Maybe it was not flagging now. Maybe it was flying. Maybe it was loop-the-looping. He was shot through with anguish suddenly for having doubted at the graveside, even for a fraction of a second. 'Thinking?' he asked.

'I wanted – to tell you something,' she said. 'Do you mind?'

'How could I?' Instantly he thought of seven different things, things he had to do for Sunday, and inhaled deeply.

'Just for a minute,' Judy said, reading him.

'Oh – right,' he said. He was rejoicing. *The pearl has changed everything!*

He flopped into the sofa, looked up at his wife.

Staring out of the window, she said: 'Derek – I – think I've – I've discovered what it's all about. You helped me, darling, along the way. I know this will sound strange, but I've taken – a step. I've committed my whole life to Christ.'

The vicar looked down at the carpet. 'All of it?'

'Yes.'

Slowly, Derek moved his gaze around the room, like a torch in a garden shed. He flashed it at his wife. He slid it down her slender figure until his eyes came to rest on her stiletto heels, the thin ankles above them, calves perfectly moulded like white marble, the whole lot parallel.

'Oh,' he said. 'Tremendous.'

She seemed not to hear, and narrowed her eyes. 'You made me realise I was ignoring it.' She rolled her bottom lip over her teeth. 'I want you to know that, Derek. It's important that you know, darling. You made me remember what we used to stand for. Maybe even more than that. What you stood for, anyway, when we first arrived here. That jewel we were always talking about, Derek – you had it then. Years ago. I think maybe I just had a glimpse. But I've been reading my Bible, Derek.' She suddenly produced one.

The vicar looked up. 'Yippety-yay. Whoopee.' But his face was serious.

'Today, by the grave – it was like a – I don't want to sound dramatic, but it was like a massive sign. The grave was. It's life and death, all this. We've been treating it like the life and death of this particular church, this particular Sunday – well, that's how it should be, I guess. And fine, you know. I mean, if my bank was threatened in the same way, I suppose people would draw swords and start lashing out. But we're different, Derek. We're not a bank. We've got souls to think of. Rex's, for a start. How did we manage to let him go like that? The whole thing – everything – has made me look – look up. To Christ. If I sound as if I'm finding it difficult to say it's because I'm used to dealing with numbers. But you've helped me, Derek. What's happened in the last couple of weeks has. Your conviction. Oh, I haven't explained it at all.' She trailed off, frustrated.

'You have, you have.' The vicar found himself staring at a candlestick on the middle shelf of a cabinet on the opposite wall. *I have a conviction for speeding.* His mind went totally blank, like a blackboard splashed with water.

'Are you all right, darling?'

'Er—' he said '—ah, yes. Yes, fine. I'm so pleased. All this has – today – has interrupted my train of thought, slightly, and—' The vicar trailed off. 'I suppose I'm thinking about Sunday. I'm just wondering how I'll feel when I get a first sight of all those people from the bishop's office.'

'God is in charge.'

'I've done a lot of work on it,' Derek said, absently.

When she had gone, he threw on an overcoat too. He climbed into the yellow Morris Minor, borrowed from George Foster, and drove to the lake at Norton Mortimer. How badly he needed to think! He set off round the lake on foot, looking out at a thin layer of mist still hanging on the surface. A bird swooped across the water, squawking. There was hardly anyone around. No wonder: Tuesday. He was trembling. *Christ? Committed herself to Christ?* The phrase flitted around his head. What was all that about? Why had she suddenly got so detailed? When had he ever mentioned Christ? Wasn't it just God, power, joy, peace and hell? Wasn't it just value, sheer human value in the eyes of a creator? Wasn't that what had been revealed to him? Why bring Christ in, except as a detail? What was she playing at?

Or is this just the first part? he wondered. *Tomorrow she's going to tell me the second. She's going to say she's committed herself to Moses. Next she's going to say she's committed herself to Obadiah. On Friday it'll be Solomon. Then she's going to say she's made a pact with Zebedee—*

This could start getting like the flipping Magic Roundabout, he thought.

The vicar slumped on to a bench, breathed in deeply, spread his arms, scratched his head, feeling the thick hair still uneven on it. *I am not going to go bald.*

Derek Weston needed the reassurance of the pearl of great price. That was what he needed. That was where it had all begun. It had energised him at the start, given him all the answers when he only really needed some . . . it would fill him with reassurance now.

Looking left and right and seeing no one, not a soul, he reached behind the folds of his overcoat, into his jacket. His fingertips touched the fabric of his shirt. They found the pocket.

Squeezing the fabric, he felt calmly for the bulge he had become so used to feeling in his pocket that it was now virtually a part of him.

He pressed the fingers into the pocket, feeling for that priceless swelling.

Then he had his palm pressed hard against the front of the shirt—

Derek Weston could not feel the pearl anywhere in the pocket. He glanced quickly left and right again. Why couldn't he feel the pearl in his shirt? An elderly couple were approaching together, arm in arm. One swung a stick. *Forget them*, he told himself. *Just find it.*

So he yanked the front of his jacket open, chin on chest, fingers prising the upper edge of the pocket away from his shirt, eyes boggling—

Where is it? Where is the thing?

He squinted into the pocket. Shut an eye. Heard fast breathing approaching.

'Are you all right there?'

He glanced over, shot up from the bench. 'Yes – yes. Fine.'

The man with the stick had apparently dropped it and charged over. 'You slumped,' he said, 'groping your heart. We thought you'd collapsed.' Derek just stood there, swaying. The man, in a dotted turquoise scarf, was breathless. He remained stock still for a moment. Then he gestured over his shoulder rapidly. Derek jerked his head an inch. The woman was standing there, hands on hips, looking worried. 'My wife is an expert in collapsing. She's retired.'

'I'm fine.' Derek swayed.

'She said she was sure you'd collapsed from the way your head rolled forward and your eyes went and you were reaching inside your—'

'Yoga,' the vicar blurted. He saw the man look him up and down, doubtless taking in strips and snatches of church clothing underneath the coat, obviously seeing his white dog-collar too. 'Christian yoga,' Derek added quickly.

'Oh – I see. Well, I'm sorry.'

'No problem,' the vicar said. As the man walked back to his wife, Derek opened the coat and snatched back the folds of the jacket, standing there at the lakeside, clawing the breast pocket of the shirt open with a curled forefinger, staring in—

Where is it? Where has it gone? I had it!

Staring in—

He glanced up, terrified. He felt the world spinning. The couple were walking towards him now, the man swinging the stick. Derek raced up to them. 'Look – excuse me – I'm sorry to—' the vicar had to pause, get his breath back '—I just wanted to – to ask – ah – I've – lost something. You haven't seen anything, have you, as you walked up here?'

'Seen anything?' That was the woman.

'A petrol station—' The man.

'Seen what?' The woman again. She was squinting at him as though he was a wild animal she had been told at school was long extinct, but which had just bounded up to her in a park. 'Seen anything?' her husband joined in, voice pumped with false urgency.

'Yes!'

'What, exactly?' the man asked. His head punched forward.

The vicar gulped. Looked left, at the lake. 'Something – round?'

'Round?' The wife.

'And glinting?'

The man frowned, cupped his chin in the inside of a fist. 'Let me think—' He stabbed the air with the stick suddenly. 'A porthole?'

'No, no – look – I'm sorry – I just—'

'Give us another clue,' the wife squealed.

The vicar apologised and raced away from them, kicking leaves off the path as he raced down it, zig-zagging this way and that, once or twice crashing to his knees frantically beside something that looked as though it might be – *where is it? Where is it? Did I drop it? Did it come out of the pocket?* – but turned out not to be the pearl, flew at a nest of branches where he saw a square of light flicker, hands scattering them everywhere . . . grabbed at the light . . . the ring from a soft drinks can . . .

Clenching his fists, a thought flashed across the vicar's mind: *I must have left it in the staples box before the service on Sunday. In the desk. In the box of staples.* Yet he tore through the insides of the Morris when he got to it, leaving the driver's door open, one leg sticking high out of the car, heel of one shoe knocking on the roof as he leant over the front seat into the back and then went scrabbling under the mat on the passenger side, ran fingers up and down the plastic moulding under the windscreen, up and down, across—

The pearl was not in the glove compartment. It was not on the asphalt beside the car. It was not lodged in a seat. It was not in the ashtray. It was not anywhere on the floor.

It must be in the staples box.

He revved the Morris like a Formula One racer and sped back to the vicarage at fifty, running two red lights, one of them in a screeching skid that would have worked in a Hollywood cop movie. His hands smeared the steering wheel with sweat. He brushed at his brow. *Where is it? Where is it?*

The car radio was on, playing 'One Day I'll Fly Away'. He banged a hand at the box, killed it. Killed it dead. He virtually smashed into the front of the vicarage. At the door, dropped the keys on the step. Dropped them. Snatched them up, fumbled one into the front door. *The wrong one, idiot.* He pulled it out, groaning, gasping, getting the right key between shaking fingertips, pushing it into the lock.

Throwing the door open with a crash, Derek turned the corner into the vicarage study like a motorcyclist, leaning so hard left that one knee was almost touching the carpet on the turn – he was like that famous motorbike racer, what was his name, Rick Tillett, the chap who always did the horizontal turns and sent himself ploughing into the grandstand once, skidding – threw the desk drawer open, threw it on to the floor, grabbed at the staples box . . . scattered everything everywhere . . .

The vicar stood up, drawing the yellow box of staples level with his eye. He breathed in. He wiped his nose. Focused. *Calm down. It must be.* Then, carefully, hands shaking still, he popped the top of the box open.

Staples.

Staples—

One eye bulging in its socket, he looked inside. *Not there! Not* – but then – *of course not* – he remembered the service, the Sunday service, he had it then, didn't he, of course he had, he had had it in his shirt pocket then, and that was after he had pushed it into the box . . . yes, he had taken it out, hadn't he . . . he could remember taking it out now . . .

The vicar felt sick at soul. He felt physically ill. He could not believe it. He could not believe it. He trembled, every inch of him, every inch trembling, from head to toe and back again. He could not bear to think what he was thinking, had not the strength in mind or spirit or muscle to think it, yet was – was thinking it – *I have lost it, I have lost it, I have lost it, I have lost it . . .*

25

Jeff Massey rolled his false tooth around on his tongue and said: 'This thing, I'm talking about. This service thing. We've got a business to run here, and—'

'Jeff – it's just one day, one favour for him and Mum. And it's on the way.'

'But we haven't been told why!'

'He wants a full church for some reason. Perhaps it's a baptism,' Caroline suggested. 'Vicars are allowed full churches from time to time.'

'Yes – at Christmas. A baptism? You mean we're going to divert a coachload of our punters to do D and J—'

'—a favour, Jeff, yes. To do Mum and Dad a favour. We don't see them often enough because of working weekends. They hardly ever ask us for anything.'

Her husband opened his mouth to reveal his tongue, the tooth sitting on it. 'Okay. Fine. The trouble with me is I don't go for all those fairy stories your dad—'

'Let me ring the curate,' Caroline Massey cut in, flicking through a book, receiver squeezed between jaw and shoulder. 'He can just confirm the thing is still on.'

'What's his name again?'

'Otis.'

'Sounds like a lift.'

'Ssshh.'

'When he answers, say you want the top floor.'

'Shut up.'

When his telephone rang, Otis was in two minds about answering it. He was lying in his bed. The first mind said the ringing could be the vicar, and he ought to speak to the vicar because this service of his was now only two days away and they had not spoken for the last three. The second mind, which started jabbering at him when he turned his head on the pillow to block off one ear, said it could be Charlotte.

Otis Cheeseman had got used to not answering the telephone when he thought it might be Charlotte, because he did not want to have to dredge everything up and risk a surge in emotion.

He was thinking he might go back to Arizona.

So the telephone rang and rang. Otis peered up at the ceiling and let it. What time was it, anyway? Past ten, probably. He cleared his throat. *Ring, ring.* Yesterday he had been bitten by a vicious spaniel in Evenham Park, which had locked its jaw on to his calf, dappled ears flapping, emitting triumphant leg-of-man-in-mouth barks as he tried to swerve away. The dog's teenage owner arrived and said a code word that made it let go, but the animal left a line of nasty bites. The curate visited his doctor and went home worrying about typhoid, tetanus, sleeping sickness, secondary infection, polio, pus and needles.

Lying there, Otis heard the ringing stop and decided he was almost certainly having the worst week of his life. He wished he could say something to Charlotte before she forgot him totally. He wished he could tell her he loved her before he evacuated the country. But all he had were lines and lines and lines from theological books – and what use was some passage on a two-thousand-year-old apostle, when he had been bitten by a dangerous dog?

Yet even at his lowest moments Otis found he could catch glimpses of his calling time and time again, and reminded himself forcefully that all the evidence suggested his soul was safe with God even if his job was not safe with the Bishop of Basildon – and that being single was not as bad as being dead, even if it sometimes felt like it (and certainly being dead would probably be less lonely). He got on with his work. Otis Cheeseman just got on with it. Visiting, mainly. Got on with the long list of demands Derek had been making. And prayed too, all day long, every day, asking for deep forgiveness for his self-absorbed, selfish, self-indulgent self-pity.

Sitting on the side of the bed, the curate stared into the

lop-sided mirror at the other end of the room. The tic under his eye triggered. The telephone went again.

This one could not be Charlotte, he decided. She was far too sensible to call the same house twice. He bounded to the phone.

'Hello?'

'Otis? It's Derek. Ringing from the vestry.'

'Oh – hi, Derek,' the curate said. 'I was just thinking we ought to get together.'

'Yes,' the vicar said vaguely. 'We must—' he changed gear '—Otis, I think I need to – there's something I—'

'What is it?'

There was a long silence at the other end, as if to let the opening flurry of words settle.

Then the vicar said: 'I have lost my faith.'

Neither had anything to add to that for a full thirty seconds.

Otis cleared his throat. 'Do you remember when you last had it?'

'I'm not joking,' Derek said in a panicked tone. 'It's gone.'

The curate almost spluttered a double-barrelled volley of laughter and shock down the receiver. 'Do you mean it?'

'Yes.' The voice at the other end sounded tiny. 'You're the only one I can tell.'

'What can I do?' Dark dread poured into the curate's stomach.

Without hesitation, the vicar said: 'Pray for me.'

'I always do,' the curate said. 'Always, anyway, Derek.'

'We'll have to cancel this service, you know.'

'Cancel it?' Otis was surprised at the tone of horror in his own voice.

'Cancel the – the extras, anyway.'

'No – Derek—'

And that was how the conversation began. It went on for more than forty minutes. Finally, because he had not been sure enough of what he was going to say when he picked up the phone to call his curate, the vicar agreed not to do anything rash. 'Can't we at least – um – cancel – um – Charlotte? And her people?' There was a frantic, loose edge to his question.

Slowly, he heard Otis reply: 'It is not really possible for me to ring her, in current circumstances. This one is kinda hard to explain.'

She is coming down . . . Charlotte is coming down. Derek could not believe he had set it all up, set up his doom, his sudden unmasking in front of everyone, in front of her . . .

The vicar replaced the handset in its cradle.

What do I do? Just get up in that pulpit and whistle?

Derek Weston turned every object in vicarage and vestry upside-down in his search for the treasure he had lost. He had even taken up the edges of the carpets. He retraced steps in and out of the church and down the gravel drive, retraced them in and out of the local optician's, which seemed to worry the staff; went back over everything, even unscrewed the mouthpiece on the telephone and looked inside. He pressed his eye so hard against the plastic that a red circle stayed on his face for two hours afterwards.

But the pearl had gone. Completely. For the first time since his visit to the Tower, a wave of guilt swept over him. It could never be replaced. Powerful voices inside urged him to confess everything. He had lost a national asset. The loss was his doing, all his . . . *I have lost it, I have lost it*, he murmured, again and again . . . but soon he was saying something else: *I am lost, I am lost, I am lost* . . . and the guilt gave way to panic, all arrows pointing at him, then to a sadness as profound as any he had ever felt. No battles were worth fighting any more.

He walked over to the vicarage. Inside, he hovered in the hallway. *Good old Otis*, he thought. *Always so stable. Such a detail man. You'll never catch him doubting, not with all those books he's read.*

Two hours later, the doorbell went.

He moved across the hallway, wondering who that could—

On the step were the same two policemen.

The same two policemen! He just smiled. The same two – Derek Weston felt as though he was in some kind of – *no, you are not hallucinating*, he told himself urgently. *They must know*, he thought. His smile must have been utterly blank.

If they don't, I am going to confess it. I am going to tell them everything.

'Mind if we come in?' That was the one with silver-rimmed glasses.

They waddled in and sat down.

'Just a quick call this, sir.' The first one again.

I am going to confess it. The vicar noticed a set of handcuffs. 'I see,' he said.

They all inhaled the cold fresh Friday vicarage air for a moment.

'We – er – well – um – one of our – ah – colleagues picked up a yellow Morris car we believe you were driving on Tuesday, on radar.'

'Oh.' The vicar frowned at the carpet. What on earth were they talking about?

'Doing fifty,' the policeman in silver-rimmed glasses said.

'Three,' the younger one added, flicking through a note-book. 'Fifty-three.'

'Through a red light, I'm afraid.'

'Ah,' the vicar said. He remembered. Yes, driving back from the lake. The shapes on the carpet seemed to break apart, then come together differently. He peered down at them. *The end of all things is at hand.*

'So – we were passing, sir, you see, and we thought we would give you a brief, informal warning to avoid any further action on our parts.'

'Yes,' said the younger policeman with the moustache. 'Especially after the jewel business.'

The vicar jerked his head up, teeth clenched.

Now. Go.

'On the subject of jewellery,' he began, 'I would like to say something.' He was aware of the ridges of bone that would be jumping up and down along his jawline.

The policemen looked alarmed.

Derek stood up to say it.

He drew himself to his full height, there in the centre of the living room.

The policemen's eyes – all four of them – rose slowly to meet his.

Derek began to move his hands, like a public speaker.

'I would like,' he began slowly, 'to inform you both that—'

The vicar was cut short by the older officer, waving. 'We apologise here and now, sir. Please don't hold it against the force here in Evenham. We were just following a remit given by Windsor.'

'Well, the Met,' said the younger policeman, wrinkling his moustache and looking down at the carpet.

'Yes,' said the constable in silver-rimmed glasses.

Derek was left chewing at air, like bubble gum. He tried to restart the sentence. Gazed out of the window, put on his visionary expression. 'You may need to open a notebook. I was just going to tell you both outright, here and now, that—'

Now the younger one was waving a hand. 'We understand, we understand totally, sir,' he was saying, cutting across the vicar. 'We just hope you won't consider making any kind of formal complaint.'

'Complaint?' The vicar had been rubbing a fist in a cupped palm. Now he withdrew it, unclenched. His eyebrows arched. 'Complaint?' He sat down again, suddenly. Dropped into the seat. 'A – complaint?' His eyebrows arched further.

'We're obviously sorry to have wasted your time the other day,' the older policeman said.

'Wasted it?'

'Well,' the other constable began, rapping his knuckles with his pad, 'now they've found the ruddy thing, wherever it was—'

'Rolled under a cabinet, apparently—'

'—yes, like my colleague says, rolled under something—'

'—a cabinet in the vaults—'

'—yes, like my colleague says, rolled under a cabinet in the whatsits – now they've found it and the whole thing turned out to be a complete waste of—'

'We assumed you would have been told, Reverend, by Sir Gearey,' the policeman in silver-rimmed glasses said in a formal, measured voice, as though he had forgotten to fill out something.

'Ah,' the vicar responded, heart thumping. 'Sir Kenneth Gearey.'

'Just so. It's a nuisance,' the officer went on. 'Obviously it's a nuisance. Apparently the cleaners must have dislodged the pearl, the wallies, and the wretched thing simply rolled underneath the—'

'—the cabinet, mmm,' the vicar put in thoughtfully, nodding where he sat. He felt he must have broken out in a sweat. 'So no one has yet – confessed?'

'Confessed?' The younger policeman laughed. He looked at his colleague, rolling his eyes. 'Well,' he chuckled, looking back at the vicar, 'I suppose someone might step forward and admit they knocked it, or used an overweight duster, or something – but at the moment it seems like a combination of carelessness and false alarm.'

They all fidgeted for a minute.

Then the policemen left as quickly as they had come, apologising profusely all the way across the hall. 'The bump's gone down,' one said, pointing at the vicar's forehead. 'Sorry,' the other added. The vicar mentioned something about the red light and it wouldn't happen again. 'I was in one of those screeching sorts of skids when I crossed it,' he mumbled. 'It wasn't deliberate.'

'Right-ho,' the younger policeman agreed genially, wrinkling his moustache and winking as Derek shut the front door on them.

He walked through to the living room, stroking his chin. *This is incredible*, he thought. The vicar tried to unpack in his mind every detail of the day he had sat with the jewel in his hands, wrapping his fist over it there in the study. He threw a glance across the hallway; remembered the way his heart and soul had sung their thanks to the heavens, there in the study . . . so what had all that been, then? Psychosomatic? Psychedelic? Psychotic, that small pressure on his palm? Psychic? Psychiatric? Was that what it was – just some chemical reaction in his head, a result of not eating enough fibre? Something he had wanted to feel, emotionally needed to feel, so his mind and body had fixed it for him when there was nothing there? *Nothing?* But it had felt so much as if God had spoken, as if God had reached out, reached down to him, touched him—

People had made things up before. There was that bank robber he met on a prison visit who had robbed thirteen banks and been up to the front at fourteen Billy Grahams.

Derek Weston rubbed his hands through his hair.

It had felt so much as if it was real.

Had he dreamt the whole thing? Had he fallen asleep somewhere and seen the whole story spool across his mind, believed it, been utterly absorbed, forgotten ever waking from it? When Judy had roused him, in the armchair, after the funeral—

The funeral, you idiot.

The vicar moved to the telephone and dialled. After a deafening silence, the high-pitched unobtainable tone cut in where Rex would normally have picked up. There was no doubting it. This was no dream.

He was gibbering to himself. His lips were moving. He was rubbing his hands. His mind was filled with electric storms, lightning thoughts forking from one side to the other. He had the pearl of greatest price, then he lost it. He had had the pearl, then he had lost it. The thing had been an agent of God. Now he had no agent of God. He lost it. He had lost contact again. He had been swept out of heaven. God's love had fallen from him, snow from a rockface, sherbet from liquorice. And in two days, just two, he would stand in his own pulpit to give the Anglican equivalent of an appeal against hanging. Everyone would be there. But now the life had gone out of him.

Come in, God.

He stabbed at the television remote control. A blurred picture unfolded on the screen at the other end of the room, flickering violently. He groaned. *Come on.* The television was broken too. Was everything in his life busted? He tried in vain to make out the distorted images, then flicked the set off.

Later, when Judy returned from work, he was sitting at the living room table. She walked in and saw him there. Her voice was tender. 'Thinking about Rex?'

He curled his bottom lip inward. 'Perhaps. A bit.' He supposed he had been. 'The police came round again.'

'Really? Did they?' She sounded concerned, almost.

'They said that jewel's been found. It never even went anywhere. Rolled under a cabinet, or something.'

'Oh. After all that.'

The sun was going down, but a late, red ray was shining across Derek's face.

'You shouldn't look into the light, darling.'

He apologised, turning his head towards Judy. But he could not see her, just scarlet shadows. He heard her say: 'Is everything all right?'

Turning towards the Green at the back of the vicarage, he bit his lip.

'Derek—'

'Sorry, darling,' he said, squinting. 'I think I've let you down.' Blinded, he felt her arm around his shoulder. After a pause, the vicar added: 'I don't really think I'm worth very much.'

'You're worth a lot to me.'

'I'm like petrol coupons. I'm not worth saving.'

'You are. Of course you are.'

'The church isn't.'

'Of course it is.'

'I don't know what the point of this Sunday is, Judy. I don't know what I'm going to say. I don't know why I fixed it all up.'

Quietly, she said: 'You've started doubting again.'

His felt his brow furrow. 'How did you know?'

'Your brow goes furrowed.'

Derek looked out into the ocean of aching red sky, wished he could be a tiny particle in it with no sense of right or wrong, no one watching him or caring. 'I've just got nothing to say.'

Judy murmured: 'The secret of it all is – is Christ. I'm sure of it. The love in his face, his eyes.'

'Yes,' he said blankly.

He felt something land in his lap, looked down and made out a sheaf of creased papers lying there. 'What—'

'I fished them out of the back of the television, darling. They're wonderful. Especially the one I put on the top there.'

'My old sermons?' She had dropped them into his lap.

'Inside the TV set. Your first ones, years and years ago.'

'When I—'

'Yes, Derek,' she cut in. 'When you had the pearl. The jewel at the centre.'

Still gazing towards the horizon, the vicar reached down. He felt the surface of the papers like a blind man. He ran a middle finger along a ridge, flicked a dog-eared corner with a thumb. Breathed in. Sighed out. Judy's hand tightened on his shoulder. The vicar pursed his mouth. He reached for his handkerchief and blew his nose with a foghorn sound.

A blackbird dipped over the Green outside, flew low parallel to the house, then swerved away into a sea of sunset orange.

26

There is a pivotal moment in the history of every church, and in the history of St Saviour's church, Evenham, that moment seemed to come soon after Wazim Bhatia and an assistant from the steering committee of the diocese of Basildon found their car jammed in heavy traffic two hundred yards from their destination.

'How can it be this bad on a Sunday?' Hawkley Castari asked.

'I have no idea, Hawk,' Wazim said, pushing the sun visor up and trying to see past a coach in front of them. 'No idea at all.'

'A fair, is it?'

'Something with tombolas? I suppose so. But it's – no, come on, it's not the season. And look – there's nothing happening on Nock Green. We're not even budging! The last time I was in a jam like this was at a carwash that was running slow.'

Hawkley Castari was looking at his watch. 'Tssk. Ten past. We might be late for the service.' He was an optometrist. 'People have parked, too. We can't just pull in.'

'I imagine Derek Weston probably delays things until he has more than three worshippers in there.' Wazim chuckled, cruelly, and revved the engine. 'Surely it can't take that much longer.'

It did. At ten twenty the car was still crawling, stuck between the coach and a Volvo saloon which had tried to overtake twice. The church had now moved into vision at the other end of the road, on the left. Hawkley Castari wound down his window and leant out.

'Goodness,' he said, pulling his head back in.

'What?'

'Half this jam seems to be – it seems to be heading into the church.'

'You're joking.'

Hawkley Castari leant out again, half opening the door this time. 'Physically. Going up the drive. We're in a huge queue of cars and coaches, from what I can—'

The sentence was drowned out by a shriek of horn and a heart-stoppingly close thud of tyre on car door panelling.

A motorcyclist had appeared from nowhere, come streaking down the inside of the line of traffic and smashed into the open passenger door. Hawkley snatched his hand away. Wazim slammed a foot on the brake.

The car door flapped to and fro on its hinge, squeaking. In the silence that followed, Hawkley Castari looked up at the biker as he pulled off his crash helmet.

The man was barrel-chested, clad in black leather from neck to toe, studs on shoulders, gloves, sides, arms and legs. His motorbike was a flashy model, with metal tubes sticking out everywhere, wide chrome handlebars, a gleaming mauve fuel tank.

'Bad idea,' the motorbiker growled, baring a line of frightening teeth set in a bushy black beard. He shook his head and burped menacingly. Thick hair tumbled to his shoulders. Tilting the bike, he dropped a foot to the ground and looked down at the open car door, making strange shapes with his mouth.

Hawkley Castari stammered: 'S-s-s-sorry.'

In the driver's seat Wazim Bhatia was rolling his eyes, pushing his head back into the headrest, breathing in and out through his nose with annoyed whistles, and drumming on the steering wheel. The Volvo lights flashed from behind.

'I think yours is all right,' Hawkley Castari offered timidly, pointing. 'Your bike.'

The man glanced down. A sticker across the top of his petrol gauge said EVENHAM GROSS ANGELS in large, flaming letters. 'Bike never let me down yet,' he said gruffly. 'Your door looks like it'll live. It bounced. Lucky I got my brakes on fast.'

Wazim restarted the car. The biker weaved away. Hawkley

slammed the door shut and turned to him. 'I am sorry.'

'It's just that I keep having crashes when I get near this church, Hawk,' Wazim moaned. 'Last time my car got burnt to death.'

A moment later the other man had his head out of the window again, more cautiously this time. 'That's odd,' he was murmuring.

'What?'

'That biker turned into the church, too.'

The coach had pulled up just ahead, hazard lights flashing. Passengers were stepping off and being helped to the kerb by the driver. 'This is ridiculous – I've never heard of a traffic jam in Evenham,' Wazim said. 'We'll have to park.' He revved the engine, grabbed at the wheel and spun the car round in the centre of the road. They drove fifty yards, shot down a cul-de-sac and pulled in.

The two men jogged towards the church. 'Better to be on time,' Hawkley said, 'even if Derek Weston does wait for us. It's worse if he does, really.'

'Well—' Wazim began breathlessly, then let the rest of the sentence go.

When they got near the foot of the drive, Wazim Bhatia stopped. He looked up towards the church, then back at the cars in the street. The jam had thinned out. Two or three were parking where they could. 'You know – I'm not sure I'm ready for what I think I'm about to see,' he said suddenly. There was a small crowd near the door of the church.

Hawkley Castari was also looking down the road and up the drive. 'Are all these cars – these cars and coaches – are they all—'

'I think they might be,' said Wazim in a bemused tone. 'Otherwise – I mean, why would they all suddenly park? I can't understand this at all.'

At that moment a large number of Americans turned the corner into the drive. The two men were swept towards the church with them. The Americans were gesturing, admiring the wooden structure, pointing at the steeple, talking about the weather, laughing. Someone mentioned having watched a public appearance recently by President Clinton and her husband, and there was more laughter. Wazim Bhatia shot Hawkley Castari a confused glance. Hawkley whispered back, 'Wedding?' The head of the steering committee grimaced, as if he had even less idea than before.

Derek was at the door to greet them both. Wazim Bhatia stretched out a hand to shake his, and was knocked off balance by someone pushing. The vicar was smiling. His eyes were utterly unreadable. Hawkley Castari shook his hand too.

'Welcome,' Derek Weston said. 'Three minutes to spare.' People were pushing past them.

'Quite a crowd,' Hawkley put in, gesturing down the drive.

'And inside, too,' said Wazim, casting a fascinated glance into the gloomy interior of the church. There was a loud noise of conversation. 'It was mentioned on the traffic reports.'

'Inside?'

'The block-up down there.' Hawkley pointed.

The vicar swallowed and told them: 'We are – having a revival.'

Wazim Bhatia rubbed his hands together. 'Ah,' he said. He was wondering – had it been formally cleared?

Several more people brushed passed them, hurrying.

'Amazing,' Hawkley remarked slowly. 'We might have to be lowered in on a mat, through a hole in the roof.'

'That happened in the Bible,' the vicar said. 'Um – don't worry. We've got two seats saved for you.' He turned towards the entrance. 'Follow me.'

They did. Walked into the church, down the centre aisle behind Derek. Both glanced quickly about. The place was packed to the rafters. Hawkley nudged Wazim and pointed at a group taking up pews on their left, all in camouflage jackets, several with peculiar visored helmets in their laps. Wazim raised his eyebrows an inch, eyes popping. Hawkley ran his tongue round the inside of a cheek. Nudging him, Wazim nodded at forty or fifty at the far end of the church with instruments. A second later they saw more squeezed in large numbers off to the right of the pulpit. Wazim's eyebrows rose another inch. Hawkley shot glances left and right, right and left, left and right and left, searching for new surprises. There were plenty. A line of Asian men bunched in one pew. The long-haired biker with seven or eight others in leather, all staring up at the pulpit as if they thought it might suddenly move. Every single seat, every space full. Loud talking everywhere. People standing at the back. Some squashed so tight into pews they would not have been able to move their arms if they wanted to.

The vicar of St Saviour's church guided the two members of the Basildon diocese steering committee to their places, then vanished. Wazim sat and saw Judy Weston out of the corner of his eye, sitting diagonally across from him. He turned, inclined his head and gave her an uncomfortable smile. She returned it with a more relaxed one. He bent forward and started on a prayer. Hawkley Castari did the same.

Derek found Otis in the vestry. 'What are you doing?'

'I can't come out, Derek.'

'Why are you sitting there like that?'

'I don't want to see anyone.'

'Come on, Otis – for heaven's sake.'

'Exactly,' the curate said, taking his face out of his hands. 'This isn't for heaven's sake at all. This is for something else.'

The vicar said, with steel in his voice that Otis had never heard before, 'Let's work out whose sake it's for afterwards.'

Otis got to his feet. 'Well, exactly,' he said lamely. 'I know you're in charge of everything, but—'

'I'm in charge of sakes,' the vicar told him.

'—I know she's out there with her keyboard, for a start, as well, and I—'

'Are they all here? Have you had a look?'

Otis grimaced. 'It's full.'

'Did the karate folk come?'

'Ju Kwon Wok. Yes, one of them climbed in through a window. He said it was a precaution.'

'The crown bowling club?' The two of them were moving out of the vestry now, back towards the main body of the church.

'Yes, yes, them, they all seemed to swerve in through the

door, plus the paintball people or whatever you call them –
your son-in-law – the clothes they're wearing are going to
make people think there's some kind of bomb threat, or war. I
can't believe they did that, that camouflage. And all the people
on my mom and dad's coach tour, they're here too but a bit
confused, that's three coaches but they have to be gone by
lunch—'

'Right—' The vicar had stopped to tie a shoelace, and they
both heard a sudden swirl of music coming from beyond the
purple curtain in front of them. 'I saw the staff from the
Tandoori.'

'Well, they wanted that promise about the catering for the
next fête in writing. We got seventy orchestra people,' Otis
was saying quickly, 'and the Hell's Angels—'

'Evenham Angels—'

'—the Gross people came, whatever, they want you to say
a prayer for Rex Gobart—' Another roar of instrumentation
beyond the curtain left Otis goldfishing, mouthing inaudibly;
Derek looked away, towards the sound, sound getting louder,
sounds piled on sounds, then turned back to his curate: 'Let's
go, let's go through now,' he hissed urgently, wheeling round
in a single, sudden movement, thinking: *there is a pivotal
moment in the history of every church.*

His mind was racing. He reached for the purple curtain and
pulled it back.

27

Derek and Otis looked out at countless faces.   .

Otis, swerving off to the right like a deer caught in car beams, glimpsed the brooch on his mother's hat poking up behind the head of someone, way back, tiny.

He dropped into his seat in front of the choir, at full strength for the first time since the bout of communal flu; undid his jacket as the music dipped and the sound of talking stopped; heard Derek say a nervous word about a song by Jimmy Kendrix, a really rather good modern church songwriter just right for revivals—

They sang. Squashed together, the musicians played loud things, difficult things, things with twirls on! Otis saw arms sweep violently across two violins, as though it mattered so much – could hear the tops of voices being sung at, see mouths open so wide hymn-books would have fitted in them, in piles of ten, and – yes, there – Marshall Kampfner near the front, glancing about like a man who had spent his life proving the strength of gravity and had just seen something float in mid-air!

Otis wondered what on earth he had allowed himself to be drawn into, yet was amazed at the success of the efforts, in practice largely his, to pack the church – to stack it, he should say, because that was exactly what had happened . . . it had been stacked like rigged Las Vegas playing cards; getting all these people here, maybe two hundred and fifty, dressing the whole thing up as revival when all he could imagine was a huge lead curtain crashing down at the end of it all, a big light going out on them . . .

Click.

What kind of accident was about to happen? He should have

let Derek call it off after that telephone call. He should have! Stupid, stupid American! He should have made the vicar put a sign on the church door saying – saying anything: closed for lunch, closed for training, rain stopped play, play stopped work . . . *anything* . . .

Anything to avoid – what accident was coming? Was this – Derek Weston, singing a tune Otis could tell he hardly knew, standing with music swirling, leaping about him as if he was going to be suddenly sucked skywards – was this the end?

Otis shot frantic glances at him. The tic triggered again and again at his cheekbone. A vast juggernaut was bearing down on them. Was this the end of all their work, their visiting, the endless teas? Would the vicar who had lost his faith show it suddenly, show it was gone, perhaps by crying or confessing just as everyone fell silent for him, or passing round a note, or using some kind of clerical semaphore; would he pick up the lectern and chuck it at Wazim and Hawkley?

Bolt upright, the curate stared directly ahead. He could not move his eyes now, not even one eye. His face was concrete. One eye did move a bit, and he regretted it. He might see Charlotte. He knew where she was. Sitting off to the side. Blonde hair like incredible flax. Don't look. Some kind of keyboard on her lap. Stop it. He prayed in his mind he might suddenly be whisked back to America. The whole of America could never, never in a million years, be as terrifying as Evenham.

He realised he had failed: all his life, he had been failing. In the second song, something about dark clouds, Otis blamed himself for this awful pass they had come to, for the cast iron sky lodged overhead. He had had all the warning signs. He should have physically wrenched Derek away from his destiny, which seemed to be to bring his church, their church, crashing down around his ears, around both their ears, all four of their ears, in as public a way as possible – but no, instead Otis had just gone on sifting Biblical obscurities, praying morning and evening for the slightest things, concentrating on Old Testament geographical borders, too taken up with staring at the stars to notice the ground opening at his feet . . .

Someone walked to the front and said a prayer. Ruth Richards. He wondered if her frizzy ginger hair had frizzed with shock when she walked in and saw the church jam-packed.

They sang again. The Evenham Gross Angels were singing as loudly as anyone, swaying left and right disjointedly as if they had tried practising earlier in the week but got called away urgently to wreck a bus shelter. Amazing to see them there. Otis squinted over at them. Ruth had prayed about Rex, and at the back of the church one of them had grunted: 'Yes.'

For a minute all Otis could think of was how much he adored Charlotte Davidson, no matter what she had done. He loved her so utterly, so unutterably.

There was a reading. Sir Kenneth Gearey marched up, sober and serious. He stood erect in the pulpit, drew their attention to Matthew, to chapter thirteen.

'"The Son of Man will send out his angels, and they will weed out of his kingdom everything that causes sin and all who do evil."' He did a kind of bicycling motion with his shoulders, as if he was hoping to avoid being weeded. '"They will throw them into the fiery furnace, where there will be weeping and gnashing of teeth. Then the righteous will shine like the sun in the kingdom of their Father. He who has ears, let him hear."' Sir Kenneth coughed, turned the page. He was speaking out of a corner of his mouth. His jet black moustache shivered on the same side, like a safety curtain. He didn't so much read a text as mention it.

'"The kingdom of heaven is like treasure hidden in a field. When a man found it, he hid it again, and then in his joy went and sold all he had and bought that field."'

His moustache did another slight tremble in the gap between sentences.

'"Again,"' he read on, '"the kingdom of heaven is like a merchant looking for fine pearls. When he found one of great value, he went away and sold everything he had and bought it."' He slammed the book shut. Dust leapt off.

Otis happened to glance at George Foster at that moment, sitting two pews back. George was perpetually glancing

214

over his shoulder for some reason. Judy Weston appeared engrossed as Derek announced another song and the musicians started again, and he stood up, and Otis stood, and the congregation stood too.

The service ran on, boisterously. Eventually there was widespread rustling of clothes in seats and the Reverend Derek Weston walked towards the pulpit. He had a sheaf of dog-eared papers in his hands. He carefully plucked the first one off the top and put it on the lectern, dead-centre.

'Thank you all for coming,' he said; 'today,' he added quickly, as if to stress that most of them came every week. Perhaps every day.

His voice was leaden, Otis thought, heart pounding. What was he going to do?

The curate wiped sweat from his brow. He pushed his hands together to stop them shaking. Derek sounded flat, toneless. If this was the sermon the vicar claimed would summarise the whole Bible into a single word, he had better leave the word quite late.

Otis felt his heart lurch with the thought: if the church closed today, he had lost her for ever.

'And thank you, Sir Kenneth Gearey, for that reading.' That was Derek.

There was a pause, in the middle of which someone sneezed.

Otis sensed the unprecedented size of the congregation. He sensed it in the form of a tingle running up his spine.

Derek Weston cleared his throat and wiped a hand on the edge of his jacket. He rearranged his posture. Then he bent closer to the lectern, hands gripping the metal rim. He began to speak as if reading a printed script word for word.

'The reason for our ministry,' the vicar began heavily, 'is to spread a certain type of good news which is better than any headline you may recently have read in the newspapers. It is better than any news you will ever have been told by relatives or friends. It is better than hearing your horse has won a race, or that your house has been selected for council refurbishment. And for those of you hearing it for the first

215

time,' he read, 'it will sound as exciting as first news of your O-level results.'

Derek paused, looked up, and added, 'GCSEs, I should say.'

Otis shifted in his seat and caught sight of Charlotte. She was staring straight at him. He jerked his head away.

'We are here,' Derek Weston was saying, 'to focus briefly on who exactly Jesus Christ was, what exactly he said, and why exactly he said it.'

Flicking at a page corner, he went on: 'Today, my sermon is entitled "The Pearl of Great Price". It's actually,' he added, looking up again, 'a theme I discover I preached on at the very start of my time here.'

In the front row Judy Weston's head jerked up an inch, no more.

The packed church was hushed.

'We all need a centre,' Derek read on. 'No one wins at roulette by chucking a steel ball around a frying pan. You have to have the right centre. The roulette ball needs the roulette wheel, and the human being who wants to win at the game of life needs to spin around the person of Jesus Christ.'

Otis felt a crease appear in his brow.

'He came to earth to save those of us who cannot save ourselves, which is all of us. His love was the most profound love anyone can ever be given. We are all sinners, however much those of us with successful professional or family backgrounds, and clean driving licences, and perhaps degrees or golf cups, or interesting anecdotes, or premium bonds, may believe otherwise. All of us.'

Otis rubbed his chin. Derek seemed to be sighing a lot as he spoke. The curate was beginning to find the sighs curiously moving.

'Christ's words, his life, are worth giving everything for. That's why the Bible calls them a pearl. If you have them, and if you know him, you wouldn't swap that for all the tea in China. You wouldn't swap that with all the ham in Evenham, or all the chess in Chessington. You wouldn't swap it with anything, no matter how high the value. You wouldn't swap your knowledge of him for a Gauguin or a Matisse – certainly not a Dali – nor for a mint Penny Black, or a tiara, or for all the popularity in the world. You wouldn't swap it for a lifetime seat in the Royal Albert Hall.'

Somewhere, someone sniggered. The snigger was followed by a high-pitched shriek halfway towards the back of the church. Otis screwed up his eyes and saw Phyllis Childs fumbling with her hearing-aid. The vicar seemed to be reading every word, he thought, turning back towards the pulpit. Reading them carefully, like a civil servant with a press statement. Where had this sermon suddenly appeared from? Had it been ghosted by one of those roving preachers? Commissioned from some bright spark on a Christian magazine? Where was all this emanating from?

'When I found God,' the vicar continued, 'it was in a hall of some sort. I didn't much notice the hall, I must say. All I noticed was that I was suddenly being told a truth I had never before acknowledged. The speaker was from Peru. That didn't matter. It was like a brilliant light. This happened relatively recently.'

He glanced up quickly, adding: 'I say recently. Recently in terms of the seventies.' Derek looked down at the script again, and breathed in. 'I was told, by this Peruvian man, that nothing I could do to better myself would ever be sufficient to bring me close to God, and to be close to God was the highest aim of any life – being close to Jesus Christ, knowing Christ. I think of it as being close to the centre, being correctly centred, having a centre, having the pearl of greatest price . . .'

Otis blinked.

It went on for another fifteen minutes. Then Derek seemed to have come to the bottom of his text, because he suddenly halted, looked under the page he was reading and saw there was nothing to follow it. The vicar seemed to get confused about what to say or do next, and glanced around.

Helpfully, music started. Derek retreated. He turned and stepped slowly down from the pulpit as they sang a final hymn. The curate kept his eyes glued to Derek's face, saw it glistening. He swung his gaze over different faces in the front row. Wazim and Hawkley were exchanging glances over the edges of their songbooks.

Then it was over. Over! Otis felt his shirt drip with relief. He stood up so fast he spent a moment swaying, dizzily: it had been an incredible sermon – incredible, just dazzling . . . impact completely understated . . . the appeal towards the end . . . three points he could remember even now . . . what had happened since that telephone call when Derek said he had lost his faith? Had he suddenly found it again?

There was a milling of people near the vicar. Otis felt panic grip his arms, one at a time starting with the left, then his legs as well. He even felt one of his toes gripped by panic, and gave it a wiggle in case it set in. He was thinking of Charlotte. Some musicians were still playing. Others were getting to their feet, shoving instruments into bags and boxes. He told himself not to look. He stood wondering what to do.

A blast of motorbiker's breath hit his right ear.

'Can I have a word?'

It was the tallest Evenham Gross Angel, the barrel-chested one in studded leathers with the long black hair and bushy beard.

'Yes,' Otis said, conscious of his American accent. 'Y-yes. Of course, sir.' He picked up a slight whiff of alcohol.

'Wanted to talk about all that,' the man said, gesturing over at the crowd at the front of the church. 'The talk.'

'Yes, the sermon,' Otis said. 'Of course.' He geared himself up for abuse, and got ready to drop into a self-defence position he had seen on cable television.

The man scratched a sideburn.

Finally, he said: 'Yup. Well, I've got the bike, I've got the road licence, the tax disc – you know, all of that – but I – I don't know. I just feel I'm missing something.'

'Right,' the curate agreed. He tried to scratch one of his own sideburns, then realised he did not have any. 'Um – an anti-theft device?'

'Eh?'

'What you're missing,' Otis said. 'I'm trying to help you find—'

'No. Not that. I've got an immobiliser.'

'Really? What, an electronic one? Zinc batteries?'

'With a combination.'

'But can't that particular model be broken into by one of those—'

'Look,' the motorbiker cut in, 'I mean, leaving out the engineering stuff for a minute, it's this God bit. This – um – this, well, this Christ thing.' He glanced absently around the church. 'Dunno if you know, mate – all of us was helped by a chap called Rex, friend of the vicar's, you see, and—'

'I was told, yes.'

'Gobart. Saved our bikes. Then he tried the other way of climbing down a staircase. Snuffed it. Hit us hard, it has. It's just that I – I feel I might've done some of these – of these – um – spins – the – the – ah – geezer was on about.'

'Spins?'

'I thought he said spins.'

'Sins, I think.'

'Well, sins then.'

'And – you say this geezer was on—' Otis had not remembered seeing an oil well at the service.

'A hundred revs per minute, or whatever you call him.'

'Oh, okay, right, the Reverend,' Otis said, feeling like a telephone engineer trying different connections. 'Reverend Weston.' His mind kept zooming to Charlotte. Was she about to leave, walk out for ever? Was that it? He was sure he would never see her again if she did. Why did these things always come in pairs, like double-decker buses? Here he was, standing next to the first convert he could remember in a place that had managed fewer conversions over the years than a one-legged rugby team—

'I suggest we pray together,' he said suddenly. Bravely, he thought.

The two bowed their heads near the front of the church. He hoped Charlotte was watching, but somehow knew she would not be. There were a lot of people bunched near them. Otis let one eye pop open and swivelled it in the socket, but he could not see anyone looking. 'God,' he began, 'we pray together now. I pray that—' he paused for a moment, and glanced up. 'I'm sorry. I never caught your name.'

219

The motorbiker kept his head down, eyes closed. 'Smasher,' he murmured.

'I pray,' Otis began again, 'for Mr Smasher. I pray that you will forgive his wrongdoings, as you forgive everyone who puts their trust in you.'

'Yes,' said Smasher.

He asked: 'Mr Smasher, do you trust in God?'

'Yes,' said Smasher.

For a second they both looked up at each other. The motorbiker leant over, and whispered at the curate: 'Lady had one of them.' He stuck his tongue against his front teeth and blew a high-pitched whistle between them. 'Wanna pray for that.'

'One of—' Otis copied the whistle '—one of them, you say?'

The motorbiker leant further forward and whispered a word in the curate's ear. Otis looked up instantly, startled. 'Really?'

'Yes,' said Smasher. His face brimmed with feeling. The bristles of his beard stood up. The crowd was still milling around them. There was a lot of talking. The curate reached forward and put a hand on the man's arm.

After a couple of minutes, Smasher said a prayer. He promised something about being a better person, and doing less smashing. He made general references to causing trouble, then brought in two instances of overtaking on blind corners and one of threats to the owner of a fish and chip shop, including a reference to hot batter.

Otis listened, hearing the man thank his creator as if a channel had suddenly been flushed clear, and reeling at the vivid sense of the present that seemed to swish past his ears like sea sounds gushing from a giant shell. Eyes goggling, wondering how much of what was real he had missed, he gazed about the building.

The musicians were all gone or going. He was supposed to be meeting his parents. He could not see them. He felt a light touch on his arm.

It was Marion Davidson, standing beside and slightly below him. She pointed at the motorbiker and mouthed something.

Otis paused. The motorbiker looked up. He had bright blue eyes.

The curate smiled. 'Thanks for coming over.'

The biker sniffed, one very long sniff. He seemed not to be in a mood to go, so Otis Cheeseman turned to Marion Davidson and said: 'Sorry. Go ahead.'

'It's just that I wanted to have a quick – er – thing with you about my daughter,' Marion told him in a low hiss. Otis drew his face level with hers, slowly. The building was emptying.

Her voice seemed to grow gradually more distinct.

'I had a chat with Charlotte and I just wanted to say I'm sorry,' she said.

Smasher was looking on, scratching his beard vacantly, but Otis was barely aware of him.

'Oh,' the curate said.

'She told me – er – things. You know, you two.'

'Right,' he said. He wondered if that joke of his about peanut mousse had leaked somehow. 'Oh, dear.'

'Whatever it is, God'll sort it,' Smasher said suddenly. 'He'll fix it. He'll do it. Trust, that's all I've got to say. He'll fix everything.'

Simultaneously, they both said, 'Thank you.'

Grinning, Otis added: 'Not absolutely everything, though.'

Smasher smiled at Marion and said: 'Smasher,' reaching out a hand.

She shook it. 'Marion Peterson.' She turned back to Otis. 'Charlotte's been upset,' she began, 'and you're obviously distressed too, and I just wanted to say what a shame it is and how I feel for you, you know, both of you equally, in these awful cases when you both love each other and it doesn't work properly.'

Otis emitted a low-pitched whistle. A horrifying thought squelched across the surface of his mind. Had he misheard the confession about the million boyfriends?

'I used to think she was someone who always had a thousand boyfriends,' Marion Davidson went on. 'But I was wrong. She was really set on you.'

Smasher leant forward, brushed the back of his hand on the front of the curate's jacket. 'She was wrong,' he said.

221

'Well—' Otis began, trying to sound casual, 'I wonder where she is.'

'Oh, she's gone, I think,' said Marion Davidson. 'A quick goodbye and that was it. I couldn't get through the crowd in time. I just gave her a wave over the tops of heads. They've all gone off in their coach.'

'Where to?'

'I don't know. It just revved up and went.'

'What's the coach look like?' the motorbiker asked.

Marion said: 'Big, green I think, with the word PEGASUS on the side. I suppose she's heading towards the M25.'

Otis was about to fold his face into the most drastic and final of grimaces, with gritted teeth, when his upper arm was snatched at by Smasher and he was pulled towards the entrance. The man was saying something the curate could not hear. He was bundled through a crowd at the door. Someone shouted: 'Otis! Are you being kidnapped?' The curate looked over his shoulder and called back: 'No. He has just become a Christian.'

'Get on,' Smasher said half a minute later.

'What – this?' Otis looked down at the huge motor-bike, chrome handlebars reaching dramatically into the air like horns.

He was being handed a helmet. 'Shove this on,' said the big man in leather.

'All the way on?'

'Don't be rocky. I can tell. You've made the biggest mistake of your—'

The bike revved at the very moment the curate hit the back of the seat, reaching forward with his arms and linking hands around the front of the biker's barrel chest, gasping as all cylinders fired under him, Smasher's booted foot pumping down on the accelerator as if they were being chased by gangs of thugs split-seconds behind them, then a roar and the thing sliding off its stand, back wheel bumping on the ground, jerking forwards—

They tore down the drive, screamed round at the end of it, gravel flying everywhere, went left down the road outside the church; Otis heard the biker shout, 'If they hit the M25, we won't—' the wind and roar of the engine swiping the rest of his words; on a corner he was almost tossed off the back, paralysed with fear, with all-out exhilaration, freezing gusts sweeping across his neck, the noise of the bike deafening him; they shot down the centre lane of Evenham High Street, slalomed in and out of a line of cars going at tortoise speed as Otis's head bounced left and right . . .

The members of the Sidney Chalet North-East Youth Orchestra were rumbling down a narrow slip road on to the last stretch of the Evenham bypass. The driver picked up speed along the left lane of the mile-long stretch of road, looked in his tall rectangular convex mirror, and put on Classic FM. The glance at the mirror, as Bach started playing, made him the first to see the big machine bearing down on the middle lane behind them. There was a huge man in black seated behind the widespread handlebars, and a second helmet that seemed to wobble in and out of vision at his rear.

The cellist in the back seat nearest to the roadside window looked up from her magazine as the motorbike and its passengers drew level with the window.

'Hey – look!'

Everyone looked. The motorbiker had started waving at the coach, left-handed, like a traffic policeman. The passenger seemed to be hanging on for dear life. The coach driver did a swift double-take, then stamped on the accelerator; an instant later the motorbiker was back level with the side of the coach, waving furiously.

All the musicians were staring out of the window, some standing up in the centre aisle of the coach. 'I think it's a hijack,' squealed one. Someone shouted: 'No way are they getting my trumpet!'

A panicked voice cried: 'We're all going to be kidnapped and held for ransoms!'

'I might have to stop!' the driver called. Now the biker had switched on a klaxon that was playing a deafening musical tune in a series of ear-splitting squawks. 'I might have to stop!' the driver called again, even louder. The coach was swerving. The man on the motorbike was hovering nearer the front end of it, making frenzied cutting motions with his left arm, a curtain of black hair streaming from the bottom edge of his crash helmet. The coach went faster; the bike slipped back.

It was at that moment that Charlotte Davidson, leaning over in her seat on the right of the central aisle, halfway down the coach, drew breath. The figure on the back of the motorbike, clinging on for dear life, was wearing a jacket she was suddenly sure she recognised. The helmeted head flicked in her direction, pressed to the back of the man in leather – and she knew in that instant whose terrified eyes were behind the visor; realised much more than that, too, all of a sudden jumping up in her seat and shouting: 'Stop the coach now!'

They hit the hard shoulder at fifty, sending up a spray of pebbles and dust. The motorbike spun round in front of the coach as it slowed, almost throwing the back passenger off the side as it stopped dead. When the coach came to a halt, the driver jumped out. 'Police?' he said.

'Nope,' said Smasher, pushing up his visor. 'Heaven's Angels.'

The driver seemed about to say something, but he was breathless and someone had moved past him so he looked at her instead. Charlotte jogged towards the passenger on the back of the bike. He pulled off his helmet.

They did not say anything. Knock-kneed, the curate of St Saviour's church, Evenham, fumbled his way off the padded leather seat and gave Charlotte Davidson the biggest hug he had ever given anyone. Perhaps the only hug he had ever given anyone: he could not, at that moment, remember any previous hugs. One of his trouser legs was hitched halfway up his leg: he did not, at that moment, notice. She kissed him on the cheek, stopped him saying something about a terrible mistake even as the words were beginning to form in his mouth; they hugged again, him holding her so tightly and managing to say, just, 'I was so wrong. I was in error. I made a mistake. I'm so sorry.'

They looked into each other's eyes.

She looked down. 'Your ankle is bandaged.'

'I was attacked by a spaniel,' he told her.

From inside the coach there was a lingering, echoing sound.

Faces pressed to the windows, the orchestra members were calling, 'Aaaaaaaaaaaaaah,' calling it all together and almost in tune, certainly enough in tune for it to be recognised by the curate's windblown ears as the most wonderful music he had heard, ever, anywhere in the world. He shivered. It seemed to him, looking into Charlotte's twinkling eyes, as though angels were singing at full volume, heaven's angels; and even when Otis Cheeseman applied his painstaking and scientific mind to that sloppy and impressionable thought, he could not be completely certain they were not.

A car skidded to a halt on the hard shoulder. A yellow Morris Minor.

George Foster sprang out of the driver's side door as a giant truck screamed past, horn blaring.

His face was crimson. He leapt towards the motorbiker and seized him by loose folds of leather around his shoulder-blades, yelling at the top of his voice: 'I am hereby making a citizen's arrest on this man for the wilful destruction of a marquee.'

Every head turned. The next half minute might have been ten years. Traffic went on roaring past. They all stared and stared. Later, Otis Cheeseman reflected that there are some rare circumstances in life which, no matter when they arise or how many people they involve, have the potential to leave all concerned feeling they were just not born equipped to deal with them.

– 28 –

'So you'll let us know, will you?'

Derek Weston could not help the nervous smile that came to his face as he twiddled a pencil at his desk and heard the question echo in his head for the umpteenth time.

And what had been the reaction of Wazim and Hawkley? It was hard to tell from looking at their faces, for sure. But then that was their job, to make things hard to tell. The Bible was hard to tell, and they worked for the Bishop of Basildon. If things got any easier to tell, whole layers of staff at HQ might have to be made redundant. So Derek Weston had never expected to be able to read their faces as they walked out of the church and he asked them the most important question in the world.

Wazim Bhatia and Hawkley Castari had simply replied, in unison: 'Yes, we will.'

The end of all things is at hand.

Perhaps it was not at hand any longer. No, perhaps it was not at hand at all. The vicar was sifting things in his mind. He wondered if he had lurched into a thornless rosebed, solved everything in his own sweet way among the blossoms – using an old sermon from the back of the television set, reading it without even listening to what he was saying . . . maybe he never needed a pearl. Maybe no one did. Maybe being a vicar was nothing to do with pearls. Maybe the whole thing was just a matter of reading things out with a straight face.

George Foster rang. Derek imagined the old man's eyes popping at the other end of the line.

'Everything okay with you this Monday morning, George?' In his mind, a shutter in his brain clicked on a hundred images from yesterday. Otis's parents asking where he had got to,

Derek suddenly wondering if his curate had resigned, Jeff and Caroline and those outdoor people of theirs, all barging out in camouflage suits—

'Yup, chum. Right as rain.' George's voice cut across his thoughts.

'You're not too unhappy about the business with the marquee chap?'

'Not at all, Derek. It's all been explained to me. We're letting him off the strimmer because he's had a change of heart.'

'I think that's right.' Otis had told him the moving story: how the biker had been racked with secret guilt after his girlfriend's abortion, how he said he had felt it slip away as the two of them prayed together.

George Foster said: 'Fourteen conversions total, someone told me.'

The vicar was thinking. *How could that happen? Nothing for years, and then I read out a crumpled bit of history and get fourteen?* He wished he had listened better, then suddenly thought: *my church is safe, I have saved it.*

'Hello? You still there?'

'Yes, George. Sorry.' Thrilled in that instant, he had begun to plan – plan bigger summer fêtes, perhaps one or two school governorships, uncuttable marquee guy-ropes. 'Hey – actually,' the vicar went on, 'one of those conversions we're not sure about. It was a chap called Allan Hottie, who's known in the Surrey area. He's been up to the front at more than seventy services around the county. There was an article about him somewhere, *Third Way* magazine I think, saying he was part of a new problem in the church. Serial converters, they were calling them. It's the attention, you see. But otherwise—'

'Otherwise, wonderful!' George Foster called. 'I spent the whole morning rearranging the books and putting the spare chairs back in the hall. Some of those Bibles hadn't even been opened before, you know. Oh, and there was a young lassie there for the first time who says she's going to keep coming. It's just marvellous, marvellous to have the place used for the purposes of our Saviour once again, after all these years of

227

– um—' he seemed to trail off, as if unprepared for his own bluntness.

'You're right,' the vicar said decisively. 'Don't worry. You're right.'

After the call, he stared out of the window for ages.

He could not help it.

Try as he might to be sober and reflective about the whole thing, the fact was that he had pulled a stroke of sheer raw brilliance and saved his church with it.

I can't help thinking it . . .

All those worries about having the pearl, having the centre to it all, being in touch with the purity of God, having the pulse of conviction – they all seemed obsolete. Leaving aside the contents of a crumpled sermon fished from a television, the fact was that he had pulled off a vast, personal triumph unaided.

For the first time in weeks, Derek Weston laughed freely.

He pulled out a piece of paper and wrote a list of things he would do when they told him the church was safe and the whole wretched business was over.

1. ORGANISE A PARTY WITH ALL THE LOCAL COUNCIL-LORS, ETC
2. READ THE BIBLE A BIT
3. BUY JUDY A NEW HAT TO CELEBRATE (+ FRENCH MEAL?)
4. TAKE CAROLINE AND JEFF OUT TO CINEMA/PLAY/ BOWLING
5. READ SHAKESPEARE, LEARN TO JUGGLE

He looked at the list and frowned, deciding it was hopelessly pedestrian. So he added, in large strokes of the pen:

6. DANGEROUS SPORTS, e.g. HANG-GLIDING

How strange the whole thing had been – how utterly terrifying at times. He cast his mind back to the start, to the fête. In some ways it had been like 'wax' hang-gliding. He had risen and risen, coming closer and closer to the heavens, but then had had his wings scorched right off him. Would he ever get to the bottom of that pearl business?

In odd, freakish moments he managed to convince himself he had never had the gem in the first place. Sir Kenneth Gearey did not even mention it when they met before the service – not even when he was shown the Bible reading, which Derek had hoped might prompt him to blurt something out. But then again, looking at his own faith, which had sprung up years back in that dingy hall with that dingy Peruvian, and then abruptly disappeared . . . well, had that not been the same? So soon after feeling its presence and power, had Derek not found himself hunting the carpets of his heart for it, probing pockets in his soul, desperately trying to remember what shape the thing was, wondering if it had all been a trick of the light?

The vicar felt comfortably middle-aged. He had saved his church, he had kept his wife. Charlotte Davidson, whose spiritual devotion he had semi-idolised, had probably left yesterday semi-satisfied he semi-shared it. The vicar had, staggeringly, proved it possible to invigorate a church with sermons prepared some time earlier. He could find out little bits to do with God as the years went by. There was certainly no urgency now.

But later that afternoon, something disturbed his new serenity.

Out walking to post a letter, Derek saw a figure strolling down the street towards him. The blurred outline was familiar. He stopped, put on his glasses. The figure waved and came into focus at the same time.

'Derek!'

'Helen! Hello.' The vicar of St Saviour's and the vicar of St Paul's both stamped their feet involuntarily, their breath joining as mist in the cold air.

'We'd better not do that,' she said. 'Price of stamps has gone up.'

The joke was too obscure for Derek, who just said: 'Faster letters.'

There was a miniature, embarrassed silence between them.

Then he asked: 'You're well, are you? You look well.'

'I am well. Thank you. Bless God! Everything all right with you?'

'Yes, thanks.'

'Judy? I haven't seen her for a while.'

'Oh, yes. Yes, very good. She's off in Bristol today, actually.'

Helen glanced around at the trees and homes. 'Nice road, isn't it?'

'Yes, very pleasant,' he said chattily. 'We had our visit from Wazim and Hawkley yesterday, of course, which was a trial, but we had quite a few turn up, and there were several questions afterwards.'

A quizzical expression passed across Helen Silverstone's face. 'Visit from—?'

'The bish bosh lot,' said Derek genially, winking. 'The – ah – competition.'

She said: 'A visit from the competition?'

He coughed into a fist, thinking: *this conversation could go on until the next Labour government*. 'No, no,' he said, 'no, not the competition visit. The visit from Wazim Bhatia and Hawkley Castari, as part of the competition. Ha, ha.'

'Right,' she said, laughing too. 'They've moved, have they?'

'Moved?'

'To a rival – what, a rival denomination?'

The cold weather has frozen the left side of her brain. Just leave it, Derek told himself. So for a while they talked about a new West End play about obesity written by two well-known Christian writers, who had put in three nudity scenes to attract a wider audience. Helen Silverstone said it was disgraceful and misguided. 'We may not have a huge number of worshippers at St Paul's,' she went on, 'but at least they know what they are getting what they arrive. It's strictly clothes-on.'

She may not have a huge number of – Derek's heart danced! He grinned as he gave whatever answer it was to whatever point it was she had just made . . . the vicar scolded himself as he did it, but he was picturing St Paul's empty as Wazim and

Hawkley strode in with wide clipboards and red pens; empty barring Helen, of course, and maybe Mickey, and a couple of cleaners, and perhaps someone in the corner doing daring drama in a desperate effort to push up the numbers . . .

Welcome to the Mouse House, someone was telling them.

But when they parted, Derek Weston was momentarily disturbed. Had the Bishop of Basildon's office not yet paid a visit to her church? And if they had not, might she still have time to double her congregation, perhaps employing the kind of artificial methods another vicar, not so very far from her, had used?

For several minutes the thought ticked away in his mind, a metronome. It was not the case at all that he wanted her out, but it was fairer for her to go. She could pick up any job anywhere, political correctness being what it was. He had once been at a dinner party where someone called Guy Chapman was introduced as 'Person Person-Person'. Well, she could take advantage of all that. Helen Silverstone could probably walk into an archbishop's office and demand his hat, and he would have to hand it over. As for Derek – he would not even be able to put in a request to borrow a spare pair of slippers.

What was that joke? Man in hospital ward told by a doctor there's bad and good news, and which does he want first? The bad news? Well, we've had to take off both your legs. The good news – the fellow in the next bed wants to buy your slippers.

Derek was the man who had only ever had the bad news. That was why he had no reservations about fighting to win. Helen was the born winner. All Derek Weston had ever wanted was to avoid dying a loser.

29

The ball spun down the alley and careered into the pack of skittles at the end, smacking the middle one dead-centre.

'Strike! Strike!' they all shouted. Derek peered at the fallen pins. *All down.* Good grief. He turned, chuckling. He could not remember ever doing that before.

He had taken the place of Otis on a Tuesday night bowling trip in Windsor with the youth group and choir, arranged weeks ago to coincide with college half-terms. Otis, for some reason, was away. With his parents, probably. Derek did not particularly mind; the fight was over. Ken O'Driscoll was in the vicarage study, doing the parish newsletter on the computer. Ken was hard work. This, on the other hand, was not.

'Well done, Derek! Everyone a winner!'

'Strike!' the vicar laughed. 'No effort! Everyone a sinner!'

Adrian Pilmer, a student at the newly-named University of Sheffield Ring Road, chattered. How was Judy? 'Oh,' Derek replied, 'away in Bristol, on business. She took off on Sunday night, in fact.'

'Took off? How was she travelling?'

'She took off in the sense of going by car.'

'It sounded like you were going to say she was on a space rocket, or something.'

'It certainly looked like a car.'

'All aboard,' Adrian laughed. 'It was a terrific service on Sunday.'

'Thank you.'

'Terrrrrrr-ific. Creamer. Most fun since the Madrigals.'

'Oh. Thanks.'

'Have you thought about building an extension?'

'Well – not really. You never know if these things are one-offs, or lift-offs.' His mind was still on rockets. 'We have pebbledashing at the back,' he added.

Adrian put in, 'There was a rumour about you two leaving.'

'Spare!' someone shouted at the scoring desk.

'Eh?' The vicar looked over, momentarily anguished. *Spare?*

'It's a bowling term,' explained Adrian. 'No, this rumour was—'

'Extremely vicious, that's all. We're not, I can promise you,' he laughed. Claire Stupples, who had been eavesdropping by a plastic chair, spun around and said: 'Oh, Derek, that's wonderful news! I know how hard it's been for you.'

Quite how the structure of that particular form of words took effect he did not know, but the vicar felt his whole frame suffuse with pride and relief. 'Thank you so much, Claire.' There was a lot of bowling noise around them – balls, skittles, laughter. His laughter, too. She moved around a bit in her billowing flowered trousers and blushed, telling him in a demure and unpunctuated sentence: 'Well Ruth sends her love and everything as well.'

Ken was gone when the vicar returned to his vicarage.

Derek poked his head around the study door, saw the computer screen still glowing in the darkness and muttered to himself, 'Yup. Thanks for turning it off, Ken.' He would have dealt with it at that moment, but the telephone rang.

'Derek?'

A long-distance voice. Bristol. Judy.

'Hello, my dearest. How's it going?'

'Have you had the news yet, Derek?'

'No, not even a murmur.' He thought of Helen Silverstone in that instant, of their strange conversation yesterday. *Best not to mention it*, he decided.

'What happened after the service?'

'Oh,' he said, 'much. I want to tell you all about it.'

'I saw some people praying.'

233

'Yes. Well, one had something caught in his eye, but the rest were.'

'I wish I hadn't had to scoot off in the afternoon.'

'Oh, never mind that,' he said. 'Don't worry about it. Everyone has to take off sometimes.'

'I had a chat with Marion Davidson,' Judy said innocently.

I had a chat with Marion Davidson . . . the words echoed painfully in the vicar's head, striking all kinds of bum notes. He said: 'Um – Peterson, do you mean?'

'Derek,' Judy began stiffly, 'don't be so childish. It all came out, because I saw her give Charlotte a most obvious wave across the church afterwards. It made me look twice. They've got the same face. You don't have to try to cover it up.'

The vicar inhaled deeply. 'Well, things were different between you and me then.'

'I know.'

'They just rolled up. Her and her husband Clive. Through the door one day. You weren't there. I felt I had to do something.'

'You can't go around covering up Davidsons in churches.'

'I know, Judy.'

'You can't. This isn't Watergate, you know. You're not Nixon.'

There was a moment's silence between them.

'Nixon of Nock Green,' he joked, at long last. 'But it wasn't so much a cover-up, as a – well, yes, I do know. But I was—' He wanted to say he was terrified. 'I was anxious. About us.' There was a crackle on the line, followed by a series of quick pips.

Judy's voice came back louder than before. 'As you say, those were different times. I feel my whole life has changed, Derek. I really have been so excited, thinking about it here in Bristol. Darling, do you think we should leave Evenham?'

'Leave it?' The question stunned him. *Leave the squash?*

'Could we serve God better elsewhere, do you think?'

'Elsewhere, Judy?' *Serve God?* 'After we've managed to – to win all of them over, to—'

'Derek, Derek, you're speaking to your wife, you know! Not Wazim or Terence or any of the others! I've seen what

234

you've put yourself through, these last few weeks. It's been really hard for us both.'

'Maybe in a couple of years, four or five years, we can see if we—'

'I'm not making the old plea here, to move closer to the office. Not at all. In fact I've been thinking whether there even ought to be an office.'

'No office? What, you want to work outdoors?'

'I'm wondering about the whole integrity of credit banking, Derek. I really meant what I told you the other day. Everything we've been through – it's made me focus on the person of Jesus Christ. I've begun to understand what it means to have the past washed, like plates. And I've kind of – returned to my roots, I suppose, if I ever had them. Really, darling. That's what I want to spend the rest of my life following. I've made up my mind. Here in Bristol, I've been making it up.'

The vicar felt himself begin to tremble. 'All I say is, let's just—'

'You know what he said, Derek? "I have come that they may have life, and have it to the full." That was what Christ said. And—'

'"A man's life does not consist in the abundance of his possessions."'

'Exactly.'

'Luckily for us.'

After a pause she breathed in unevenly, adding softly: 'Our lives, Derek. We've got to follow it. Him. Together, the two of us.' She paused. 'Derek, think about what was in that sermon you read out. Think about what you were telling them.'

Yes, the vicar thought, *but there's no need to go around having that effect on people every day of the week*. He ran a nervous hand through his hair. *I am not going to go bald*. They talked about Caroline and Jeff for a minute, about a new toll system for people who wanted to jump off Clifton suspension bridge, about perhaps having the vicarage cladded because of VAT on fuel . . . Derek's mind was elsewhere.

He felt rebellious, suddenly. He and Judy would be asked

to stay, and he was going to tell them they were staying, and that was that. *Wives, obey your husbands*. It did not matter what zany ideas she had. All these wild cards she was dealing, like a croupier on crack – serving God better, the integrity of credit banking; what on earth was Judy throwing all this around for now? Things had got so good between them, ever since he had

No, he did not want to complete that sentence.

He did not want to complete that sentence at all.

Ever since I found the pearl.

He kicked himself for completing it.

He booted himself for completing it.

In the kitchen, the vicar heaped some baked beans into a pan and warmed them on the stove until they sizzled. A slice of toast popped up black. He scraped burnt parts into the sink with a kitchen knife. Well, one thing relieved him. Getting that silly Peterson business out of the way was a weight off his mind. He had not expected Judy to be so forgiving on it.

He ate from a tray by the electric fire, one bar glowing the same orange as the beans. Important to save money on heating. The cladding was a good idea. As long as it wasn't that DSC stuff. He did not want his vicarage looking like a birthday cake. Well, anyway, the diocese would do it. He was sure they would find the necessary funding. The bishop could use some of the money saved with his huge economy drive.

The television flickered, still blurred without the lost sermons its electronics had become so used to, but Derek made out footballers on a field and followed the game for a bit after putting on his glasses. Then he thought of the computer Ken had left on in the study, slid the tray to one side and walked across the hallway.

Clearing his throat, Derek felt for the light switch.

He turned on the light and walked over to the computer.

He had a look at whatever it was Ken had left on the screen. Something to do with polo necks for Christmas – ah, yes, now that had been a clever suggestion from Charles Mannox-Lloyd and he was jolly glad to see it going ahead. The vicar hit a key and a green border appeared around the words, covered them, flipped and shrank.

Now, let me see if I can remember how this thing turns off
. . . a long list of files unfurled down the right edge of the
screen in a grey-cornered cube. The cursor blinked on one
of them. Derek pressed a key and it dropped five lines with
a series of bleeps. Frustrated, he hit *Return*.

That threw a different file on to the screen, a short
paragraph all in capitals with a date in red at the top.

'Silly. Come on,' the vicar whispered genially to himself.
He was about to hit F7 or F8, which he was now certain was
the way out, when the first line of the block of print on the
screen caught his eye.

Derek Weston read the words, and his stomach turned
over.

30

Otis Cheeseman was not, as it happened, with his parents at all.

Charlotte Davidson was not with hers.

Gasping, they had just finished the long walk up hundreds of stairs to the top of Durham Cathedral. There they talked, gazed down at the city peninsula mapped out beneath them – and, a couple of times, kissed.

'I'm so sorry,' the curate kept saying.

'Sorry for what? I'm not sorry, Otty. It's nicer to make up, you know, than never have a row. I just thought you'd gone for ever. Back to Arizona. Whoosh. Zip.'

'I got too bogged down in detail,' Otis said. 'I've been so selfish.'

'You keep saying that. You haven't – not half as selfish as me, anyway.'

'And argumentative.'

'You haven't.'

'I have.'

'No, you've not.'

'Have too.'

She giggled. A man in train-spotting glasses turned and looked.

Charlotte and Otis wandered over to one corner of the towertop and leant against the cold wall together, heads poking over the thick stone lip, fringes ruffled by the breeze, looking miles down and across and away.

'Derek's weird,' the curate said, at last.

'I know.'

'I still can't believe that service. It sounded like one of our preachers, a fellow called Wraggage from Vegas who got arrested for making things up. Perhaps he lifted it straight out of a theological textbook.' He laughed loudly.

'Perhaps he did. Have you lent him one?'

Otis grinned. 'My books are all too stodgy. I've even got one called *The Significance of Beds in the Prophecies of Micah.* Now that's what you'd call—'

'Do you think he's been happy?'

The curate paused before answering. 'I guess he's – he's lived.' He went on, quietly: 'These last few weeks, he's been living like he never has before. Really! He's been – I don't know how else to put it – he's just – it's been a bit like – like someone's connected him to a power point, or something. Just – I don't know – he's just been so completely caught up in it all. Before, all he was interested in was taking things easy, playing squash, walks, the odd film. Then suddenly he gets completely caught up in the church, caught up in absolutely everything – it's very hard to explain it unless you saw it. He's had – a kind of zeal. It's worried me,' Otis added, 'like I told you it did. But you know, I've been envious of it as well.'

'Envious?'

'I suppose I wanted to get caught up too. I was never able.'

Charlotte coughed. 'He wasn't taking things that easy before, Otty. He was always conscious he needed more – that he'd lost something. He didn't have a centre, that's what he said. He was always on about it. That's what he used to tell me.'

'If that's true, he never showed it. The only thing he ever told me he'd lost was a squash match.'

'Well, he covered it up. But you're right – the bishop saying the church might close, that made him panic. He rang me in a panic.'

'Vicars ring lots of people in a panic.'

'It's part of their training.'

'It's part of the advanced training,' Otis said. 'No, it was more than just a panic. It was as if he'd touched something.'

'Mmm.'

The curate added: 'He even rang me in a panic, saying he'd lost his faith.'

'Well—'

'Oh, he's been doing the whole caboose at a hundred miles an hour, in every direction, you know, with no centre to it at all, but—' A gust of cold wind forced the curate to flick his head to one side, and in that fraction of a second he thought of how he had flicked his head away from Charlotte on Sunday; now, gloriously, he found himself staring straight into her sparkling, twinkling eyes. 'What was I saying?'

'Don't know.'

'You've given my life a meaning,' he said seriously.

She gave him a genial frown. 'I thought it was your job to have some meanings already.'

'I did get jealous of him, Charlie,' the curate said, reflectively.

'I like you calling me Charlie.'

'I didn't really want to start doing it,' he said. 'I thought it was inaccurate.'

'What?'

'Calling you—'

They hugged and kissed.

'—Charlie,' he said in a subdued voice. Drawing away, she saw the familiar twitch trigger in Otis's cheek. 'Your little eye.'

'I know,' he told her. 'It's – well, the thing is, when I was a kid I used to get beat up a lot at school. Maybe that did it. When I grew up and stood on my own two feet, I was – I suppose I really wanted love from somewhere. Which I suppose is why I was receptive to – to the love of God, of Christ, which is where everything started for me, all the professional stuff, I mean.'

She was staring at him intently.

'I got sort of fixed on books and study,' he continued easily, 'which I think made me a little bit shy, a bit over-cautious about everything. And – well, I never told you about my sister, I didn't want to, but she – my sister died. Quite suddenly, though I suppose it always seems sudden. She was very young. I was young too.' He brushed a hand across his face, shook his head. 'I used to count up the number of verses in the gospels and learn the square roots. And I didn't like using the phone in case I got a wrong number. That sort of thing. Now my books seem to control me, Charlie. That's my problem, I think. I used to never want to start a prayer for someone unless I was sure I could pronounce their name exactly right.'

'It's lucky you didn't take a job in Wales.'

Adjusting a glove, the curate concluded: 'Which is why Derek keeps me on church notices, mainly. And of course I've been really into the studying, too. Private study. But the trouble is, I think it all took me away from the truth.'

The wind picked up. Charlotte drew the heel of a hand across a teary eye.

'I never knew about your sister. I'm really, really sad. You never told me—'

'It was years ago. I didn't want to spoil anything.'

'—and you know – hearing you say that, it makes me think of the problems my parents are having with Adam – well, yes, how tiny they are by comparison.'

'Mmm. Sometimes I felt the grief might tear my stomach out.'

'Oh, Otis. Even now?'

'Do you think it might have made me what I am?'

'Possibly. But I don't really – I suppose some things, maybe, come from that.'

'Well,' the curate went on cheerfully, 'all I'm saying is that I got too keen to do a lot of examining, learning, mulling and what-not – I didn't actually start living it.'

'You mean living – what, living like Derek has been?'

'Exactly! That's just what I mean! He's certainly been living something – and I've played things so safe all the time! He's had everything on the go but missile launchers!'

'You say that, but I even saw one of them parked in the driveway.'

'Really?'

'No.'

The curate chuckled, almost to himself. 'That's my problem, Charlie, you see. I've been taking it all too literally. Even your jokes.'

Going down the long staircase leading to the cathedral nave, their footsteps echoing off the stonework, Otis asked: 'Are you happy about tomorrow?'

241

'Perfectly, yes.'

Keen to meet her, his parents had invited them to spend the afternoon in London. They had paid for Otis to travel up to Newcastle with Charlotte, as she had a Tyne Spanish Music Group concert which could not be cancelled; they even insisted on funding her journey back down with him. 'They're so kind,' she put in. 'Beautiful people. Bo and Chipperton.'

'Chippendale,' Otis corrected her. 'If you want to shorten it, his friends call him Chips.'

'So it's either furniture or food.'

'You're right,' said Otis, misunderstanding. 'We must get them a present.'

He pitched up in Yan's room. Yan was apparently away with his girlfriend, an Olympic javelin-thrower. So Otis dumped his stuff there, a sports bag with three toothbrushes, and spare batteries for his shaver in case there was no socket the right shape, and a small number of books. He was in the best mood he could ever remember being in. The word 'Evenham' set off a concert orchestra in his head, and he had all the tickets to it. He imagined staying there for years, Charlotte coming down and doing something nearby, maybe him taking the church over and turning it round with her as his wife when Derek and Judy finally threw in the towel.

Pulling the bedclothes up to his chin, he thought of Smasher, of Marion Davidson, Claire Stupples, George Foster . . . of his dear sister . . . heard a small sound next door, where Charlotte was sleeping, and thought of her as well as all of the others, thought of them all together, and then only of her.

For no reason, Otis swung his legs out of the bed. He stood up and scratched his chin, moved over to the window and looked out.

A small car parked half on the kerb at the mouth of a driveway across the street chose that instant to burst into life, jerk forward three feet and shoot away, headlights blazing . . . as he watched the vehicle speed off down the road, something in the curate's memory shifted an inch; he opened his mind's eye too late to catch it moving.

What tiny thing had he just been reminded of?

31

The chicken was overhot, the roast potatoes not properly roasted, the white wine tepid and the serviettes misfolded. That, at least, was the gospel according to Chips Cheeseman, who barked out every verse within earshot of an uncomfortable waiter.

'Pa—' Otis began, then stopped.

Embarrassed, Charlotte squirmed herself into the puffed fabric of her seat. She had not eaten many lunches at restaurants in Piccadilly with floor-length velvet curtains. Bo Cheeseman, mousey face delicately made up, caught her eye and winked, making a structural movement inside a dress spattered with sequins.

'As I was saying, son,' Chips began loudly, 'you've got yourself a woman here who has music, she's got twirls, she's got fascination, she's got Shakespeare—'

'I've seen Hamlet,' Charlotte offered.

'Glory,' Bo Cheeseman said in her high-pitched, fluting voice, laughing, striking a match, pointing across the table and creasing her face into the most generous of smiles around a cigarette. She sucked at the filter. 'Hey,' she said suddenly, 'I meant to say, that service of yours was *fun*.'

'Which? The one on Sunday?' Otis asked, as if there had been others.

'Yep – Sunday. I came close to believing everything that guy said.'

Wide-eyed, Charlotte inquired: 'Derek Weston?'

'Whoever it was.' She coughed politely.

'Bo and I,' Chips blurted, 'are in drawn-out anniversary wonderfulness. Thirty years come December! Now – I'm testing – which anniversary do you think that is?'

'I think I know,' Otis commented, staring vacantly out of the window.

'Just testing,' said Chips again, winking at Charlotte. 'He would.'

She thought about it. 'Um – ruby?'

'Pearl, pearl, pearl!' called Bo. 'Pearl!' added Chips, a cigar moving in his mouth like a joystick. 'Pearls! Big round ones! Like the preacher said!' He guffawed. So did Bo. Charlotte blushed, swallowed, moved her gaze around the rim of her plate.

But the day did get better. The sun surprised everyone by shining. They saw the City, the West End and Billingsgate.

Charlotte looked at Otis at one point, head down, sandy fringe swinging like a frayed curtain, eyes fixed on the pavement – and knew in that instant she loved the curate dearly, knew it for the first time if she had not already been certain of it; knew she would love him forever.

They wrapped up warm and walked through Hyde Park, saw St Paul's Cathedral from the outside. They even made it to the Tower of London, and goggled at the torture instruments and the jewels.

– 32 –

'Hello, my dear. It's absolutely lovely to be back.'

Judy hugged Derek on their doorstep. She held him tightly for a few seconds, then he broke away and reached for her overnight case.

'Watch your back, Derek.'

He heaved it over the threshold with a groan.

'Don't hurt yourself.'

Derek Weston smiled weakly, picked up the case and hauled it to the other side of the vicarage hallway. Judy said as he straightened up; 'Thanks – oh, it's so nice to be home, darling. There's such a lot to talk about.'

She spun around in the hall, peered into the living room – 'I just wanted to check we weren't about to have another surprise party!'

'No,' the vicar said. 'No parties.'

She peered into his face. 'Are you all right?'

He filled his lungs with air, like a climber within ten feet of the mountaintop needing one more gulp to make it. 'Yup,' he said.

'Sure?'

'Yes, yes,' Derek said, looking down at the floor. Quietly, he added: 'Perhaps I'm irritated there's been nothing from Basildon. It's been nine days. What are they waiting for? I just want to get it out of the way, get on with everything.'

'You sounded strange on the phone.'

He jerked his head up, as if surprised to find someone standing in the hallway with him. 'Strange? Did I?'

'Cold.'

'Sorry.'

'Chilly.'

'Hmm.'

Tenderly, she asked: 'Have you been dwelling on Rex?'

The vicar did not answer.

'Well, anyway, I'm the one that's sorry, because it was a much longer trip than it was supposed to be.' She grabbed his arm enthusiastically, 'Derek, why don't we plonk ourselves down in here? There's so much to talk about. Come through.'

The vicar moved into the living room with his wife. She sat in an armchair opposite him, pulled a band out of her hair and shook it loose.

'Your trip was a success, anyway.' He put the question as a statement.

'Oh—' she waved it away '—yes, yes – like I said, we just took a few extra days to tie the whole thing up. I'm sorry it was longer than I – than we both—'

'Don't worry.'

'—expected, especially as I know this is – well, a really tough time for you.'

'For me?'

Judy had been twisting her fingers, wrapping them around each other. Now she stopped moving them, found herself caught in his gaze. 'For us, I mean. For us.'

The ancient grandfather clock in the corner counted out forty seconds, spreading full stops around the room like Italian pepper; the vicar thought of all the late-night conversations its ticking had punctuated.

'I've been doing a lot of praying,' Judy said, finally.

'I've been doing a lot of Hoovering.'

'I'm serious.'

'Right.'

'Praying for some guidance for us. Where we should go next. It really is quite exciting,' she added, smile flickering on and off.

The vicar did not say anything. He just looked down at the carpet.

'Derek – have I done something? Is it something I've said?'

'You've only been back five minutes,' he replied. 'How could it be?'

'There is something, isn't there?'

The vicar paused. He ran his tongue across his lower lip, raising a corner of his mouth so one cheek bunched under an eye. He brought up a hand to run it through his hair, then thought better of the gesture and replaced it in his lap. Finally, in a tone of utter seriousness, he said: 'Yes. Yes, I think so.'

'Well – what, then?'

The vicar did not reply. He got to his feet and walked out. Frowning, Judy cocked her head to the right and watched him move across the hallway, into the study.

Sitting there alone, she thought she could hear the sound of her heart racing.

She thought she might have been sitting there for two thousand years.

When Derek came back, he was holding a sheet of A4 paper.

'You've had a letter?'

'Someone's had a letter,' Derek said, and passed it to her.

Judy Weston took one look and gasped, putting a hand over her mouth. Eyes clamped on the paper, she wrapped the hand tightly around her face, stare roving across the print.

'I found it stored in a file in the computer,' Derek said. 'I knew it was you.'

She handed the document back to her husband, and he stole a hundredth glance at the typed words on it – the high-stacked capitals, the uneven spacing . . .

THIS HAS BEEN FOUND TODAY – IS IT YOURS? PLEASE ACCEPT IT BACK, IF SO. APOLOGIES FOR ANY TROUBLE, ALL GOOD WISHES (ANON)

. . . and then scrunched up the paper and threw it into a wastepaper basket by the television. 'I killed the file,' he said. 'You should have done.'

'How did you know it was—?'

'The date at the top of the screen,' Derek sighed. 'The day

I lost it. And the way you signed it.' He shrugged. 'Or didn't, as the case may be.'

Judy was clenching her teeth. The ridge of bone in her thin jaw went up and down. She stared into his face. 'Derek, my sweetest, it was just the most obvious thing in the world. I didn't realise for ages. But when I did – oh, Derek, it was the most obvious, obvious thing in the world, my—'

'So how did you know, then?'

'How – oh, come on, darling! On that Sunday – when Otis led the service after Rex – um – after the accident – I – well – you were off to one side, and I saw you reach into your jacket, and then you pulled your hand away so guiltily when you saw me, and that's when I suddenly realised – and it all flooded in – all the things – you'd told me in so many ways, Derek, so many things had been telling me and I'd just ignored them – the police coming round, your tatty little green Bible in there—' she pointed over at the study '—yes, that, because I picked it up soon after the whole thing started and found the bit about the pearl of great price with thick red rings around it – and you were always going on about it, too, Derek! On and on about pearls and gems! Pressing my snooze button and talking about jewels! And we had Ken Gearey ringing up saying he was missing one! I mean to say, how on earth you thought I wouldn't—'

'So you took it.'

'Derek, *you* took it. And there you were, just after the funeral, dozing on the sofa, and I leant over and peeped in your top pocket and saw it sitting there, big as anything. Can you imagine how I shook when I fished it out? Like a leaf, Derek – and then Ken and Sonya and Connie suddenly appeared, with the flowers, ringing the bell at just the wrong moment, and you suddenly jolted awake! But I mean, do you realise how close you must have come to losing it, or—' she moved her head sharply '—do you realise how near you came – how near you came to—' Judy brought the back of a hand up to her face, as if unable to say it. 'You might have been caught!'

'I was borrowing it. To tide me over. Sometimes you have to take risks.'

'Not – Derek, no, not risks like that! I took it out of your pocket, typed out that note, put my coat on and zipped into town and posted it back.'

'You said you were going into work.'

'I—' She waved the comment away. 'Luckily – if that's the word – luckily, when the Tower got it back – well, I think they must have decided not to admit it had ever gone because this story about it rolling under a cabinet or some such thing started coming out in little paragraphs in the papers. So the upshot is – you don't have to worry.' She forced a smile. 'I guess they didn't want to admit that new security system of theirs could be beaten by a vicar.'

'Don't have to worry?' Derek's voice was toneless, ironic almost, as though he did not want it recognised in any words he might be about to speak. 'Do you realise how close this whole church came to total demolition because of what you did?'

Judy Weston said nothing. She just stared at him, open-mouthed.

'You never understood, Judy. You never, never understood.'

'I'll tell you one thing I understand, Derek.' She spun her bracelet around her wrist. 'If you think some chunk of oyster from a steamed-up glass case is going to bring you one inch closer to your creator, you've lost your marbles.'

'You said you were going to leave because I didn't have the centre any more. You kept saying it. I never planned to steal that thing. You musn't think I did. In fact I didn't steal it. I took it, almost by accident. On an impulse. And when I got it home, everything—' he broke off, adding: 'You see, you can't even begin to understand.'

'Try me. Explain.'

'Everything was different suddenly. Every single thing seemed possible, all of it. I held it in my hand, Judy, right here, in my hand, and it was as though I was in touch with – with some sort of value at last. Or – holiness. Real value. Like it had proved what the Bible said. Like I had made a connection with God.'

'But you hadn't. It's not the pearl Christ talked about.'

'How do you know that?'

She paused. 'It's not – mentioned.'

'So how did you come to be so excited by the change in me? You were off, praying and studying – I even found your Bible in the fridge once, next to some lard. And look at the church that Sunday, look at the numbers we had!'

'I didn't know what was behind it,' she said. 'It was all an illusion.'

'But it wasn't, was it? Not if it's changed things. How can it be? I can't accept that. It changed something in me. It's changed something in you.'

'God changed something in me. And you changed yourself, somehow – maybe. You've been following a mirage, Derek. Just accept it.'

'No. I can't. Something changed in me. I don't have the power to make changes in myself – I've found that out the hard way. It wasn't a mirage. I can't accept that.'

'You can't accept it because you haven't got anything that's real,' she told him.

The vicar shouted suddenly: 'Don't talk to someone in the Church of England like that!'

Calmly, after a moment, Judy went on: 'What I've found since I started searching, praying, leaving my Bible in the fridge and so on – darling, what I've found is more real than anything. I promise you. I've found love, Derek, I really have. And I was so hoping—' she broke off, holding a trembling finger up to her mouth.

'Hoping what?'

She paused, gathered herself. 'Why do you think I fished out that sermon? It was the most beautiful thing you've ever preached. You preached it right at the beginning. And then, the Sunday before last, you only had to read it out to have everyone in church on the edge of their pew. And what was the theme?'

He turned his hands upwards, showing them empty. 'The pearl.'

'No, Derek. Jesus Christ. That's what the sermon was about. The text was the pearl of great price. The sermon was about Jesus Christ. You weren't listening. I've found him, Derek. You ought to start looking again. That's what I was hoping for.'

'Don't you think I know all about that? Years ago, I had it. For real. But it went. I must have a leak somewhere. All I've been trying to do is get it back.'

A bird squawked outside.

'Well, I wanted us to talk about the future,' she sighed. 'Pray, discuss, sort out what you and I – oh, I don't know, I don't want to go on with this treadmill in the City. That's why Bristol took so long. I had to get a few things fixed finally.'

'You keep moving the goalposts,' the vicar said. 'First you wanted me to become Superman, then a bishop, then save my church – and I try and try, but no sooner do I pull it off than you're asking me to forget and become some sort of sage.'

'Don't you see? The pearl was a sham.'

Derek looked down at the floor. 'I can't admit that, Judy. I don't have anything else. A sham is better than nothing. You'll laugh, but when I had it in my hands I felt I was worth something – me, worth something – for the first time in years.'

'You're worth everything. Not just something. And look – I'm not laughing.'

Derek placed his palms together and rested the end of his nose on the tips of his index fingers. He sniffed, as if trying to find out a fact from the aroma in the room. Then he let out a deep sigh. The skin around his eyes leant inwards, giving his face a mournful look. Thoughtfully, he said: 'Maybe one day I'll look back and be grateful. I'm sorry if I sound a bit overwhelmed. Perhaps I've been a bit confused all along. If that's been the case, I'll apologise here and now.'

He withdrew his hands, and Judy watched a wry smile pass across his mouth. Then he pursed his lips, and it vanished. 'But look – there's one thing I'm absolutely set on, you know,' he went on. 'I'm not going to leave this place. That's final.'

33

The next day began with stunning normality.

Judy was up first. She gave Derek a peck on the cheek as he appeared at the bathroom door. 'You need a trim,' she said, pointing at his head. He replied in a gravel voice, 'It's the only thing I've got lots of.'

'It looks like a hat,' she sniggered. 'Or a tree.'

The vicar watched his wife apply her make-up with laser precision. 'I'm sorry if I – um – got a bit worked up last night,' he mumbled. 'I'd had half a glass of wine before you arrived. I think it made me—'

'Don't mention it, don't worry,' she said, snapping her blusher shut.

'I feel quite bad about it.'

'Let's just take things easy. Look to Christ, Derek.' She was dabbing mascara on an eye. 'He loves you, Derek.' She looked at her watch. 'I'm in a rush.'

'I need to be told he does,' the vicar said.

'I'll do the telling.' She switched off the light over the mirror.

'Forgiveness.'

'You need a holiday, Derek. I'll bring a couple of brochures back tonight.'

Judy left at seven fifteen on the dot, as always. Half an hour later, the telephone rang. Derek trotted down the stairs to get it.

'Yo.' He felt invigorated, trendy. He had an exciting life. A wonderful church, too. Things were gradually getting back to normal. He had ridden out the storm.

'It's Marshall, Derek. How are you?'

'Good, man. Thanks. Judy's back.'

'Really? Long trip, that one.'

'She had some things to tie up,' the vicar said, thinking: *get to the point, please*.

'To get to the point,' Marshall began, 'I had a letter this morning saying we'd won the pebbledashing case. After arbitration. I thought you'd be delighted. It means the builders must replace a number of the pebbles without charge.'

Derek's eyes slid across the study window, out on to the drive. He wanted to hurl the phone at the ceiling and shriek with laughter, throw several parties at once, roll about the floor crying hysterically, call for Prince Charles to be publicly flogged, pop a million bottles of champagne, shout at vast congregations through high-powered megaphones . . .

The pebbledashing case has been won! The pebbledashing case has been won! The pebbledashing case has been—

'Hullo?'

'Hello – yes, sorry, Marshall. Still here. Well, that's a real tribute to your efforts.'

'As you know, I defended the case myself.'

'I hope it didn't cause you too much inconvenience.'

'Not really. The only expense I incurred was in buying a secondhand wig, which I was then told I didn't need to wear as it was a small claims court. Still, I argued very forcefully, using diagrams, and it was adjourned and then recalled three-ish weeks ago and I was able to put our case quite strongly to them. I just got the news this morning.'

'Terrific. Very well done.'

'It means a new look to the back end of the church.'

Derek fought an uncontrollable urge to burst out laughing. 'Hullo?'

'Yes. Still here. It's great news. Really well done.'

'Just one other thing, Derek – about the congregation on Sunday.'

'It was huge, wasn't it?' The vicar was still thinking about a different Sunday.

'Well – I mean – no, that's what I wanted—'

'Oh, I see! This Sunday just past.'

'Yes. We had a hundred and ten, Derek, you see. I was

253

counting at the door, because when you get a revival you want to be sure it doesn't suddenly stop. And – um – I mean, a hundred and ten is all right, you know, but considering the week before was more like three hundred—'

'Three hundred? Was it?'

'Two hundred and eighty-four.'

'Two eight four? As in – nearly two eight five?'

'Including the choir, yes. And there was a fifty in the collection.'

'Well, we often get fifty pence—'

'A fifty pound note!'

'Two eight four,' the vicar murmured, basking in it.

'Eh? Oh, yes. Sixty-four over capacity. With the choir.'

'Well, you have to include the choir.' The vicar felt himself swell with renewed pride. *Two hundred and eighty-four*. It was an extraordinary achievement, with or without pearls. It was his achievement.

'It's just that last Sunday's number – three days ago, I'm talking about – was so drastically down, Derek, that I wanted to mention it to you. It was less than half.'

'A hundred and ten? Well, that could be natural fluctuation.' The vicar had never imagined he would be put on the spot like this. 'It could be seasonal.' *What am I supposed to say?* 'The figure should be seasonally adjusted. We'll go on fighting, Marshall, that's what we'll do. Fight on, fight to win. Like Thatcher. And they'll all be back, every one of them.' Only Otis knew about the way he had planned it, the reasons it had to be planned that way. Trust Marshall to start kicking up a fuss. 'I don't think we want to get too snaggled up in numbers.'

'All right. Just wanted you to have the exact figure,' Marshall said. 'I mean, for a start, we seemed to have a lot of Americans the time before last. I even saw a coach. So if you think varying the hymns would bring them back – perhaps putting in the one that goes to the tune of "Stars and Stripes", or doing a sermon on gun control – well, however you want to play it, you've got my support. Our first aim has to be to get them through the doors.'

'I agree. That said, two or three of those motorbikers came back, didn't they?'

'True.'

'So we are making some progress.'

'I suppose so. Okay. Cheers, Derek.'

'Bye.'

For no reason, the vicar dialled Otis Cheeseman's number. He held the receiver to his ear, then heard an engaged tone cut in and put it down.

Derek Weston tried to formulate a strategy in his mind. Bit by bit, he would start to read his Bible again. That would keep Judy blissfully happy. Persuade her to stay in her job a little while longer.

Then he would set some goals. A hundred and ten by Christmas, a hundred and thirty-five by March. Capacity – two hundred and twenty – eighteen months later. Then Judy would see the point and want to stay. *Two hundred and twenty*. He mulled over the magical figure. That's what vicars called The Big C. *Capacity*. A slab of mail dropped through the front door. He could afford to move more slowly now, take the whole thing more deliberately. No fast car chases after flashing jewels and gems and sudden revelations . . . no rocketing through spiritual red lights . . . wasn't that where the whole trouble had begun?

Oh yes, the vicar told himself. *Yes, yes, yes. That's where every kind of trouble begins*. He was convinced of it. The problem with Christianity was exactly the same as the problem with film advertising. It sold itself too hard by half – nothing could ever be that exciting in reality, not even fiction. You had only to look at the number of disappointed people filing out of cinemas to know it. The poster campaign for Christianity was still more audacious: golden dreamworlds, glowing horizons, clouds at the end, sunbeams, unlimited love, the man always getting the girl. If only it could be like that for more than a fortnight.

But it never lasted. The chasing Christians did in search of the poster image of their faith! *That's where all the trouble begins*, he told himself again, brewing a cup of instant coffee.

The vicar sat on a stool at the kitchen table in his dressing gown. His eyes glazed over. The coffee grew cold. He slugged it back. The little portable radio warbled away by the sink.

Oh, his mistake had been the most common error in Christendom. For a tiny moment, for a moment the radius of a dust-speck in history, Christians might grasp perfection in their hands – yet it was fatal, lethal, to think it was a matter of mere concentration to make that perfection permanent in their lives. With the Peruvian, he had felt God's breath on his soul . . . well, lucky him. He had felt God's breath on his soul with the Peruvian; that was all that could be said about it. Recently he had had another experience that gave him a blistering insight into holiness and flawlessness. Well, lucky him. He had had a blistering insight. That was all that could be said about it. None of these things lasted longer than the glow left by a half-good feature film. He had twice in his life fallen into the terrible trap of thinking that perfection ought to be seized, when in fact seizure killed it . . .

Better just to look at the posters, he reflected. *Don't go inside the cinema at all*.

The only thing that was permanent was his tenure of St Saviour's church, Evenham. The vicar had no doubt that he could use it for good. But it would take a long time. He needed to go back to basics, build something solid where previously there had just been a vacuum and sudden heavenly flashes. He saw the future stretching out before him, a long and painstaking attempt to build up certainties, possibly by reading serious books. He smiled at the idea. *Perhaps I'll go for the Otis Cheeseman approach*, he told himself. *Lots of books, lots of study*.

He felt suddenly enthused, as if he had solved a mathematical theorem that had baffled everyone for decades. Then he stopped the train of thought dead. What if he still had the pearl? Any pearl? Would he be going on like this? Would he be telling himself about painstaking study and serious books if he still had the thing in his hands? The vicar shivered where he sat, slid the half-empty cup six inches across the table, suddenly missing mindblowing revelations. Where was his vision now?

Combing his hair in the full-length hallway mirror, he remembered one of his old conversations with his reflection: *Sir Derek Weston*, he had called himself. He studied the outline of his head in the glass, smiling. *Nothing bald about Sir Derek. Lord Derek Weston, chief of an international conglomerate.* He grinned at the newspaper headline he had dreamt up standing in the bathroom, months before: POLLS MAKE WESTON FAVOURITE TO SUCCEED PM AS HE SURVIVES STRIMMER ATTACK.

Yes, he pondered, remembering the marquee day, *that'd be it. Glass desks by the dozen. Millions of pounds just lying about.*

Whoosh, Derek teased himself.

I'm on my way up.

He thought: *I am not going to go bald*.

He slid the comb into the front pocket of the dressing gown and caught sight of a jagged white island hovering at the mirror's edge – the mail, sitting where it had fallen from the letterbox. Pushing his hair down on his head, Derek Weston turned and walked slowly across the hall. He picked up the pile of letters from the mat.

34

Judy put the key in the lock, turned it, walked in.

'Hello? Hello darling? I'm home.'

No reply.

That seemed strange. The vicarage front door had been on the latch.

Leaning against the panelled wall, the vicar's wife lifted each foot in turn and pulled the stilettoed heel off it. She grimaced at a buckle, hanging by a thread; then walked to the bottom of the stairs and called up them: 'Derek! I've brought a couple of holiday magazines! Guess where to!' She was dangling the shoes from a hand.

There was a moan from the living room.

'Perth.'

Judy Weston jumped, dropping the shoes. She looked over her shoulder.

'Derek—?'

She strode across the hall and into the room. There was her husband, sprawled over the sofa, half-sitting, half-lying, one leg dangling from an armrest, an arm splayed out. She walked across to him. His face was drained of colour, eyes narrowed.

He smiled weakly. 'Afternoon, Judy. Or – or evening, is it?'

'Derek—'

'Sorry, Judy.' His lips trembled as he spoke. 'Thinking.' He seemed to shiver. 'Did I say Perth?'

'Perth?'

'Scotland.'

'Derek, what on earth are you—'

'Not Australia.'

258

'—doing, sitting here in your—'

'Do you remember that couple we had from Australia, Judy? The two who wanted to get married, and I had to tell them not to? Because the only thing they had in common was surfing?' The vicar rolled his eyes away.

'What are you talking about? What are you doing, Derek, sitting here in your dressing gown?'

He did not answer; just pursed his lips and clenched his jaw, turning his head from her and looking into the fireplace. 'I have no logs to put on my fire,' he whispered.

'Derek—'

The vicar moved his gaze slowly back to her.

Then he pulled a creased white envelope from the front pocket of the dressing gown and offered it to his wife, hand trembling.

'Have a look. Came today.'

She bent down towards him, heart thumping as if a rabbit was stuck in it and had suddenly sensed danger, not moving her gaze from him, taking the envelope, rabbit's back foot pounding, not shifting her eyes from him even for a fraction of a second; his face was wan, drawn, pale – she pulled a letter from the envelope.

A folded letter. The thing was flapping in her hand, unfolding. She had to yank her eyes off his face to read. Her hands were flapping.

The rabbit thumped and thumped.

She heard someone in the room gasp. No, not someone. The gasp was hers. Judy held the paper in front of her face. A sound beyond it, a muted sound, must have been Derek moving an inch on the sofa.

A minute later, Judy Weston lowered the sheet of paper six inches and saw her husband's eyes appear over the top of it, except that they were not looking into hers but away across the room.

'Derek, I'm so sorry.'

He did not reply.

'I really am sorry. I know how you—'

Judy could not finish the sentence, because she realised no one could ever know how Derek Weston was feeling at that moment, not even her; perhaps especially not her. She swallowed. 'Have you been sitting here since you—'

'Yes,' he croaked, still staring away.

'At least he signed it.'

'"Terry,"' he said. 'He signed it "Terry". I've never called him that. It's like me signing something "Del". It would look ridiculous.' His voice was a whisper.

Feeling short of breath, feeling cramped as though the walls were closing in, Judy glanced at the type again. It was a brief letter, considering what it said under the stupid mauve Basildon diocese letterhead: the church was closing, St Paul's had been designated principal site for the Evenham parish, the Reverend Helen Silverstone would remain in overall charge there and use her broad knowledge of the area to expand her ministry, the contribution Derek and Judy had made to Evenham would long be remembered, his future would be something all interested parties would gather to discuss in due course . . .

'She must have beaten me,' Derek murmured.

'Broad knowledge of the area? She's only just arrived,' Judy mumbled, looking down at the letter.

'She beat me.'

'Oh, darling—' she let the piece of paper fall to the floor, dropped to her haunches and placed her hands gently on his knees '—no, no darling, don't think of it like that – it could just be—'

'She must have done. Two eight five. She must have got two eight five.'

'Derek, please don't – don't let it get you like this.'

He stared ahead, his jaw going up and down slowly but no sound coming out.

'Have you really been sitting here since you opened the letter?'

Now he was chewing his bottom lip.

'Derek – please – please don't let this destroy you, darling. Don't let it get to you like this. You'll have so much to offer, Derek, somewhere else – somewhere – wherever it might be—' she was squatting in front of him, squeezing his limp hands between hers. 'Dear Derek, really, it all comes down

260

to Jesus Christ, darling – it really, really does – his love for us, the things he did for us – dying, Derek, you know – darling, come on, please don't lose sight of how much love there is for us, how precious we are to him—'

He shifted his position on the sofa, smiling weakly.

'Our contribution will long be remembered,' he muttered, staring ahead like a man in a trance. His eyes seemed to have glazed over in the last two minutes, as though he was closing himself into his own world and had hired small invisible glaziers to complete the job. 'Tommy Trinder,' he added quietly.

'Tommy Trinder?'

'Yes, exactly. That's what they said about his contribution.'

'Look, Derek—'

'Where did we go wrong? Was it the third hymn?'

'Thirteen?' Judy could hardly hear his voice.

'The third hymn.'

She stared down at him. His eyes rolled upwards, then closed.

He pulled one hand away from hers, then reached out with it like a blind man feeling for the face of a friend. 'She must have had more than us.'

'Derek—'

He was silent. He curled his fingers into fists, rubbed a bare foot on the carpet.

Firmly, she said: 'Derek – listen Derek, think about it – think about all we've been through, darling – all the things we've said to each other, all the things we've been through – ask yourself, my love – couldn't this – might this not be for the best? Really speaking—' she flicked her wrist, snatched the letter off the carpet, jerked it in the air – really, truly speaking – this – I mean, what have you really lost? Ask yourself, what have you lost?'

He breathed in and out, slowly.

He moved the tip of his tongue left and right across his top lip.

'The pearl,' he said.

It was as if he was deep in a cave somewhere. She could not reach him, not even by pot-holing. Judy expected to feel anger burst banks inside her, volcanic anger erupt at him for not realising this could so easily happen, for not being ready . . . but no, she found herself more sad than anything, more terrifically sad than she could ever remember or imagine feeling. She closed the door behind her as she left the room, walked into the study, sat at his desk and prayed.

She asked God to touch her husband's soul with his warm forefinger.

Then she picked up the telephone and rang Otis.

'There is some not-too-hot news,' she said gently.

The American voice came back: 'The pebbledashing?'

Judy was silent for a moment.

'I'll come over,' she said.

The curate's flat was a tiny collection of rooms over the town bakery. He had hung views of Arizona in every room, and one or two of Scotland.

'The walls are bowed,' the American said as she looked at the pictures. 'I can't put up shelving here. That's why all my books are stored in the church. Anyway, it's too tiny to keep them here, this apartment.'

'Your beloved books,' Judy remarked, staring at a kettle sitting on the floor.

'I sometimes think I've loved them too much.'

'How is Charlotte?'

'Um – great, thank you,' the curate replied, rather formally. He opened a door at the end of the room. 'I say "all". I keep a fifth of them here.'

'Goodness,' she said. The cupboard was piled high with volumes in every colour. Brown, red, grey, green, blue, two or three pink even. There were stacks and stacks of them. There was nothing visible but books. She peered at them. Five deep, they must have been piled forty high. One-fifth?

'One-fifth. These are my books on – well, anyway. Never mind.'

The spines and titles seemed suddenly to arrange themselves into a huge swirling question mark, which buzzed out of the cupboard and hung in the air over them both until he turned and slammed the cupboard door and she saw the image fizzle into a hundred million humming squares and dots, then disappear.

Judy gulped. How could she tell him?

She would be ending everything for the curate. His place on the Church Swap Scheme would be terminated. He would be sent back to Arizona, without Charlotte Davidson, and probably have to live by a cactus somewhere. He would be forced to do things she imagined pastors did in Arizona, like appearing on television game shows and creative swindling.

'Do you like this one?' he was saying.

She looked at a framed print at the end of the room.

'The Tower of London,' he said.

'Oh – very nice.'

'We were there just last week.'

'Really?'

'It's beautiful. They have some beautiful things there.'

'Yes,' she said, 'they do.'

'I've bought a book on it, but you can't capture it in a book.'

She found herself blinking back tears. 'The church is closing, Otis,' she said, the words rushing out. 'I'm so sorry. I'm really so sorry for the trouble we've put you through. Derek got a letter from the bishop today, thanking us for everything we've done. That's the English way of saying please go as soon as possible. I'm sorry you came to us. I'm so sorry. We've not been very good for you.'

Otis Cheeseman was silent for a moment, glancing about the ceiling as if he had been told earlier that this was the moment it would suddenly disappear and he would be whisked away into space, and he was now wondering why the whisking was not running to schedule. He put his hands in his pockets, then pulled them out again. He asked sombrely: 'How is Derek?'

She was sobbing. 'He's on the sofa.'

They drove back to the vicarage together. When they walked into the living room, the vicar did not seem to register them. 'Hi,' Otis said cheerfully. Derek did not even look in his direction. He was now stretched out across the full length of the cushions, head lolling on an armrest, eyes closed, lips moving as if in silent prayer. Judy clenched and unclenched her jaw. The curate cleared his throat and rolled his shoulders. They stood over him.

'He's suffering from shock,' Judy said.

'He's certainly in a state of something more than surprise.'

'Hold on – isn't he whispering something, Otis?'

'A message of some sort?' The curate bent down towards Derek. There was sweat on the vicar's brow. He looked as though he had gone a shade of pale green; he was unshaven. The curate slowly moved his left ear closer to the vicar's mouth.

As he did, Otis heard the whispering become two tiny words.

'Her bedroom . . .'

The curate frowned, moved his head closer to the vicar's mouth, catching Judy's thin stockinged calves in the corner of his eye as he did so. 'I think I'm picking something up,' he muttered.

'. . . what was in her bedroom. That's what gave it away. The maps. Now I know what they were doing. They planned it. Her broad knowledge of the area, they said. That's why the maps were in her bedroom. On her bedside table. I jumped out of her bedroom window, didn't I, hung off the gutter? Wazim brought them. Piles of them. Maps. They planned it. They were in her bedroom . . . the maps . . . I jumped out of the window . . .'

On and on. Circles and circles. Reddening, the curate straightened up. Avoiding Judy's eye, he cocked his head to one side, as if the words were a jumble of nothings he was trying to shake out of one ear.

'It's possible that he might need a doctor,' Otis pronounced.

'What was he saying?'

'Er – something to do with maps.'

'Mats?'

'Maps.'

'Maps? Maps? Of what?'

'He didn't go into that.' Otis leant down again, put his ear next to the vicar's mouth as the lips moved. 'Ah,' he said a moment later, drawing himself up again. 'Maps of Evenham.'

'Maps of Evenham?'

'Yes,' the curate said. 'I think maybe he needs to see a—'

'Cartographer?' she asked tonelessly. 'No, you're right. Yes, he needs – look, I'll ring the doctor now.'

She clicked her tongue against her teeth and sighed deeply to herself, as if she could barely believe the scale of this reaction to what had happened – and yet she was not tutting and sighing because she begrudged it to Derek, but because she was furious at herself for failing to see all this coming and what it would do to him when it finally came; perhaps it had even been coming when the Stitts arrived at the summer party, all those months ago, maybe even before the creak of the marquee centre-pole . . .

She felt as if rocks were falling on her head. There was no dodging them. A doctor came, in a car and a beard. He fished a stethoscope out of his bag. 'I visit your church on Christmas Day, regular as clockwork,' he said. 'I take belief very seriously. Looking forward to this Christmas, are you? Nearly upon us, isn't it?'

'Nearly,' Judy replied, nervously fiddling with a blouse button. 'Well, nearly two months, actually.'

'But I like a warm-up period,' the doctor said. He took Derek's temperature, listened to his chest with the stethoscope, then said 'Testing' a number of times.

At last – 'He's not responding,' the man ended up telling them, and Judy wondered if you really needed six years in medical school to learn a trick like that.

After a moment spent scribbling on a pad, he announced: 'Well, I must say, it's rather strange. He has all the symptoms of shock. Do you have a loose power point near here? Dangling wires?'

'No,' Judy said.

Otis put in: 'I think it might be something else. We both think we know what.'

'No, Otis,' Judy sighed.

'Oh,' said the doctor, grinning at him. 'What?'

'Nothing major,' Judy broke in urgently before the curate answered.

The doctor noticed the brochures. 'I see you're thinking of going to Paris.'

'We were about to look at them,' she told him. 'Actually it's Bonn.'

'*Très bon*,' Otis agreed, seriously.

'Well,' the doctor breezed, 'there's no reason for you to worry, but he seems to be running quite a high fever. He needs to be kept warm. See that sweat there – that's a cold sweat. He may also have a small infection, or some sort of food poisoning, which is why he's got that fishy complexion. That should clear in a couple of days. If you can get him to slurp a couple of spoonfuls of this a day—' he tore the top slip from his pad '—just antibiotics, just as a precaution – I think he'll be as right as rain in no time.'

Judy Weston took the square of paper from the doctor, and gazed down at her beloved husband. He did not look as if he would ever be as right as rain again. He did not even look as if he would be as right as scattered showers.

35

That night, Judy had said to Otis: 'I think he's going to die.'

No, the curate told her firmly, he would not, Derek was just deep in shock, it happened to people during the World Wars, in fact there was one occasion when two hundred Italians suffered it simultaneously after being given orders to advance.

'I really think he will. I'm so scared.'

Otis wanted to reach out and say – say something caring to her, something of God; but his heart and soul felt cramped, squashed, like books in boxes, and he could only think of things he had read. Tic flickering under his eye, staring down, he breathed: '"What in our lives is burnt in the fire of this?"'

He could feel her looking at him.

'Isaac Rosenberg,' he told the carpet, lamely.

Leaving the house that night, the curate agreed to return early so Judy could go to work. Why were so many feelings so difficult to experience, he asked himself, except schematically?

He would be sent back to America. That was now certain. And he knew he could never, never, never, summon up the courage to do what he so needed to do before he bought that ticket.

His insides were snarled up with orange frustrations, like traffic cones the vehicles of his emotions could only crawl between.

He conjured up his sister's tiny face, and apologised to it.

When Otis returned to his flat that night, he opened the cupboard at the far end of the largest room, grabbed handfuls of books and threw them at the walls with a cry of naked rage.

One, a dense volume on Isaiah, struck the Tower of London picture and smashed the glass. He sent the tallest pile flying with a sweep of an arm, then kicked them black and blue where they lay strewn on the floor. But he knew he could not break their hold on him. And as long as that was there, he would never ask Charlotte Davidson to be his wife.

36

At ten the next morning, Otis walked past the southern edge of Nock Green on his way to the vicarage. The air was still. The sky was cast-iron grey. His face was blank. It was freezing cold. At least it would never be this cold in Arizona, USA. He went 'Brrrrrrrrrrrr' with his lips, then tweaked them to get rid of the itching.

Turning the corner, he caught sight of a parked car.

His memory was instantly jolted.

There at the kerb was the small green car he knew he had seen before, sitting in the same position opposite the mouth of the driveway.

He walked towards it, quickening his pace, craning his neck to see anyone inside, momentarily anxious at the thought that someone might be paying a visit to the vicarage and happen on Derek.

And then Otis knew. He realised exactly when he had seen it last. The day he delivered the laundry. He remembered handing the mended suit to the vicar, the wire hanger dangling off his finger, that stilted exchange about it tearing on a gutter, some conversation about money, and then how he had strolled off down the drive and caught sight of the car, seen the man in the back glance up sharply and tap the driver on the shoulder, another in the passenger seat looking over and saying something as the vehicle rolled into the road with a bump and shot off.

The same three men appeared in front of him.

Just as Otis approached the rear of the car, they came into sight. Gathered on the other side of the big square pillar at the end of the church driveway.

'Hi there.' That was the man in the front seat. He was

now standing half on the pavement, half on the church gravel.

'Good morning.' Otis realised he was not wearing his curate's outfit.

'Hello – hello there,' the other two said, self-consciously. They seemed embarrassed, being found hanging around outside a church.

'Lovely day,' said the curate, in a casual voice.

'Tell me—' the first man began, scratching his chin '—do you know anything architectural about this place, in the way of acreage at the back?' He sounded as if he had deliberately chosen the question a burglar was least likely to ask.

'It's quite big,' Otis answered. 'But I'm not sure how much of that is Nock Green and how much is church land. Are you—?'

'Property,' the second man said quickly. 'Buying and selling, developing.' He was pulling at a wallet. 'Oh – you're American, aren't you?'

The curate's thoughts whirred like screaming circular saws. *Property?*

The first man leant towards him. 'We had a tip-off a few weeks back—'

'Months,' the third man put in, furtively glancing left and right.

'—that this place was going to be shut down. It came from the top, see, because I think they wanted to be ready to sell the land as quick as they—'

'We gather those concerned have had the bad news,' said the third man in a low voice, thumbing at the church buildings.

'So we don't have to be so secretive,' the second said, handing Otis a business card. 'We've got a contract from a strip cartoon wholesalers, and this might be ideal. Printing and selling strips. Butthead and Beavis, that sort of thing.'

The first man looked into the curate's face, a glimmer of suspicion kindled in his eyes. 'Are you – hey – you're nothing to do with this place, are you?'

Otis Cheeseman felt his mind sprint hundreds of yards in the instant it took the answer to tunnel to his mouth.

'No.'

He was falling over a finishing line, sobbing, gasping, tangled in tape.

'You're not involved here?' That was the second man, blowing his nose loudly.

'Er – no.'

'Not at all?' The third, looking at his watch.

'Nope.'

Somehow, mind boggling, breathless, Otis ended the conversation. He had denied it three times! He walked further down the street, then doubled back by moving through a bush, trembling. He hopped on to a section of driveway out of sight of the street so they would not see him. *Property?* Crazy thoughts came at him in charges, raging bulls. His stomach ached. The circular saws screamed in his head. *Property?* Suddenly he remembered Derek's words, muttered on the sofa . . .

They had planned it.

Is that what he was talking about? That there was no competition, never had been, they were just going to close it and that was that? Walking up the drive, shuffling up it at tortoise pace, thoughts raced through his head so fast Otis felt he almost had to duck to stop them smashing into his brain. They had planned it, they had planned it, they had planned it. The property people knew weeks ago. They had been casing the joint! Sizing it up for bulldozers and steamrollers! Measuring it! That's why they shot off in their car when he suddenly walked out of the drive!

Otis found the vicar still prostrate on the sofa, covered by two large duvets and a flowered cushion. He seemed to be asleep. His face had a pallid, dry look to it, as if someone had sprinkled it with flour. He had shaved, or been shaved at least. The curate walked up and gazed down. He desperately wanted to apologise for his cowardice. He discovered he did not have the courage to.

'Derek?'

After a moment, the eyes opened a merest millimetre.

'Are you okay?'

The vicar's face stayed put. His lips stayed shut. They had

271

a bluish tinge. Otis thought: I am in the gutter. He found his mind ticking out its own rhythm, replaying words Derek murmured yesterday on the sofa, something about gutters – a gutter? Something to do with maps and bedrooms; a gutter? Was that the day he gave back the laundry, then, when Derek talked about ripping his trousers on one? Climbing out of her bedroom? *Her* bedroom? Whose? Someone Wazim Bhatia gave maps to?

A bell went. Otis moved across the hallway to open the door.

The smiling face on the other side took his breath away. Instantly, it all fell into place. He knew whose bedroom it was, how the vicar's trousers had been torn, what the maps of Evenham had been for—

'Hello, Helen.'

—and now he was panicking, terrified the woman vicar would step into the living room and see what she had done.

'Otis! Hi. What brings you here? Silly question, I suppose,' Helen Silverstone said cheerily, the long lines dropping from her nose, past her mouth, hemming her smile in. 'I suppose you're here all the time.'

She looked carefree, Otis thought. 'Minding the shop,' he said stiffly.

'Tra-la-la. Is Derek at home?'

'He's a little unwell,' the curate said, motioning at the shut living room door. 'In fact he can't really be disturbed at the moment.'

'Ah. You don't – Otis, you wouldn't have a minute, would you?'

The curate and the woman vicar ended up in Derek's study, sitting on the wooden vicarage chairs. Otis had turned his backwards, protectively.

'I'm just a little bit confused about a piece of news I've had,' Helen Silverstone began. 'I wondered if you might be able to clarify it for me.'

Otis was about to nod, or say, 'Yes, I'll try,' when there was a deafening yell from the living room.

'Waaaaaaaaaaaaaaaaaaaaaaaaaaaaaaaaaaaaaaaa—'

They both jumped. Helen Silverstone shot a glance over

her shoulder. The curate sprang off the chair and looked around the study. 'Um – excuse me,' he jabbered.

He opened the living room door. Derek's eyes were flickering; open-close, close-open, open-close . . . the curate knelt at his side. He wondered if the vicar might be dying. He put a hand on his arm. It was warm, thank heaven. He prayed: 'Lord God, be with Derek Weston. I know the pair of us have really wrecked things here. Please be with Derek now. Comfort his soul with your love. Forgive both our sins.'

Utterly motionless, he felt his sandy fringe sway to and fro, brushing at his forehead. 'I mean, forgive the sins of both of us,' he added quietly, in case God might think he was saying there were only two sins.

All Otis could think was – what if he dies?

'No more shouting, Derek,' the curate whispered. 'There's really no need.'

To his surprise, the vicar began to murmur. The curate moved his ear into place six inches above the vicar's mouth.

'I lost it, I lost it . . . I lost it . . .'

'You didn't lose, Derek,' Otis muttered. 'It was all decided long before we even started trying.'

Back in the study, Helen asked nervously: 'Is he all right?'

'Yes,' said Otis. 'He'd just lost something.'

The woman vicar was silent for a moment, as if wanting to give the startled expression on her face time to clear. She breathed in and out in a way that might have been taken for yoga, under different circumstances. Then she said: 'The – um – the thing is, Otis, when I took over at St Paul's I was – ah – you will obviously have known this – I was told it would be leading up to responsibility for all the churches in Evenham, Hullbridge, Rettendon and Norton Mortimer.'

'Oh,' the curate said. He amended it to: 'Oh, yes.' He had not heard this at all.

'They gave me maps, and so on. And a history of the way things had come together here, thick records of the budgets, staffing, and all that kind of thing. Quite a lot of paperwork to read up on. Lots of paper clips.' She laughed. 'Ha.'

'Oh, yes,' the curate said. 'Ha.'

'Wazim Bhatia,' she smiled, rolling her eyes.

'Ha,' the curate put in.

'And I gather this is all happening in the new year,' she continued. 'Actually – well, to tell you the truth, I'm not much of an administrator, more of a pastoral person, so – well, anyway—'

'I know what you mean,' the curate said.

'Yes. Still, it's an honour to become a rector.'

'Oh, yes.'

'But what I can't quite understand, Otis – and maybe you can help me here – is that I gather from a letter I've just had that this church isn't going to be in the picture. Your church, I mean. I can't quite work it out.'

The curate paused.

'I was wondering if you had any light to shed,' the woman vicar added.

Otis chewed at the inside of his mouth, wondering how on earth to answer.

'We are becoming a cartoon shop,' he said, finally.

37

The ladder looked secure enough.

Marshall Kampfner stared up at it, then closed his fists around two of the lowest rungs and heaved it a few inches to the left. The top end came to rest on the brickwork directly below the bedroom window.

He stood there for a moment, hands on hips, just gazing up.

This, Marshall understood, was a fairly desperate measure. But maybe something fairly desperate was needed.

He was concerned. Derek was never usually out at this time on a Friday morning – and when he had rung the vicarage half an hour earlier to say he was popping round, the phone had been picked up and there had been a strange sort of gurgle at the other end before the receiver seemed to be dropped on something hard and the line clicked off.

Appearing at the top of the church driveway, Marshall had looked at his watch. Quarter to ten. Judy would be at work. He rang the bell. Nothing. He scoured the front of the vicarage for clues. A light was on in the study. He peered through the window. No one. That's where he would have expected Derek to be, preparing a sermon.

His gaze had moved from window to window, come to rest on the bedroom.

The curtains were closed. For some reason, that struck Marshall as very peculiar indeed. He had checked his watch again and walked round the back of the building.

He stood in the grass at the rear, staring up at the bedroom window. This really was strange. The curtains were open, a light was on inside. He shouted: 'Derek!'

That was when he noticed the ladder.

Marshall had spent a few minutes working out how, and whether, he could use it. He wandered around the thing, rubbing his hand across his throat, looking at it from every angle.

Then he heaved the ladder out of the grass and hoisted it on to his shoulder, walked to the corner of the building and dropped an end directly below the window, holding it in place with a foot. The whole business was done in one continuous, professional movement. This was a chartered librarian in full swing.

Taking great care, he tipped the ladder at a shallow angle so the strut-ends connected gently with the wall just below the sill.

Now he was staring up at it, thinking it looked secure enough.

Marshall had a foot on the bottom rung when he caught sight of the back end of the church and paused for a moment, thinking thousands of irrelevant thoughts about why he went there, the odds and ends of work he did for the place; he remembered something from ages back, one minute singing a hymn about the cross, the next realising what it all meant – that God had sent a precious thing to be slashed and slaughtered on his behalf. The following day he quietly returned thirteen cassette tapes from the library that had found their way into his own collection, gave two hundred pounds to someone he knew was having a problem with a pest control bill, and apologised to his wife for having so often been in his own world.

Foot on ladder, he wondered: was he about to climb into heaven?

'Tssk,' he said to himself. He was about to see what on earth was the matter with Derek, why the vicar had answered his telephone with a strange noise, why his bedroom light was on with curtains closed around the other side; this was not the moment for reminiscences about loyalty to the church. He climbed the ladder.

At the top, Marshall poked his head over the sill and looked into the bedroom.

Peering, he could just about make out the vicar, lying there on the bed.

Was he asleep?

Marshall frowned. He wondered if Derek might have suffered a collapse while praying. It was most unusual for him to – no, it was more than unusual, it was unprecedented for the vicar to be in bed near ten on a Friday morning, making gurgling sounds into the telephone. Had he had some kind of seizure?

He rapped on the window.

'Derek?'

Marshall stared. There was no movement inside the room. The vicar's face was directed at the ceiling, in an imprecise, impassive sort of way. Marshall said his name again, more insistently this time.

The vicar did not respond. Did not even look over.

Now Marshall feared the worst. He was about to shout instead of just speaking, perhaps try to scramble in through the window and administer first aid, when he heard his own name called from the foot of the ladder.

'What—?'

He looked down, suddenly dizzied.

Otis came into focus.

'Marshall! Don't move your head!'

The curate had remembered what the PCC member had at that moment allowed himself to forget – that ever since the accident with the marquee pole, any sudden backwards jerk of his neck could cause him to black out. Marshall froze at the top of the ladder, felt himself start to shake with fright at what had nearly happened . . . and then slowly, very slowly, began to climb down.

'Derek is unwell,' Otis said at the bottom.

Marshall leant against the ladder, gingerly. 'I wanted to discuss an orange juice stain with him.'

'He's not really up to that, I'm afraid.'

'On the lobby carpet.'

'I think it'll have to wait.'

'I very nearly – hum,' Marshall said. 'Very nearly – sssweeeeee.' He whistled the word for falling unexpectedly. 'Thanks, Otis. I'm really grateful. I so nearly—' He trailed off, and coughed. 'Phew.' For the first time, Marshall felt

277

a bond with the curate. He never had before. He thanked him again.

'No problem,' Otis said, distractedly. 'Um – Judy's at work. I've been checking everything,' he went on. 'The doctor's coming at any moment.'

Marshall was feeling more conversational than he ever had. After a minute, he asked: 'What's wrong? He made a strange noise.'

'He is – I'm not sure what the medical term is,' Otis said. 'He's suffering from shock, I think.'

'Why?'

'I don't think I can – well, okay, I'll tell you, but I'd be grateful if—'

'Understood. I won't tell—'

'Helen Silverstone knows, and she's promised it'll go no further.'

'—a soul.'

'The church is closing, Marshall.'

The librarian took a deep breath. 'I was tipped off,' he said quickly. 'Ages ago. The marquee pole—' He motioned at his head, shrugged, abandoned the sentence.

'I think Judy is going to ask for the reasons, formally.'

'And Derek—'

'—hasn't spoken since he got the letter,' Otis said, slowly and sadly.

'Not a word?'

'Hardly any.'

'It must have been a terrible shock.'

'Yes. Well, worse than that.'

'Dreadful.'

'Yes.'

'He loved this place,' Marshall said. 'I don't mean he was Britain's Number One Vicar, or anything glamorous like that – he wasn't ever going to win a prize for Cleric of the Century, or Most Dynamic Sermons in Essex, but—'

'I know.'

'—he loved this place, he really did, and a lot of us loved him,' Marshall went on. 'Charles, Ruth, Ken, the Geareys, George – you know. Me too. I did. Do, I mean. Sometimes you get a church where it looks like God is not at work – but he is, he's always there, just buried.'

Otis blew a line of vapour through his teeth. 'Yes.'

'And there are lots of brilliant vicars with smaller congregations.'

'Yes.'

The two men stood there for a minute, thinking their own thoughts.

'I was worried,' Marshall muttered. 'The ladder—' he gave a vague wave in its direction. He shook his head. 'Derek was doing the sermon when I found the meaning of it all. Actually it was a hymn that set me pondering. I used to think the whole business was good behaviour, except I wasn't much good at it. Then I realised it was just a matter of—'

'Free,' Otis cut in.

'Eh?'

'It was free of charge.'

'Yes, I realised it was free,' Marshall chirped, grinning. 'The whole bang-shoot.'

They both fidgeted where they stood.

'Heaven,' Marshall added. A dog was barking somewhere. He asked: 'You'll be going back to the States, then?'

'I think so.'

He risked: 'No girlfriends here, or anything?'

'Someone. But I spoke to her this morning. She seemed to understand.'

'What, you leaving?'

'No other option makes its case – um – with sufficient strength,' the curate said stiffly, hating himself.

'So you're taking your books back, are you?'

'They're taking me,' Otis mumbled, almost inaudibly. He added: 'Yes.'

They walked to the front of the vicarage in time to see the doctor, Justin Rutter, jump out of his car.

'Well I never!' he said. 'Is that head of yours all right now, Marshall?'

'Fine,' the PCC member told the doctor as they all shook hands. 'Hello, Justin. I didn't know you were dealing with this.'

'Blackouts?' the doctor asked.

'Well – thanks to—' Marshall glanced at Otis, and was put off explaining. 'No, none. I've been taking care.'

'Where's the vicar, then?'

'Upstairs,' Otis said. 'He's been moved to the bedroom.'

The examination took more than fifteen minutes. Derek seemed to come close to waking at times, then fell back into a deep sleep that was almost a stupor. The doctor looked into his eyes, took his blood pressure with a small gadget, managed to get his temperature, turned on the bedside light and examined the vicar's face minutely.

'Let's talk outside,' he said.

In the living room, Justin Rutter asked: 'Is Judy Weston here?'

'I've been recommending she goes to work,' Otis said. 'Just for her own peace of mind.'

'Well,' Dr Rutter began, 'to be frank, I've got no idea at all what the problem is. At first I thought he might have some sort of muscle wastage. That is patently not the case. I thought it could be ME, the very debilitating viral condition yuppies have been getting, but that tends not to come on so quickly and it doesn't usually affect vicars, particularly not in this area. You'll find this peculiar, I imagine, but he actually has all the symptoms of shell shock.'

Marshall said, 'Really?'

'From what I've read. His temperature is stable, and there is a small white line across his lower lip,' the doctor said. 'It allows you to rule out a lot of things.'

He was packing his instruments into a bag.

'I'm a little bit concerned. It's rather as if he has gone into a very long faint. How long has he been like this?'

'Since you first came,' said Otis. 'Two and a half days.'

'And he's not been near any explosions?'

'There have been no explosions in Evenham,' Marshall said authoritatively.

'He's been eating?'

Otis replied: 'Toast. He's had some bits and pieces, Judy told me. He's not been out cold the whole time. He'll wake and eat a little, then he'll just groan and sink back into the bed without saying anything.'

'Strange,' the doctor said. 'Look, it's Friday. I am a trifle worried. This is rather like a very bad flu without any of the symptoms, and that does concern me. That said, his complexion has cleared. So the antibiotics may have acted. But what I would like to do is have him into hospital on Monday, if he's still flat out like this. We'll do tests. And he may actually need someone to talk to him, professionally. So—'

'Evenham Hospital?' Marshall asked.

'Yes, exactly, where you went after your accident.'

'Talk to him professionally?' That was Otis. 'You mean a psychiatrist?'

'I just wonder if he might be in some sort of first-stage coma, induced by a kind of emotional trauma triggered by some event or other. He might need to be talked through it. There might be – well,' the doctor chuckled through his beard, 'I'm getting out of my own terrain here, but—' he shrugged '—there might be a key word, or a key event, that'll make him suddenly spring out of it. Otherwise he could be like this for the rest of time, frankly.'

The other two looked aghast.

'Oh yes, it's serious. But he's just as likely to get better here as anywhere – if he does get better, that is.'

When the doctor was gone, Marshall asked Otis: 'Wouldn't it have been better for us to have told him?'

'It's just that Judy thought it might make him worse, if he woke up and found the news had gone round. Dr Rutter sometimes goes to the church. She thought it might give Derek a relapse.'

'Oh.'

'I know what you mean, though,' Otis said, uncertainly.

'You were just doing things by the book.'

'Yes.'

Marshall said: 'Otis, do you think we should pray for Derek? Perhaps get some people round to pray for him?'

'Who?'

'Ruth and Claire, perhaps? Eunice Cooper, John and Sonya Todd?'

'The trouble is, half the country would find out about it.'

'Yes, but Derek's health is more important than—'

'I know, Marshall. I know.'

'We could bring them round here for a vague reason.'

Which is exactly what they did. Later that afternoon, seven members of the congregation who answered their home telephones agreed to come to the vicarage to pray for what they were told was 'a matter'. Ken O'Driscoll, for one, kept asking where Derek was. Marshall Kampfner just said the vicar was indisposed.

Claire Stupples seemed to realise early on that something was seriously wrong. She prayed: 'Lord God, whatever this matter is, we pray for your healing hand upon it. We thank you for Marshall's head. We pray that your light will shine upon those concerned. We thank you for all the love you have shown those of us, in this church, who have never seemed to feel we do anything right. Lord God, we are all failures. We are ashamed of the way we go on and on failing. And yet your son, Jesus Christ, is there, loving us all the time, his beautiful face staring into our horrible ones. We pray that if the church is about to turn a corner, you will be the steering wheel.'

38

They both apologised to Judy when she returned.

'We didn't tell anyone,' Marshall said. 'We just prayed in a general way.'

'It was so general someone even brought in Northern Ireland,' Otis added. He was about to tell her not to bother trying to contact Basildon, because they had planned the whole thing ages ago and there was never even a slight contest between the two churches, there was never any point – he could not bring himself to say it.

She thanked them tearfully.

That night she climbed into bed next to Derek and noticed he was not snoring. He always snored. Lights out, she whispered: 'Derek?'

No answer.

'Derek, please come back,' she said quietly. 'Don't go.'

Judy must have slept for all of two hours. She kept turning on the light and looking at him. Sometimes it seemed as if he was just sleeping. At other times, frighteningly, his eyelids were open the width of a hair and she could see the whites of his eyes through them. His face was still and blank, his head cricked back unnaturally as if he was cradling a table-tennis ball in his neck. She almost rang the hospital twice, lifting the telephone by the bed out of its cradle, then forced herself to accept that the doctor was probably right to say Monday. And what if Derek went in, and never came out again?

Judy had a sudden memory of the two of them lying there, arguing . . . her bringing up Charlotte Davidson, of all the silly things.

She looked over at the window.

She had been standing there, at the glass, had seen Derek

down below reach out frantically for her, like a removals man stopping a piano tipping . . .

If only she had known then how desperate he had been for just an inch of truth, the merest murmur of it, how desperate they had both been, she would never have so thoroughly misunderstood his stupid, stupid gesture, never used it as a broken bough to beat him with.

Now she lay, staring at the ceiling, begging God to save her husband from whatever sharp jaws were chomping at his soul.

When dawn broke she could not remember having slept at all.

Helen Silverstone rang early.

'Are you awake?'

'Yes, Helen. Hello.'

'Hello, Judy. I don't know if Otis told you, but he mentioned to me the church was closing and I just wanted to say I'm thinking of you at every moment of the day.'

Judy felt so upset she just said, 'Thanks, Helen,' and promised in a choked voice to call round before they left the area.

There was a telephone call from Mirabel Weekling, saying Derek had promised to visit and she was just sitting here wondering . . .

'I'll get him to reschedule, Mirry. I am sorry.'

Others came round during the day, though not for any particular reasons, and Judy said Derek was under the weather and unable to get down to see them. So they left messages. She started thinking how much she was going to miss the church, and kept telling herself she should not be thinking that; it would make things even worse.

She spent most of the day at Derek's bedside, much of it praying or talking to him, but being ignored. Marshall Kampfner rang, and she said: 'Thank you for organising that time of prayer yesterday, Marshall.'

'The doctor seemed hopeful,' the librarian said.

'He's rather relaxed, I think.'

'Yes, I know what you mean. He'd probably say it was good news if your blood pressure was three.'

She swallowed and heard Marshall burble at the other end, 'Oh – sorry. Not that Derek is in any difficulties, serious ones.'

By four o'clock the sun was almost down. Judy sat on the edge of the bed, a Bible in her lap. 'Derek, Derek – can't you say something, my dear? What's wrong with you?'

He did not even shift an inch in response.

She moved over to the radiator and switched it to full power. Back on the bed, she said, 'Well, look, I'm sitting here with my Bible and I can read something to you, if you want.'

Judy thumbed through it, feeling her lips thicken with emotion. Pulling a handkerchief from her pocket, she sniffed into it.

Grimacing, she thumbed through the pages, opened it four-fifths of the way in and started reading in a quiet voice. '"The kingdom of heaven is like treasure hidden in a field. When a man found it, he hid it again, and then in his joy went and sold all he had and bought that field."'

She blew her nose. '"Again, the kingdom of heaven is like a merchant looking for fine pearls. When he found one of great value, he went away and sold everything he had and bought it."'

Judy looked up, sighed, and closed the book. He was as motionless as tarmac. The doorbell went downstairs. She murmured: 'I'll get that, sweet. I won't be a minute.'

She jogged down the stairs, walked across the hallway and turned on the exterior light. An unfamiliar face was illuminated outside. She opened the front door.

It was a young man, smiling broadly, brandishing a camera. 'Mrs Weston? Hi. John Gracey, from the *Gazette*. I was just wondering if you might be able to help me this evening.'

She hesitated, looking down at her hands. 'Yes, John – erm – what?'

'We're compiling a pre-Christmas feature in the *Evenham Gazette* on the councillors, and the prominent businessmen, and the golf club chairman and so on, everybody important in the area and what Christmas means to them.' He rattled the strap on the camera and grinned. 'I'm doing a spot of pre-shooting.'

'How can I help?'

'It's vicars too.' He wound on the camera. He looked ambitious, keen, young, fresh-faced, she thought.

'I see.'

'Oh – and their wives, obviously. Obviously wives as well.'

'Thank you.'

'In fact,' he went on, 'I noticed that the last picture we have in our library of Derek was when that "Rocketbomb" record was in the charts, so—'

'That was a few years ago.'

'—yes, and he was in a sprint at the time and had covered his face with a folded newspaper, so it was a bit tricky catching him. Is he in? Would you mind if I—'

'Oh – oh, no, sorry,' Judy said quickly, 'I'm afraid he's not – well, he's not really available. He's under the weather.'

'Right.' The photographer looked disappointed.

'Sorry,' she said. She hated to disappoint him.

Pushing his camera into a case, he said: 'Okay, well – it wouldn't have taken that long – I mean, just a minute or—'

'I'm really sorry,' she said.

'Look – I'll be passing here again at about seven, seven thirty, tonight. Do you think he might be up to it by—'

'No, I'm afraid he won't,' Judy broke in. 'I really am sorry.' She wanted to suggest another time, but knew that was out of the question. They would be gone by Christmas, she guessed. How could she tell him they were leaving?

He looked into her face, with curiosity and a measure of annoyance, she thought. 'Don't worry,' he said. 'No problem. I'll be back another time. Thanks. Bye.'

Judy made herself a cup of coffee, went up to the bedroom and sat in the wicker chair by the dressing table. She was telling herself she was too strong to cry, too strong to scream in despair – then she remembered some verse that said your weakness is my strength, or whatever it was . . . she took a sip of the coffee, set the cup down by the dressing table mirror . . .

When she opened her eyes it was seven. She had fallen asleep. It was too warm in the bedroom. She took a swig of coffee, making a face as she swallowed because it was stone cold. Picking up the Bible, she walked over to Derek.

The vicar of St Saviour's church, Evenham, was lying prostrate on the bed, his arms outside the quilt, stretched down and quite lifeless. His head was completely still. His chest moved a little . . . up . . . down . . . but no more than a little; his face was gaunt and pale, the thick hair oily and unwashed, springing up in large mounds from the top of his head, one tuft shooting forward untidily, the whole lot looking like a winter warmer left by a well-wisher; his eyes were open the smallest fraction of an inch, though she could see no pupils behind the lids.

The sight of him there made her heart quicken. A sense of terrible sadness, of waste, tore through her. What struck her hardest was that his fingers were completely motionless.

'Derek, if you can hear me,' she began, leaning over him, 'I'm going into the church to read my Bible and pray. It's too warm in here for me. It may be all right for you, darling, but I'm falling asleep.'

That said, she walked out of the vicarage and across the top of the gravel drive, then took a few steps down the mossy knoll to the church entrance.

She brought a key up to one of the locks in the doors, and tutted; someone had left them unlocked. Otis, perhaps. She walked into the dark lobby and groped for the light switch.

Suddenly, she jumped.

She stood there, shaking.

'Is there someone here?'

Her heart was pounding.

'Hello?'

She held still for a minute in the dark, afraid to turn on the light. Had she heard a noise? Now she could hear nothing.

For a second she had thought there was someone in the narrow wooden corridor that led along the main body of the church.

Then she decided – no, silly, no one there at all, come on.

She switched on the light.

Breathing more easily, she walked across the lobby and into the gloom of the church. She felt for the switches on the right, by the wall, just above the wooden collection box, turned on the lights at the end; they lit the altar, the front rows . . . there was a strange smell, she thought. The place needed cleaning.

She put the lobby lights out.

Judy Weston walked slowly towards the dusty light at the front of the church, a million images piling on top of each other in her head, superimposed slides with a brilliant pure beam shining through them.

It was more than just a change of temperature that had brought her. She badly needed to walk into the church where they had spent so many years, she and Derek; walk down the aisle.

What would become of her husband?

She sat at the front, in the orb of orange light from the bulbs in the rafters. Behind her, the lobby door squeaked. She jerked her head around.

She peered back at the entrance to the church. The lobby was dark. The door had – oh, yes, surely it had just swung an inch this way or that.

Nothing there, silly.

Judy Weston stared at the altar, trying to form something in her head that could even half-say what was in her heart. What was it? Gratitude, drowned in panic? Fear? Pain? Agony? Love, even? Could she say something of love?

The altar table looked sepia yellow under the lamps.

And there was that smell again – what was it?

Her dreaming things up, that's what.

Squeezing her eyes tightly shut, Judy prayed. She went through the whole gospel story in her head, from cradle to cross to empty tomb, and begged the God in heaven, who had taken so many pains to activate that train of events there and then, to spend a moment attending to things in the here and now.

John Gracey was turning the corner at the edge of Nock

Green when he saw the aura of light playing around the roof of St Saviour's church and wondered why they might be having a service on a Saturday night.

He swore under his breath. The vicar had obviously not been unavailable at all, not under the weather – he was probably just busy, preparing for whatever it was he was doing now; why were these Church of England people always so reluctant to help with articles and photographs? They had no idea of the real world. They did not even live in it.

He shook his head, peering up at the church as he passed it. The stained glass windows came into view at that moment, lit from inside with an almost blindingly bright light.

He had just passed the mouth of the church when a sound caught his ear and an image repeated itself in his head – a rectangle of stained glass, the blinding light behind it—

His heart lurched. He stamped the foot on the brake. That was not—

Those were not lights.

That was a fire.

He turned the car into the kerb, grounded the front of it and leapt out, almost tripping and falling in the gutter.

Carried to him on the wind was a terrible sound, the roar of wood burning, crackling and popping. As he stood there, staring up the drive for an instant, the roof of the church exploded in flame.

John Gracey raced up the driveway, tore up it like a champion sprinter, the camera jumping this way and that around his neck, feeling the heat from the fire race down towards him.

He had to move away from it as he drew level with the church and saw white flames roaring out of the woodwork fifty yards down one of the sides; then on the other side too, then at separate points on the side nearest the road, then all the different flames suddenly joining together as if a massive fuse had been lit across the wall of the church; he ran to the front door of the vicarage and banged on it.

Were they in there? Reflections of the huge flames leapt in the upstairs windows. He smashed the front door furiously with his fist.

Then he turned, and what happened next seemed to move in the slowest slow motion.

As the photographer screwed up his eyes and gazed at the burning building, momentarily hypnotised by the heat and light, hearing a siren wailing in the distance and seeing the lobby collapse in that instant, the entire thing go up in a storm of white sparks . . .

He saw a figure appear at a doorway at the side of the church, towards the back of the building, two figures, stumbling out of a door somewhere, one holding the other in its arms . . .

Not even thinking, John Gracey reached for his camera.

It felt hot in his hands. He felt his thumb burn as he wound it on.

The taller figure was carrying the other down the side of the church as flames shot out of the windows above them. Now he heard a fire engine screaming up the gravel drive.

He tried to move towards the two figures. They were coming towards him.

He could not get closer. 'Come on! Nearly there!' he was yelling, but his shouting was drowned out by the roar of fire and siren and then the barking of firemen leaping out of their vehicle behind him.

John Gracey had his camera up to his face when the man finally cleared the front of the church, a flame flickering on the material at his shoulder, a woman in his arms; his flash bulb went off a fraction of a second before the man collapsed into the arms of the first fireman.

He took only one picture, then someone shoved him in the chest and he was pushed right to the back of a crowd of men in uniforms, a hose unrolling past him.

The man said something as he appeared in the frame, and only John Gracey heard it.

He caught the image there, on his camera, in the only instant it existed: the vicar of St Saviour's church, Evenham, holding his wife in his arms, her clutching a Bible to her chest, the cross visible on the cover, as their church burned down behind them.

39

By the time the last of the boxes from the living room had been taped up and pulled into the hall, Otis and Derek were ready for lunch.

Judy brought soup and brown rolls, and a big bowl of crisps.

'Phew.' That was the American.

'Phew to you too,' Derek said. 'Thanks for—' he gestured around '—all of this, Otis. It's really good of you.'

They ate for a while in silence.

'Strange to be leaving,' Derek said.

The telephone rang in the study, and he left the room to get it.

Judy said: 'We're going to miss you, Otis.'

'I'll miss you,' the curate said.

'We will miss you very, very much,' she said.

'I'll miss you the same amount.'

Derek came back in. 'It was a diocese in Wales,' he said. 'Offering a rectorship, or something, I think they said. I couldn't understand his accent. He seemed to be talking about mountains.'

'Mountains of money, I expect he meant,' Judy joked.

'Perhaps he meant mounting a pony to get to the place,' said Otis.

Judy asked: 'Did you take their number?'

'I put it in the book with all the other ones.'

There had been a lot of numbers after the fire. The photograph taken by John Gracey, of the *Evenham Gazette*, had missed the deadlines on the Sunday newspapers. That had turned out to be hugely to his advantage. By the following Monday, he had managed to sell it to every single broadsheet national, as well as the *Sun*, the *Mirror*, and the *Daily Star*.

It was on the front pages of five of them, an extraordinary image: 'Essex vicar Derek Weston escapes burning church, wife Judy and Bible in arms, saying: "I have the whole world in my hands," as firemen come to rescue,' one caption read.

There was Derek, eyes popping in panic, a sheet of orange behind him. Six of the newspapers reproduced it in colour. One gave it almost half a page.

Neither of them was badly hurt, though Judy had suffered from smoke inhalation and a bad burn on an elbow, and the hair had been scorched clean off Derek's head. After three days of checks in hospital, they had returned home to find a hundred messages from well-wishers up and down the country, distraught that a vicar and his wife could lose their church in such tragic circumstances . . .

'Yes,' Derek was saying, 'I stuck it in the book – Otis, have you seen the updated list?'

'Nope.'

The vicar walked back in with it a minute later. 'Lay caretaker at St Paul's Cathedral – believe it or not – rectorships in Northern Ireland, one in Bradford, that one in Wales we just heard from, vicar of Clapham, vicar in Stratford, vicar somewhere near Richmond—'

'North Yorkshire,' Judy put in.

'—vice-chairman of a Christian bookshop in central London —' he adjusted his spectacles '—as well as president – it says here – of a charity that's something to do with buying telephones for separated French families – I didn't get the gist of that, it was a bad line – and some sort of senior position in a soup place—'

'Croutons?' Otis suggested.

'—yes, croutons probably, Head of Croutons – then there's – hold on – vicar of about five churches, two in Cornwall, a suggestion from Ken Gearey that I sit on something at the Tower,' he said quickly, 'as well as – here – secretary of the Church of England Overseas Funding Board, it says—'

'Which sounded really interesting,' Judy put in.

'—and, finally – ready? Dean of Middlesbrough!'

'What was he offering?' Otis asked.

'No, Dean is one step below bishop,' Judy laughed. 'And – Derek, don't forget the Australian one – you know the one I mean.'

'Bishop of Wonga-something,' he said. 'Yes, that photo must have gone round the whole world.'

They were all laughing, all three of them.

'So you've got no shortage of offers,' Otis said.

Derek grew serious. 'What about you?'

'What do you mean?'

'You and the future. I know I keep asking.'

'I've got some ideas,' the curate said. 'Ideas involving churches.'

'But generally—'

'Generally, finding out more about real life.'

'And specifically?'

'Specifically, secret plans.'

Judy looked pained. 'I'm – I'm dreadfully sorry about your books. I know I've said that almost every day since—'

'And, as I've been saying,' Otis broke in, 'there's no reason for you to—' he trailed off, then said: 'I'm delighted. I'm delighted they got incinerated. I've lived my whole life in a succession of indexes. I wouldn't even mow the lawn without looking it up. It's time for me to step through the ashes of all that, to reality.'

'Yes,' Derek said. 'Beautiful, Otis.' He was trying to picture himself in a tall Australian hat.

'It'll be fun for you, spending Christmas on the coast.'

'It will,' Judy agreed. She was watching for the tic under the curate's eye, but it seemed to have gone. 'They've given me a break from work,' she added.

Someone had made a personal donation of two thousand pounds to the vicar and his wife, to give them a rest from everything. A total of seven thousand had come in. They had given three to Otis, two more to Helen Silverstone's church.

Otis left soon afterwards. The removals men were due the following day. The boxes would go into storage while they were away, deciding what to do.

'He was quiet, wasn't he?'

'I thought he was louder than usual,' Judy observed. 'He'd left a couple of buttons undone on his shirt, too. He's terribly relaxed.'

'Yes, I noticed a tartan sock,' Derek muttered. 'Strange.'

'Why? He's stopped getting so wound up. All that study and everything. He was so fixed on all the jots and tittles and the full-stops. He's obviously going to ask Charlotte to marry him,' Judy went on. 'He'll go back to America after that. Both of them. You watch.'

'You're so clever,' Derek said. 'How did you become so clever?'

'I don't know.'

'I was lucky to marry you.'

'I was lucky to get married.'

Derek said: 'I can't believe what we've been through in the last—'

'Sssshh,' she said, putting a finger to her lips.

She looked into his face. It was as healthy-looking and as tanned as it had ever looked. But there was only the thinnest hint of hair on his head, a grey bed of prickles slowly growing back. For now, he was bald.

Marion Davidson knocked on their front door, requesting prayer.

'What for?'

'For Adam,' she said.

'And the problem is—?'

'No problem,' she said. 'That's the thing. No problem at all.' Tears were streaming down her cheeks. 'I think I told you about this condition of his, this problem he had, this genetic thing – you know he's adopted, don't you? This condition means some kind of moral impairment, you know, he's bright but he just can't tell the difference between right and wrong, that's the thing—'

'Slow down, slow down,' Derek said.

'He's cured, he's better,' Marion suddenly cried. 'I don't know why or how. He had been particularly difficult and – just in the last month, something must have shocked him, I don't know what – but I wanted you just to say thanks for that, to say thanks for the wonderful thing that has happened here, because—'

'He's better?'

'He asked me if he could become confirmed. He's shown remorse for the smallest things. The doctor says the whole thing is in remission. He must have had a shock, somehow. I hope he may become a great spiritual leader, or bishop.'

'That's wonderful,' the vicar said.

'He says his prayers at night, he even says sorry for things.'

After she had left, Derek and Judy looked at each other.

'I saw him,' she said, finally.

'I know.'

'I told you I did. I was certain I did.'

'And you did.'

'He started all those fires – Wazim's car, everything—'

'Good grief. I won't ever ask him to babysit.'

'I saw him through the window just before I got trapped in there,' Judy said, and shivered. For a minute they just looked at each other, shaking their heads.

'We're back where we started, aren't we?' Derek asked.

'If you mean back at the very beginning—'

'I'm not sure what I mean,' he said.

'We're further ahead than that,' she told him.

'Where are we, then?'

'At a crossroads.'

'It feels like an accident blackspot.'

'It doesn't have to,' she said.

'I didn't mean that,' he added after a moment. 'I didn't mean that at all.'

40

They sat at the dining room table that night, staring out at the dark sky.

'Look at all the pearls, twinkling there,' he said.

They were both silent for a moment.

'There's only one pearl,' she muttered, finally.

'You love him, don't you?'

'Who?'

'Him. Not hymn, as in hymn number. Him.'

'Yes.'

'Christ,' he whispered. 'Oh, dear.' He went on quietly, 'When I was – I don't know, wherever I was, wherever I went on that terrible day – it was as if there was no God, or there had been a lot of them but they had all resigned – I just lay there – I know I was conscious of things vaguely, but—'

He breathed in deeply, and snatched a glance at her. She was staring at him intently. He looked back out of the window, out on to Nock Green.

'The only other time in my whole life I felt shock like that was when someone kept an election promise recently.'

'You're always joking, Derek.'

'And you're always right. You were right about Otis.'

'Back to America, with Charlotte.'

'And no books on the plane,' he said. 'Not one.'

A minute later, he told her: 'I nearly died, Judy. It was as if everything I believed in had collapsed in front of me. I really thought I had done it on my own, you know, saved the church from – from – and – and then I thought, I thought Christianity was just a matter of reading up – just sitting and reading – and I presumed I'd spend the rest of my life here, we both would, and then the letter came – and now, you know, I look at Otis, and what he's been through with those books, and I realise how futile all that sort of behaviour is—'

He was shaking his head.

'What, reading?' she asked.

'Anything that's not direct contact with God. I'm not blaming Otis.'

'I agree,' she said. 'I tried to escape through banking.'

'I saw the flames, Judy. It was like hell, or something, just outside my window. It woke me. I knew what I cared about. We've been such fools, rowing.'

'I know,' she said. She had clenched her hand into a fist and held the thumb side to her mouth. 'Well, having said that, we didn't—'

'Most of my rows were with myself,' the vicar said.

'You didn't like yourself.'

'Teach me to, Judy.' He smiled. 'Marshall's delighted, you know, about the pebbledashing. He's been telling everyone that's what saved us. It was the only fireproofed part of the church. He's completely changed his tune on it.'

Staring out at the sky, he said: 'Do you think, Judy, if I reached for one of those stars, I could hold it in my hand?'

'You have something much more precious in your hand,' she said.

'The newspaperman made up that quote.'

'He didn't, Derek, and you know it.'

'I do know it.'

Then he asked: 'Where do we begin, now that everything has ended?'

She placed her palms flat on the dining room table, spreading the fingers. Glancing up, she followed his gaze outside.

'We go out to our field,' she said, 'and we dig up our pearl, and we make sure we never lose it again.'

'I'll spread my gloves with Superglue, to make certain,' he added, after a while.

His face turned serious. 'Judy, is there – hope? For us?'

'Yes,' she said.

'How do you know that?'

'Love goes on for ever and ever, as far as those stars,' she said. 'God's love.'

'Further, I bet.'

'Yes.'

'It sounds a bit soppy, though.'

'It's reality. Truth.'

'One day, I'll have it in my hands.'

'No, Derek. That's the whole point. That's what caused all the trouble, from day one. You and your pearls, Otis and his books. You don't hold truth. It holds you.'

'So all the effort—'

'All the reading, all the effort—'

'They're just—'

Neither of them completed their sentence. After a moment Derek sniffed, and said: 'I really believed I had it all—' he clapped his hands together '—right here. I thought I had it all in my hands.' He stared down at them.

'No, Derek,' Judy said. 'He's got us in his. Can't you feel it?'

They sat there for hours. Then they went to bed and held each other.